WILD MAGIC

ANN MACELA

Medallion Press, Inc.
Printed in USA

DEDICATION:

To my readers, with heartfelt thanks for all your support

Published 2009 by Medallion Press, Inc.

The MEDALLION PRESS LOGO
is a registered trademark of Medallion Press, Inc.

Typeset in Adobe Garamond Pro
Printed in the United States of America

ISBN: 9-781-93383699-7

10 9 8 7 6 5 4 3 2 1
First Edition

ACKNOWLEDGMENTS:

Thanks to my critique group—MJ, Rita, Sherry, Jan, Noirin, Barbara, and Chris—plus Paula and Kelle. Ladies, I couldn't have done it without you.

Thanks to all those with whom I played fantasy role-playing games in the past. You really taught me to throw fireballs and lightning bolts.

About the location of the HeatherRidge Center. I have rearranged a few sub-divisions in the vicinity of Barrington, Illinois. When I began the book, the land was vacant. So, if you go looking for the HeatherRidge, it won't be there.

Special thanks, as usual, to my own hero and the love of my life, Paul. He's also the best research assistant a writer could hope for. And you can take that statement any way you want to.

PROLOGUE

Twenty-five years ago

"Are you sure we're in the right place?" Bruce Ubell asked his cousin, Alton Finster, as he looked around the dingy storeroom in the basements of the hundred-and-ten-year-old ancestral mansion in Chicago. It was midnight, and their flashlight beams barely penetrated the cold gray gloom in the never-electrified space.

"Yes, I'm sure," Alton replied with the edge he used to let Bruce know he had asked a ridiculous question. "Granddad's diary is extremely specific, and I spent a lot of time as a kid exploring the cellars. I never noticed this place, though."

Bruce straightened his red and black practitioner robe, settling it more carefully on his shoulders. This dusty, musty, dark corner of the basement creeped him out, and he reminded himself of the prize hidden here somewhere. To find it, he simply had to put up with Alton's bossy tendencies. One day he'd show his two-years-older cousin who was really the smartest—and make him acknowledge it.

"Man, I thought my parents would never go to bed," Alton said. "I expected any minute my mother would tell us it was past our bedtimes. You'd think they could treat us like adults. After all, I'm twenty-seven, and you're twenty-five."

"Yeah, my mother's the same way. Given your father's hatred of Granddad, I doubt they'd have joined in the hunt for what the old man called the *secret* of his success."

"You've got that right. If Dad knew Granddad had ordered his lawyer to give me the diary ten years after he died, with instructions to show it to you, he'd have a fit."

Bruce wondered for a moment if he would have showed the diary to Alton if he'd been the recipient, but put the thought out of his mind as unproductive and irrelevant. He stepped closer to the back wall and shined his flashlight behind a pile of wooden boxes. "Here's the door."

"Give me a hand," Alton ordered as he lifted the top box and placed it behind them. A long smear of dirt trailed down his robe when he turned around.

Bruce grimaced. Alton never worried about ruining his robes—which matched Bruce's since they had both inherited the family's accounting talents. Bruce, however, did. The damn things didn't always clean easily, and they cost a lot to replace because of their protective enchantments. For a CPA, Alton threw money around in a way Bruce couldn't bring himself to emulate. Granddad's instructions had been explicit, though: "Wear your robes."

Bruce picked up one edge of the next box with his fingertips and helped carry it to the other side of the room. It was lighter than expected—the empty boxes were simply stage dressing.

"Only one more," Alton said.

They moved the container and turned their attention to the dark wooden door. A black metal handle was bolted to the right side, but there was no visible lock mechanism.

"Okay." Alton pulled a red-leather book from his pocket and opened the slim volume to the third page. "Shine the light here."

Bruce did as he was told and reviewed the instructions along with Alton. "The *resolvo* spell is required to open it. Want me to cast?"

"Yeah," Alton replied, "I've never used it."

Of course he hadn't—Alton was too lazy to learn any enchantment unless it directly involved his talents. Bruce cast the spell at the door.

It swung open, slowly and silently. A gust of stale, frigid wind blew out of the room behind it and ruffled the bottom of their robes. He shivered when, despite the protective spells, the chill penetrated the cloth.

When both aimed their flashlights at the opening, the darkness inside swallowed up the beams.

"Damn," Alton said. "Looks like we have to use the candles."

"Personally, I'd rather not chance exploding flashlights. If the magic in there is as old and powerful as the diary suggests, it may not like newfangled gadgets." Bruce wished he'd paid for more safeguards in his robe, but nothing had fried him or Alton when they opened the door, so they were probably all right. After all, Granddad wouldn't want to destroy his heirs—would he? He pulled a candle and holder out of a robe pocket and lit the wick with a small *flamma* spell.

Alton put the little book in his pocket and did the same. "Granddad wrote that he cast extremely powerful shielding spells around the entire section of the basement, and especially this room. Can you feel anything?"

Bruce concentrated on the blackness. Nothing made him want to turn away. "No. Let's be careful no matter what."

Holding the candles in outstretched hands, they stuck the lights through the doorway into the dark. The flickering flames illuminated only a small room, as dingy as the one they stood in. When nothing happened, they entered—Bruce letting Alton go first.

The walls of the ten-by-ten space were rough-hewn stone, granite by the looks of it. The only furnishings were a scratched and dented wooden table and a matching chair, both dark with age and dirt. A tarnished-to-black six-branch candelabra, a supply of white candles, and a few sheets of blank, yellowing paper sat on the tabletop. Propped in a corner was a gnarled black stick about six feet long. Its top looked like four dead fingers trying to grasp something.

Bruce quickly put candles in the candelabra and lit them.

Alton turned in a slow circle before pointing at a corner. "The diary says to look three hand-spans south and four up from the northeast corner. Find a man's face."

Bruce raised the candles while Alton scooted the chair out of the way and knelt by the wall. They both jumped when a devilish stone face with a gaping grin leaped suddenly out of the black gloom.

Alton gave a nervous laugh and held his solitary candle closer to the carving. "Looks like Granddad, doesn't it?"

"Now you're supposed to put your fingers in the mouth and pull."

"Whoa. Not me. Not when the instructions don't say what's in there or what happens next." Alton stood and backed two feet away. "You do it."

"Coward."

"Just cautious. Granddad always liked you best,

although why, I could never figure out. So, he won't hurt you, but where I'm concerned . . ." He shrugged.

Glaring at his cousin, Bruce had to admit Alton was right. Their grandfather had shown a preference for him, the younger grandson, and even predicted he'd grow up to take control of the entire family shipping empire. Bruce knew that prize wouldn't be his. Even though his own mother was the eldest child, control of the Finster conglomerate always went down the male line. Besides, Alton wasn't about to give up his privileged place in the succession, even to a smarter male cousin with a higher magic level than his.

On the other hand, for all his accounting ability, Alton wasn't the most complicated spreadsheet on the computer. He couldn't even understand Visicalc and was perfectly happy to let Bruce do the thinking. As a result, Bruce could usually manipulate him to do whatever he wanted, as long as Alton got the credit and none of the blame.

"All right, but you owe me for this." Bruce handed Alton the candelabra.

In the glimmering candlelight, the stone face seemed to move, almost to laugh, almost to lick its lips, almost to be looking forward to chomping on some juicy fingers.

Bruce felt his own hand twitch and reminded himself he was a higher level than the old hedonist had been. He could protect himself. He thrust his index and middle fingers into the mouth.

Nothing happened.

He wiggled his fingers. The space around them was empty.

He reached farther in. The tips hit something. He withdrew his fingers enough to insert his entire hand into the hole and explore. The object at the back became a handle.

"What's there?" Alton asked. "What's inside?"

Bruce grinned as anticipation of what they'd find behind the stone in the wall rippled through him. He knew, absolutely *knew*, his life was somehow about to change enormously. He ignored his cousin and hooked his fingers around the bar. He pulled, first carefully, then harder.

CLICK.

He took a firmer grip and exerted more pressure. With a harsh grating sound, the whole face and the nine-inch-by-twelve-inch stone into which it was carved slid an inch out of the wall.

"Oh, shit," Alton whispered. "What do you suppose is behind it?"

Bruce ignored his cousin, braced his feet, and pulled harder still, grunting with the effort. Stone scraped on stone, and he managed to haul the damn thing out only about three inches. Panting, he looked up at his hovering cousin. "Granddad must have used a strength spell to move this. Do you know one?"

"No, never learned it," Alton replied. "Or a telekinesis spell, either."

"Neither did I." Bruce stood up and waved at the protruding face. "Brute-force time and your turn. Get it out a couple more inches so we can get a better hold around the edges."

Alton put the candelabra on the floor, knelt, wiped his hands on his robe, reached into the mouth, and began to pull.

When the rock protruded another three inches, Bruce said, "Stop."

He grabbed one of the candles and held it by the wall above the face. A deep groove was gouged in the stone's top. The thing was not a stopper protecting a hole behind it, but a drawer.

He put his fingers into the groove. "Come on, Alton, pull."

With the two of them working together, they brought the drawer out another foot. Alton held up the candelabra, and they peered into the small pit.

The groove was not empty.

A red leather-bound book, a duplicate to the diary in Alton's pocket, and a drawstring bag lay in the bottom. Bruce picked up the book and riffled through its pages. "It's a spell book, I think, and some of it looks like a list. It's written in a weird language with strange letters."

"Oh, great," Alton said, rolling his eyes.

Bruce put the book in his robe pocket and studied the bag, a dark red silk with embroidered gold runes and glyphs and black drawstrings. It appeared to be about ten or twelve inches square. Whatever was in it pushed out the sides to make it six inches thick.

He held his hands over it, but could detect nothing to indicate either a threat or the contents—not that he would have been able to recognize a spell, but it seemed the thing to do. The bag itself, however, glistened as the candlelight hit the symbols. Granddad was nothing if not meticulous in his magic and protective of his secrets.

Whatever was in the bag, Bruce knew he didn't want to discover it in this cold darkness. He carefully picked it up by the drawstrings and laid it on the table. "Let's close the drawer and get out of here," he told Alton. "We can investigate our 'inheritance' better upstairs."

"Fine with me," Alton said with a shiver. "I'm freezing."

With both of them pushing, the stone drawer slid back into its place in seconds. Bruce took up the bag, Alton blew out the candles, and they exited the chamber, closing the door firmly behind them. Flashlights worked out in the storage room, thank goodness.

"Let's put the boxes back," Alton said. "We don't want one of the staff finding the door by accident."

Although Bruce doubted anyone had been in this

room in decades, he went along with the idea. Alton was so damn picky—obsessive-compulsive, in fact—about how he put stuff away, and Bruce had long ago given up arguing about it. They restored the wooden boxes to their previous position.

"Come on, my father's study is the best place for privacy," Alton said, and he led the way up the stairs to the book-lined room on the first floor.

The only light came from a green-shaded lamp on the desk, barely enough to illuminate the portrait on the wall over the credenza behind it. Otto Finster, the previous owner of the book and the bag, glared down at them with his perpetual expression of distrust and disgust.

"You have no power now, old man," Bruce said to the picture.

"I wish I was as sure of that as you are," Alton muttered.

Bruce placed the bag on the desk under the lamp and looked through the book again. He had no clue what language it was written in—Greek maybe?

Alton went straight to the bar where he poured himself a stiff brandy. After swallowing it quickly, he poured one for Bruce and refilled his own.

Bruce raised his glass in a small salute to his grandfather and took a generous swallow of the amber liquid. He felt every fiery drop all the way down, and his sense of anticipation returned. "All right, let's see what we have. The diary says it's potent magic, so let's take the precautions it outlined."

"Right. I'll get a bowl from the dining room." Alton left and came back in a minute with a clear crystal bowl. He carried it to the desk, sat in the big leather chair behind it, and put the bowl directly in front of him.

Bruce pulled up a chair and sat across from his cousin. He gently picked up the bag, first by the drawstrings, then cupped it in his hands. The runes and glyphs glowed when the lamplight reflected off the gold threads.

"It's not very heavy," he said, squeezing it slightly. "I can't tell what's inside, however."

"Get on with it, man," Alton gritted.

Bruce took a moment to study his cousin. Since he'd laid eyes on the pouch, Alton had become nervous and sweaty, whereas he himself felt calm and collected. He shut off his curiosity about their different reactions and turned his total attention to the container.

Careful, very careful not to touch the contents, he loosened the drawstrings. Holding the bag by its bottom corners, he slid the contents out of their covering and into the bowl.

The two of them sat until dawn, staring at what fell out.

The contents stared back.

CHAPTER ONE

Present Day

Good, the don't-notice-me spell is working. Irenee Sabel sidled out of the packed second-floor ballroom and into the hall.

Nobody paid the slightest attention, and a couple she knew well passed her without so much as a flicker of acknowledgment or recognition. After a quick glance around, she started walking toward the stairs to the first floor.

She had to admit, Alton Finster knew how to throw a party. On this early summer night, his Chicago Gold Coast mansion was wall-to-wall with the rich and famous and their wannabes. The charity for which the auction gala was being held would rake in a bundle.

Holding her long skirt carefully so she wouldn't trip, she hurried down the stairs and turned right into the darkened corridor. The guards were on their rounds, and she had only a short time to accomplish her task.

A little buzz of excitement—and anxiety—skittered

along her nerves. Her first solo assignment as a Sword! She would accomplish her task, whatever it took.

The carved oak door was locked, of course, but an *adaperio* spell opened it. After another glance around, she slipped inside. She locked the door manually and leaned against it while she studied the room.

Only a lamp over the portrait of Otto Finster on the left-hand wall and a small green-shaded one on the desk illuminated the high-ceilinged study, leaving the bookshelves and corners shrouded in shadows. The elder Finster glared at her from his frame, his hooded eyes seeming to follow her movements. The man had been an unscrupulous scoundrel in business, a ruthless robber baron like his fathers before him. His craggy face with its bushy eyebrows and fierce expression confirmed his determination and implacability.

"You old warlock," Irenee muttered at the portrait, "What do you think of your grandson and the uses to which he's putting your treasure? Or, were you the source of the item we're after? I wouldn't put it past you." She scanned the room. No sign of what she was looking for, of course.

"*Deprendo incantamentum*." She cast a "discover spell" over the room. A faint glow outlined the edge of the oriental rug in the corner to her right. She stepped onto the hardwood in the corner, knelt, and laid her purse on the floor. If anyone had noticed how much larger it was than a regular evening purse, no one had said a word. Let them think she was out of fashion. What did it matter?

Now to see if she'd found the right place, where the spell-sensitive spy they'd inserted into the event catering staff had reported picking up emanations of powerful casting. She knelt and lifted the rug by its tasseled edge.

The hidden safe pulsed faintly with protective enchantments—stay-away and do-not-touch as well as lock-tight, according to her discover spell. To gauge their strength, Irenee held her hand close to the glow remaining from her first spell. She shook her head in disgust when she realized they offered only minimal protection, the kind that would deter only a non-practitioner burglar. Alton must be an idiot to think a simple spell would keep out a Sword.

All practitioners knew certain extremely sensitive Defenders could pick up the vibrations set off when someone used an evil magic item unless the spell caster took elaborate precautions with shielding. True, the vibes Glynnis Fraser, their evil-sensitive expert, felt were faint, but clearly the signature of an ancient, extremely powerful focus for casting. Maybe Alton believed he had been sufficiently protected when he cast spells using the item and had no idea the Defenders were after him. After all, it had taken time—three weeks altogether—to track down the source of the evil. He might believe he was in the clear.

She doubted Alton even knew she was a Sword. The Defenders didn't announce their membership; neither did they keep it a secret. Surely he would have reacted differently to her if he thought she was after him or his treasure. No, his reaction when he greeted her upstairs had been his usual cordial self—exactly as it had been at all the other society functions where they ran into each other.

Irenee, however, had to control herself firmly when they met. Evil people, practitioner or not, gave off an aura, almost a miasma, of *wrongness* Defenders could identify. Where Alton hadn't before, he certainly did now. His recently acquired emanation raised the question of how long he had been using the item. Finding that answer, however, was not her goal.

Her task was clear: bring back the item to her team and help them destroy it. When she succeeded, she would be a Sword in every sense of the word, and also able to hold her head up as an accomplished member of the Sabel family.

She was stretching to lay the carpet back away from the safe, when faint noises came from the door into the hall—a scratching, a click, and the doorknob turning. Someone was picking the lock.

"Damn," she breathed while she let the rug drop over the safe and intensified her don't-notice-me spell to full invisibility. She could see the shimmer as light bent around her, and she smiled with satisfaction. She wouldn't be seen even if somebody looked directly at her.

The door opened slowly, only a crack, just far enough for a figure to slip through.

A tall, dark, curly-haired man in a tuxedo entered quickly and locked the door behind him. Although from her corner and in the darkness, she couldn't get a good look at his face, she didn't think she knew him. He stared at the portrait for a long moment before striding over to it. After tugging at the sides, he swung the picture on its hinges, revealing a black safe door.

A lighted bank of eight red zeros marched across its front. The man pulled a rectangular box out of his pocket and held it to the door. Two green lights on its side blinked alternately while numbers flashed through a complicated sequence.

Irenee smiled to herself. Primitive technology, compared to her magic.

In a few seconds, the green lights stayed on, the zeros had changed to a set of numbers, and the man twisted the handle to open the safe door. He searched through its contents—some papers; a small pistol; a few small, possibly jewelry, boxes—but he must not have found what he wanted because he put it all back. She heard him curse before closing the safe and the portrait.

His hand still on the frame, he suddenly froze for a few seconds, then whipped around.

And looked right into her eyes.

He could see her.

How was that possible?

Irenee stood as he approached, the V of his white tuxedo shirt gleaming in the dim light. Who was this man who clearly saw right through her spells? How did he do it?

He wasn't a warlock. If he was, he wouldn't have used the gadget to open the safe—or not without checking for enchantments. He certainly hadn't cast a discover spell to find her or she would have felt it. Besides, she knew every practitioner capable of recognizing, by sight or otherwise, that she was in the room.

Was he a thief? Who would dare to steal from Alton? No common criminal would trifle with the Finster security forces. Those who tried were usually beaten to a pulp. Corporate espionage? Maybe. What would he expect to find here?

Despite his lock-picking entry, the man wasn't evil. Not a whiff of corruption radiated from him.

If he wasn't a thief, and he wasn't evil, what was he? What was he after? Whatever it was, she knew its likely location—in the safe under her feet.

She was running out of time. The auction would be starting, and the guards would be making another round. She had to get rid of him. If she helped him find his objective, he might leave her alone—after all, he was here as secretly as she was. As a last resort, if he objected, she could always stun him and make her escape.

Although . . . she really hoped she didn't have to do that. The man intrigued her for reasons she couldn't identify—or were her own reactions surprising her?

As she looked at him, a pulse of excitement ran down her backbone, and she was suddenly filled with a sense of well-being and . . . joy? Her magic center under her breastbone fluttered.

By sheer force of will, she succeeded in quelling her peculiar response to this stranger, who was moving silently and lithely, staring into her eyes as if he meant to mesmerize her, his prey. She cancelled her invisibility spell. It obviously wasn't working. He couldn't hurt her, she told herself. She was a Sword.

As he walked around the desk and headed toward the woman, Jim Tylan could still feel the tingling in the back of his head from what he called his "hunch mechanism." That physical response always meant something important or dangerous was about to happen. Why hadn't it alerted him when he walked in the room? He'd probably been so focused on the wall safe, he—and it—simply didn't notice her crouched in the corner.

He mentally cursed when he stopped before her. It was bad enough he hadn't found Finster's clandestine financial records, even though his informant said they were in a safe in the study. No one, however, was supposed to know he was executing a secret search warrant under Homeland Security and Department of Justice auspices. Now he had to deal with a witness.

A witness with a *glow*, both around her and in the rug in front of her.

The radiance cloaking her abruptly vanished when he came within two feet of her. He sent her one of his most accusatory cop glares. She only returned a distinctly puzzled look with no hint of guilt at being caught inside a locked private room.

"Who are you, and what are you doing here?" he asked in a low voice. He'd seen no one in the hall, but the last thing he needed was for someone to hear them and come in.

"Did you find what you were looking for?" she returned in the same tone.

"What business is it of yours?"

"I think I can help you."

"How?"

"You're standing on it." She pointed to the carpet.

"What?" He glanced down. The rug still glowed.

"Step back," she ordered, crouching to lift the rug's corner.

He understood then, knelt, and pulled the carpet back himself. A safe was set into a depression under a clear cover level with the floor. "Why is it shining? Why were *you* glowing?"

She gave him no answer, only shook her head, as if she didn't understand a word he was saying.

He turned his attention to the safe. When he reached for the cover, she put out a hand to stop him. As they touched, a jolt of heat raced up his arm and through his body. They both jerked back, so she must have felt it, too. Despite the shock, he somehow managed to keep a poker face. What the hell was going on here?

"Let me," she told him. She held her hands over the safe for several seconds, and the glow diminished until it disappeared altogether. She removed the cover, turned the handle, and opened the door. A tiny light came on inside the opening.

Together they peered into the foot-square compartment. The contents consisted of three manila envelopes, a black plastic four-inch-square box, a red leather-bound paperback-sized book, and a red drawstring bag embroidered with symbols. The bag glowed—probably the gold embroidery reflecting the dim light.

She picked up the black box and held it out to him. "Is this what you're looking for? Or one of the envelopes?"

Jim stared at her for a moment. Nothing was making any sense. What had happened to the glow around the safe? How did she know what he wanted? Who was she?

The cop in him immediately categorized her: five-foot-seven or eight, dark red hair, dark eyes—too little light to tell the exact color—slim, dressed in a dark blue or black dress. Then the man in him took over. She was gorgeous, curves in the right places, skin almost luminescent. Her wavy, shoulder-length hair made his fingers itch to touch and find out if it was as silky as it looked. She smelled good, and he inhaled deeply as her scent wound its way to him—and through him. Her full mouth was made for kissing—an idea that caused him to lick his lips in anticipation.

She nudged his hand with the box and brought him back to business.

"Yes," he replied, took the box, and opened it. Success. The two small flash drives inside had to contain the data his informant described. He took his specially constructed PDA out of his pocket, plugged in one of the drives, and hit the buttons for copying.

While the machine worked, he watched the woman pick up the book and look at a few pages, a puzzled look on her face. She put it and the bag in her purse, her slightly *glowing* purse, took out an envelope, and laid it in the safe. Was she a thief who left a receipt?

His gadget signaled completion of the copy, and he began the process for the second drive.

"Who are you?" he asked again. "What are you after?" He put his hand on hers, as if the physical connection would gain him answers. It only raised more questions when the jolt went to his toes this time, after making a couple of stops, one behind his solar plexus and the other lower down. He tried to ignore both the itch in his middle and the hardening in his loins.

She frowned. "Nobody and nothing that concerns you," she answered as his PDA clicked again. "We need to hurry. The auction begins in three minutes, I must be there, and I have to reset the alarms on the safe."

He restored the second drive to its box and handed it to her. She replaced it in the safe and, after she closed its door, said, "You'd better leave while I do it. The guard is due on his rounds, and it wouldn't do for both of us to be caught here."

He didn't like it, but he acquiesced. He rose. "I'll see you outside."

He silently unlocked the door and checked the hall. It was empty. He looked back at her, and she was putting the cover on the safe. He stepped into the hall and took up a position close to the stairs where he could see her when she came out. They had some talking to do.

CHAPTER TWO

Ten minutes later, Jim lounged inside the wide doorway leading into the gold-and-white ballroom, where chairs had been set up auditorium-style. His plan to wait for her had been interrupted when a guard had come along, tried the study door and found it locked, then looked pointedly at him. He'd had no choice except to come upstairs.

Damn the woman. His quarry came in a side door in the middle of the left-hand wall. She took a seat on the end of a row, one obviously being saved for her by a short, balding older man who stood and gave her a peck on the cheek. Okay, at least he knew where she was.

He turned his attention to the front of the room where Alton Finster was standing by a lectern on a small stage elevated between large round columns. The man certainly didn't look to be in his early fifties. He was a good-looking SOB, dark-blond hair going gray at the temples, his body showing he exercised regularly. He gave the impression of being in control, both of himself and of Finster Shipping, a global company of trucks, ships, and planes. He came over to Jim's mystery woman, leaned over, and said something. They and the balding man all laughed.

Jim stopped himself from growling. What was the redhead to Finster? Why this rush of anger at the sight of them laughing together? He thought about taking the open seat behind her. They couldn't talk in the middle of the audience, however, and he didn't want to draw attention to himself. No, he'd grab her on the way out.

Finster left the redhead and spoke to a man who had come in the side door. Jim recognized him—Bruce Ubell, Finster's cousin. A "person of interest" in their investigation. Tall like Finster, but Finster was solid, and Ubell was skinny. Where Finster stood out in a crowd, Jim doubted anybody would notice Ubell with his thinning light brown hair and ordinary looks. Just the kind of face eyewitnesses would have trouble describing. No distinguishing marks or features.

A few in the agency questioned which cousin was running the show. Most put their money on Finster. Seeing them together, however, Jim wasn't so sure. Ubell's body language said he was in charge. Jim studied them for about thirty seconds and turned his head when both men scanned the audience. He felt his hunch mechanism tickle again, but he couldn't tell whose gaze had crossed him. Whichever it was, that one was the boss. His hunches were never wrong.

He looked at the redhead again, talking animatedly to the guy next to her. Nothing from his hunch apparatus. Sometimes he thought he had wiggling antennae attached to the mechanism. Neither was fidgeting or tingling. He idly rubbed an itch under his breastbone and turned his attention back to the cousins.

Ubell exited, and Finster walked back to the lectern, picked up a microphone, and spoke some words of welcome, encouraging everyone to bid lavishly during the auction for the good cause. He turned the proceedings over to an auctioneer and stood by the side of the room. As the auction progressed, he gently heckled the bidders to give more and applauded the winners for their generosity.

Jim studied his "complication" while she bid on several items. She appeared to be as innocent as everybody else, but he noticed she kept a firm grasp on her purse with the mysterious book and bag in it. Who was this woman? Too bad he couldn't ask Finster directly. He surveyed the crowd again. Somebody in the bunch of society types ought to know her.

Spotting an ambassador whose life he'd saved several years ago, Jim worked his way around the crowd to the man. Bill Anderson was delighted to see him and happy to provide information.

"She's Irenee Sabel," Anderson said. He pronounced the name *I-ree-nee.* "Sabel Industries, the big conglomerate run by her mother and her brother. Father's Hugh Sabel, the economics genius who left academia to 'dabble' in the stock market, where he made millions. The whole family keeps a low profile. Very old money. Irenee's an event planner, puts together fancy shindigs, although I don't think she handled this one. She's definitely in the background, keeps her name off letterheads and her picture out of the papers. Hasn't been in the business long, and already has a good reputation." He shot a glance at Jim. "She's a beauty, isn't she?"

"Yes, sir, she is." Let the ambassador think he was attracted to Sabel as a woman. The fiction obscured his true objective. "Who's the guy sitting next to her?"

"Dylan Hampton. Does something in a medical field, I believe. They're related somehow. As far as I know, she's never been linked with a boyfriend." Anderson smiled faintly. "Your coast is clear."

Grinning like Anderson had given him the best possible news, Jim shook the man's hand. "Thanks for the information, sir. I'd appreciate your keeping our conversation confidential."

Anderson grinned back and winked. "Don't worry. Your secret is safe with me."

Jim kept a careful eye on Irenee Sabel for the remainder of the auction. At one point, the infuriating woman actually waved merrily at him, then pointed him out to Hampton.

When the bidding was completed, the buyers congratulated, and the floor being cleared for dancing, he started across the room to her. Unfortunately, the crowd was packed together, and he lost her.

He stalked out the side exit she'd used previously, and it took him into a hall, around the ballroom, down the stairs, and into the entrance hall, where she was walking out the door. He tried to reach her, but a group of people suddenly blocked his way, and by the time he came out on the steps, she was climbing into a limo, which quickly moved away from the curb. It turned the corner and was gone.

Grimly he stalked down the stairs toward his car several blocks away. He had a name. He'd find out more about the woman soon. First, he needed to deliver the information burning a hole in his pocket.

Irenee hugged her purse with glee while the limo left Alton's house and headed for the Kennedy Expressway. *She had the evil item!* She'd accomplished her first solo mission. Now to get to the HeatherRidge Center in the northwest suburbs where she and the Defender team could find out exactly what it was and destroy the object.

After checking to make sure the bag and book were still there, she pulled her cell phone out of her purse and hit the speed dial. "Hi, Fergus, it's me. I have the item, and I'm on my way home."

"Excellent!" His voice boomed out of the phone. "Come to the large conference room in the Defenders' building when you get here. Everything go all right?"

"Yes, well, only one small problem, and I handled it. I even spoke to Alton afterward, when I had the item with me. The shields on my purse worked fine. He didn't bat an eye. No way will he connect me with the confiscation."

"Good. The man has proven to be too vindictive when crossed to give him a target."

"I'll see you soon," she replied and hit the disconnect button. She'd tell him about the "small problem" later. Discussing the mysterious man over a cell phone connection wasn't a good idea.

Besides, she needed to concentrate on the object in her purse. If it was as ancient and high a level as Glynnis thought from the vibrations, it was going to be a bear to destroy. Doing so would also be the first real test of her ability. She and the team had only practiced on insignificant evil items, tiny pieces of shattered or misshapen crystals or rocks or metal the Defenders kept for training. Annihilating a major item would put her in the big leagues. She barely stopped herself from wiggling with excitement at the prospect. Never in her wildest dreams had she envisioned the kind of future opening before her.

What a roller coaster ride she and her magical abilities had been on during the past eight years. In a family of overachieving practitioners—her mother, a level eleven, and brother, a level thirteen, both with business mega-abilities, and her father, a level fourteen, stock market genius and Defender—what was she? A lowly level five with some organizing talent. If anybody didn't fit into her family, she was certainly the one.

Oh, she knew she was loved and supported and her level didn't matter, but still . . . So she'd worked extra hard—she *was* smart—and parlayed her meager talents into a career as an event planner after she graduated from Northwestern four years ago. In fact, she'd actually gotten her organizing start while an undergraduate. Somebody with attention to details and willingness to take on the job was always needed in campus activities and organizations. She'd interned with a firm for a year before going out on her own. Thanks to her family's connections and her abilities—both magical and non-magical—she was doing all right.

Her biggest problem after all this was combining her world of business with her world of magic.

How surprised she, her family, and the Defenders had been when she suddenly developed new talents, extra talents, wonderful talents—the kind that usually kicked in at ages eleven to thirteen, not eighteen. Not simply Defender ability to share magical energy. No, the jackpot, *Sword* talent, the power to destroy. Swords, the special forces of the practitioner world. Her magic potential had shot up to a level ten. Then she'd had to learn how to control her new powers.

The Defender Council had taken one look at her and immediately assigned as her teacher not merely any old Sword, and not one of the excellent teachers in the Center, but Fergus Whipple, at level twenty—the top one—the most powerful Sword alive. Between the demands of his tutoring and her college and job activities, she was surprised she had lived through the long years of study and preparation.

It hadn't been all drudgery, of course. What fun she'd had learning to cast or "draw" her sword, to throw fireballs and lightning bolts, and most of all to focus her energy down to a laser beam of incredible power and destroy evil. What a rush!

Best of all, she could truly hold up her head as an accomplished member of the Sabel family.

She'd have to tell her Defender team about the man in Alton's study. Uncle Dylan would work the crowd to find out who he was. She smiled at the thought of her uncle on her mother's side. He looked so innocuous and bland that people told him more than they realized. Behind his balding facade, however, lurked the mind of an excellent psychiatrist. With any luck, Mr. Mysterious would try to pump Dylan for her name and become the pump-ee instead of the pump-er.

Perhaps the man was in law enforcement. Once the Defenders had started investigating Alton, they'd discovered the extent of the evil in his criminal activities—drug smuggling, weapons dealings, money laundering. If the authorities had discovered Alton's crimes, they would be after him, and Mr. Mysterious was one of theirs. The Defenders had made plans to inform relevant agencies of Alton's deeds, but only after they had the evil item—their first priority—in hand.

As for her attraction to the man in the office? She was a young, healthy woman. Who wouldn't be attracted to a handsome man with a square jaw and broad shoulders? She found interesting a man whose nose looked like it had been broken once, just enough to make him look rugged, not male-model-pretty, and whose hair curled just enough to make her want to run her fingers through it. And she mustn't forget his piercing gaze. Too bad she didn't know what color his eyes were. It had been too dark to tell in the study, and she hadn't gotten close enough in the ballroom.

She thought she'd handled him well. Thank goodness he went along with her suggestion to leave, and she didn't have to stun him. A body lying in the study would really have alerted Alton to something amiss.

Irenee dismissed the mystery man from her mind

to concentrate on reviewing the procedures for destroying an evil item. Eventually, the limo pulled up to the HeatherRidge Center and dropped her off at the building housing the Defender offices, classrooms, and training facilities.

The center, the practitioner complex of training, meetings, research, and condo/hotel, was the only site in North America for advanced Defender and Sword education. Destruction of major evil magic items took place here in an extensive underground network of rooms. Although practitioners loved the original HeatherRidge Hotel close to the edge of downtown Chicago, nobody wanted to destroy major items in the middle of a city where a mistake could cause disaster.

When she started training, she'd moved to the Center, but she didn't drop by her own condo in another building to change out of her evening dress. First she had to report, and she hurried down to the conference room where the team was waiting.

"I have it!" she announced when she entered the room. In addition to the six members of her team, four other Defenders—including her father—were present. The only other Sword besides Fergus was John Baldwin from New York, a member of the Defender Council. The item had to really be important if a council member was here.

Everyone burst into applause.

"Excellent," Fergus said and gave her a hug. It was like being hugged by a combination bear and Santa Claus since Fergus stood six-five and had a full beard and flowing white hair.

Irenee stepped up to the table between Fergus and Glynnis Fraser, their resident expert in the power and character of magical items, and opened her purse. "I found something else and brought it along." She held up the book. "It seemed to go with this." She handed Fergus the book and took out the bag and laid it on the table.

Fergus opened the book and looked at a few pages. "Looks like Greek combined with another language. Here, Jacob, what do you think?" He passed the book across the table.

Ancient-language expert Jacob Mbuto leafed through it. "Yes, at least one other. I can see Cyrillic, maybe some Sanskrit, and a few letters that appear to be totally made up. I'll consult with a few scholars tomorrow."

"Fine. Now let's see the real prize. Irenee, you do the honors." Fergus waved at the bag and the crystal bowl in the middle of the table.

"Wait," Glynnis, a tall woman with light brown skin and salt-and-pepper hair, spoke. "First, everyone put on your robes for protection. We don't know exactly what we're dealing with here."

"Here, Irenee, I brought yours," her father said, handing her the garment, after giving her a little hug.

"Thanks," Irenee said and hugged him back.

She shrugged into the flowing, hooded, midnight black robe but didn't bother to close it. Her fellow Swords, Fergus and John Baldwin, wore the same color, and their greater experience and power was displayed in the many glyphs appearing—to those few with the talent to see them—on the bands down the center and on the cuffs and around the bottoms and hoods of the robes. By contrast, Irenee had only a few of the symbols; she'd accumulate more with experience.

Defenders wore the colors associated with their everyday talents, and several shades of blues, greens, browns, reds, yellows, metallics, and others swirled when they donned theirs.

Telling herself to be calm even though she was about to burst with excitement, Irenee picked up the bag while Glynnis positioned the bowl and the plate under it.

"Be careful," Glynnis warned, "not to touch the item. Evil has a way of 'rubbing off' on the handler of some of these stronger articles."

"I'll watch out," Irenee assured her. She loosened the drawstrings, grasped the two corners at the bottom, and slid the contents into the shallow receptacle.

A couple of people gasped. Several drew their robes tight around them. Everyone stared at what had appeared.

Irenee had expected some sort of crystal or polished rock or metal brooch with a gemstone or even a small dagger, like the pictures of various ancient evil items. She'd studied misshapen objects, semi-melted jewelry, crystal clusters in grotesque shapes, and nausea-inducing carvings.

Nothing she'd seen or heard of looked like what lay in the bowl.

An obsidian crystal about three inches long, the item was shaped like one end of a large egg. The rounded portion held many facets, but they absorbed, rather than reflected, the overhead lights. The rest of the egg had been sliced off with a slanted cut or perhaps broken along an oblique fault line, leaving a smooth, sloping side. Even more than the facets, this surface sucked in light like a miniature black hole.

"This cannot be right," Glynnis stated, bending over the bowl. "It is not whole. Where's the rest of it?"

"Th-that's all there was," Irenee said as nausea roiled in her stomach. Oh, God, she'd confiscated the wrong item. Or only part of it. She had failed. She had to clear her throat before she could say, "Nothing else was in the safe except for some envelopes and a black box with flash drives in it."

Glynnis patted her arm. "I know it's all you found, honey. The rest was probably destroyed long ago when the break occurred."

Although the comment helped bolster Irenee's confidence, disappointment still ate at her insides.

"What is, or was, the whole?" Fergus asked.

Glynnis hesitated, studied the object for a few minutes with a magnifying glass as she used a pair of tongs to turn it over. She held her hands over the bowl to measure its vibrations. She stood unmoving, eyes closed, for a number of minutes. Finally she opened her eyes and said, "Assuming it did look like an egg, I'd estimate the intact item would have been about seven or eight inches on its long axis. Taking into account the slanting cut, I estimate this is about a third of the intact whole. The vibrations from this remaining piece are incredibly strong. It's definitely what I felt when Alton Finster used it to cast. Do any of you feel anything?"

Several Defenders reported a much higher level of dizziness and queasiness than evil items usually caused.

Irenee pushed her personal feelings of possible failure aside. She wasn't having her usual reaction to an evil item, either. "My magic center feels like something's tugging on it—or trying to get in."

"That's the item looking for a victim. Fasten your robe," Fergus said. "Everybody, even you two at the end of the table, button up."

Irenee kicked herself mentally for not remembering to follow one of the basic rules for dealing with nasty items. The robes, with all their heavy-duty protective enchantments, were their first line of defense, able to repel harmful spells on their own. She quickly pulled the sides together, hooked the loops over the buttons, and tied the sash. "It stopped."

"With me, too," Annette Chang reported.

Glynnis nodded. "As for its identity, I can't be totally certain without more research, but it's ancient and extremely powerful, even in its fractured state. The total blackness and the absorption of light have been documented in only a few items, and all except two of them have been found and destroyed. If it's what I think it is, we may be fortunate to have to deal solely with this portion. It's a coup for us that we confiscated it. Since the fifteenth century, Defenders have been looking for the Cataclysm Stone."

CHAPTER THREE

While Glynnis and Fergus moved the Cataclysm Stone to the specially spelled and protected underground chamber where they would destroy it, Irenee ran over to her condo to change into comfortable clothes. There was no telling how long demolition would take with such an ancient artifact, even a somewhat diminished one. It was midnight already. She might be standing for hours.

Fergus had taken her aside for a moment to say she had accomplished her mission exactly as required and with great success. If the piece of the Stone was all Alton had, so be it. There was nobody else they could have sent or who would have confiscated the item with so little furor.

She'd smiled and thanked him. Although one part of her knew he was right, the other part wasn't totally convinced. Should she have looked around more? No, she couldn't have. Not with that man in the study with her.

Oh, goodness, she hadn't told anyone about him.

How could she have forgotten him? Even with all her attention on the Stone? She'd tell the team immediately after they took care of the item. For the moment, she'd put him out of her mind. The destruction process required that she pay close attention. One tiny mistake, one break in concentration, one weakness in her blade could bring horror to them all.

She could do this, she assured herself.

She headed for the other building's basements, fastening her robe securely as she went.

The team had gathered in the larger of the two "D" rooms, those used only for practice with and actual destruction of items. Her Defender team members were colorful as always: Glynnis in her purple robe; Thomas Canterbury, jewelry maker with copper, gold, and silver tracings; Bill Trusdale, landscaper with green leafy designs on his; Annette Chang, a meteorologist showing off dark blue swirls reminiscent of weather patterns; Denton Jones, tall in his banker's robes, with multicolored engravings like money. A healer in yellow, nurse Mary Ann Matlow, was on the side preparing her medical kit.

Those in the conference room had also accompanied the team, including her father Hugh in his gold economics robe, Jacob Mbuto with black and white letters from varying alphabets on a beige background, and John Baldwin in his Sword black.

As she had been trained and was her duty, Irenee surveyed the room carefully to make sure all was ready.

The five stone-clad walls glowed with spells designed to restrain unleashed, undisciplined power, and those were at full strength. Stone benches were set about two feet from the walls. Candles in sconces along the walls provided more conventional light.

A large pentagon, fifteen feet from center to corner point, was engraved into the floor. When activated, it would become their fortress. In its center a five-sided stone pedestal rose to a height of two feet. On the top sat the crystal platter and bowl containing the Cataclysm Stone.

A shiver snaked through Irenee when she glanced at the evil item. If she didn't know better, she would swear it was looking back at her.

"Don't stand directly in front of its broken smooth face," Fergus said. "I don't like the feeling I get from it."

"Neither do I."

"We'll attack the Stone from the sides. The key to destruction is to kill the facets, and they're reached more easily that way. Is everything set?"

She nodded to the big mage. "All's in order."

"Team members, take your positions," Fergus said. "The rest of you get comfortable. I hope we won't need you. Thank you for being our backup in any case. Mary Ann, are you ready?" When the nurse answered yes, he and Irenee stepped into the pentagon and placed themselves on either side of the pedestal, the length of their individual swords away from it. One Defender stood inside each corner.

"*Munire aegis. Castellum. Tenere,*" they all said together and pointed at the pentagon in the floor. *Build protection. Fortress. Hold.*

Multicolored lights flared along the five-sided figure, which glowed as shimmering walls formed and climbed to the ceiling, where they met overhead to form a roof. The walls did not prevent people or objects from passing through them in either direction, but the spells as cast would contain an inside discharge of harmful magic. Without the "hold," the fortress protected against magic from outside. Every team member fed power into the shield until it was a gleaming rainbow.

When Fergus nodded, he and Irenee both cast their swords, holding them firmly in two-handed grips. She cast her spell to create an energy weapon looking like the gladius, a Roman shortsword about thirty inches long overall. Since the weightless magical blades required both hands to wield, she had modified the original design to increase the length of the grip. Her sword was elegant, she thought, and it fit her perfectly. She started hers on a lower seventh level, green laced with yellow swirls and brought it up to blue.

To match his size, Fergus's weapon was a massive claymore, fully five feet from pommel to tip, and he also began at a lower level before raising it to a silver-striped gold. Both pointed their swords toward the ceiling.

A low hum vibrated through the air, and the light generated by the energy in the swords, plus the pentagon shield, made the room brighter than day.

She and Fergus saluted each other and brought the tips down to point directly at the Cataclysm Stone. The evil item seemed to grow blacker in the bright light.

"Is everyone ready?" Fergus asked. They all said yes.

"One, two, three," he said softly in a measured cadence.

The Defenders focused and put their hands first on their magic centers, then extended them palms up in front of them. Magical energy poured from their hands, shimmering with rainbow colors. The individual streams spread horizontally, linked up with those of the others, and began to melt together. What began in various colors coalesced into a shining circle of gold floating midway between the Defenders and the backs of the two Swords.

The hum increased in resonance and went lower in pitch.

As she felt the power growing, Irenee took a firm, centered stance, made sure her shoulders were relaxed, and concentrated on her own magic center. The area under her breastbone, which some called the energy well, came to attention. She nodded at Fergus.

"One, two, three," he said again.

She tapped into the power source swirling behind them, gathered energy into her well, molded it into a form she could use.

"One, two, three."

Irenee aimed the power into her sword, and a laser beam of energy shot out of its tip directly at the evil Stone. Fergus hit the item with his beam from the other side at the same time.

"One, two, three."

They both flooded their swords with energy. His turned pure gold. Hers intensified, moving up the levels from blue to blue with indigo streaks. Where the beams met the Cataclysm Stone, they combined into a pure white. The light flowed like water around the black item, over the facets, down the sheer slope of the ruined side. The surface of the black facets turned shiny, as if the Stone no longer tried to absorb, but to repulse the light. The hum dropped an octave, took on the rhythmic aspects of a slow and steady heartbeat.

They held the pose, deluging the object in good, white power. Irenee lost track of time as she modulated the energy passing through her center, being careful to maintain an emergency reserve while making sure she was reaching all of the Stone facets she could see.

The Stone began to tremble like the facets were moving or the pedestal shaking. A sensation like the rising of a strong wind snaked around the interior of the pentagon. A low moan sounded at the edge of hearing.

"Ignore the moan," Fergus ordered. "It's at the

frequency that causes unease and often terror in human minds. The Stone's fighting back. We're making progress."

Irenee said nothing, took a deep breath, and blocked the sound out. It wasn't easy. She could almost feel icy tendrils of evil reaching for her from the Stone, almost see an oily mist of nauseating colors begin to pool in the crystal bowl, almost smell noxious fumes rising from the mist.

She shook her head and reached for a bit more energy. The illusions vanished. *Hah, take that!*

The damaged crystal continued to shudder, and its faceted surface rippled as though its insides had turned molten and boiled. It began to roll from side to side in the bowl like a boat in heavy seas. The damaged slice, which had been facing between the two Swords, began to shift in her direction.

"Watch out, Irenee," Fergus said, "the damn thing is maneuvering its smooth side to aim right at you."

"I see it," she answered and increased her power output as the Stone turned its fractured face to her. "From this angle, it appears almost transparent or hollow, but there's something like a black flame burning inside."

"Pure evil power." Fergus poured on more energy from his side.

The Stone's facets began to undulate, trying to throw off the attacks. She and Fergus had tight control, however, and forced the reflected beams right back on their target.

"Give us more, Defenders. We're beginning to havc a real effect." Fergus's sword took on tinges of white when he increased the power of his output.

Irenee threw more energy from the team into the mix and forced it through her sword until blue and indigo swirled together equally along the shining blade.

The Stone's undulations quickened. The facets twisted, writhed, threw off one beam of light only to be deluged by another, until the surface appeared liquid.

Irenee knew they were succeeding as one, then another facet faded, gave off a brief burst of blackness, and sank into the heart of the Stone.

Good, progress. Maybe she could relax a little, build up some reserve energy. Breathing easier, she set a part of her mind to the task, flexed her shoulders, lifted her beam the tiniest bit.

The black flame at the Stone's center lunged at her.

"No!" She jerked her sword beam down and forced the flare back into the Stone.

Another blaze of black struck out. She hammered that one into retreat.

And another and another.

She pulled all the power she could—more than she ever had before—from the team, but the flame kept attacking. First to one side, then to the other. Twice in a row she barely managed to bring her beam to bear in time.

She grabbed for more energy. The team responded.

A flare shot out.

"Oh, no, you don't!" she snarled and threw it back into the Stone.

Breathe, relax the shoulders, keep the wrists flexible.

Another strike. Another block.

How much did the team have in reserve? How long could she keep this up? What would happen if they ran out of energy?

She stopped yet another assault from the Stone and braced herself for its retaliation.

She vaguely heard Fergus shouting, "John, Hugh, the rest of you! Get in here! Mary Ann, call for every Sword and Defender in the Center."

John came through the shield to stand beside her, and his pure silver blade began to work with hers on the evil reaching out of the Stone.

She increased her power and speed. She wasn't going to relax her guard again.

She felt her father at her back, his hands on her waist, feeding his energy directly to her, and oh, it was so powerful and so welcome. Her sword glowed pure indigo.

The Defender reinforcements added strength to all three Swords.

More people, including two Swords, joined them inside the pentagon. Irenee ignored them. All she could see was the black fractured face with the hideously obscene flame behind it. The evil continued to attack her alone.

Brilliant light surrounded her and all the Swords as they poured energy onto the Stone. The hum had become a deep roar, and people were shouting or screaming with the effort to produce more power.

She found support. Physical in the bulwark of her father. Mental and magical in the energy the Defenders were pouring into her. She embraced both to increase her output. Her sword developed a violet tinge and settled into violet streaks through the dark blue.

Attack. Counter. Attack again. Counter again.

She had no idea how long they battled.

A cheer rose when facets finally began to die once more. Slowly, so slowly, the Cataclysm Stone began to shrink.

At the last, the smooth face collapsed in upon the flame, and the Stone lost facets at an accelerated rate. It dwindled rapidly to a six-sided cube, then a four-sided pyramid on a square base, and finally to a triangular structure of only four facets.

"Strike now!" Fergus thundered. "One, two, THREE!"

Irenee threw every bit of energy she could grab into her blade's beam. Blinding white light hit the dying Stone from all sides.

A shrill cry of rage and despair filled the room as the black flame flared one more time. What was left of the

Stone disintegrated into a small pile of ashes.

The cry continued until only its echo reverberated off the walls.

Finally, silence, except for everyone's harsh breathing.

Irenee let her hands fall to her sides, dissipating her blade. So drained she couldn't have even cast *flamma* to light a candle, she looked straight across the remains of the Stone at Fergus and said, "Well, that was exciting."

Then she fainted into her father's arms.

CHAPTER FOUR

"Alton!" Bruce let himself into the Finster mansion and put the keys into his pocket. He'd been jolted out of a sound sleep by the sure knowledge something was horribly wrong. He had the distinct impression his Stone was calling to him. Since it never had before, he thought the feeling must have come from the bad dream he'd been having—until the phone rang.

The house was silent. The caterers had all left, and the staff had gone to bed.

"Alton?" Bruce called again. "Where are you? What's so important to get me over here at two thirty in the morning?"

"Here." Alton appeared in the hall and beckoned him into the study. His cousin looked like shit—pale skin, dark shadows under his eyes, his hair sticking up, his clothes disheveled. Quite a contrast to the debonair host he'd been at the party.

"What's the matter?" Bruce asked as he entered the room.

"It's gone," Alton wailed. He pointed to the corner of the room where Granddad's old safe lay. The rug was folded back, and the safe's door was open. "You gotta help me."

Bruce looked around the room. Except for the safe, nothing seemed disturbed or out of place. "Take it easy. What's gone? What are you talking about?"

Alton handed him a piece of paper.

Bruce glanced at the paper, and his center contracted into a cold, hard ball. Displayed on a black pentagon, the Defender golden shield with two silver long swords across it practically leaped off the page. He quickly moved over to the desk to read it under the light.

NOTICE OF CONFISCATION

By order of the High and Defender Councils:

Alton Finster:

You are hereby notified that the Defenders have confiscated an evil magic item or items found to be in your possession.

This seizure was made in accordance with Section LX, Paragraph 1, of the Practitioner Constitution; Section XII, Paragraph 2, of the Rules Concerning Magic Items, the High Council Procedures; Section II, Paragraph 1, of the

Defenders Mission; and your oath as freely given on your eighteenth birthday to abide by all practitioner laws, rules, and codes of ethics.

The item or items will be destroyed as quickly as possible.

Note: If you have attempted to or have actually used the item to cast spells:

You may be physically or mentally harmed in the destruction process.

Your magic level may be decreased by the destruction process.

You may be in need of medical attention after the item is destroyed.

By authority of Section XII, Paragraph 10, of the Rules Concerning Magic Items, the High Council Procedures; Section III, Paragraph 5, of the Defenders Mission; and your oath referenced above, neither you nor any member of your family may sue or otherwise attempt revenge on the High Council, the Defenders, or any other person involved in this seizure and destruction. If you take any such action, none of the above are liable for the outcome, which may result in greater physical harm to you, up to and including your death.

Members of the High and Defender Councils will call at their earliest convenience to investigate your possession of this item and to determine the effects it may have had on you, your actions, your environment, and other persons.

You may be subject to a fine and/or a censure and/or required to make restitution for harmful effects caused by you, the item, or you and the item acting in concert.

It is in your best interest to cooperate with the investigation.

Fergus Whipple,
Sword and Defender

The freeze in his center became an arctic blast that almost congealed his gut. Bruce waved the sheet of paper at his cousin. "What the hell is this, Alton? What did they confiscate?"

"It was here before. They must have taken it during the gala, but the door was locked," Alton mumbled while he paced around the room, gesturing wildly.

"Alton!" Bruce grabbed him by the shoulders and gave him a shake. "Stop it. Tell me what happened. What's missing? What evil item did they take? How did they get into the basements without somebody noticing?"

Alton seemed to deflate. He pointed over to the open floor safe and shook his head. "I had my Stone in there. I've been using it lately to make sure the deal went through—the new one with the Iranian group."

"You had your *Stone* up here? You *used* it up here? You *left* it up here in the safe?" Bruce's voice rose, and he shook Alton harder with each question. Finally he flung his cousin into a chair. "You damn idiot! You shit-for-brains fool! How many times have I told you to *never* cast a spell with your Stone *anywhere* except in the shielded room downstairs? And *never* without me, without our using the Stones together for maximum power? And *never* to take it out of that room?"

"I know," Alton sniveled. "The deal looked like it was going bad. Their numbers weren't adding up. You've been out of town for the past month, and the people from the gala were driving me crazy, and the Iranians were pressuring me for answers. So I cast a few spells to get the weapons buyers off my back."

Bruce ran a hand through his hair. What a time for Alton to develop an independent streak. He thought he'd cured the jackass of acting on his own initiative long ago. "You're all wrong about the deal, but that's not the most important thing. Why did you keep your Stone here? *It was only yours, wasn't it?* Alton, if you brought mine upstairs and they took it, so help me . . ."

"No, no, it was only mine. You know yours doesn't like me. It won't let me use it like you can do with mine. Besides, I like having mine around. It feels good. I feel good."

"Goddamnit, you're addicted to it. I've warned you about the dangers, haven't I?"

Alton wiped his face with his sleeve. "How did the Defenders find out? We've had the Stones for twenty-five years, and we've used them over and over again. We wouldn't have been able to build that side of the business without them."

"How the hell should I know how the Defenders do anything? Maybe they have antennas on the Hancock Building or the Sears Tower to pick up spells being cast with items like the Stones. Granddad told us in the red book to never take them out of the special room, remember? He obviously had a reason. I did what he said. Why didn't you?"

"Oh, my God. The red book." Alton's face went even paler. He jumped up and ran over to the safe, knelt, and rummaged through the remaining contents. "It's not here."

"They got the book, too? Oh, great, just great." Bruce took a deep breath and concentrated on getting hold of himself before he really did kill his cousin. *Think, man.* "Look, maybe it's not so bad. They probably can't read it. We couldn't—not until we took over the Stones. They conferred the power on us."

"How can we get mine back? The letter says they're going to destroy it." Alton stood up and went back to slump in his chair.

"Who specifically took it? When exactly?"

Alton leaned forward and put his head in his hands. He spoke slowly, as if reciting his actions carefully. "I know my Stone was here before the gala because I looked at it during the afternoon. There were people, gala organizers, caterers all over the place for the last three days. I kept the study locked and posted a guard to make sure none of them had access to the private parts of the house. Somebody must have taken it during the party. But who? It could have been any guest or staff. Maybe we can ask the guards who patrolled the hall if they saw someone."

"Wonderful. We'll have to compare the entire guest and staff lists to the practitioner registry to find our likely culprit."

"The registry doesn't tell who's a Defender. Except for the people on the Defender Council and Whipple, their names don't get broadcast around." Alton was whining now, and Bruce wanted to slug him to shut his cousin up. The man was such a wimp.

"No, but it will help us narrow the field, and I have a couple of sources for gossip." Bruce started pacing between the desk and the door while he ran through possibilities and probabilities—not, however, about retrieving the idiot's piece. The notice of confiscation said Alton's Stone would be destroyed as soon as possible. They could be working on killing it this very minute. Probably were. No, that Stone was gone.

His, however, remained. His, the larger piece, with the greater power to go with his higher magical level. His magic center seemed smug all of a sudden—exactly like it was when he was casting spells with the Stone. His Stone. He'd miss having Alton's piece to boost his power, but he didn't really need it.

He almost laughed. Without his Stone, Alton would cease to be a nuisance, would have to get out of his way completely, even as a figurehead. Bruce would be the one in complete, unquestioning control. He'd finally get what was due him. Looks like Granddad's prophecy was going to come true. He'd be in charge of the companies—and *all* their activities.

Bruce stood staring at the door and beyond it, contemplating his wonderful future, when a strange noise, a drawn-out grunt from Alton, turned him around to face his cousin.

Alton gasped, groaned, and fell out of his chair to the floor. He curled up in the fetal position and began moaning and rocking from side to side.

"What happened? What's going on? What do you feel?" Bruce leaned over him without touching him. Alton was obviously in pain. The Defenders must be destroying the Stone, right this minute. He had no idea what would happen to Alton when they did, and he'd be damned if he was going to hang on to the man and get caught in a backlash.

Alton rocked more violently, his moans became shouts, and his eyes were wide open but focused on somewhere out of the study. "No! No! I won't let you! Bitch! Son of a bitch!"

"What, Alton? Who? Do you see someone? Who's the bitch?"

Alton looked up at him, seemed to actually see him. "Re-re-red . . . B-b-b . . . I- . . . Sa . . ."

"Who, Alton? Read? Read what? A book? The red book? You what? You say what?"

The writhing man shook his head and began to shout again. "No! You can't! I'll get you, I'll get you!"

He reached out and grabbed Bruce, who recoiled and fought to free himself as enormous fear, pain, and anger spread through him from Alton's grip. He had to kick Alton in the ribs to break loose, and he retreated across the room until he was sure his cousin wouldn't be able to seize him again.

Alton yelled and thrashed around, cursing, trying to cast spells on whoever was tormenting him. At times he seemed to be dodging a missile; at others, he was plainly taking a direct hit.

Bruce moved a chair and a small table out of Alton's way, but did not approach him. He needed to find out who the bitch or the son of a bitch was—or were. As powerful as the smaller Stone was, he assumed it would take more than one Defender to kill it. He wanted to know his enemies. It was quickly clear, however, that Alton could not supply the information.

As Alton's torture went on, Bruce felt a familiar stirring in his magic center—his now warm center. Gone was the frozen lump of ice. His own portion of the Stone was responding, reaching out to help its severed third. Magical energy coursed through his body until he felt like he could take on the world. There was clearly no way he could help his cousin—he couldn't see whoever was killing the other Stone, and Alton had gone beyond speech to incoherent cries.

Maybe what was happening to Alton didn't matter. The influx of magic infusing Bruce's brain and muscles was conferring new powers. He could actually feel his knowledge, abilities, and spells growing. When the Stone granted them the power to read the red book, the process had been pleasurable. This gift surpassed the previous ones by a magnitude of hundreds or thousands—ecstasy.

As he watched his cousin writhing on the floor, Bruce smiled. When he found out who was behind the attack, he now possessed the ability to destroy them. He intended to take every iota of pleasure out of doing so.

Suddenly, Alton went stiff, arched his body so only his shoulders and feet touched the floor, and screamed, a long, drawn-out wail of anger and pain and despair. Bruce thought he heard another deeper cry, this one coming from under his feet where the secret room lay. An immense sorrow engulfed him for a moment. Then Alton collapsed—out cold or dead.

Bruce knelt beside him and put his hand on Alton's neck, searching for a pulse. Just as he found a faint beating, the door flew open, and Sedgwick, the butler who had been with the Finsters since before Bruce was born, burst in, his robe askew, his thinning hair flying.

"What's the matter, Mister Bruce? What's wrong with Mister Alton? Was he screaming? It woke me up. It sounded horrible."

"Call 9-1-1, Sedgwick. Alton's had some kind of a fit. Don't worry about anything except him. I'll take care of everything else."

CHAPTER FIVE

Fireballs and lightning bolts came at Jim from every direction, singeing his body as they passed. A black hole was opening at his feet, and he fought against its pull, scrabbling backward on a slick, uneven surface and losing ground with each breath.

He couldn't get his shield up, couldn't fight back.

The hole grew bigger, the surface became slicker, and the darkness got blacker. A flame burned at the bottom of the well.

He was sliding into the horrible pitch-dark maw, when a brilliant white light speared past him and blew the hole to smithereens.

He yelled and woke up, gasping for air and sweating like he'd just run out of hell.

"Holy shit! What was that?" he mumbled while he hauled himself out of bed and into the bathroom. After splashing cold water on his head and chest and drinking some out of his cupped hands, he felt a little better.

He staggered back into the bedroom and flopped on

the bed. His breathing and his heartbeat still weren't back to normal, and he rubbed his aching, itching breastbone.

He peered at the clock. Three in the friggin' morning. He'd only been asleep for an hour and a half.

Where had his crazy dream come from? Black holes? This damn case was a black hole. Finster's activities all by themselves were enough to give him nightmares—already had, as a matter of fact.

If he'd found the right information last night, however, he would look forward with great relish to seeing the bastard brought to justice. If they couldn't catch him outright in drugs or weapons smuggling, they would catch him the same way they caught Al Capone—tax fraud and evasion.

Jim had delivered the flash drive copy to the office after he left Finster's, and the techies went to work on it immediately. As ordered, he'd phoned the task force head to report his success, and Ken Erlanger had praised his work.

But . . . Jim had left out part of what had happened in Finster's study. He couldn't bring himself to mention the redheaded woman—who glowed. He had to learn who she was and how she fit into the mess before he told anyone about her. He had to see her again.

Because? Because another hunch was driving this decision. One of the most powerful he'd ever had.

At first, the guys in his police squad and then the Drug Enforcement Administration and now a combined task force had ridiculed him for his intuition, his premonitions, his out-of-left-field notions like he was a weirdo or a charlatan. When his hunches started to pay off, everybody shut up. Next, they were asking his help.

Sometimes he wondered where his ideas came from. They didn't really come all that often, and the big, solve-the-case ones didn't show up until he and the others had gathered reams of information. It was like the data had to sit in his brain and percolate, drip down from his subconscious. He'd be doing something totally unrelated when, all of a sudden, *wham*, and everything was laid out in his mind like rolling out a carpet.

Having a quick strong hunch, like with this woman, was rare. Something would be behind it. What, he didn't know—yet. Could she be the real key to nailing Finster?

He almost let himself follow the road of wishing he'd had a quick hunch about his sister—hell, any hunch about his sister. Almost. He shut off the thoughts, stuck them behind the wall in his mind, and remortared the stone. Finster would pay for what he did to Charity. Patience and good police work were the keys.

He turned over, punched the pillow, rubbed his itching sternum, and willed himself to sleep.

In a private dining room at four in the morning, Irenee took a break from stuffing herself and looked up. Everybody in the room was eating like they hadn't seen food in a month. One of the wait staff brought her favorite dessert, warm fudge cake and raspberry sauce. Could she truly eat more? When the warm chocolate smell hit her nose, she realized of course she could.

Because energy in the human body was caloric and spells required use of that energy, she'd known she needed to eat to maintain her Sword powers. She never expected, however, to be eating like a teenaged boy or a farmhand. On the other hand, she could indulge her sweet tooth. She'd probably lost five or ten pounds in tonight's endeavors. Maybe a hot-fudge sundae would top off her appetite—after the cake, of course.

The food was definitely helping her headache, and she didn't feel at all wobbly anymore. She hadn't been the only one to fall over when the Cataclysm Stone finally died, so she wasn't embarrassed by her fainting. Two team members and two backups had also.

She did feel somewhat guilty and chagrined about relaxing her guard for the moment when the black flame almost burst out of the Stone and hit her. Her training had emphasized the need to maintain concentration.

Better to face her lapse, learn from the mistake, and go on.

Turning to Fergus sitting at the head of the long table next to her, she waited until he put down his coffee cup before speaking softly. "Listen, I'm sorry I almost blew it."

His bushy eyebrows shot up. "What are you talking about? When?"

"I made a mistake, relaxed when I shouldn't have. When the facets first started dying, I jumped to the conclusion the Stone was much weaker than it actually was. It almost got loose, and it was my fault."

"Nonsense. I was assuming the same thing. The attack surprised me, too. No, you have nothing to apologize for."

"But—"

"Hush, Sword. You did your job." He smiled at her. "I, for one, am very proud of you. We'll have to test your level again. From the way your sword changed colors, I think you went up during the battle."

A little thrill of excitement zinged through her when she remembered the color changes. At the same time, praise from her mentor choked her up so much she couldn't get a word out in return—not that he gave her the chance. He stood up and clinked his spoon against his water glass.

When he had everyone's attention, Fergus said, "We have done some great work tonight. Thanks especially to those who answered our call for help. I've never had an item cause so much unexpected havoc. I particularly call to your attention the actions and abilities of Irenee Sabel, our newest team member. Her blade was pure lightning. I doubt very much I could have risen to the challenge the way she did at the same stage of my career."

Someone started clapping, and the entire group rose to applaud her.

The praise totally discombobulated her, and it took all of her control to say simply, "Thank you," and not burst into tears. Her father, standing next to her, gave her a hug.

Fergus waited until everyone was seated again before speaking. "We should be proud of all of us. However, I fear we are not finished with the power residing in that Stone."

Unsure what he meant, Irenee stole a glance around the table. Several Defenders were nodding. All looked worried. She sat up straight as tension from her center tightened her muscles.

"I would venture a hypothesis," Fergus went on. "First, the remainder of the Cataclysm Stone, the larger portion, has *not* been lost to history. And for the sake of argument, let's propose only one other piece exists and the original has not broken into multiple parts—a nightmare we definitely don't need. Second, this other piece is close by. Third, someone other than Alton Finster has it."

Several Defenders nodded in agreement.

"Here is my reasoning: Usually, once facets or other physical attributes of an item start dying, that's its death knell. It will continue to fight, but only with defensive, not offensive action. This Stone, however, attacked us, Irenee specifically, after its facet decline. Therefore, it had help, more power from a different source, which could only logically come from its mate, the other piece. The missing remnant, larger by Glynnis's extrapolative measurements, probably more powerful as well, still lives. The proof is in the scream at the end that went on after the reduction to ashes. While I've had many an item cry at its end, I've never heard a sound so late or with an echo. Does anyone disagree with my theory so far?"

John Baldwin spoke up. "I concur with the defensive versus offensive action also. I've never seen one begin to lose mass and then come back. Let me point out also, the aid from the other remnant pierced all our shielding on the building, in the D chamber walls, and in our pentagon fortress to reach the smaller piece. I've never heard of such a possibility in modern times, although I can think of a couple of legends telling of similar powers. We may be very lucky the monster is in pieces."

"That brings up my second point," Fergus said. "It has to be close by. How close, we can only guess. The most powerful items, whether good or evil, can have effects from halfway around the world. In the hands of a very high-level caster, an intact Cataclysm Stone might have been one of those."

"Remember, we're dealing with a damaged Stone," Glynnis interjected. "The broken items I've come in contact with in previous encounters have always been less powerful than the whole. The distance over which they could act was also greatly cut. Furthermore, the pieces of an item give off different vibrations from each other. Having felt the original vibrations when Finster was casting and then from the item we had, I can confirm they are one and the same—identical modulations, identical energy. Wherever the larger piece is, I have not directly felt it—yet."

"Exactly," Fergus acknowledged. "Before we get into actual distance, let me bring up the third point. Someone other than Finster possesses the remnant. If Finster did have the other piece, why wasn't he casting with both for greater power? Why was only one piece in the bag Irenee brought back? I think someone else has the greater section, and Finster knows who."

Mary Ann, the team's healer, spoke up. "We're all aware destruction of an item harms its possessor. For those of you who have only dealt with much weaker items, let me point out demolition can physically damage brain cells or the magic center. Destroying the stronger ones can trigger various psychoses and cause a total breakdown. Doing the same for the ancient monsters can kill. After what we all went through, Finster has to be in much worse shape. He may not be able to tell us anything, now or ever."

"I'll send someone over to Finster's to see what they can find out. Would anyone like to estimate where the other remnant is?" Fergus asked.

"I think it's somewhere close to Finster," Irenee's father said. "I'm willing to bet he's had the thing for a number of years because of the magnitude of his criminal activities. You don't build a sizeable organization in a day. Neither do you create it without a lot of power. Those actions imply, if not a whole Stone, certainly pieces of it working together and/or a partner. And another question, was this accomplice on the other end of the line, so to speak, casting at us during destruction?"

"I agree with your points, but I don't think there was a human looking through that black flame at us. I've been in a similar position, and there's a different feeling entirely," John said.

"If Finster and another person have been casting over years, especially close by, they must be in an extremely secure environment, or I'd have picked it up," Glynnis said.

"Looks like we have some investigating to do. Glynnis, you put some scholars to researching the Cataclysm Stone. If we're going after a larger piece, we need to know what we're doing," Fergus concluded. "First, we must get rid of the ashes from our most recent project. John, do you have the vials?"

"Yes," John replied. "I divided the remains into portions so all who participated in the destruction could have one. They're in the box by the door. Be sure to take one when you leave."

"As usual," Fergus said, "please scatter them in many places. The last thing we need is the abomination or even a part of it reconstituting itself. We'll meet this evening at seven to discuss the situation and make plans to find the remains of this abomination. Okay, anything else before we adjourn?"

Irenee tugged on Fergus's sleeve, and he bent down to her. "Could you ask our team to stay for a minute? I forgot something I'd rather discuss with them alone. Oh, and Dad can stay, too."

Irenee fidgeted until her team members were the only ones in the room. During the previous discussion, she'd thought about telling everybody, but the task was somehow too much to take on, exhausted as she was.

"Here's the thing," she said when all were settled again. "When I was about to open the safe in Alton's study, a man picked the lock and came in. He could see right through my invisibility, and he asked why both the safe and I were glowing. I don't know, however, if the safe radiance was from my discover spell or Alton's protective ones."

She related the events without mentioning her more personal reaction to him. What possible importance could it have to the larger problem? "Uncle Dylan said he'd find out who the man was after I left."

"This guy specifically mentioned seeing a glow from the spells?" her father put in.

"Yes, but he didn't say a word about magic."

"What about evil? Was there any taint?" Glynnis asked.

"None I could identify. He certainly didn't want Alton to know he'd been there, so I'm guessing he's connected with law enforcement."

"It would stand to reason," John said. "We've been assuming one agency or another must be after Alton after all he's done."

"He didn't threaten me with either arrest or harm, even though he was angry," Irenee continued. "I think we were under the same time constraints because he didn't argue when I suggested he leave first. He simply left. I finished up and heard the guard try the door right on schedule. It was still locked, so he didn't come in. If Mr. Mysterious thought to waylay me in the hall, the guard must have chased him away because there was nobody there when I came out to go to the auction."

"Very puzzling." Fergus stroked his beard. "You're sure he's not a practitioner."

"I don't think so. He used an electronic gadget to

open the wall safe, and he didn't know how to handle the spells in the one in the floor. He was actually going to touch it before I stopped him. No practitioner expecting magic protection would have done so, whether or not they could see a spell glow."

Fergus leaned back in his chair. "He didn't take anything—not from either safe. He only copied some drives and put them back. Interesting. Is there anything else you haven't told us?"

Oh, damn. Might as well make light of it. She smiled and said, "He was good-looking and wasn't happy when I pointed him out to Uncle Dylan. Is that what you mean?"

"How good-looking?" Annette asked.

"Very, in an I-can-take-care-of-myself way."

"I'm really puzzled by his ability to see a spell glow," Fergus said. "Did you get the idea he could also see your spell aura?"

"I don't think so. From what he said, I didn't glow after I cancelled invisibility, and he didn't mention my shining when I dispelled and unlocked the safe."

"Interesting. The talent to see a spell aura around the casting person's body is common among family members. The talent to see the aura of a nonrelated person is much rarer. To see spells glowing without casting a spell to do so is extremely rare. Only a couple of people on this continent can do it, and I know both. Neither of them is this fellow. He seems to be able to see spells, not auras, yet he doesn't know what they are."

"Seeing either takes more than a simple sensitivity to magic," Irenee's father said.

"Yes," Fergus agreed. "It's even more curious that he actually saw *through* Irenee's invisibility spell. I would have expected him to see the shell of bending light, not her inside it. We'll have to find out how he did it." He stroked his beard again and stared into space. "I wonder . . ."

"You have a look in your eye like you're about to pull a rabbit out of a hat." Glynnis shook her finger at him. "Come on, give. What do you think he is?"

"I'm not going to speculate until after I've met the man. I will go so far to state unequivocally that he'll be showing up soon. We'll find out who he is, and he'll find out who Irenee is, and he'll come looking for her." Fergus sat back in his chair with a satisfied look on his face.

"Oh, no, I didn't think of that," Irenee moaned. "What am I supposed to do with him when he finds me?"

"Bring him to me. I'll take care of him," Fergus said.

"And me," her father added with a frown. "I'd like to meet a man who's impervious to your spells."

Irenee refrained from rolling her eyes at her father's statement. There he was, being overly protective again. Her whole family—mother, father, brother—had always protected her to the point she wanted to scream—she assumed because her level was so much below theirs. The problem was, it didn't stop when she shot up in level and abilities. Indeed, her parents' reaction to her becoming a Sword had been close to dismay. Oh, they were proud, too, but she could tell they didn't like the idea of her being a frontline fighter.

However, she was a Sword, no matter what, and she knew her father, as a Defender himself, understood how well she'd done with her first big assignment. Her next one was to turn her attention to Mr. Mysterious and lure him into Fergus's clutches. How hard could it be?

"Everybody get some rest," Fergus commanded. "It's late, or rather early in the morning. Remember, we'll meet at seven to see what information has come in." He shooed them out the door.

Irenee gave her father a hug, picked up her vial of ashes, and headed for her condo, where she concentrated solely on getting ready for bed. She had no choice. It was concentrate or fall over from sheer exhaustion.

Once lying there, however, the encounter with Mr. Mysterious played out again on the backs of her eyelids. Her magic center fluttered, and she smiled while she rubbed it. She was looking forward to seeing him again, she decided—purely for answers to the puzzle of his abilities, of course.

CHAPTER SIX

Early Sunday afternoon, Jim went into the task force office, located in a nondescript building close to the Loop. After getting a cup of coffee, he stopped by Dave Richards's desk to see what progress they had made on the flash drives.

"We're going to nail this guy," Dave reported gleefully. "The schmutz didn't encrypt the files at all. He used a simple password we cracked in seconds—*cataclysm*, can you believe. The forensic accountants are going over the financials, and I've sent you the file of his 'business associates.' Finster had those all set up like a Christmas card list. Incredible. Now if he just doesn't die on us."

Jim almost choked on his coffee. "What? Die?"

"Yeah, haven't you heard? Finster's in the hospital. He collapsed about three in the morning and seems to be in a coma."

"Son of a bitch!" Jim dropped into a chair and slammed his fist on the desk. "The bastard cannot die. He deserves to be alive and suffering, not dead to the world. Hell, I'll haul his ass into court if it has to be on a gurney."

"Believe me, a lot of us will help push."

"What about our investigation?"

"Erlanger's called a meeting for seven tonight. From the rumors, we continue as planned."

"Good." Jim stood. "I have some people to look up. Let me know if you hear news about Finster."

"Will do."

A couple of hours later, Jim had more data—and wished it was more helpful.

The bad news: A still unconscious Finster had been moved from the hospital to a private clinic where it would be extremely difficult for the task force to monitor him. An agent was looking for a way in, but the staff turnover was practically nonexistent, and the clientele exceedingly private. The only reports said that the butler and Finster's cousin, Bruce Ubell, had found him unconscious on the floor of the study.

Finster's cousin. What was it about the guy that bothered him? Jim remembered the odd feeling he'd had at the gala when the two were together. Which one was really the boss? They'd have to see how Finster's collapse changed the criminal activities.

The good news: Jim had better info on Irenee Sabel. Date of birth, Social Security number, education, occupation, family, net worth—she certainly didn't need to work for a living. Address—the HeatherRidge Center? In Barrington? Where the hell was that? Out in the northwest suburbs?

He looked her up every way he could, and found few references except to charitable causes and various kinds of corporate special events. Some she organized and some she only attended. No pictures or reports of her at clubs or parties. No connection at all with any men. She certainly wasn't playing the celebrity circuit—or circus—like some women her age.

The only color close-up he could find was her driver's license photo. Eyes brown, hair red, fair skin. It didn't do justice to her.

Her small business, Sabel Events, had organized parties and conferences for some big names and companies, but it, like its owner, kept a low profile. Her office address was in the Sabel Industries headquarters building in Schaumburg. According to the building diagrams, instead of a location in the upper-floor, plush executive suites, her small three-room office was in the lower-rent middle.

To all appearances, she was a young woman living quietly, concentrating on her job.

Somehow, the description did not match her dark red hair or the way she took control last night. It certainly didn't go with a woman who'd sneak into a locked room and burgle a safe without turning one of those red hairs.

Oh, yes, he wanted to see her again—for all kinds of

reasons. The only questions were when and where.

He rubbed the itch in his chest and got to work on Finster's list of business associates.

Monday morning at ten o'clock Irenee hurried into the Sabel Industries building not far from Woodfield Mall. On the way she'd visited several forest preserves to scatter her portion of ashes, and she was running late. Fortunately she had no pressing events upcoming, and she'd planned on devoting the day to paperwork and some phone calls to prospective clients. She juggled her purse, briefcase, and a box full of promotional items to push the elevator button.

As the elevator took her to the third floor, she went over her mental to-do list. The way her business was expanding, she really needed a full-time administrative assistant. Someone who could keep the books and back her up with all the details. She'd hired a couple of women from her mother's office for past individual projects outside of normal business hours, but such sporadic part-timers weren't reliable in the long run.

Her planning efforts were complicated because, although she was a full Defender team member after four long years of study, she was still in the dark about how much time her Sword activities would actually take. In general, the teams saw real action only once or twice a year. Practitioners were like everybody else, a mix of normal, honest people and a few bad ones. Only a very small number of the criminal types had sufficient power and talent to create even tiny evil items. The ancient, powerful monsters only showed up every fifty or a hundred years.

This business with the Cataclysm Stone, however, was clearly a special case, and her active role was yet undetermined. At the meeting last night, they had only decided to keep investigating. Various Defenders, both on her team and not, were working on Alton's and Bruce Ubell's movements and activities, searching for any trace of the larger remnant, or monitoring Alton's condition. Until they knew more, she was to go about her regular business. Even with no team task, at least she could think about the situation.

Alton was out of commission, so he couldn't tell them who had the rest of the Stone. Several team members thought his cousin might be the second villain and possibly, even probably, the holder of the other remnant. Their reasoning was based mostly on Ubell's close association with Alton since childhood, his ambiguous "vice president" position with undefined duties within Finster Shipping, and his reputation for being the power behind Alton's throne.

Until they could do so from a position of certainty, however, nobody wanted to ask Ubell where the rest of the evil item was. Indeed, practitioner law was against accusation without proof. If Ubell had found the notice she left, he certainly hadn't contacted them, and his lack of action raised everyone's suspicions even higher.

Irenee had never met Ubell face-to-face, only seen him at a distance—like at the gala—a situation the other Defenders shared. They were working on ways to get physically close to him without making a formal call. One good sniff and they'd know if he was evil. Unfortunately, you had to be standing next to the person to pick up the odor of evil. Thank goodness she hadn't had to spend much time near Alton on Saturday night, or she might have thrown up from the stench.

Oh, wait a minute. Alton hadn't reeked of evil when they crossed paths before, had he? Before he'd used his Stone out of the protected place he'd obviously been casting from. Ubell might not smell, either. Nobody had thought of that particular point yesterday.

On the theory Alton and another had been casting with the pieces for years, several people, herself included, thought the remnant was hidden in the mansion under a pile of shields and protections. It was the only way the item could be used in total privacy. The nineteenth-century building was sure to have nooks and crannies modern construction lacked. Oh, to be able to get into that house for a more thorough search.

Ubell, however, had moved into the family homestead from his high-rise condo by Lake Michigan. According to their surveillance reports of this morning, he was running the companies from there and, except for Finster executives and his administrative assistant, not accepting visitors. Since Alton's transfer to the private hospital Sunday morning, Bruce had not visited his cousin's bedside.

Did his reclusiveness guarantee the location of the Cataclysm remnant in the house? If so, where exactly? Had he and Alton truly been casting evil spells for years? Again, where? What had possessed Alton to cast with his piece out in the open? Too many questions, not enough answers.

At least Uncle Dylan had found out who her fellow thief was—Jim Tylan, a DEA agent who had once saved the life of an ambassador. Assuming his agency was going after the Finster drug activities, what effect he and his agency might have on the Defenders' search for the rest of the Stone concerned them all. Fergus had people researching Tylan also.

Forcing her mind back to business, she exited the elevator on three and walked quickly down the hall. The box was beginning to slip off her hip, and her grip on the briefcase was loosening. Good thing her office was right around the corner.

"Let me help you with that," a deep voice said when she ran right into the man standing in front of her door.

She froze and stared up, directly into the eyes of Mr. Mysterious. He caught the box just as she lost control of it.

Now she knew what color his eyes were—green with gold flecks, a golden green. A stormy golden green. The turbulence in them went with the determined expression on his face. At the same time, the heat in his gaze made her want to throw herself into his arms so much she almost would have—if not for the box between them.

She broke eye contact to look at the rest of him. His nose had still been broken. His hair was still curly. His shoulders were as broad in a sports jacket as they had been in a tux, but he seemed taller today.

Idiot! You had on three-inch heels at the party, not flats. Wake up! He's found you. She blinked a couple of times and took a deep breath. Saw his gaze travel down to her chest, then back up. *Men!*

"We need to talk," he said, frowning at her.

"What do you want?" she asked in, she hoped, a no-nonsense tone, and she forced herself to stand still when a hot shiver ran up her backbone and heated her center.

"Do you really want to discuss our last meeting standing in a public hallway?"

She gave him a hard look, which he returned—doubled. Reminding herself she was strong and couldn't be intimidated, she opened the door.

He followed her in, right on her heels as if he thought she'd try to shut the door on him.

"Put the box over there," she told him and pointed to the desk where her assistant would eventually sit.

He did as she ordered.

She continued into her own office, where she laid her briefcase and purse on her desk. She decided to see how much she could get out of him before luring him to the HeatherRidge and Fergus. Her hands on her hips, she turned to face him. "All right, who are you, and what do you want?"

He came only as far as her doorway. Arms crossed over his chest, he leaned against the jamb and looked around her office as if he was taking inventory.

Not that there was much to see—desk, chairs, computer, printer, filing cabinets, a bookshelf, a couple of plants, a desk lamp, and some promo goodies she'd used in past events. True, she did have a nice colorful print by a contemporary artist on the wall, but, except for a photo of her family, no fanciness or personal stuff. The office was neat because that's the kind of person she was—organized. She rarely met clients here, and the decor suited her work style. If he didn't like it, too bad.

His gaze returned to her. "What did you take out of Finster's safe, and why? What was the book, and what was in the bag?"

"Why should I tell you anything? I don't even know who you are."

"My name is Jim Tylan," he answered.

"And . . .?" She made a coaxing gesture with her hands.

"And what did you take out of Finster's safe?"

"Why should I answer your questions? Are you with the police? You were evidently after something also. What was on those flash drives you copied?"

"Let's just say it's a matter of homeland security."

"Show me some identification if you want answers."

"ID is on a need-to-know basis. You don't qualify."

Irenee shook her head. "If you use the words *homeland security*, are you a government agent? If so, what agency and what kind of officer? Don't you have to identify yourself? Are you going to take me in for interrogation?"

He straightened off the doorjamb and took three steps to loom over her and stare down into her eyes. She glared right back.

He was so close, she could feel the heat in him. She could see the little golden flecks in his green eyes and smell him, too—an alluring, indefinable scent that made her nostrils flare, and which was *not evil* in any way, shape, or form.

A strong urge struck to move into his arms and discover if his body was as hard as it appeared. She actually felt her muscles prepare to take the step, and she relaxed them by sheer force of will. Where had such an idea come from? She recovered her focus and concentrated on standing her ground.

"Answer my questions, Ms. Sabel." Obviously intent on domination, he bent farther, and they scowled at each other for some seconds, nose to nose.

Or rather, her straight nose to his once-broken one. She wondered what he'd do if she did something outrageous, like bite his nose—or kiss those lips drawn into a straight line by his anger.

The thoughts—irreverent and unexpected as they were, under the circumstances—tickled her funny bone. She couldn't stop her lips from quirking up in a smile. The smile became a grin. She struggled for a few more moments to keep a straight face—until she lost the battle irrevocably.

When she started snickering, he drew himself up as if she'd insulted his parentage.

When she started giggling, he blinked first, but regained control before his shock at her reaction lasted more than a second.

He must think she was a wimp. Irenee the Sword, a wimp! She started laughing.

"Look, lady . . ."

His clear exasperation, accompanied by his leaning on her desk and bending over to put their faces at the same level—nose to nose again—set her off completely. He actually thought he could bulldoze her into talking.

She took a step backward and held onto her sides while she laughed so hard, she lost her breath and began coughing.

"Oh, shit," he muttered and, straightening up,

thumped her back until she waved him off.

"I'm all right," she wheezed after a moment. She grabbed a tissue and dabbed at the tears in her eyes. When she could see again, she snuck a glance at him.

"I'm glad you find it funny. Let me assure you, however, this is no laughing matter," he growled.

She sighed. "I realize that, but I don't know you. Honestly, why should I even talk to you?"

Before he could speak, a new voice called from the outer office.

"Irenee, are you here?" Tiffany Blake and her mother, Bitsy, breezed into the room and stopped abruptly inside the doorway. Both women gave Tylan the once-over and smiled appreciatively.

"Oh, are we interrupting something?" Bitsy asked in a tone full of innuendo.

Oh, great, what a time for Chicago's most notorious celebrity darling—and her mother—to show up. Irenee and Tiffany had known each other since grade school, but had never run in the same social circles, and never would. Wishing she could throw a go-away spell at the intruders, Irenee put a smile on her face. "What can I do for you ladies?"

"We need to see you about organizing an extremely important, wonderful, once-in-a-lifetime event for us," Bitsy answered, never taking her eyes off Tylan.

"I'm sorry," Irenee said, "but my calendar is full for the next year, and I don't have the time to discuss taking on any new work at the present time."

"Oh, Irenee," Tiffany said, her little high-pitched voice grating on Irenee's frazzled nerves, "you must, simply *must* manage our event. There's no one else in the world who can." She sauntered in and took a seat like she owned the place.

Tylan cleared his throat. "Excuse us, ladies. If I could speak to you for a moment, Ms. Sabel . . ." He hustled Irenee into the outer office and closed the door behind him. "Look, we do have to talk."

Irenee grabbed his arm and tugged him toward the door into the hall. She wouldn't put it past Bitsy to put her ear to the door to eavesdrop. On the other hand, the interruption gave her the chance to get Tylan out of her office and to put the man in Fergus's clutches.

"I agree," she whispered. "Look, it's going to take me a while to get rid of the queen and the princess in there. Why don't you meet me at the HeatherRidge Center in Barrington at five this afternoon. We won't have these disruptions. Do you know where that is?"

"Yeah, I'll find it," he grumbled. Then he glanced at the door to her office and shuddered. "No tricks? You'll be there?"

"My word on it." She held out her hand to shake and raised her eyes to his.

He gave her a distrusting look, but locked gazes and took her hand.

She felt the zing clear to her toes.

He seemed startled, too, as their fingers tightened.

They stood unmoving for a long moment, until they both let go at the same time.

He recovered first, opened the door, and said, "Five o'clock."

"Ask for me at the reception desk."

He nodded and left.

Irenee took a long, deep breath while she watched the door close. Wooooeeeee. What was that? She'd never had such a reaction to a man before. Her insides were practically tingling, and a sliver of heat rolled up and down her backbone to settle in her middle.

She probably would have stood there longer, replaying their conversation, remembering his eyes—and the look in them. Unfortunately, the sound of Tiffany's high-pitched giggle penetrated the walls. She turned around to face her office and squared her shoulders. Now to get rid of the Blakes. No way was she going to get involved in their celebrity shenanigans.

Just before she opened her office door, she paused to rub her slightly aching, slightly itching breastbone. Even her body was repulsed by the idea of dealing with them.

She plastered a professional smile on her face, marched into her office, and sat behind her desk. "What's going on, Tiffany?"

CHAPTER SEVEN

At five minutes to five, Jim climbed out of his car and looked around at the buildings and grounds of the HeatherRidge Center. In appearance, the center matched corporate establishments for retreats, training, and conferences, and it was nestled in an area of subdivisions with high-dollar homes. In their parklike setting, none of the contemporary-style buildings were higher than five stories, and the landscaping was immaculate, the garden areas filled with colorful flowers, large trees, and nice places to sit.

Except . . .

He didn't know exactly what went on at the center. Who was trained? In what? Who met? For what purposes? He couldn't find a corporate or institutional connection.

Searching the Internet yielded not even a mention. The place had no Web site. Neither did the HeatherRidge on the fringe of the Loop. He'd called both places—at least they were in the phone book—to see about reserving a room or holding a meeting. The reservations clerk informed him that all of the buildings under the HeatherRidge banner were only open to members, not to the general public, and therefore not available for rental.

Jim actually went over to the nearby one, an old, gracious, hotel-and-condo landmark occupying a complete block and dating back to the nineteenth century, where the concierge at the front desk had likewise turned him away. When Jim inquired how one became a member, the guardian looked down his nose and said, “Only by referral.”

The suburban center also guarded its exclusivity carefully, evidenced by the lack of an identifying sign and the presence of security at the gated entrance. The guard did not simply wave him through, but actually checked by phone to be sure he was legit. For all their fancy filigree ironwork, the gates, which swung open silently, looked like high-end security barriers. Jim had a faint impression they and the serious fence around the property were glowing—surely only the effect of the bright sun.

What was with this “glowing” business, anyway? First in Finster’s study and now here. Did he need to have his eyes checked?

He would have liked to take a stroll to check out the place. Because there was no visible parking lot, however, he had no choice except to follow the tree-lined drive to the front door. A valet appeared immediately to give him a ticket and drive his car away, around a hedge to who knew where—probably underground.

Two men and a woman, dressed in casual business attire, came out of the front door, and another valet materialized to go after their car. The threesome looked at him and smiled vaguely. He nodded back as he walked past to enter the building.

Once inside the thick glass door, Jim stopped again. The three-story open atrium space looked like every other hotel or conference center, with seating areas, trees and flowers in large tubs, and a fountain in the middle. The building's wings, presumably with living quarters, rose another two stories on each side. A man behind the reception desk to the right was watching him expectantly, so he walked over.

"May I help you, sir?"

"I'm here to see Irenee Sabel," he answered.

"One moment, please." The desk clerk picked up a phone, punched some numbers, and said, "Your guest has arrived . . . Immediately." He put down the phone and smiled at Jim. "Someone will be right here to escort you."

Interesting—they wouldn't let him wander on his own. Jim thanked him and turned away to walk over to the fountain. The gold, white, and black koi that swam in its pool immediately flocked to him with their mouths open. He shook his head at them. "Sorry, fellas, no food."

When he walked farther into the space, he could see a restaurant entrance on the back right wall and an exit to an outdoor terrace on the left. A couple of small groups were talking at tables strung along the rear wall while a waiter served drinks.

Everything looked excessively normal.

Except . . . something was definitely in the air—or more accurately in his hunch mechanism. His antennae definitely shivered or wiggled. These particular feelings usually preceded important discoveries, ended in revelations solving a case, or warned of an imminent threat. He wasn't so sure what they meant this time, however—discovery or danger.

He still hadn't told his boss or fellow agents about Irenee Sabel. Back in the office when he'd actually started to, his antennae had shimmied like a hurricane was blowing through them—an alarm that had saved his life too many times to discount. So he said he was only pursuing a slim lead from the party. It was easy to rationalize his decision—he wanted to find out details, and he considered her nothing more than a possible source of info. He'd play his hunch out first and deal with repercussions later.

Within thirty seconds, a young man in a blue blazer with a gold-and-silver *HR* embroidered on the chest pocket showed up and led him to an elevator on the left side.

On the way up, Jim wondered if she'd actually be

there. He wouldn't be happy if she wasn't. She'd given her word. And looked at him with those dark brown eyes promising her agreement. And shook his hand—rattling him to the core with one simple touch.

She was definitely intriguing. No other woman laughed at his intimidation tactics as if she wasn't afraid of him one little bit. If he hadn't been in the middle of the biggest case in his life and she wasn't involved in a yet-to-be-determined fashion, he'd really want to know her better. Much better. See if her redhead complexion was as creamy all over her body.

As the elevator bell dinged and the door opened, he told his body to relax. It didn't pay much attention. Instead, the place right under his breastbone practically quivered with anticipation. What was the woman doing to him? He hadn't felt this excited on his first date.

They exited on the third floor and walked along the corridor to the end, where his escort knocked on the last door on the right.

It was opened immediately by a big man with a white beard and mane of hair. He looked like he'd be right at home playing Santa, but his shrewd gray gaze warned Jim to watch his step.

"Welcome, Mr. Tylan," he boomed. "I'm Fergus Whipple."

Not at all what Jim had expected. Where was Irenee Sabel?

Whipple held out his hand, and Jim shook it automatically. The man had to be at least six-foot-five and didn't have an ounce of fat on him, just solid muscle. It was anybody's guess how old he was—fifty, sixty, even seventy? No matter his age, he wouldn't be easy to take down. His conclusion wasn't a hunch on Jim's part, only his usual automatic assessment and police experience talking.

Jim followed his host into a living room with colorful, comfortable furniture and serious artwork on the walls. Filmy drapes were pulled across the big windows to mute the brightness outside.

There she was, sitting in an easy chair, with her hands clasped in front of her and her dark red hair shining like a beacon—danger or something else? She regarded him soberly, seriously. She didn't smile or seem apprehensive. He nodded, and she returned the greeting.

Jim concentrated so much on the woman he didn't notice the man on the couch next to her chair until he stood. Damn, what was the matter with him? He quickly glanced around the room to make sure he hadn't missed someone else before turning his attention to the new guy. This one was about six feet, wiry rather than solid, with iron gray hair and brown eyes like Irenee's.

"Hugh Sabel," the man said.

"Jim Tylan." He recalled the info on her family and shook hands with her father. He hadn't expected either man, but maybe having more people would elicit more info. He used the idea to squelch the little pang of disappointment hitting his middle.

"Have a seat, Mr. Tylan." Whipple waved him to the couch and took the other chair, a tall wingback.

Jim sat on the opposite end from Hugh Sabel. Three pairs of eyes were aimed at him. Whipple's gray ones almost twinkled, Sabel's were calculating, and Irenee's guarded. He'd better take control of the gathering, or he'd never get his questions answered.

Before he could open his mouth, however, Whipple said, "Mr. Tylan, I'm sure you're curious about what went on in Alton Finster's house on Saturday night. We're also curious. If you don't mind, I'd rather we start with our questions. You have my word we'll get to yours. That okay with you?"

No, it wasn't really. Sometimes, however, questions told him more than answers, so Jim mentally told his inner hunch to stay alert, and said, "I'll go along for the time being."

"Good man," Whipple nodded approvingly. "You're aware Alton Finster is in the hospital today, correct? He collapsed sometime in the early morning hours Sunday, and his cousin, Bruce Ubell, found him?"

"Yes," Jim answered. It had been on the morning news, so no surprise the trio knew it also.

"Saturday night, at the gala, you picked the lock and entered Finster's private study, from what Irenee tells us."

"Yes."

"Then you searched the wall safe and didn't find what you were looking for. When you turned around, you saw her in the corner. Am I correct?"

"Yes." So far, nothing new.

"When you noticed her, what did she look like? How did she appear? What was the light like around her? Or was there light at all? Be as accurate as you can, please."

Jim blinked. This he hadn't expected. However, he couldn't think of a reason not to tell them what he saw—only he wouldn't mention his *hunch* someone was watching him. "I closed the portrait and was wondering what other hiding place Finster might have in the room. I turned around, and there she was, crouching in the corner."

"How was the light shining on her?"

"The only lamps were dim ones above the portrait and on the desk." He paused, replaying the moment in his mind. "The light wasn't exactly shining on her. I don't remember a reflection like off jewelry or shiny clothing. The corner was almost smoky or foggy. It was weird, though, because the stuff seemed 'contained' somehow. You know, like when fog or smoke swirls inside a glass, and you can see through it but still see *it* at the same time. It gave the impression of a halo around her."

Whipple nodded, said in a low voice, "Go on."

Jim looked straight at Irenee and locked gazes. "She

stood up, and I walked around the desk to her. When I got about two feet away, the fog vanished. So did the halo. When I looked down, the carpet glowed around the edges, and when she flipped it back, so did the safe in the floor. We both knelt by it, she did something with her hands, and the glow disappeared. She opened the safe."

It took him a few seconds to break the eye contact with Irenee. For some reason, he didn't want to look at the men—who could blame him with her in the room? He turned to Whipple. "That what you wanted?"

"Did the glow have colors?" Sabel asked.

He had to think about his answer for a few seconds as he visualized the study. "Yeah, the one around her was sort of dark blue and the one on the safe was reddish. Neither was bright."

"Only a couple of other questions," Whipple said. "Did you see this glow elsewhere in the house? In the private areas, for instance?"

"No. I didn't go into any of those except the study. The wall safe wasn't shining either."

Whipple waved a hand toward the rest of the room. "What do you see glowing here?"

Jim frowned. Was the old guy a nutcase? To humor the man, he glanced around, and lo and behold . . . He pointed. "Yeah, the little dish on the coffee table, and the painting on the wall, and that tall stick with the glass sphere on top in the umbrella stand by the door."

Whipple chuckled. "Oh, I had forgotten about my staff. Very interesting. All right, Mr. Tylan, let's try something else. Look at Irenee. What do you see?"

He looked. "Only her."

"Irenee?"

Jim almost jumped when a shining bubble appeared around her. How? He could have sworn she didn't move a muscle. Did one of the men flip a switch? No shadows gave away the position of a light source, however. "She's glowing, and there's a yellow shimmer around her."

"Light yellow or dark yellow?" Whipple asked, his voice soft and low.

"Light."

"Next, Irenee."

"Damn. Now it's blue." This was getting crazier and crazier.

"The real test, Irenee. Full strength."

"Whoa." Jim drew back, then leaned forward. He knew his eyes were bugging out. "The smoke or fog or whatever the hell it is just appeared."

"You can see her through it." Sabel made it a statement, not a question.

"Yeah."

"I'll try to make it stronger," Irenee said, a very irritated expression on her face.

"The fog got thicker, and it's dark blue, and the light seems to . . ." Jim's voice petered out when he realized what he was describing.

"Seems to what, Mr. Tylan?" Fergus said softly.

"It seems to bend around her." He stood up, took a step closer to her, and studied the phenomenon. Reaching out an arm, he waved his hand through the edge. Nothing. Not cold or warm. The smoke didn't move with the shifting air currents either, as it would if it was real.

He stepped back and looked around. No fog machine or mechanical contraption or light source accounted for it. Sweeping back his coat to put his hands on his hips, he looked from one to the other of the threesome. "All right, what's going on here? Cut the crap, and tell me now."

Whipple looked at the others. Sabel shrugged, and Irenee winced. The fog dissipated.

"Sit down, Mr. Tylan, and we'll explain," Whipple said. "Please hear us out before you come to any conclusions. We usually don't share our secrets with outsiders, and we tell our story with some trepidations. Because you are with a federal law enforcement agency, we can't ask you to keep the information confidential. We can only hope for your discretion if you choose to share it with your superiors."

Jim stared at the big man. They knew he was an agent. He'd ask later how they discovered it. As for what they would tell him? His hunch said *he absolutely had to know.* He sat down and rolled his shoulders to relax them. “I can live with that.”

“Hugh, why don’t you begin?” Whipple said and leaned back in his chair, his elbows on the armrests and his fingers steepled under his chin. Under his bushy eyebrows, his eyes were aimed at Jim, and he seemed incongruously amused.

Cognizant of the big man’s scrutiny and studiously ignoring it, Jim turned to Sabel.

Irenee’s father sat sideways on the couch to face him. “I need to lay some groundwork, and I can’t tell this without it sounding like a lecture, so bear with me, please. Our story starts long ago. In ancient, prehistoric times, a few humans developed the ability to harness their internal energy and use spells and enchantments to make their lives and their everyday jobs better and easier. In other words, they could work magic. It helped immensely in their survival.”

Jim felt his eyes squint and his chin lower, but he managed to keep his lips together. Man, just when he thought he’d seen and heard it all. *Magic?*

“These people found others like themselves,” Sabel continued, “and they married and produced offspring, who turned out to have the same sorts of innate gifts. Sometimes the children’s talents matched those of their parents, sometimes not. When this ‘inheritance’ became clear, they began to keep detailed family histories. Today we’re their descendants. In addition to living in the world like normal people, we also exist quietly unto ourselves. We call ourselves 'practitioners' because we have to learn and practice our skills. We use our powers to make our livings and to protect ourselves. Other than using our talents, we live ordinary lives with ordinary lifespans. We're as human as anybody else."

"Exactly what do you do with these 'magic' abilities?" Jim asked, intrigued and puzzled despite his usual skepticism about all outrageous claims. He was also more than a little irritated. Were these people weirdos or what? What had he gotten himself into?

"We use our magic in our occupations." Sabel shrugged. "After all, everybody has to make a living. Our 'talents' are specific to each individual job. Accountants can cast spells to help them keep financial books, engineers figure out how to put something together the best way, mechanics use them to decide how to fix a car, and so forth. Fergus was a veterinarian before he retired, Irenee is an event organizer, and I'm an economist, for example. Think of those people—musical prodigies, 'born' engineers, or whatever—who are so good at what they do, but you have no idea how they do it."

Sabel's explanation made a bizarre kind of sense, but Jim stopped himself from pursuing the ideas. He needed to concentrate on his main mission. "Okay, so what? I don't care if you use magic or voodoo or fairy dust to do your jobs. What does it have to do with Alton Finster?

What did you"—Jim pointed at Irenee—"take out of his safe?"

Irenee didn't answer. Whipple took up the tale instead. "Some of us have additional, more esoteric talents. We're charged by our governing bodies with maintaining our ethics and rules—we're the police officers, basically. A few of us have the power to share magical energy, transfer it from one person to another, multiply it so several people can use it at once. Those we term 'Defenders.' A very small number of Defenders have an extremely rare talent. We can use the offensive and defensive kinds of spells you find in fantasy games, movies, and novels—fireballs, lightning bolts, and the like. Most important of all our gifts, we 'Swords' have the power to destroy items of evil magic."

"Evil magic?" Jim couldn't help sneering. "Oh, come on. You expect me to believe this far-fetched story? I mean, I could see where somebody might think an expert could be using magic if living in a primitive society, but your explanation puts us into fantasy movies and games. Next, you'll have a dragon in the basement."

"No, no dragon," Whipple said with a chuckle before he frowned. "There are, however, bad practitioners as well as good—in the ethical and moral senses, I mean. In the past the bad ones created items to enhance their powers, to make evil deeds and their influence greater and more successful."

Jim sat back and crossed his arms over his chest. The situation was getting more unbelievable by the minute. "I repeat, what does any of this have to do with me and Finster?"

"Alton Finster and his family, including Bruce Ubell, are practitioners," Whipple stated with absolutely no humor in his voice or expression. "Alton had possession of one of these evil items, an extremely powerful ancient crystal. Every practitioner takes an oath to abide by our code of ethics, part of which obliges us to turn over to the Defenders all evil artifacts we may find. The oath includes an agreement that Defenders can at any time confiscate such items we may possess—with or without our consent."

He pointed at the other two. "Irenee and I are both Swords. Hugh is a Defender. On Saturday night, Irenee confiscated Alton's piece of an item called the Cataclysm Stone and a book connected to it. You saw her take them out of Finster's safe. Early Sunday morning, we destroyed the crystal. An evil item is linked psychically to the person who possesses it, and when the item disintegrates, the process affects the possessor. The destruction of his Stone threw Finster into a coma. There's more, but are you with us so far?"

Jim glared at Whipple. What a load of crap. What world did these people live in? He was sitting with a bunch of loonies.

Except . . .

He could feel his brain beginning to churn. Feel the synapses start firing. Feel facts and ideas coming together in the back of his mind until they practically exploded into an enormous hunch. Whipple was telling the God's honest truth and had *The Answers.* Closing his eyes, he laced his hands together on his head to keep his skull from cracking with the force of the hunch. A mushroom cloud rising above him wouldn't have surprised him.

He opened his eyes and looked around at the three who were studying him closely. Irenee's eyes were round, and her lips formed an *O*, and the men were stoic. He lowered his hands and took a deep breath. *Slow down. Take the new info logically and in order.* "Personally, I'd like some proof about this magic business."

"Big proof or little proof?" Sabel asked. "Here's little—a lightball."

Swirling with rainbow colors, a glowing, basketball-sized sphere floated suddenly in the air. Jim felt his eyes bugging out. The ball disappeared.

"Here's a medium illusion—your dragon," Whipple said, and, without a sound or flash, a big white lizard with furled wings and gray eyes was sitting in his chair. The dragon grinned at Jim for a second, then Whipple was there, also grinning.

Holy shit! Jim managed to keep his seat and close his mouth only by sheer force of will. He looked at Irenee and had to clear his throat before he could ask, "What about you?"

"Well, my best magic is a big proof, and here is not the place to do it. How about this?" She waved her hand at herself. "What do you see?"

She began to glow again, and he squinted to focus better. "The shape of a big cat outlines your body. It's outlined in a dark red, like your hair. It's like you have a transparent mask on too."

She grimaced, waved her hand again. "Now?"

"The cat is coming into focus, but I can still see you through it." He blinked several times. The special effects did not go away.

"That's really puzzling." Sabel cocked his head from side to side. "I can see only your panther."

"It's frustrating." Irenee ran her hand through her hair, and the panther outline disappeared. "What's the matter with my spells?"

"Not something we should worry about at the moment," Whipple said with a small, secretive smile. "I have an idea we'll discuss later. Tylan, do you believe us, or do you want more proof?"

Yeah, Jim wanted a hell of a lot more. Magic or not, however, what counted was his mission. What should he be asking? He let his hunch guide him. "Okay, let's say for the sake of argument, you three are what you say you are—these practitioners. What I really want is more info about Finster and his activities. Yes, we're investigating him. I fully expect to bring him to justice for a number of criminal acts—once he wakes up."

"You may have some unexpected problems. We have reason to believe there's another piece of the Cataclysm Stone, and it's being manipulated by another person."

Jim felt his hunch mechanism fire up again and supply the answer. "Bruce Ubell." As he said the name, the pieces fell into place and locked like a jigsaw puzzle. By himself, Finster couldn't do all the things they thought he had—he would have to be in two places at once to do so. Ubell had been so far in the background that few had noticed him.

A mental vision formed of the two cousins standing by the wall at the gala. The shiver caused by one's glance made a reappearance now, running up and down his backbone. His hunch said the surveyor hadn't been Finster. Ubell's gaze had been the one setting off his instincts. Ubell had been the hunter looking for prey or the sentry searching for the enemy.

"Our conclusions agree with yours," Whipple said.

Whether he believed in their magic hocus-pocus or not—and he wasn't ready to agree to their claim yet—Jim knew he would be a fool to discount the worth of the inside information these practitioners seemed to have. Any help in bringing down Finster, Ubell, and their organization was welcome. "Okay, what does this

'Cataclysm Stone' do? Where is it? How does Ubell use it? What for?"

"When you're casting a spell," Sabel explained, "magical items like crystals can help focus your energy and result in a stronger incantation and more powerful results. Usually your inborn talents confer on you the abilities connected with your profession. The most powerful and ancient items—and there are a few 'good' items also, by the way—not only make your spells incredibly effective, they can also give you powers *not* related to your talents. For example, it might let you cast a lightning bolt, a spell your natural talents don't include."

Whipple took up the tale. "Let's say Ubell wants to get a shipment of drugs through Customs. His Stone could help him cast spells affecting the inspectors so they either find nothing or don't even look. With the power of his item, he could cast these spells from far away."

"Or," Irenee said, "it could enchant his buyers to give him more money."

"Or," Sabel added, "influence a judge or jury in his favor."

"The Stone has that kind of power?" Jim asked. Whoa. If, and it was still a big *if*, this kind of magic actually existed, he had to reassess the situation. The task force might have some real problems.

"Yes," Sabel answered. "You may have a more immediate difficulty. If I may ask, was the information you took from those flash drives financial?"

"Yeah, it was. Extensive accounting records, from what the bean counters are saying."

"The Finsters are a rare family where the inherited talents stayed in one area—numbers, accounting, and finance," Sabel went on. "Both Alton and Ubell are CPAs and have MBAs. Under ordinary circumstances, their non-magic skill to manipulate the books would make them extremely difficult to audit. With the Cataclysm Stone enhancing their inherent powers, it might be impossible to find enough illegal manipulations or discrepancies in the accounts to stand up in a court of law. Even an auditor practitioner would have only a small chance of negating the spells."

"Then we need to get our hands on his Stone," Jim said. "If we have it, he can't use it, right?"

"There we have a predicament," Whipple admitted with a grimace. "We don't know exactly where it is. We think it's in the Finster mansion and shielded by very powerful spells. Finding it will take a team of experts and be extremely dangerous."

"Oh, great." Jim sat forward and rubbed his hands over his face. This mess was giving him a headache.

"There's more we need to discuss, but it's almost six thirty." Whipple rose. "Before we go farther, I have an idea I'd like to check out, and I need Hugh's help to do so. Why don't you and Irenee have some dinner, and come back here in about an hour and a half? I should have some answers by that time."

Jim looked over at Irenee. She was frowning at Whipple, and he thought she might refuse.

"Yes, go on, my dear," her father said. "You really need to replenish your energy."

"But . . ." Irenee glanced from Whipple to her father and finally to Jim, who stood.

He wasn't sure he wanted to let the men out of his sight. On the other hand, having dinner with her sounded like a great idea. He'd have her to himself—to question, of course. His middle gave a little flutter. See, his stomach liked the prospect of food, too. "Works for me. How's the food in the restaurant here?"

She sighed. "It's excellent. Let me tell Fergus something first." She stood, walked over to Whipple, and when he bent down, whispered something in his ear.

"You don't say. How intriguing," the large man said with a smile that turned into a grin.

"Come on," she said to Jim and started for the door.

He followed her out, not even trying to repress his satisfaction. Alone at last.

CHAPTER EIGHT

"You hardly said a word in there," Jim remarked on the elevator.

Irenee shot him a glance. "Fergus and Dad explain things better than I do." She wasn't about to tell him Fergus had suggested her silence and total concentration on him and his reactions. Why she should see something they wouldn't was a mystery, but she hadn't minded. He was nice to look at, and his responses to their explanations had been fascinating—from disbelief to almost grudging acceptance.

She'd almost fainted, however, when he had closed his eyes and put his hands on his head, and he *glowed—blue!* Whatever was going on was way beyond her experience. She'd told Fergus. Let him figure it out.

She had enough on her mind in the person of Jim Tylan. Merely his nearness in these close confines was enough to tighten all her muscles and cause her center to jump around. Was her reaction fight-or-flight . . . or something else?

Once seated in a quiet and almost private corner of the restaurant, Irenee leaned back in her chair and tried to relax. Her growling stomach told her how right her father was: she wasn't totally back to her normal energy levels. When the waiter came, she said, "My usual."

Jim looked up from his menu and asked, "What's your usual?"

"A filet mignon, rare, with baked potato, vegetable, salad, and dessert."

"Sounds good," he said, handing the waiter his menu. "Make it two."

They both declined wine. She was not about to befuddle her mind while in his company, and he gave every indication of being "on duty."

"Oh, also, put our dinners on Fergus Whipple's tab, please," she added to the waiter. When Jim raised his eyebrows at her, she shrugged and grinned. "Dinner was his idea, after all."

"Okay," he said, but she couldn't tell if he was pleased or not.

"You're not a member, so your money's no good here," she added.

"Okay," he repeated, glanced around, leaned a little closer to her, and whispered, "So, everybody here is a 'practitioner'? The diners? The waiters? They can all cast spells?"

"Yes, everybody—to varying degrees of power." She

paused and studied him before saying, "You don't completely believe our story, do you?"

His expression—raised eyebrows, squinting eyes, cynical smile—proclaimed his skepticism. He played with his silverware before meeting her gaze.

"Honestly, I don't know. It's so completely fantastic that a group of people like you exist." He shrugged. "Believe or not, I'd be an idiot not to take advantage of every bit of info you have. Especially since you have sources I don't. I'm for whatever will bring Finster and Ubell to justice. Let's put it this way—I'm keeping an open mind."

It was clear he was holding something back—maybe what had caused him to glow. Short of showing him some "big proof," like her sword and a fireball or two, she knew she wasn't going to be able to convince him. Under the circumstances, she'd fall back on her curiosity. If he was going to work with them, she wanted to know more about him. "Well, let's talk about something else. Where are you from, originally?"

"California, San Diego. You?"

"Here in the Chicago area. Both my mother's and father's families."

"Oh, yeah, you keep track of your genealogies."

"We have to, for the magic. All it takes is for one parent to be a practitioner, and the child will be one, too, with full powers."

"You marry 'outside the faith,' so to speak?"

"Yes, although personally I've never met anyone with a non-practitioner parent or spouse. Fergus and my parents have, though." He seemed interested, but practitioner life was really none of his business, and she wasn't going to go into the more personal aspects. "Anyway, I was born to all this. What about you? Do you come from a long line of cops? Or should I call you 'Special Agent Tylan'?"

"Jim is fine." He buttered a roll while he talked, and he didn't meet her eyes. "My dad managed a grocery store, and my mom was a legal secretary. They were gunned down outside his store by a druggie trying to score for a fix. I wanted to be a cop all my life. That cinched it."

"Oh, no, I'm so sorry!" Irenee said. She couldn't even imagine going through such a horrible experience. "How old were you? Did you have other family?"

"Twenty-two. Only my sister, Charity. She's dead now, too." He almost mumbled the last part.

She was about to reach out her hand to offer more physical support, but before she could, the waiter brought their meals. When he had finished serving, Irenee looked again at Jim. His attention was totally on his steak. She wasn't going to let him stop there, however. "Were you a regular city policeman, or more?"

"This is really good," he said, taking another bite.

"Or did you go straight to the feds?"

One side of his mouth quirked up in a half smile. "You're going to make me talk to you, aren't you?"

"Hey, you're the one who 'wants to talk,' remember?" She grinned and raised her eyebrows. "Talk."

"Okay, okay. I always wanted to be in law enforcement. Majored in criminal justice in college. Worked on my Spanish, too. After I graduated, and my parents were killed, I went into the San Diego department. After Charity died, I joined the Drug Enforcement Administration, and I've been with the DEA since then."

"Now you're after Finster and Ubell."

He sighed. "Yeah, I thought we had the case sewed up with the info from the flash drives, but you people are changing my mind." He waved his fork at her. "How about you? How'd you get into planning events? I'd have thought you'd be like those two who showed up at your office. The Blakes?"

"Oh, please, don't remind me," she said with a shiver of repugnance. "Tiffany's getting married, and they wanted me to manage her wedding. No way. In the first place, I don't do weddings, and in the second, I wouldn't run hers, no matter whose daughter she is. It would be a fast trip to either insanity or homicide. No, I run charitable and corporate events, period. My talents for organizing and detail came to me early—I guess I've always had them. My brother always teased me about how tidy my room was. Of course, he lived in a pigpen."

Jim laughed, and his golden-green eyes twinkled. He looked so darned wonderful Irenee suddenly wanted to throw herself into his arms. She was barely holding onto the chair arms as it was. His expression abruptly sobered, and he stared right back at her.

Only the waiter's return to remove their dinner plates broke the impasse. She rearranged her napkin, took a sip of water, and pretended nothing had happened. Jim didn't say anything and only looked off into space—although he seemed as baffled as she was.

Jim's eyes grew round when he saw their desserts—large pieces of fudge cake with raspberry sauce. "This is your 'usual'? Where do you put it all?"

"Casting spells uses energy. It has to come from somewhere, and since we don't have a god to give it to us or a long extension cord to a power plant, it's our body's internal caloric energy. The higher the spell level, the more often you cast, the more energy you use. If you don't replenish yourself, you'll lose weight. The only fat practitioners you'll see are usually pretty old and not casting much. I've been casting a lot of spells lately." She took a bite. "Hmmmm. It's warm, too."

His eyes zeroed in on her lips when she licked them. His gaze had a tactile quality, and she wondered how it would be if he touched her mouth—or kissed her. She blinked and came back from her reverie. Where was she going with these crazy notions? Where were they coming from?

He seemed to be caught up in the same sort of problem—she wasn't alone in these long eye-locks. To see what he'd do, she savored every bite of her cake, making sure she licked all the fudgy goodness from her fork.

On her third lick, he groaned and applied himself to his own dessert. She stifled a giggle. When he finished, he studied the other diners, but she could tell he was watching her out of the corner of his eye.

When she put her fork down for the last time, he leaned back and pointed upward. "What do you think we're going to learn when we go back up there? What idea do you think Whipple had to work on? Do you think he'll figure out where the 'item' is?"

She took a sip of coffee and pondered. "I honestly don't know the answers to any of your questions. This is my first experience with a major artifact."

"So, you're a what-did-he-call-it, a Sword?"

"Yes, I developed my talents late, and I've only been a Sword since I was eighteen. I didn't start training in item destruction until four years ago."

Jim leaned on his elbows toward her across the table. "How do you do it, destroy one of these items? What kind of sword do you use?"

"It looks like a Roman shortsword, and it's made of magical energy, not steel. Let's simply say destruction is not easy." She repressed a shudder at the memory of the Stone's attacks. Not a story she wanted to tell at the moment. Pushing her chair back, she said, "We're due upstairs. I hope Fergus and Dad have some answers for both of us."

CHAPTER NINE

"Come in, come in," Whipple boomed when they returned. "I have some interesting ideas to discuss."

Jim let Irenee precede him into the condo while he wondered what surprises Whipple had conjured up while they were gone. Before they had walked three steps in, an older woman came out of the kitchen.

She approached him, held out her hand, and said, "Hello, Jim, I'm Bridget, Fergus's wife."

"Nice to meet you." He shook hands with her. Whipple's wife was stunning—tall, imposing, silver hair, and like her husband, it was impossible to tell her true age. She had an air of calmness about her, putting him—and probably everyone—at ease.

"And Irenee!" Bridget gave her a big hug. "I heard we had some excitement while I was gone. Are you all right?"

"I'm fine. How was your medical conference?" Irenee answered.

"My wife is a pediatrician," Whipple informed Jim.

"The usual—a few good papers and lots of medical gossip," Bridget said, dismissing her meeting with a wave of her hand. "Since you're in my living room, I've invited myself into your discussion. Can I get anyone something to drink before we get started?"

Everyone declined, and they all took seats again—Irenee in her original chair, Whipple in his. Jim snagged the end of the couch closest to Irenee, and Bridget sat on the other end. Sabel pulled up a chair from the dining table.

Whipple stretched out his legs and studied Jim over steepled fingers. "We have a puzzle to solve where you're concerned, Tylan."

His statement made Jim sit up straight. His hunch antennae quivered—not in a warning fashion, but more of a wait-and-see mode. A small wave of electricity rushed through him, as though something good was about to happen. He squelched his reactions. *Don't get excited. No telling what this bunch would come up with.*

"First, we have a few questions," Whipple added.

Figured. Jim crossed his arms over his chest and gave the older man one of his "cop" looks—the kind declaring, "This had better be good."

"Since Irenee reported your being in Finster's study and your surprising ability to see her, we've been investigating you." He held up a hand when Jim rolled his shoulders in a get-on-with-it fashion. "Not in the way you probably think, however. We've been looking into your ancestry in particular, because the evidence points to your having some magic skill."

"Wait just a damn minute," Jim said, shaking his head. These people were incredible. Him? With magic skill? "That's screwy. I am not one of you."

"So it would appear from your family lineage, at least as far as we can trace your bloodline," Sabel interjected. "We're only to about 1850 at the moment."

Jim shot a glance at Irenee, who appeared to be as surprised by the news as he was. It was curious, though—despite the outrageous claim, he wasn't picking up any premonitions about their statements' truth.

"However," Whipple continued, "there are more than a few instances throughout our history where a person unconnected to us developed practitioner talents on his own. Through a quirk in DNA or some lucky convergence of the stars? We don't know. Such spontaneous development is probably the way talents started in the first place. We haven't been able to track our talents to specific genes, by the way."

"What, I'm a *mutation*?" This was getting weirder by the minute. First, his hunch mechanism was sitting there like a lump, seemingly asleep despite these wild allegations, and now Whipple thought *he* could do magic stuff. What next?

"The term is a little harsh, but exactly what you are has yet to be seen." Whipple stroked his beard. "There are two aspects of magic to consider in our decision: spell radiances and spell auras. First, you can see spell radiances. Casting a spell on an object causes it to glow. If a practitioner has the innate ability or casts the specific spell, he can see the luminescence. You saw the glow from the spells I cast on the bowl, the picture, and my staff, correct?"

Jim looked at the objects in question. They still glowed. "Correct."

"You saw the protective spells on Finster's safe, and you saw Irenee's invisibility radiance."

"If you say so. I'm not convinced of that."

"If the practitioner casts a spell on himself, he will also glow," Whipple continued. "We don't know why or how you are able to see *through* her spells. We have some theories, but no firm conclusions."

Man, this magic stuff kept getting more and more complicated, Jim thought. He said only, "Okay."

"Second are spell auras. When actually casting, a practitioner creates a spell aura around his body, and it can often be seen by family members. The proficiency to see a nonrelated person's aura is rare, and you don't seem to have that. What you can do, spontaneously see spell glows, however, is much rarer."

"Maybe I'm peculiar that way." Jim shrugged and turned to Irenee. "What do you think?"

"I think you should listen to Fergus and my father.

Something's going on, because you're seeing through my spells." She smiled at him. "Besides, if it's your innate talents, I'm not making a mistake with my magic."

"Great," Jim muttered. "Okay, I have some abilities—maybe. What's next?" He unfolded his arms, snapped his fingers on both hands, and pointed at the coffee table. "Abracadabra! It's a pony?"

Whipple chuckled, Sabel shook his head, and the two women smiled.

"Not exactly," Sabel said. "We also learned you have a reputation within your agency for your intuition, prescience, capacity, whatever term you like, to put two and two together and get answers when nobody can even frame the questions. You solve the case when others are totally mystified. A couple of your fellows think you're psychic, while others call you a wizard. You merely say you have a 'hunch' about something."

It took effort, but Jim kept his expression flat. "How did you find all this out?"

"Let's simply say we have our sources," Sabel answered dryly. "Did I state the situation correctly about your hunches? Did you have one a little while ago when you shut your eyes and put your hands on your head after we told you about Finster and the Defenders?"

Jim crossed his arms again, let his eyes go unfocused, and thought about those questions for a long moment. While he did, his hunch antennae didn't move, didn't even twitch, although the area right under his sternum heated up considerably. Oh, great. Heartburn, too. He glanced around the circle. They waited with an expectant air.

He couldn't accept their words as gospel. Not yet, anyway. "Maybe I was trying to wake myself up or calm myself down. My God, you'd just told me my prime suspect was one of these practitioners, he had an evil magic item, and you destroyed it. Because of all these events, I may never bring him or his coconspirators to justice."

He shrugged. "Or maybe I decided I was with a bunch of crazies and needed to humor you because you might really know something. What makes you think I was having a hunch?"

"Because you were glowing," Irenee said. "You had a spell aura about you. Why or how I could see it, I haven't a clue, but it was a bright blue."

"I was glowing?" Her statement brought him to his feet. He pointed at her, then himself. "*You* saw *me* shining like a lightbulb?"

She rose also and pointed back at him. "Yes, you," she answered, raising her chin, almost daring him to dispute her. She poked him in the chest with her finger, hitting him right in the solar plexus, punctuating her comments. "*Glowing.* Exactly like the floor safe. Only *blue.* That means *magic*, and the *color* indicates you have a *high* level potential, the power to cast some heavy-duty spells."

Jim gasped when her finger hit his chest again and a bolt of fire spread from it throughout his body. He grabbed her hand before she could poke him again. Their connection only increased the heat. Every muscle in him tightened, and a fierce arousal prowled through his bloodstream. And went south.

He stared into those dark eyes . . . and tugged her closer . . . and lowered his head . . . and was about to kiss her . . .

. . . when he heard Whipple say, "I told you so," and the sound pulled him back from the brink.

Her eyes wide, her lips slightly parted, Irenee blinked at him, but didn't otherwise move.

Jim looked at their hands—which radiated a faint, flickering glimmer—and slowly released hers. The vague shine vanished. She abruptly sat down and continued to gaze at him with an expression of both confusion and alarm.

He turned toward the two men. "All right, what happened here? What did you do? Cast a spell on me or us? What the hell is going on?"

"I think your magic talents are beginning to reveal themselves," Whipple said and grinned.

"So?" Stepping past Irenee, who still seemed shocked, Jim paced around the room for a few seconds. Their claims were unbelievable, totally ludicrous. Why couldn't he seem to find any reasons or facts to deny them? He extended a questioning hand to the group.

"This is absolutely crazy. How in the hell could I be one of you? How could I do magic?"

"You could," Sabel said, "if you're what we call a 'wild talent,' someone who develops talents spontaneously. As I said, we don't know how it happens, because there haven't been enough people available to study or we haven't gotten to them in their formative stages. We have learned that abilities do seem to show up more readily when one is around other practitioners. You've probably had dormant talents at least since puberty."

"You're damn lucky we found you," Whipple interjected. "Wild talents have been known to become seriously disturbed trying to reconcile their magic with the everyday world."

"Oh, for God's sake! First I'm a mutant. Now I'm going to go *nuts*?" Jim threw himself back into his seat on the couch.

As he did, his hunch antennae quivered and, he could swear, began to jiggle and wave and almost do the boogie. If those effects weren't bad enough, a spear of heat, then cold, then heat again, hit him right in the breastbone. He doubled over and groaned, "Holy shit!"

Irenee knelt immediately in front of him, and he grasped her hands as if holding on to a lifeline. Bridget slid over to hold his arm and rub his back.

"Take it easy, Jim," Bridget said, and her calm voice and touch somewhat soothed the tumult inside him.

Irenee held his hands inside hers, and warmth—or something—flowed from her to his middle. A sense of contentment settled on him when the bombardment of hot and cold stopped.

In the center under his breastbone, however, something grew. Another organ? No, impossible. But something was there that hadn't been there before.

He sat up slowly and locked gazes with Irenee again. Because it vaguely seemed the thing to do, he brought their clasped hands up to his chest. When they touched the spot in the middle of his body, everything in him—his hunch mechanism, his muscles, whatever was beneath his sternum—all relaxed.

"Are you all right?" Irenee asked, almost whispering, her big brown eyes as soft as melted chocolate.

He took a deep breath. No pain. Only contentment. "I think so. My insides seem to be working properly again."

Bridget put her hand on his forehead, before moving it to take his pulse. "No fever, and your heartbeat is a little rapid but strong. Any trouble breathing?"

"No. I think my chest was about to explode." He rubbed his hands and Irenee's—he hadn't let go of hers yet—over the end of his sternum. His eye and hand contact with her formed a bond he wouldn't, he couldn't, release. He did manage to mutter, "What the hell is going on? What did you do to me?"

"We did nothing. You didn't have a heart attack, either. What you felt was your magic center coming to consciousness," Bridget said, sitting back in her spot on the couch.

"Magic center," Jim repeated. He straightened Irenee's fingers and flattened her hands on his chest on either side of his breastbone. Warmth and pleasure and peace spread from her touch. He wouldn't mind staying in such a state of euphoria forever.

Irenee stared into the golden green of Jim's eyes while his magic energy pulsed under her fingers. The man truly was a wild talent, one of some strength and power. Her center thrilled to the energy flowing from him to her and back again. He must be a Defender, as well. How else could they be sharing power like this?

Before she could say anything, her father was helping her to rise. Jim released her hands, and the movement took her away from him. Her center seemed to sigh.

She could see Jim's eyes focus when he came out of the trance they had both been in. He looked around the group. "What the hell just happened?"

"How do you feel?" Bridget asked.

"Fine . . ." He studied his hands, rubbed them over his chest, and took a deep breath. "At least I think I do. Most of me does. Right here"—he pointed to his sternum—"feels different somehow."

"It's your power reserve, your magic center," Irenee

told him. "Remember when I said casting spells uses your body's internal energy? The spot behind your breastbone is where your magic energy resides. You'll concentrate on it when you want to cast a spell."

"That's the damnedest thing I ever heard." Jim shook his head, and when he spread a hand over his center, he frowned. "Something's vibrating inside me."

"You've never felt it before?" Fergus asked. "Not even during one of your hunches?"

"No. They're all in my head," Jim answered. "The 'big' hunches come to me in a huge rush. I can almost feel my head exploding with the knowledge. For the little ones, it's like being hit over the head with a hammer. Oh, wait a minute. Lately, they've been more like a punch in the stomach."

Irenee leaned forward. She would have liked to touch him, but would doing so throw them into that weird state where the world came down to the two of them and nobody else existed? Definitely something to think about later. Right this instant, they had to help him. "The first time I cast my sword, it felt like a blow to my center. What was the hunch you had here before, the one where you held your head and shut your eyes? Was it big or little? What was it about?"

"Big. It told me to believe you about this magic stuff." He scratched the back of his head like it itched.

"It looks to me like your talent has to do with these

hunches," Fergus interjected. "Anybody disagree?"

"I concur," her father said. "It might be related to probability-theory spells. I've known several people involved in theoretical activities—physicists, economists—and they have told me their best ideas often come to them after much study, but not much actual conscious examination of the details. They'll be doing something totally unrelated when, suddenly, it all fits together. Does yours work the same way?"

"Yeah, that's pretty much it." With a thoroughly glum expression, Jim looked around the circle. "So, I'm a practitioner? Hooray. What does it mean? What happens next? I learn how to do hocus-pocus? How am I to use it to catch the bad guys?"

Irenee stifled a sigh. He didn't totally believe his changed circumstances yet, and she had no idea what to do with him. Could he cast a spell if he didn't really believe in his ability to do it?

Fergus seemed to have the same reservations because he said, "Why don't you go home and get a good night's sleep, Tylan? Let your hunches tell you if you are, in fact, a practitioner. Come back here tomorrow, and we'll do some conclusive, determining exercises."

"What's wrong with right now?"

"I'm not putting you off for no reason," Fergus replied. "It will be better for all of us if you let the ideas and reality settle in your mind and your body. Magic isn't to be done without a great deal of care."

"I've got a big meeting on the case tomorrow morning," Jim said.

"Are you going to tell your agency about us? Or have you already?" Hugh asked.

"No, I didn't tell them about Irenee at Finster's or where I was coming today. 'Something' told me not to." Jim rubbed his center and stopped when he glanced down and saw what he was doing. "I don't like keeping quiet. But I won't say anything about all this 'magic stuff' until I have to. Hell, nobody would believe me anyway."

"Let us know when you can be here," Fergus said. "Irenee, why don't you give him your phone numbers, and you can be our liaison. Escort Tylan to his car, and come back. We have some other business to discuss."

The walk to the elevator, the wait, and the ride down were quiet. Jim seemed lost in thought, and Irenee didn't interrupt him except to hand him her card with her phone numbers.

Poor guy. What a lot to learn about yourself from strangers and totally unexpectedly. If she had been in his place, she would be stupefied and flat on the floor.

As they waited for his car, he turned to her. "I'll give you a call when I find out what time I'll be free to come out here."

"Good. Listen, are you okay?" She stopped herself

from putting a hand on his arm to offer support. From his previous attitude, he might not want it.

"Yeah." He rubbed the back of his neck as if it was stiff and gave her a part-perplexed, part-uneasy smile. "I'm just—I don't know what I am."

"We threw a lot at you at one time. I remember being extremely confused when my levels shot up, and I knew what was happening."

"Whipple was right—I need to sleep on all the ideas, come to terms with them. Do you really think he and your father are correct? What will these 'exercises' be?"

"Yes, I do think they're right." She wouldn't tell him yet about the magic energy vibrating between them or the possibility of his being a Defender, however. That was an unnecessary complication right now. He needed to accept being a simple practitioner first. She smiled, she hoped, with encouragement. "You're the first wild talent I've ever met. What he plans, I'd guess, has to do with learning and managing your skills."

"Great." The valet brought his car up. Before Jim got in, he nodded at her. "I'll see you tomorrow, probably in the afternoon."

On the way back upstairs, Irenee rubbed her temples. She'd get some aspirin from Bridget before they started talking. Jim Tylan wasn't the only one who had to come to terms with a new situation, and it was giving her a headache. What was going on between them and causing her strange reactions? How could he see through her spells? What could Fergus want? Please, not anything major.

Her center quivered, and she patted it. She was looking forward to getting the discussion over with. She needed some rest.

CHAPTER TEN

"He's my *WHAT*?" Irenee looked from her father to Fergus and back again. "*My soul mate?* Where did you get such a preposterous idea? Jim Tylan can't be my soul mate! That's impossible!"

"It's the only explanation for his being able to see through your spells, honey," Hugh said. "Since the spells of soul mates don't work on each other except for healing and defense, your invisibility spell didn't phase him. He saw right through it."

"Through your panther illusion, also," Fergus put in.

"Maybe it's part of his quirky ability to see spell glows."

"He didn't see through Fergus's dragon," Hugh added.

"But . . ."

"The clincher is," Fergus said with a grin, "the way you look at each other."

"Oh, please." Irenee waved her hand as though she

could wipe away the comment—and the idea behind it.

"Think about it, Irenee," Bridget said, her voice low and calm.

Irenee eyed her suspiciously. Bridget wasn't going to suck her into their idiocy with her comforting pediatrician's manner. She wasn't an unruly child who didn't want to get a shot.

Bridget, however, kept talking. "Remember when you poked him in the chest and he took your hand? How the two of you froze and forgot we were here? He was about to kiss you when Fergus said something. Again, especially again, when you were kneeling in front of him on the sofa? He raised your hands and put them on his magic center? I could almost see the energy flowing between you. You were definitely feeling a soul mate's attraction."

Irenee sat down with a plop and put her head in her hands. Yes, she remembered every single detail. And her reactions to him in Alton's study and in her office.

She'd heard about practitioner soul mates all her life, of course. As a teenager, she'd even wondered about who hers would be, what he would look like, what kind of talents he'd have. When her levels had shot up and she became a Sword, all thoughts of soul mates had disappeared. She'd had more important problems to overcome.

Now, out of the blue, her father, her mentor, and his wife were telling her this man, this stranger, whom she'd known for only a few hours, was the *soul mate* with whom she would spend the rest of her life?

It was so damn hard to believe.

She looked up at her father, Fergus, and Bridget. She knew they were telling the truth as they saw it and had her best interests at heart, but she couldn't help putting up some resistance. "Are you certain you're not mistaken? I'm twenty-five. Maybe all my reactions are only my hormones telling me my biological clock is running."

All three shook their heads like three bobble-head dolls.

"We're sure," Hugh said. "We discussed it while you were at dinner and again while you escorted him out. Are you feeling an itch in your magic center when you think about him? A warmth? That's the soul-mate imperative at work."

"What about him? When are you going to tell him?"

"We're not. It's up to you," Bridget said. "We think it best, however, if you wait until he accepts what he is and learns to control it some. I also recommend the two of you get to know each other better."

"Thanks so much." Irenee sat back in her chair and crossed her arms in front of her.

"Telling him about soul mates really is your call," her father said, "and I think you'll figure out when the time is right."

"What about Mom? What will she think of your

idea?" Her mother had been twenty-seven when she married her father. Surely she would be on Irenee's side for not rushing into telling Jim—to make absolutely, positively certain he was her mate first. A hot shiver ran up her back when the word *mate* crossed her mind, but she held herself rigid.

"I spoke with her while you were at dinner, since she's flying to New York tonight. She's delighted. Even began talking about when you'd have children."

"Children! Isn't she rushing things a little?" Irenee had barely met the man, and her mother had given them children? Oh, this was entirely too much.

Hugh chuckled. "She's been wondering for a while about both you and your brother. I think some of her friends are teasing her about the lack of grandchildren."

"Has she told Dietrich?"

"Of course not. We both know you and your brother will find your true mates, and there's absolutely nothing we can do about the timing. Since you have, however . . ."

"Dad"—Irenee pointed at her father—"you stay out of whatever's going on here. I don't know for a fact there's any soul-mate connection between me and Jim Tylan, and the poor man has enough to worry about without complicating his life even more. I had a devil of a time coming to terms, not simply with a level increase, but with becoming a Sword, too. He probably feels like he's been transported to another planet."

"Okay, honey, I'll call your mother off—if I can."

She gave her father a squinty-eyed, you'd-better-succeed look before continuing, "I'll tell you another, greater possibility besides his being an ordinary practitioner. When my hands were on his chest, magical energy was oscillating between us."

"The exchange was probably the soul-mate connection," Bridget said. "You'll see what I mean after you've mated."

Although Irenee felt her face grow heated, she persevered. "I don't think so. It felt exactly like what happened when we were destroying Alton's piece of the Stone and Dad stepped up behind me for support. He fed me power directly, through his touch. It also felt exactly like what happened when you, Fergus, taught me to use my sword. In each case, you had your hands on my waist and fed it directly into my center, and I sent it out to my sword. There may have been the phenomenon in the mix with Jim, I'll concede, but it wasn't all soul mate."

"Hmmmmm. If you're right, Irenee, and you may well be," Fergus admitted, "it makes the situation even more complicated. Tylan's going to have to accept many new ideas in addition to his new abilities."

"What are you going to do tomorrow? He thinks he won't be here until afternoon, by the way."

"You and I are going to teach him to cast a spell or two."

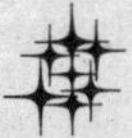

When Irenee finally made it to bed about an hour and a half later, she couldn't fall asleep without replaying the detailed discussion about soul mates to which her father, Fergus, and Bridget had subjected her. They hadn't told her anything she didn't know—well, not about the woman's perspective. Her mother had covered that already.

From her father and Fergus, Irenee did have a better idea how a man approached the situation—lust!—and how a man understood the reality—more lust! with growing love. The knowledge did not, however, lessen the embarrassment of having to talk about it with "older men," one of whom was her father and the other her mentor, for pity's sake.

She took to heart Fergus's warning about the soulmate imperative. The whole phenomenon—practitioners *always* found their soul mates and true love—was like a fairy tale, but the imperative, which Fergus called the phenomenon's enforcer, had to be reckoned with. If she or Jim tried to reject one another, or if they simply didn't accept each other fast enough, the imperative would "nudge" them together. The nudges could be painful.

Meanwhile the attraction between her and her soul mate would become increasingly intense. Or, worse, totally overwhelming and out of her control.

Oh, great.

She could only hope the imperative would leave her alone when she had her sword in hand. The last thing she wanted to do was become distracted and slice her supposed soul mate—or anybody else—in half.

The possibility, however, was probably the least of her problems. More important was when and how she was to explain soul mates and what he would think of them in general—and of her in particular. He was so new to the concept of practitioners. Maybe, if they could convince him he was one of them, the rest would follow naturally. She could only hope.

What would it be like to have a soul mate? It was supposed to be wonderful. What would it be like to have Jim in particular as hers? Even without the impressions encouraged by the phenomenon, he was an attractive man. Tall, broad-shouldered, with great eyes, and curly hair—and once-broken nose.

Besides the physical person, she liked his intensity, his attention to his work. She didn't know if she could have kept in mind a main objective—learning what had been taken from Alton's safe—when bombarded with all the information about practitioners for the first time.

From what Bridget said, the physical attraction would come first for him. If that weren't enough, he would probably act on it, whether or not she told him about the phenomenon.

What would it be like to kiss him? Her center definitely warmed at the thought. As she gave it a rub, other parts of her body tingled and some ached. She had to laugh. Lust was not confined to the males, it appeared.

She'd kissed a few boys in her time, purely in the spirit of experimentation, and she was sure none was her soul mate. Her attraction to them had been too mild. Truth be told, she'd expected more of an inner explosion when she met her mate-to-be.

On the other hand, "getting lost in his eyes" had taken on new meaning. His touch alerted every cell in her body. Feeling magic energy move between them had been exhilarating. She had a lot to look forward to when they came together.

When would they? Or, first, *would* they at all? Fergus, her father, and Bridget could still be wrong, and Jim might not be her mate. He might still reject her—from confusion, refusal to accept his new reality, or sheer cussedness, for all she knew.

She absolutely had to protect herself in this situation. Keep an open mind, be open to the process, while being prepared for anything and everything else.

She would explain the soul-mate phenomenon soon—but not until he got used to the idea of being a practitioner. Take it slow. There was no rush. Her center itched like crazy at that thought.

Hey, imperative! Give the guy and me a break. The

Cataclysm Stone is our first priority.

Her center itched a few seconds more, then subsided.

Hoping the phenomenon got her message, she turned over and punched her pillow into a comfortable shape. With her soul mate on one side and an evil magic item on the other, both demanding her energy, she should get to sleep. She'd need it.

CHAPTER ELEVEN

In the study of the Finster mansion, Bruce Ubell worked on matching the gala's guest list with the registry on the practitioner Web site. It had not been the fairly easy job he had envisioned. The registry was huge and worldwide; searching took time. The guest list wasn't very long, but so many people had similar or ambiguous names. For example, J. B. Jones. Was this person John Bartholomew Jones or James Bolton Jones? He often had to look at the entire entry for picture or location to make sure the person listed was not the same as the guest.

Even though there was no one else he could trust with the job, he resented taking time from his company work, from bringing Finster Shipping and all its parts into more efficient alignment and profitability. Alton had delegated some very important duties, and his minions had not been up to their tasks.

Furthermore, there was the problem of his cousin's little spells cast on the Iranian group. Bruce had reversed the enchantments and sent the Iranians to another dealer, "convinced" they would get a better deal there. By the time they figured out the new man was cheating them and removed him from competition—a nice side benefit—Bruce would have all his legal and illegal activities working perfectly. Best of all, he'd be able to charge them double the original price.

He'd also use the respite to protect himself and his Stone and to take revenge on the Defenders who destroyed its severed section.

He did wonder why, as the notification had stated, the Defenders had not visited the mansion. He assumed it was because the notice had been for Alton, not him. Did they suspect the larger part of the Stone existed?

As the red book had instructed, he'd been extremely careful to keep everything in the old man's specially shielded room. At first, Bruce had wondered who was keeping up the spells since Granddad was dead and he and Alton weren't supplying magic energy. Then he'd figured out that the Stone was protecting itself—an added bonus. The deeply buried and enspelled space kept all emanations safely inside, undetectable by even the most sensitive enemies. Casting from there might actually be easier than in the open—the shields could be boosting the strength of his spells, if he had read the book correctly. Damn Alton for losing the text before he could study the last chapters more closely.

Bruce had been surprised to discover he didn't miss

having the extra power Alton's smaller piece provided. In fact, he was beginning to think his Stone was giving him even more potency, as though its severed third had somehow leached energy from its larger brother. The same way dealing with Alton had drained his own regular enthusiasm. With his item concentrating solely on himself, he was certain all his capabilities were growing. Look at what he'd learned and accomplished already.

He wouldn't, however, underestimate his enemies. He'd assume the Defenders were looking for his piece, and they'd show up sooner or later. He and his Stone had some surprises in mind for when they met—and he knew they would.

He'd need every ounce of his energy against the Defenders, but with his Stone on his side, how could he lose? He wouldn't hesitate to bring about a true cataclysm, whereas they, poor weaklings, were bound by practitioner conventions no longer applying to him.

He heard the mantle clock strike two and groaned. Only two more pages to go. He'd made it to "S." The first name on the page was Irenee Sabel. Ah, yes, the daughter of the renowned Sabel family. She'd been talking to Alton right before the auction began. He knew her family were high-level practitioners, but she'd always been a little guppy—some sort of event planner—in their group of corporate and Wall Street sharks.

He was about to dismiss her when the familiar

oozing of his Stone's magical energy began to seep through his bones. With it came an impression of a command: *Look at her.*

Calling up the Sabel woman's information, he started reading. Address—hmmm, the Center. Why out there? Education, age, profession—yes, her business as an event organizer. Level . . . ten. Ten?

How on earth did she become a level ten? Her previous level was a five.

Bruce swiftly read through the rest of her listing. No clue there.

While he stared at her photo, he felt his Stone flare and its energy flow become more rapid. The power heated his blood from slightly warm to boiling hot to molten lava, and a furious wrath permeated his consciousness. Every cell in his body hated the woman in the picture, and every molecule wanted to annihilate her. His gaze alone should have burned a hole in the computer screen. With an effort that left him limp, he gained control over himself and his Stone before he threw a fireball at the monitor.

Here was the thief. As if to prove his contention, his Stone sent him images of the destruction of its stolen section. Horrible, terrifying, hideous, tragic images. From inside his own piece, he experienced the other's defense and his own's valiant attempt and devastating failure to counter the onslaught of Sword and Defender power—led by Irenee Sabel.

The woman was a Sword. Oh, yes, *she* was the *bitch* Alton had named in his throes of agony.

"Irenee Sabel will pay," Bruce said aloud. In his head, his Stone laughed.

CHAPTER TWELVE

"Nooooo!"

Jim sat straight up in bed as the echo of his cry reverberated in his bedroom.

"Oh, shit," he panted as he tried to catch his breath and control the shakes left over from the terror of the nightmare.

Irenee was in danger. He dreamed it, he felt it, he knew it, and every hunch antennae and even the strange area under his breastbone agreed.

The red clock numbers showed 2:10. Hell, he'd only been asleep for a couple of hours. He grabbed her card and his cell phone off the bedside chest, read the card by the glow of the phone screen, and punched the buttons.

The phone rang three endless times.

"Hello?" her sleep-laden voice mumbled.

He sagged back against his pillow as relief jellified his backbone. "Are you all right?"

"Jim? Jim Tylan?" Her voice rose on his last name. Had she forgotten him already?

"Yeah. Remember me? Tall guy, wild talent, magic man, Hunches 'R' Us?"

"What's the matter?" She definitely sounded awake and alert now.

Hell, what was he going to tell her? He'd had a bad dream? On the other hand, she was the perfect person to understand—if he used the right words. "Nothing here, except I suddenly had a *hunch* something was wrong with you. It was so strong it woke me up."

"Oh."

He could hear her moving and the sheets flapping. Of course, she was in bed.

The mental picture of her snuggled into her blanket, all warm and gorgeous and with her red hair spread across her pillowcase, immediately turned him hard as granite.

"Are . . ." He had to stop to clear his throat. "Are you there?"

"Yes, I'm here. What kind of hunch?" Her voice sounded scratchier than it had a second ago, sort of lower and sultry and . . .

He had to stop his line of distracting thinking. *Concentrate on the immediate problem, dammit.*

"Look, I'm sorry I woke you, but this hunch came out of nowhere. I've never had one wake me up before. It wasn't just a bad dream. All my usual hunch reactions are still going off. You're in danger."

"No, I'm fine. I'm at home in the Center. Alone.

Not a threat around, and believe me, my condo is well protected. What was going on in the dream?"

Her question brought it back in startling detail, and worry replaced relief. "There was a big, black void or shadow about to grab you. In the center was . . . a flame, a really strange one because it wasn't red or yellow . . ."

"What color was it?" she asked in an excited whisper.

"Black. I don't know how a flame could be black, but it was flickering lighter and darker than the void. Seeing it made my skin crawl. It was reaching out, or the void was. You were standing there, too close, and I couldn't get to you. You had something shining in your hand, and you pointed it at the flame, and there was a big flash, and I woke up."

Reliving the dream broke him out in a sweat. He wiped his face with his hand, then used the sheet to dry his chest.

"Oh, wow, oh, wow! You *have* to be more than a simple practitioner." Her excitement came right through the phone.

"What do you mean?"

"Did you feel anything else? Like a sensation of good or bad or . . ."

"Yeah, it all . . . felt evil." Almost embarrassed to say them after ridiculing the idea, he blurted out the last two words in a rush.

"Oh, double, triple wow!"

What was the matter with her? She sounded almost happy. "What was it? You know, don't you?"

"This could be great, our chance to catch him. Jim, you have to get to the Center as soon as you can tomorrow. I have to call Glynnis and Fergus and see if one of them picked up—"

"Stop!" He slapped his hand on the bed, but of course she couldn't see it.

She stopped, and he could feel her excitement coming through the phone.

He spoke carefully. "Take it slow, and tell me what I dreamed."

"You described what could have been our fight with the first Cataclysm Stone remnant. There was a black flame in the middle of it, too. I wonder if your dream means the holder of the larger section brought the bigger piece out of hiding. I want to call to see if the sensitives felt its emanations."

"Wait. Hold on a minute. You were alone in my dream fight. That flame thing was about to eat you alive."

"Oh, it was just a dream," she scoffed. "I was definitely not alone in the real fight. I'd never go up against such a powerful item by myself. Besides, I *do* know what I'm doing. I *am* a Sword."

"Hey, remember me? The guy who doesn't know anything yet? What I saw is what you actually faced destroying even a little piece of the thing? How could you put yourself in such awful danger? How can your father let you do it?"

There was a small silence on the other end. When she spoke, it was with a calm, slow, implacable voice. "Listen to me, please. I am a Sword. Swords destroy evil items. It's our mission. Yes, it can be dangerous. That's why we do it in teams. My father is a Defender. He is aware of all the risks. He's very proud of me, and he would *never, ever* try to keep me from doing my duty and following my calling."

"Okay, I understand, but—"

"You're not one of those men who always think they have to protect the 'little woman,' are you?" She gave the question a distinct edge—a sharp one, like on a sword.

Hell, even if he probably was one, he knew enough to say, "No, but—"

"I'm sure you've put yourself in danger many times. What if I asked you those questions, Mr. DEA Agent?"

"Point taken," he said quietly. He'd evidently hit a hot button, and this wasn't the time for an argument. Especially when he didn't have enough info to win one. To bring them back to the original subject, he said, "You think my dream could have come from Ubell's actually using the Stone?"

Another little silence. He could almost feel her shifting gears.

The excitement had returned when she answered, "I think it's possible. Even allowing for the strange way dreams change reality, yours was so accurate, especially about the black flame. That's exactly what I thought was inside the piece we destroyed. I hope someone picked up on its use besides you so we can find out where the Stone is. No matter what, however, Fergus will want to talk to you about your experience."

"Speaking of Whipple, do you have any more ideas about what I'm going to do tomorrow? What kind of test he was talking about?"

She paused, then asked, "Have you decided you are one of us? You might be able to do magic?"

"I'm still getting used to the idea," he answered. It was the truth. To forestall more questions, he said, "I'll get to the Center as soon as I can, but when depends on the meeting and my boss."

She didn't pursue the subject, only replied, "Give me a call when you're on your way?"

"Will do. You stay safe in the meantime."

"Yes, sir," she said with a groan. "You, too. Bye."

Jim put the phone down and lay back in his bed. What in the hell was going on?

First, he had hunches that scared him half to death with black flames. Complicated by a prickly woman who'd sounded like she wanted to kick his ass for questioning her right to throw herself at the exact same hideous fire. A gorgeous redhead he wanted to keep safe right here in his bed.

Second, his investigation had gone, if not totally bad, definitely weird, with an even weirder villain. Ubell had to be the one with the Cataclysm Stone, an evil magic item, of all things. Assuming Sabel was correct about the guy's ability to warp financial records, how were they going to make a case against him? How was justice to be brought to bear on Finster and Ubell?

How was he ever going to avenge his family?

By casting a spell on the bad guys? By using *magic*? This was really the crux of the matter. If he believed he was a practitioner, with all being one entailed—the magic, the evil, the community, the Swords—then he had to believe he and they would overcome Ubell, the Stone, and everything connected to it.

Even though he'd thought long and hard about the entire situation after he'd returned to his apartment, he hadn't been able to come to any firm conclusions. His hunch mechanism hadn't helped at all. It seemed to be exhausted after the evening's workout. He couldn't blame it—he was pretty tired himself.

His fatigue showed in his inability to keep his mind focused. Other, unwelcome memories fought their way through the wall in his mind—of his sister and how he hadn't been able to help her and how suddenly it was too late. How much he still missed her and his parents.

God, the damned addict had killed his parents ten years ago, and Charity had died five years later.

Where were his vaunted hunches when all that happened? Absent. Nowhere in sight. Either time.

They sure as hell showed up tonight.

In the midst of a bunch of "magic practitioners," no less.

In front of the most attractive and exasperating woman he'd ever met.

Irenee Sabel. Merely the thought of her, her red hair; her feistiness; her big brown eyes; her pride; her luscious, surely kissable self; and her smile—all banished the residual loneliness he experienced every time he thought of his family. How and why did he react so intensely?

Maybe he was horny.

Duh! Of course he was horny. Irenee would turn on any man.

He couldn't help wondering what it would be like to have her in his life. Someone who cared for him and about him personally. To be part of her circle of family and friends. To have a real home again instead of a barely furnished apartment.

"Family," his dad had always said, "is the most important thing in our world."

His breastbone, which was supposed to have his "magic center" right under it, began to vibrate. When he put his hand on the spot, it radiated warmth, and despite all of his confusion and apprehension—and other feelings he squelched and stuck back behind the wall—he felt . . . content. Yeah, that was the word.

In the middle of the chaos, confusion, and sheer, absurd improbability of his situation.

Content.

His contentment might be the weirdest thing of all.

What a position to be in—caught between his agency and this bunch of magic spell casters. If he told his boss about the practitioners, Ken Erlanger would probably take him off the case and commit him to a psycho ward. His career would be down the drain for sure. If he didn't, he might be obstructing justice and certainly wouldn't be doing his job or helping his team.

Would the practitioners tell his boss the truth if he dragged Erlanger out to meet them? They were obviously extremely secretive about their abilities—he could understand why. No, he wouldn't count on even the slightest help from them with his boss.

But, push come to shove, he had to find out if he could actually be one of them. Try to discover some evidence on Ubell clean enough to use in court. Or get help from the practitioners in finding some. Maybe one of them could unhex those damned financials.

Okay. He'd go out to the Center today. If his boss didn't have any orders, he'd ask for a few days of personal time. He'd been working nonstop for over a year and could do it without mentioning names or details.

He'd see if Whipple, Sabel, and company could prove to him he was a magic guy.

And he'd do everything in his power to get closer to Irenee.

His center hummed in agreement.

CHAPTER THIRTEEN

Jim notified Irenee he was on his way and made it out to the HeatherRidge Center about one o'clock Tuesday afternoon. This time the guard at the gate didn't check with anybody, simply waved him through. Irenee and Whipple were waiting for him in the lobby by the fountain, black garments of some kind over their arms.

"Sorry I couldn't get here sooner," Jim said when he reached them. She looked good enough to eat, and he had to stifle the urge to give her a hello kiss.

"That's all right," Irene replied. "We just arrived ourselves."

"Let's go where we can try a few spells," Whipple said.

Jim followed him and Irenee through the lobby, out the back onto the terrace, and down a walk where they climbed into a golf cart. The big wizard drove them to a two-story building some distance from the main one.

"This is one of our classroom and office buildings," Irenee said as they went in. "The offices and conference rooms are all aboveground, and the classrooms and labs are below."

"Safer in case a spell goes awry." Whipple led them to an elevator. "It's primarily a building for higher levels. We have another for training novices and young practitioners, but since we aren't sure exactly what you are, we thought we'd be prepared for any level."

The elevator came, and they entered it.

"Whoa," Jim said when he turned to face the door. "Lots of glow."

"What's shining?" Whipple asked with a grin.

"All the buttons, and they're not the usual lighted kind, either." He pointed to a clear square on the button panel. "That blank space is almost blinding."

"It should be," Irenee said and put her hand on it.

The elevator started without her pushing a single button. He had the distinct impression they descended farther than the two basement levels indicated on the panel.

When they stopped, the back of the elevator, which had not appeared to be a door, opened behind him. He turned and stood, staring at what should have been a simple corridor—if they'd been in a castle—gray stone walls, floors, ceilings, about fifteen feet wide and ten feet high. The doors were dark wood with metal latches and hinges. If there were lights, he couldn't see them for the spell radiance. He squinted at the luminescence.

"More glow, I presume," Whipple said.

"Yeah, everything's lit up, floor, ceiling, doors. Lots of colors, too." He also took note of the gold shield and silver swords displayed on a black pentagon—more like what he'd expect to find in a magic castle.

"What you're seeing are mostly defensive and protective spells," Irenee told him as they walked down the hall. "The training rooms themselves are covered with particularly heavy containment enchantments. Is it too bright for you to see?"

"No, I think I'm getting used to it." He blinked and was able to stop squinting.

"We'll have to find a way to cut the glare for you," she said. "I wonder if sunglasses would help until you can control it internally."

Standing next to a bulletin board filled with announcements and notices, a man and a woman in colorful robes were talking, but they smiled and nodded to Irenee and Whipple. Jim noticed their curious glances at him.

They came to a wide door, the top half of which was open. A shelf on the lower part formed a counter. Inside the room, Jim could see a series of open cabinets containing garments on hangers. Attached to the wall, a white sign said "Wardrobe" in plain type.

Whipple leaned over the counter into the room beyond. "Tameesha? Where are you? We need a robe."

A short, stout woman with light brown skin and

short black hair came around the corner of a cabinet. "Hold your horses, Fergus. And who's this?" she said when she spied Jim.

"Tameesha, may I present James Tylan, whom we believe to be a wild talent. We're about to test him to make sure. He needs a practice robe. We don't know his level yet, but it may be in the nine-to-ten range. Tylan, the imperious lady is Tameesha Washington, Keeper of the Wardrobe. She'll be the one to make your robe when you're ready for one."

"Oh, my, I'm so happy to meet you, Jim. A wild talent? You're only the second I've ever met. What kind of talent do you have? It's never to early to plan a formal robe."

"Nice to meet you, too," Jim said, "but I don't know what my talent is."

"This one will try your expertise, Tameesha," Whipple said. "His talent seems to lie in having hunches. Once he learns a few spells, we may have a better idea. In the meantime, we'll make do with the basics."

Her brown eyes grew thoughtful, and she tapped a finger on her jaw. "I like challenges. I can think of a couple of possibilities. For practice and since we don't know your level, however, I recommend a stronger robe than a novice." She looked him up and down. "What's your height and weight, Jim?"

Jim told her, and she vanished into the cabinets.

Within seconds, she returned with a light gray garment and passed it over the counter to him. "Try it on. You might want to take your jacket off first."

Jim took off his coat and laid it on the counter. No one said a word about his weapon in its holster on his belt, so he left it in place. With its hood and long sleeves, the robe looked like something a medieval monk might wear, only it was a thick cotton or linen, not wool. Around the edges of the hood, the front opening, the hem, the sleeve cuffs, and an attached tie belt, symbols flickered. Heavy in his hand, the robe was weightless on his body.

"Turn around and let me see," Tameesha ordered. As he did so, she asked, "How does it feel?"

Jim flapped his arms and rolled his shoulders. The robe moved with him easily. "Fine. What are these little symbols?"

"You can see those? Fergus, he can see the glyphs?"

"Yes, he can see spell radiances, too."

The wardrobe mistress grinned at Jim. "Outfitting you is going to be fun."

"Let's get to it," Whipple said after Jim had thanked Tameesha and picked up his coat. The big wizard led the way along the hall, past a cross corridor and several doors to a chamber on the left. He stopped outside a room whose sign proclaimed it to be "Practice Room 3—up to and including level 15 spells." On the whiteboard under the sign were the neatly printed words, "Reserved, F. Whipple" and the date and time. Whipple wrote "FW" on it while Irenee opened the door.

They entered first a small vestibule separating the hall from the room behind. Both the hall door and the one into the room itself were about three inches thick with metal handles and latches worn shiny with use. The stone-clad inner room was shaped like a pentagon about twenty-five feet across. The ceiling was high—Jim estimated fifteen feet at least. Electric fixtures on the walls lit the space, and next to them were sconces with candles—not that Jim needed the light to see with the spells glowing here.

A table against one of the walls held a full glass water pitcher, some glasses, and a number of tall, thick-bodied pale yellow candles in individual saucerlike holders. Several wooden chairs with heavily carved backs and arms stood against another wall.

"You can put your coat over on the table, Jim," Irenee said, "and please put your gun over there too. I'd hate to have you set it off inadvertently with a miscast spell."

He followed her instructions, carefully unloading the weapon first.

She and Whipple put on their robes. Cut on the same pattern as his, Jim saw, they were made of pitch-black, velvety, finely woven material, obviously much better quality than his gray one. Multitudinous glyphs shimmered, not only at the edges but all over the robes. Whipple's had more than Irenee's.

"What's the significance of the symbols?" he asked.

"They're spells and enchantments, designed to protect us and enhance our spells and talents. Practitioners, including Defenders, wear robes identifying their career talents. Swords always wear black," she answered. "The more symbols, the higher in level and more powerful the person. As you may have figured out from Tameesha's surprise, very few practitioners can actually see the glyphs."

"The robes also help shield you if a spell goes wonky," Whipple said and nodded at one of the walls. "Here, let's move the chairs. We want a semicircle facing that way."

Wondering how "wonky" a spell could go, Jim helped move the chairs and sat in the middle one as directed. Whipple and Irenee placed ten candles in their holders on the floor about three feet from the wall and separated from each other by a foot or two. They sat down also. Jim was about ten feet from the line of candles.

"Before we get started, I'd like to know if you were able to find the source or cause of my dream or whatever it was this morning," Jim said.

"Sounds like quite an exciting event. Unfortunately"—Whipple shook his head—"you were the only one who felt any vibrations or effects."

"What was it, then? Only a dream? Some wild figment

of my imagination? Something you told me earlier that came back to haunt me?"

"Not according to Glynnis Fraser, our team member who's extremely sensitive to evil items," Irenee said. "She's positively identified Alton's piece as part of the Cataclysm Stone. She's been investigating both how the Stone might be used and how practitioners like her perceive evil items in general."

"She's developed a theory," Whipple interjected, "that Bruce Ubell—we are assuming he has the rest of the Stone—was using his piece somehow, but it wasn't out in the open like Alton's when she felt the first vibrations. She thinks you tuned in to his casting, as it were."

"Ubell himself wasn't protected?"

"Evidently not enough."

"Is the sensitivity distance-based?" Jim asked.

"It depends primarily on the strengths of the Defender, the item, and the shielding. Distance can, however, play a role," Whipple answered. "Are you getting a hunch about it?"

"No," Jim said. "I'm simply using common sense. My place isn't very far from the Finster house. Ubell's staying there. Since I seem to be sensitive to magic, maybe I picked it up."

"Not knowing what to do with the information, your mind must have translated it into a dream," Irenee suggested.

Whipple rubbed his hands together and gave them both a huge grin. "This gets better and better, doesn't it?"

"Depending on your point of view," Jim stated dryly.

"You're probably feeling rushed, aren't you?" Whipple said.

"That's putting it mildly."

"Understandable, but unavoidable," the wizard continued. "Ubell is not giving you time to become comfortable with the idea of being a practitioner. We, however, need to protect you as soon as we can. If it's any consolation, he's pushing us also. We need to take care of his Stone quickly."

"It doesn't look like we're going to distract him by arresting him soon, either," Jim said with a grimace. "Sabel was correct about those financials I copied. They're giving the forensic accountants fits—all the names are in code, and some of the info and figures seem to change from day to day and when printed out. The computer guys are looking for hidden files and programming causing the changes. The head of thc task force doesn't want to move until we have firm numbers."

"Are you getting anywhere with the more overt crimes?"

"We're still investigating the drug and weapons dealings, of course. It looks like business is slow at the moment on the drug side. No product is being moved on the street at all. The weapons guys thought they had a buy going down soon. All of a sudden, it was called off. Everything's changing on the bad guys' side, too."

"Not surprising with Alton in the hospital so suddenly," Irenee said. "Bruce has a lot to contend with on legitimate Finster Shipping activities, let alone the illegal ones."

"Yeah, I agree," Jim agreed. "My boss let me take a couple of days of personal time while the accountants and geeks work and since I'm not part of the group on the weapons activities. So I have a little time to try out whatever you're going to teach me."

"Excellent!" Whipple rubbed his hands together and grinned. "Let's get you started. Irenee, you begin with the basics."

"Okay," she answered, looking so earnest and serious that Jim almost smiled. Then he remembered what he was there for—*magic*—and the area under his breastbone vibrated like it could hardly wait to get moving.

"First of all, you've had overnight to think. Do you believe us? You probably are a practitioner?" she asked.

"I believe you think I am," he answered, "and I'm willing to try hard to do what you want me to. I myself need to see more tangible proof to be truly convinced."

"A fair answer," Whipple said.

"There are three determining factors in casting a spell," Irenee stated. "Your personal magical energy, your particular talent, and the exact spell you're casting.

We use our internal energy, the magic power within us, to cause something to happen. Oh, energy and power are interchangeable terms, by the way. You're born with a certain amount of energy and the potential to reach a specific level of ability. Your energy amount and ability level are set and do not normally change. This rule has one general and at least one specific exception, but we won't bother with them at the moment."

"That's what you were replenishing with that meal last night—this inner energy," Jim said.

"Correct. Second is your particular talent. You have the capability to cast spells only belonging to your talent. For example, I can cast organizing spells, Fergus can cast spells relating to veterinary medicine, and my dad casts ones to do with economics. I can't cast either of their spells because I don't have the talent. Are you with me so far?"

"Yeah, I think so. How do you learn what your energy and level are?" Jim asked.

"We'll get an approximation of those with a spell you're going to learn today—one of the universal spells everybody can cast," Irenee answered. "The third factor is the individual spell itself. Spells have levels, degrees of difficulty. Higher level spells are more complicated and require more energy from the caster. If I'm a level-five in power and an auto mechanic, I can cast only mechanic spells up to and including level-five ones, but I can't cast a level six."

"So, everybody specializes and has limits," Jim said, "and your abilities as Swords are on top of those talents."

"Yes," Whipple said, "and we'll cover those later."

"There's also the matter of practice," Irenee continued. "We aren't called 'practitioners' for nothing. We must practice and practice. Using your powers builds stamina and expertise. You have to build up your 'magic muscle,' so to speak. Every time you cast a spell, you deplete your energy reserve residing in your magic center. Low-level practitioners have less energy to use than the higher ones. Or, to put it another way, it costs more of your total energy to cast the same spell if you're a low level than if you're a high one. Practice helps you make more efficient use of your energy, however much you have."

"It's like sports, then. Exercise to increase your muscles and extend your range and endurance. Practice to increase your skill." Jim nodded. "Okay, I get it."

"The present emergency notwithstanding," Whipple said, "it's vitally important you, a wild talent, learn to handle your power. Untrained practitioners are menaces to everyone. They will use magic without even realizing it, or they will sense the magic inside them and be unable to come to terms with it. You seem to have escaped this latter fate, which can lead to mental imbalance and worse. Okay, what do you say? Shall we try a spell?"

Although Jim felt distinctly uncomfortable, he knew he couldn't back out now. He had promised to try. What the hell, it might be fun. His center grew warm and seemed to be laughing at his last thought. All he let himself say was, "Yeah, I'm as ready as I'll ever be."

"Good. You're going to try two spells, the first spells novices formally cast before masters to prove they are indeed practitioners. Note that we're not going to *teach* you the spell—you're going to *cast* it on your own," the big wizard said.

"Remember, magic is all about using energy. In the first spell, lighting and extinguishing a candle, you have to place energy accurately in a short burst. The second, a light spell, involves harnessing energy, placing it somewhere, sustaining it, moving it, and then dispelling it. We'll start with lighting a candle."

Irenee took up the explanation. "Casting spells can be highly individualized. Not all practitioners cast lower level spells exactly the same way, because these spells don't require the preciseness of higher level ones."

She pointed at the line of candles. "There are several ways to light a candle, for instance. The point of the spell is to deliver, shoot, present, throw, transfer, however you want to think of it, a tiny bit of hot energy right on the wick of the candle. Practitioners usually have their personal ways of bringing off their spells. There is no prescribed hand or body movement for this spell."

She lifted her hand from the chair arm. "You may choose to use a gesture."

She pointed, and one of the candles suddenly started burning. "Or not . . ." She glanced at it and it went out.

"Whoops, almost forgot . . ." She waved a hand at the candles in the wall sconces, and they flamed as she rose and turned off the electric lights at the switch by the door. The electric light fixtures slid into recesses in the wall. "Magic can be hard on lightbulbs and electrical circuits."

"The name of the spell is *flamma*," Whipple continued. "My students have had the most casting success if they move a tiny hot spark from their energy center to the wick or they coalesce a small hot bit of energy right on the wick. A few have pictured the flame in their mind's eye and transferred this visualization to the candle. Some find it helpful to say the word *flamma* out loud or in their minds to trigger ignition. We want you to try it, using whatever method or methods you can think of." He waved a go-ahead gesture at Jim.

Jim squirmed slightly on the chair, leaning forward with his elbows on the chair arms. He glanced from one to the other of his companions. Clearing his throat, he said, "I really feel weird about this, you know."

"You don't ever have to worry about embarrassing yourself with us," Whipple answered. "Just relax and concentrate."

Jim sighed, sat back, and looked hard at the candle

directly in front of him. He still wasn't completely sure he believed in all the hocus-pocus, but the evidence was mounting, and he wouldn't know unless he tried. Therefore, he concentrated—man, did he concentrate—right on the wick of the candle directly before his chair. After a few minutes, it was clear his staring at the wick did absolutely nothing.

Wait a minute. Irenee didn't say to stare, she said to send energy somehow. He pictured throwing a little baseball of something—energy? heat?—at the wick. Nothing.

He created a flame in his mind and moved it out to the candle, mentally settling it right over the wick. Nothing again.

He shot the wick with a movement of his hand like a kid playing cowboy. Still nothing.

He pictured having a flame on the end of a long matchstick and touching the wick with it. Ditto.

He used Fergus's suggestion of a tiny hot spark. Cold. Not even a whiff of smoke. He couldn't bring himself to say the spell word out loud.

He looked again at the two practitioners and shrugged.

"Don't stop," Irenee encouraged. "The glyphs on your robe are sparkling, so something's happening with your energy."

Jim shifted in his chair, sitting upright, hands gripping the chair arms, eyes unfocused. He started thinking about energy as a tangible thing that could be shaped, compressed, heated, chilled, that came from inside him, that could be given force and substance. What had they said last night when he thought his stomach was going to explode? His magic center had come to consciousness?

He took a long, slow breath and imagined the source for the energy right in his middle, lying under his breastbone, next to his heart. He concentrated on the spot, turning his mind inward, losing contact with the rest of his body.

And he felt the "new organ" he'd grown last night stirring, expanding, gathering energy from his cells. It grew warmer, then hot, and finally . . .

Delight, exhilaration, and a deep satisfaction exploded through his nerves like molten silver, and they left in their wake an enormous sense of sheer *power*.

Yes! The unspoken word roared in his head. *He could do this!*

He focused his eyes, framed the spell word in his mind, and shot a glance at the wick on a candle in the middle of the row.

The wick exploded in a two-foot tower of red and yellow flame, and the entire twelve-inch candle dissolved into a puddle of wax overflowing its slightly warped holder.

"Scale it back a little." Whipple's voice was low, barely audible.

Jim struggled with his internal bonfire, tamped it

down some, and flicked his gaze at a new target.

The second candle ignited, melting only half of its length, but it remained burning.

"Again," Whipple rumbled.

Frowning at the difficulty of control, Jim closed his eyes briefly, then opened them in a slit he hoped would reduce the *what*, muzzle velocity? He looked carefully at the next candle in line.

The wick caught perfectly, exactly as though he had held a match to it.

"All right!" Jim said under his breath. He had the idea now. In swift succession, he lit the remaining candles. Before he turned in triumph to his two teachers, he shut his eyes and asked, "Okay, if I look at anything or anybody else, I'm not going to fry them, am I?"

"No, not unless you mean to. Casting is an active, not a passive endeavor," Whipple answered.

"Good," Jim breathed in relief. He opened his eyes and looked at Irenee.

Her face was split in a huge grin. "Congratulations! You did great! I've always liked to see novices cast their first spell, and this time was special. I knew you could do it!"

"Very good," Whipple said. "I don't think, on his first try, even one of my students has ever melted the whole candle and almost the holder as well. Now extinguish them."

Jim's euphoria disintegrated when he realized what Whipple had said. "How do I do that?"

"Think about it. Think it through logically."

Jim glared at his teacher for a second before concentrating on the problem. If the energy was cold instead of hot . . . He envisioned cold energy in his center—it felt like he'd swallowed an ice cube—and aimed his eyes at a candle. It sputtered and died, a thin stream of smoke rising from its wick.

Or could he take the flame back into himself? He concentrated on one flame, trying to absorb the energy back into himself, willing its return. The flame died slowly, finally completely, the wick not even glowing as it went out. His energy center seemed to grow a tiny bit warmer in consequence. He tried alternating methods with the remaining candles and extinguished them all.

"Good work, my boy!" Whipple leaned over and thumped him on the arm.

"How do you feel?" Irenee asked.

"I'm fine, I think," Jim replied, slumping back in his chair. "I feel a little like I've run a ten-mile race, though. How'd I do?"

"Splendidly," Whipple beamed at him.

What he had done finally dawned on him, and Jim gazed at the candles, as a sense of wonder spread through his mind. "God! I can't believe I did it! Once I concentrated on energy itself, it was like something was waiting inside me to do that very thing."

"It's a rush, isn't it?" Irenee grinned at him, rose, went to the table, and brought him a glass of water. "Here, you may need to cool off."

"I certainly do," he replied and thirstily drank while she resumed her seat. His mind was whirling, and he looked again at the candles. *Holy shit!*

What would they want him to do next?

CHAPTER FOURTEEN

"We've established you have the ability to manipulate magic energy," Whipple stated after Jim put his empty glass on the floor. "Next, we'll work on sustaining and controlling. The *lux* spell will also give us an indication of your potential. The idea is to create a source of light that can be brightened or dimmed and moved from one place to another. *Flamma* and *lux* are two of our most ancient spells, which only seems reasonable since practitioners have always needed a light source for their work."

Whipple held out his hands and brought them together so his fingertips touched and his palms did not. He bent his wrists so they came together also. "Make a cage," he instructed, and Jim followed suit.

"Here's what you're going to do. Create a small ball of energy in your cage. Magic energy naturally shines, although hot energy is brighter than cool. I recommend you keep it cool right now for comfort. Encapsulate the ball in a shell of more cool energy. Or you can create the shell first, then put the ball of energy into it.

"Think of an egg. The yolk is the light, and the shell keeps the light inside it from dissipating or changing shape. The shell can also be cool while the yolk is hot. That way you won't set fire to anything if the light gets too close. You can brighten or dim the light inside by feeding the yolk more or less of your internal power, and you can increase or decrease the size of the shell to change it from a small focused beam to a more diffused illumination. I'll cast very slowly. *Lux!*"

Jim watched Whipple's hands start to glow. A little golden ball of energy appeared in the middle of his cage, and just before a silver layer seemed to swallow it.

The ball glowed brightly—about the strength of a hundred-watt bulb, Jim estimated. It made no sound.

"I'm going to vary the energy," Whipple said. Golden rays shot out from between his fingers as he brightened and dimmed the light.

"The lightball will exist as long as you supply energy to it," he said. "At first, you'll probably need to concentrate most of your mind on sustaining it. When you and your magic center get used to the spell, you'll be able to set the light on automatic, the same way you do many tasks. Your mind and your center will carry on until you cut the energy flow by canceling the spell or you run out of energy altogether."

"Think or say *resigno* to cancel the spell. Shut off the

energy at the same time," Irenee put in. "Once you've canceled a spell, your center will know what to do the next time."

"*Resigno*," Whipple said, and without a sound, his lightball ceased to exist.

"Okay, let me see if I've got it straight." Jim held up his hands in the cage and concentrated on his inner spot again. A reservoir of energy seemed to be waiting for him, ready to do his bidding. He felt like he had more control, too, but he decided to build the shell first, just in case.

Don't forget to keep it cool, he warned himself, *you don't want to burn your fingers.*

He mentally pinched a little bit of energy—he envisioned a kid's cold marble—from his center and moved it to his cage. A swirling, foggy, colorless mass with a diameter about the size of a quarter appeared inside. Taking another tinier piece and thinking *hot*, he "pushed" this spark inside the marble. Still no color. His fingers tingled, though, so something was definitely in there.

He shook the cage lightly. Nothing happened. No illumination. What was wrong?

"Think 'light,' and say *lux*." Irenee suggested.

"*Lux!*"

Dark blue light poured from between his fingers.

Hot damn! The light flickered, and he gritted his teeth to keep his concentration, but he managed to say,

"It's not the same color as yours."

"I'll explain that in a minute," Whipple answered. "Try to dim and brighten the light by raising and lowering the energy you're supplying."

Jim worked so hard at maintaining his light he started sweating. It was a nice surprise when his robe began to cool him.

"Relax with it if you can," Whipple said. "Let active maintenance float back in your mind so it's not your primary concern. Keeping the light going will get easier the more you practice. Eventually you won't need to form the cage physically and can simply create the light."

For several minutes, Jim brightened and dimmed his light. He realized he could relax a little, but he wasn't confident enough to try "automatic." He did find, however, that he didn't have to look continually at his hands to keep the light functioning. Irenee gave him an encouraging smile when he glanced her way.

"You're doing well, Jim," Whipple said. "Next we're going to try releasing the egg and letting it move. Irenee, show him, full power."

Irenee stood up, moved to stand in front of Jim, and created her own light in the cage of her hands. When indigo and violet light shone out, she and Whipple both started.

"Fergus?" she asked as she peered at the lightball inside her fingers.

"It looks like our bout with the Stone definitely enhanced your powers, Irenee. We'll have to test you soon," the warlock answered with a huge smile on his face. "Release your light."

Irenee opened her hands and the golf-ball-sized light floated free. "Nudge it with your mind, and you can put it wherever you want it." She demonstrated, and the ball moved up and down and from side to side.

"You can get fancy, too" She bounced it off the floor and the ceiling and stopped it directly in front of her, capturing it in her hands again. "You try it."

Jim had to send a burst of energy to his light since he'd been watching Irenee's instead of maintaining his. He reestablished its glow and opened his hands to release his ball.

At first it simply hung in the air. He tried thinking of it as a balloon and gave it a mental poke. It lurched about a foot away and stopped. He tried a right side punch and one from the left. With a few more tries, the ball moved spasmodically up and down and from side to side.

"This is like learning how to drive a stick shift," he complained. "Or I'm drunk."

"Take it easy," Irenee said. "You're getting the hang of it."

Before long, he had it moving more smoothly and was able to move it in a circle around him, out of his eyesight for a few seconds. Eventually he brought it to a stop before him. Tentatively, he reached out a finger, stopping about an inch away.

"It's okay to touch it," Irenee said, "as long as you're using cold energy on the outside."

Jim grasped it between thumb and forefinger and squeezed gently. It felt like a cold helium-filled balloon. He batted it gently from one hand to the other. Finally he let it sit in the air in front of him and grinned at it, then her.

Irenee released her own ball, and the two lights began to drift together.

Closer and closer to each other they floated.

"Fergus, I'm not controlling its movement. My light should be hovering about a foot from me," Irenee said, concern evident in her voice.

"Ditto," Jim said, rising to his feet.

All three watched the two lights literally melt together until they combined and grew into a basketball-sized shining globe swirling with blue and violet-laced indigo and hovering between Irenee and Jim.

He looked at her across the top of the glowing orb. Simultaneously they raised their hands, palms out toward the ball, and cupped their hands around it until they touched the sides. The surface felt smooth and cold. His hands tingled like they were waking up from being asleep.

"Let's see what happens if we squeeze it," Irenee suggested.

The swirl of light increased in tempo, before the brightness slowly dimmed while they pushed to decrease the size of the cage their hands had created. When their fingers were intertwined, the light went out altogether.

Her hands in his, Jim looked into her eyes, and his center rejoiced. His lungs were working like he'd run a mile, and Irenee was breathing hard, too.

Only Whipple's words brought him back to reality. "My goodness. I don't think I've ever seen anything quite like what you just did. I know of one other couple whose lights can combine into one. I don't believe they ever touched the result."

"What's going on here?" Jim asked. "What's with the colors? Did we do something wrong?"

"Not at all, not at all," Whipple reassured him. "Normally when a practitioner casts *lux* for the first time, the color of the light indicates his energy and level potential. A red light would mean the person has the potential to become a first- or second-level practitioner and has a small amount of energy. An orange would be third to fourth, yellow fifth to sixth, with corresponding increases in energy amount, and so on up the spectrum. Those who cast a silver light usually top out around seventeen or eighteen. Gold goes all the way up to twenty. Twentieth is the highest level a practitioner can attain alone. After gold is white light, and the only way we can produce that is to combine energy when we're destroying an evil item."

"Sounds kind of indefinite to me," Jim said.

"The levels aren't precise because there's so much chance for variation. Irenee's level-ten light has always been a blend of more blue and some indigo. From the colors of her light today, it appears her powers have grown, and not by a small amount." Whipple's eyes squinted in thought, and he tapped a forefinger against his lips. "It will probably take some time before we know exactly what level you are, Jim. From the shade of blue, you're a nine or ten. The vast majority of practitioners, by the way, are below level ten."

Whipple sat back, stroked his beard, and sent an almost mischievous glance at their still clasped hands. "What gave you the idea to cage the light and hold on?"

Jim looked at their hands and let her go. His center gave him a little punch when he did so, but he ignored it and said, "It seemed to be the thing to do."

"I agree. Something in me said to squeeze," Irenee said, holding out her hands and studying them as if they had somehow changed from the experience.

"For the couple whose lights combined," Whipple continued with a gleam in his eye Jim wished he could figure out, "the blending had specific significance and was a distinct predictor for their future abilities. In the 'light' of what happened here, I believe you are correct, Irenee, in your conclusions about Jim. And, yes, the couple were—"

"I get the picture," Irenee interrupted. "I'll tell him soon."

"Tell me what?" Jim asked.

Irenee took a step back and rubbed her forehead, effectively covering her face. When she lowered her hands, her face was blank. She sighed. "There's so much about everything to tell you, Jim—spell-casting, practitioner life and ethics, discovering your specific talents, Defender teams, and more. Right this minute, however, I suggest we stick to one task—manipulating a lightball. It will help you learn energy control faster than any other spell."

Thinking to himself that he wasn't going to wait very long for more explanations, Jim nodded—for now. From her air of unease and her slight blush, he was willing to bet whatever she was holding back was a doozy. His hunch antennae gave a little wiggle in agreement. He sat back down. "Okay, what do I do next?"

He spent the better part of three hours playing with *lux* and *flamma*. Whipple and Irenee were good teachers, able to deconstruct their own casting to lead him through the processes step by step. By six o'clock he was able to maneuver the ball around the room at will, create it at a distance—on the other side of the room, for example—and even start it out at a lower level than his own intrinsic one.

The last he found particularly difficult at first, but

Irenee assured him it was necessary, as level modulation conserved energy. He had already showed he could when he cast *flamma*—full power at the candle in his first attempt and much less by the third.

Once he got the hang of it, starting his light at red, bringing it up through the rainbow to blue, and taking it back down was easy—well, if not totally easy, at least *easier.*

Also exhausting.

"Resigno." Jim cancelled his spell and stretched in his chair. "Can we take a break? I'm starving."

"I'm not surprised," Whipple said. "We've put you through a lot. Most new practitioners don't make it through half as much and remain conscious. Look, it's getting late. I have a call to make to a couple of people from the Defender Council. As you can imagine, they want updates on our efforts toward finding the rest of the Cataclysm Stone. Why don't you two get some dinner? Irenee, you can tell Jim more about practitioner life while you eat."

Whipple looked innocent, but Jim heard an undercurrent in his words. Irenee must have also because she said with a set jaw, "I'll take care of it, Fergus."

"How about Italian?" Jim said, more to get them moving than a desire for spaghetti.

Irenee stood and started removing her robe. When she finally turned to him, she had a smile on her face.

"That sounds good. Let's get out of the Center, too. I know a good place on Golf Road that makes the best tiramisu. I'll run over to my condo to get my purse, you hand in your robe, and I'll meet you in the lobby."

After her fast exit, Jim looked at Whipple with his eyebrows raised. "Something you'd like to tell me?"

"No, it needs to come from her. Don't worry, it's good, not bad."

Although Jim wasn't so sure about that, he'd be patient—up to a point. Probably about the time he brought her back from dinner. Then he'd get her by herself if it killed him.

His center gave him a jolt while he took off his robe, picked up his weapon and jacket, and followed Whipple out the door of the practice room. His idiotic irritating magic center was also on the discussion list. If it drove every practitioner as crazy as it was doing him, they could have their damn magic.

CHAPTER FIFTEEN

In a corner of the cozy restaurant, Irenee studied the menu. The smells of good Italian cooking permeated the room, and she knew she'd smell like tomato sauce and Italian herbs when she left. No matter. She was ravenous.

"What'll we have for an appetizer?" Jim asked.

"Calamari. They really know how to fix it here."

The waiter came over with bread, and they discussed their menu selections versus the specials and ordered. Jim picked a wine—he was evidently off duty, and she needed to relax, if possible—and the waiter left.

Jim poured olive oil into a shallow dish, soaked a piece of bread in it, and took a big bite. "Mmmmm. I needed this," he said between more bites.

"Wait," she said, "you're doing it wrong. Here is the Chicago way." She picked up the Parmesan cheese shaker and shook it into the dish, added more olive oil, and mushed the mixture together with her fork. After sprinkling on some pepper, she dipped a piece of bread in the paste, held it out to him, and said, "Try this."

He looked at the dish, then her, and took the bread. One bite, and he was nodding his head. Two, and he was dipping a bigger piece into the oil-cheese mixture.

"Okay?" she asked.

"Oh, yeah." He nodded and reached for another piece of bread. "Chicago, huh?"

"Wait till you taste it with roasted garlic." She pulled the bread basket closer. She wasn't going to let him have it all.

They'd hardly said a word to each other on the trip there, and Irenee could almost feel his curiosity and determination growing. Before he could ask any questions she didn't want to answer, therefore, she'd see if she could lead the discussion where she wanted it to go. "If you feel light-headed, it's normal, and food will help. You did really well. Young practitioners, even knowing what to expect, don't come as far in a week as you did in a few hours."

"I'm surprised how . . . *depleted* is the best word, I guess, how *completely depleted* I feel. Like all my energy has been sucked out of me."

She glanced around. There was enough ambient noise to cover their conversation, they were sitting side by side, not across the table from each other, and nobody would overhear them if they kept their voices low. "Some call their center a 'power or energy well.' Since you haven't truly been using your abilities, you haven't been exercising or practicing to build stamina and automatically replace the energy as you use it."

"I thought you said my color meant I have lots of energy," he said around another bite, but in the same tone, so he evidently understood the need to keep their discussion private.

"The color indicates your *potential*, not what you can use this minute or without work. Reaching your potential takes a lot of practice, and there are tests involved along the way. For example, from my present color, I seem to have increased in potential in the fight with Alton's Stone. To be 'officially' listed at a new level, I must learn the spells and be tested on them. Unofficially, I can cast lower spells to greater effect with the new power."

He was silent while the waiter returned with the wine and went through the opening ceremony.

When the waiter left, Irenee raised her glass and said, "Here's to our newest practitioner."

"Thank you," Jim answered, looking both pleased and dubious at the same time. He clinked his glass with hers and took a sip. "How do you go up a level, and how long does it take to learn spells? I don't think you explained that."

She ate a piece of bread to gain time to think. His questions worked to her advantage. She could discuss the specifics of her own situation without treading into dangerous soul-mate territory. "I'm some kind of special case nobody completely understands. I was a level five until I turned eighteen, and all of a sudden, my potential, energy, and talents increased."

Over the appetizer and dinner, Irenee told him what had happened to her, how long it had taken to learn all the new Sword and Defender spells, how difficult it had been getting through college and starting her business while dealing with the change. As she expected, he asked lots of questions.

They were eating the famed tiramisu of sponge cake, liqueur, and chocolate, when she said, "Nobody from Fergus on down, including master teachers and our scientists who study our abilities, has any idea what caused my change. I'm not the only practitioner such a transformation ever happened to, but I'm the first one in this country since 1850. Except for other wild talents, I'm probably the only person alive who can begin to understand what you're going through."

"Yeah, I can see that. I can also see I have a hell of a lot to learn." He didn't look overjoyed at the prospect. He finished his coffee and said, "Let's go back to the HeatherRidge. I have some more questions about practitioner life."

Was it her imagination, or did he emphasize those last two words? Was she going to have to tell him about soul mates tonight? Was she ready? Nooooo, not if she could put it off. Maybe some excuse would come to her on the way home.

When the check came, she offered to pay her half, and he gave her a part-insulted, part-incredulous look. The man was definitely "old school" at times. He paid the bill, and they walked out of the restaurant.

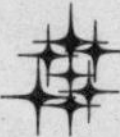

It was a lovely summer evening, and something of a shock to come out of a dimly lit restaurant to daylight. The sun was still up at seven thirty, of course, but it was rapidly setting.

Saying he always prepared for a fast getaway, Jim had parked his car—a nondescript dull brown-and-rust sedan where she had been expecting something sportier—by itself and facing outward three rows from the building in the strip shopping mall. Now, however, the lot had filled in, thanks to the two other restaurants there.

As she preceded him between cars, she saw his lights flash to show he'd unlocked it. He was reaching to open the door for her when two men appeared, one at each end of his car, blocking them in. Two large men—with guns.

"You're coming with us," the one behind Jim said. "Keep your hands where I can see them."

Irenee turned to the man at the back of the car and glared at him when anger replaced the shock of their threat. Of all the nerve! Who did these guys think they were, fooling with a Sword? After half a day dealing with puny lightballs, she was itching to cast something of substance. Here was her chance. She shot a glance at Jim, who was facing the other thug, then brought her eyes back to her opponent.

"No," she said.

"Irenee . . ." Jim sounded like he was speaking through gritted teeth.

"No, we won't go with you," she continued, "however, I will keep my hands up." She extended both hands, palms facing the thug, and cast "puff of wind" at hurricane force. She pushed her hands forward. *"Flabra!"*

"Aaaahhhhh!" the would-be kidnapper yelled as he flew through the air, landed with a thump, and slid into a car in the next row.

Irenee turned, ready to stun the other guy, but Jim had taken advantage of her diversion and slugged him. He dragged the groaning man to the side and ordered, "Get in the car. There are more of them."

Only when she looked to her left did she notice two similar men running toward them from the edge of the lot. She quickly climbed in and buckled up.

Jim got in, started the car, and roared out of the parking lot.

"Head for home," she told him.

"Right." He had to wait precious seconds to get across Golf Road, and he made the turn across the eastbound lanes and the left-turn-lane median with a squeal of tires.

Irenee squirmed around to her left to see out the back. "There are two cars coming out of the parking lot—two black SUVs."

Jim must have glanced in his rearview mirror because he said, "I see them. When we left the HeatherRidge, a vehicle like that was pulling out of the road across from the entrance. I waved for him to go ahead of us, and he waved back, so I went. He must have tailed us."

Still sitting halfway backward, she dug in her purse for her cell phone with one hand while she braced herself with the other. He zigged and zagged through the traffic until there were several cars between them and the thugs.

"I'll get us some help." She opened her phone and hit the speed dial for Defender emergencies. When the dispatcher answered, she set the phone on speaker so Jim could hear. "This is Irenee Sabel. I'm with Jim Tylan in a car traveling west on Golf Road between Higgins and Barrington. A couple of men tried to kidnap us, and two black SUVs are following us. We're heading for the HeatherRidge Center."

"Understood," came the answer. "Stay on Golf and turn north on Bartlett. We're sending people to meet you."

"Roger that," Jim said when they had to stop for a light. He used the pause to click his seat belt together. "I bet Ubell sent these guys."

"I don't think they're practitioners, though." Irenee said, craning her neck to see around cars. "They were totally surprised when I hit the one with the puff-of-wind spell."

"Defenders are coming to meet you on Bartlett Road," the dispatcher announced. "Don't stop for them. Come straight to the Center, no matter what happens. We have your phone on the GPS tracking program, so we know right where you are."

"Roger," Jim said. The light turned green, and the cars in front of them began to move.

"The passenger in the closest one opened the door and stood on the door frame to look at us for a couple of seconds," Irenee said. "The nearest SUV is four cars back. I can't see the other."

"Let's hear it for Chicagoland traffic. They won't be able to gang up on us easily. If the truck behind me will just let me in . . ." He maneuvered the car into the left lane. "There. We have some cover between us and them. What did you say you hit the goon with? A puff of wind?"

"Swords have an arsenal of offensive and defensive spells," Irenee explained, rather proud of herself for being able to act in the face of such a threat. "I cast *flabra*."

"You scared the hell out of me when you threw that thing." He sounded angry.

"It didn't stop you from decking the other man." Why was he angry? She'd helped them both.

"Of course not. What's the traffic like on Bartlett this time of night?"

So, he could hit someone but she couldn't? She'd have to make some things about Swords clear to him. First, they had to deal with the jackasses in the SUVs. "There's hardly any, and we'll go from two lanes to four. They'll have lots of room to maneuver in the middle of the forest reserve."

"Yeah, I know," he said with another glance at the mirror when they crossed Barrington and the road through the Poplar Creek Forest Reserve narrowed to one lane in each direction. "Damn. One of them is closer. Once we make the turn, I'm going to hit the gas, so hold on. I can outrun them. My car has more under the hood than meets the eye."

"A team is on its way to you," the dispatcher said.

"If they get too close," Irenee told Jim, "I'm going to hit their car with a *fulmen*—a lightning bolt." She loosened her seat belt and squirmed to face totally backward, kneeling on the seat with the shoulder belt across her back for support. Even if she couldn't direct the spell from a point inside the car without risking a ricochet off the metal or glass, she could aim by sticking her left hand out the passenger-side window and directing the energy out through it.

"What? No! Sit straight. Here comes the turn." He twisted the wheel and accelerated. The car fishtailed a little when it came around. He corrected and floored the gas pedal as the road rose slightly before them.

Irenee paid him no attention, only held on until they were straight again. They were in the right-hand lane. She hit the window button to roll it down, and the resulting rush of wind blew her hair around. She could still see, so she ignored it to hang on to the seat with her right hand and brace her body against the seat belts. The thugs' cars made the turn, shifted to the left lane, and roared up after them, but didn't gain much.

She held her fire. They weren't quite close enough yet.

"Oh, shit!" Jim snarled and slowed the car as they came to the top of the rise.

"What?" she asked without turning to see.

"The light up ahead is red, and there are cars in each through lane on both sides. The left turn lanes are open, so I'm going to go through them and hope the others don't start fast when the light changes."

"Okay," Irenee said when Jim moved their car to the left lane, "Stay straight in this lane for a second."

She stuck her left hand out the window and pointed at the fast-gaining pursuer.

Dial down the power. You don't want to blow them up. She waited a few seconds until the SUV came a little bit closer . . . *"Fulmen!"*

CRACK!

BOOM!

Smoke began to pour out of the car behind them, and it swerved from side to side.

"Hot damn!" she yelled. Her bolt had hit the front tires as well as the engine.

Sparks flying from the tire rims, front bumper scraping the road surface, the damaged SUV slowed abruptly—too quickly for its partner immediately behind to dodge, and the second one hit the first on its left rear bumper. The impact stopped the second and threw the first to the right, over the short grass next to the road, and into a wetland full of water and cattails. After a huge splash, the vehicle came to a stop, smoke still pouring from under the hood while it settled into the mud. The second SUV sat in the middle of the road not moving.

Jim had pulled back into the right lane and slammed on the brakes after she cast the spell. He turned in his seat in time to see the SUV hit the water, and he stared at it through the passenger window. "Holy shit! What about the guys in there?"

The men in question climbed out of their sinking vehicle. One of them fell on his face into the muck, and the other one fished him out.

"It looks like they're okay." Irenee knew she was grinning like a loon and wished she had room to dance. Her spell had worked perfectly! Being a Sword was so much *fun*! Take that, you scumbags!

The two staggered out of the water and across the road to the other vehicle. Just as they clambered into it, two white Hummers passed Jim's car headed at the thugs. Its front fender somewhat bashed in, the remaining black SUV lurched into a U-turn and headed south.

"The Swords are in the Hummers," she said and wriggled around to face Jim again. He gave her one of his trademark scowls. Still grinning, she leaned forward, touched the tip of his nose with her finger, and said, "Zap!"

He jerked backward far enough to grab her hand in his and shake it. "Are you crazy, woman? What if you had missed their car? What about innocent bystanders?"

"I knew what I was doing, and I wasn't going to let them catch us. Nobody else was in my line of fire. My lightning bolt worked, didn't it?" She glared back at him.

"Oh, for God's sake," he snarled, and then he kissed her.

She hardly had the chance to register the feel of his lips on hers, his tongue demanding entry and sweeping inside her mouth, before heat and his scent and a glorious sense of belonging flooded over her. She was reaching for him when a loud horn blast caused him to break the kiss, abruptly swing his head around, and stare out his driver's side window.

One of the white Hummers was alongside, and John Baldwin leaned out the window and pointed toward the HeatherRidge.

Jim cursed, let go of her—when had he grasped her shoulders?—and put the car in gear. They headed for the Center at a sedate pace. Jim didn't say a word.

Irenee worked on slowing her fast-beating heart and gaining some control over the sparks shooting through her nervous system. Those fireworks weren't the result of her spell. They came directly from that kiss.

Take it easy. It's only the imperative pushing you. His kiss meant nothing. Probably his way of working off the adrenaline rush from the chase. He didn't feel a thing. The conclusions—or were they hopes?—didn't help calm her nerves. All she seemed to know with a certainty was that she wanted another kiss. She did wonder, however, what would have happened next if they hadn't been interrupted.

She sat straight and studied him. He had both hands on the wheel and wore a grim expression. Nothing indicated to her he had been affected at all by their oh-so-brief kiss. Until she noticed how flushed his skin was, how set his jaw, and how tight his grip. How he took a long, deep breath and let it out too slowly. He seemed to be simmering.

They pulled up to the HeatherRidge gate, and Gary, the guard, told them to go straight to the Defenders' building. Jim asked how to get there, and Gary gave him the directions—turn left before going into the underground parking, follow the road, he couldn't miss it. Jim nodded and stepped on the gas without giving her so much as a glance.

Yep, he was definitely on a slow boil. She'd wait until they got inside before saying a single word. Then she'd use more than a couple of words to tell him about Swords in general and herself in particular. Didn't he have any confidence in her?

CHAPTER SIXTEEN

Jim followed the drive around and pulled into one of the parking slots on the back side of the Defenders' building. Avoiding even a glance at the woman next to him, he carefully took his hands from the wheel and exited the car. He honestly didn't know whether he wanted to shake her until her teeth rattled or kiss her senseless.

What a fool stunt! What if she had missed? What if the spell had backfired? Would they have been fried? She didn't ask permission or even discuss it before she threw those spells—either time. She shouldn't act like such a loose cannon. She could get hurt. He certainly had a couple of things to tell her about letting him, the one with experience against bad guys, take the lead. Didn't she have any confidence in him?

Irenee had already climbed out when he went around to open her door, so he stalked to the building and held that door for her. Nose in the air and gaze straight ahead, she sailed through. She wouldn't even look at him. He hoped she was sorry about her impulsiveness, although deep down he knew she wasn't. What was he going to do with her?

The kiss had shaken him to his toes. What the hell was going on with him? He'd never had the reactions to a woman like he was having to her. He realized he was still standing there holding the door when the man and the woman from the Hummer came up the walk. He let them precede him inside the building and into a conference room. At least they smiled at him.

Whipple and Sable were seated at the table waiting for them.

"Nothing like a little unexpected excitement to get the blood flowing, is there?" Whipple said, grinning and rubbing his hands briskly together. "Tylan, these two are John Baldwin, Sword and member of the Defender Council from New York, and Johanna Mahler, Sword and teacher of our young Defenders here at the Center."

Before taking a seat, Jim shook hands with both of them. Short, sturdy Baldwin had an air of command reminding him of one of his best captains in the San Diego PD. Mahler, a pretty dark-blonde in her early- to midthirties, projected both calm and confidence.

Irenee sat next to her father and directly across the table from him. Good. He could keep an eye on her. He could almost laugh at the way she was pretending he didn't exist—except he was still strung so tight, his face would probably crack if he tried to.

"Okay, what exactly happened?" Whipple asked.

Jim spoke before she could—he'd tell it his way, objectively. "We came out of the restaurant, and two men jumped us and trapped us between cars. They had guns. One told us to come with them, but he didn't say where. I could see two similar men heading our way. Irenee hit the guy on her end with a puff of wind, and I slugged the one on mine. We jumped in the car and took off."

He stopped to take a breath, shoot a glance her way. She said nothing, so he continued, "She called here, and we were given directions to take Bartlett Road. Thanks to the traffic, we were able to maintain some distance between us and the two SUVs—Suburbans by the look of them—coming after us. When we turned on Bartlett, they followed. We had a good lead before I had to slow down when I saw cars in the through lanes ahead at the light. I moved to the left to pull into the left-turn lane and run the red light."

He looked straight at her and worked hard to keep the anger out of his voice. "That's when Irenee threw a lightning bolt at the first SUV. It swerved and slowed, was hit by the second, and ended up in a swamp off to the right side the road. The two men in it got out and climbed into the second vehicle. The Swords showed up, and the other guys beat it. Have we heard from them?"

"Our people in the other Hummer called and said they lost them when they turned east on Golf and crossed

Barrington," Baldwin answered. "Once the lanes expanded from two to four, they sped off, and we didn't try to keep up—too dangerous for other motorists. We've alerted the people we have watching the Finster mansion to see if they show up there."

"I figure Ubell sent them," Jim said. "When we left here, I noticed a black Suburban in the road to the subdivision across from the Center's entrance, and I think it was the same people. Ubell wouldn't have any reason to know who I am, so they must have been after Irenee. They were probably going to bring me along as a possible bargaining chip."

His last words brought her gaze back to him. Looking genuinely puzzled, she said, "I thought they were after both of us. Why only me?"

He refrained from pointing out she couldn't think of everything and didn't have the experience to think like a bad guy. If it was up to him, she'd *never* have that kind of knowledge. Instead, he explained, "Our investigations have shown Finster—and we must assume Ubell also—are really sick puppies. In their various criminal activities, nobody crosses them and lives long. I think he's connected you to the theft of Alton's piece of the Stone."

"I concur with your conclusions," Baldwin said. "The Finsters in general are very difficult to do even legitimate business with. Most practitioners avoid it if possible. How did Ubell find out about Irenee? It was a clean confiscation."

Jim's hunch antennae quivered. "You remember the dream I had last night where something was attacking Irenee? She said my description matched the actual fight with Alton's piece."

"Yes," Baldwin nodded. "Fergus told us about your dream. Pity nobody else caught it."

"Well," Jim continued, "what if Ubell cast some kind of spell with his Stone, and the spell revealed something about the destruction, and the revelation involved Irenee?"

Irenee picked up his idea. "What if his Stone told Ubell I was the one it was fighting?"

"Wait a minute," Jim interjected. "*Told* him? I thought you said you used crystals and stuff to focus, sort of like a telescope or a magnifying glass. What are you telling me? Are these things able to *think*? They actually communicate with you?"

"The best answer is that we're not totally certain." Whipple shook his head unhappily. "Here's the difficulty. Very few of the really powerful items exist because they are extremely difficult to make in the first place and for a variety of other reasons—necessary size, strength, composition of the item itself, among others. A practitioner must also be a very high level to create one like the Cataclysm Stone. Ninety-nine percent of spell-enhancing instruments of any level are neutral, and only two or three truly good items have come to us through the centuries—probably because there are so few truly good people to make them."

Whipple frowned, leaned forward, held up a finger. "Many more evil items exist, however, because practitioners trying to get an advantage over their enemies fell into evil ways. To change an item from neutral to evil is not difficult. It's a matter of spell intent. Using an object to cast an evil, or harmful, or hurtful spell changes it. If you continue to cast those spells, the item becomes more and more evil."

"Therefore," Jim interjected, "if a bad guy who's really powerful pushes a lot of evil through a big one, it becomes one of these monsters?"

"Exactly. A crystal like the Cataclysm Stone has centuries of evil in it," Whipple answered. "To come back to your original question, their possessors or manipulators seem to be more under the control or influence of the items than the other way around. The users have often acted so far out of their original characters there is no other explanation. The items are somehow affecting or even communicating with them. As for an actual dialogue . . . ?"

"It's a nasty dilemma," Baldwin said. "The only way to be absolutely certain would be to let yourself come under one's influence—that is, we surmise, by using it to cast a spell with evil intent. No sane practitioner would agree to be the guinea pig to try such a thing. Once in an evil item's clutches, the *sole* way out is for someone else to destroy it, and in every single recorded case, the user is damaged in the process. With the small items, he can lose talent, energy, and/or levels. With the most powerful, he can lose his life. You know what happened to Alton Finster. I would be surprised if he ever regains consciousness."

"Has a possessor ever been conscious after you killed one?" Jim asked.

"None of the three people I knew who survived a medium-sized object ever remembered exactly what was going on between themselves and the items. All they could come up with were vague, scattered, incoherent impressions, some pleasant, some awful. With the smaller ones, the manipulator is certain he was in control, not the item."

"Wonderful." Jim rubbed his hands over his face. Whether the items were conscious or not, he wasn't going to worry about it now. "Okay, we don't know. Back to my hunch. Somehow Ubell's Stone connected Irenee with the theft—"

"We prefer 'confiscation,'" Irenee interrupted. "Every practitioner has to sign an oath to turn over an evil item and agree to its confiscation."

"—confiscation, whatever, and I picked up on their 'communication.'" Jim waved a hand at the word and looked directly at her. "The point is, he knows you were involved. The further point is he's coming after you. We were lucky this time. We might not be so the next."

Irenee had a mutinous look when she said, "Didn't I just prove I can handle myself? Do we need to explain more to you about what a Sword does and is?"

"We were lucky. If those guys had been practitioners, they'd have expected a counterattack. You wouldn't have had the chance to throw so much as *lux*." The woman was worse than a rookie cop, Jim decided, ready to go tearing after the bad guys with no preparation. Why hadn't he realized that earlier? This was her first big job. She was a *rookie*.

He needed to be careful here, though. He didn't want to alienate the Swords by yelling at her. Since he lived in the real world of bad guys, he said, "Next time, no matter what they are, they'll be ready. Nothing I've learned says you or your magic can stop bullets. Is that correct?"

"Well . . ." She at least looked a little thoughtful, but he could practically see her mind working to refute him.

"He's right, Irenee," Whipple said, "none of us can stop bullets. Our shields keep out only magical weapons and spell-cast missiles and energy beams."

"Then we won't let Ubell have another chance at her." Hugh Sabel pointed at his daughter. "Irenee, you won't leave the Center without a team of guards."

"Dad, I have a business to run, clients to see. What kind of impression do you think I'll make if I pull up in a Hummer with an entourage? The gossip will start flying, and we'll have more attention than we want."

"Fine, in that case, you'll stay here until we get the situation under control." Sabel crossed his arms and sat back in his chair. "Say you're sick, got the flu, make all your contacts over the phone or e-mail."

"If Ubell is as smart as I think he is," Jim put in, even though he would have liked to watch the battle between the two Sabels to see if her father could make her see reason, "he won't send simple muscle again. In fact, he'll think up the most evil way he can to get hold of Irenee."

"Why? Why me?" she asked. "Alton's piece of the Stone is gone. He can't get it back. Surely he knows that from Alton's collapse. If he were to kidnap a single one of us, he must expect we'd go after him in force. What does he want with me?"

"Revenge, or a hostage. Maybe he thinks the Defenders will back off the search for his Stone if he's holding you," Jim said.

"Probably also to torture you," Johanna Mahler interjected. "Remember the case ten or so years ago in Oregon? A witch had two items, and a Sword confiscated one—much the lesser of the two. His team destroyed it. The witch had been working with the power of the greater item, and it protected her from harm. She went after the Sword and managed to capture him. Defenders rescued him, but not before she'd almost killed him. He said all during her abuse, she screamed about the pleasure her second item was getting from his pain."

"There's a cheery thought," Irenee retorted. "Look, I can't stay locked up forever. When are we going to go after Ubell?"

"Good point, and exactly what I've been pondering. Okay, why don't we do this." Whipple leaned forward in his chair and pointed to Baldwin. "John, you, Hugh, and all the Defenders here keep investigating. Also arrange a meeting with Bruce Ubell to confront him with the fact of his cousin's Stone. Aim for a meeting on Thursday if possible, Friday at the latest. I signed the notice, so he'll expect me. See if the head of the Defender Council is available. Maybe a member of the High Council. He can't refuse to see them."

He looked around the table. "People, our first priority is to get our hands on Ubell's Stone. We need proof to even begin the procedure. We need an exact location. Lacking the bare minimum, at the very least we'll make sure he understands the consequences of his actions."

He turned to Jim. "You have a lot to learn. If you're free, let's put your time to good use."

"Fine with me," Jim said. "I need to check in with my boss from time to time, but I have the rest of the week off."

"Good. Stay here at the Center. We'll assume you'll be targeted because you were with Irenee tonight. We'll supply you with a room and send a Sword to pick up whatever you need from your apartment tomorrow. The travel ban outside the Center applies to you, too. For training, we'll put you with our best."

Whipple looked at Johanna. "You work with Jim on spell-casting. Concentrate especially on defensive spells and energy manipulation. I can't imagine how novice skills will help against a monster like the Cataclysm Stone. It can't hurt, however, for him to be comfortable with them. Irenee thinks he may have some Defender-type sharing ability, and even if it's only with her, we need to know how much, if possible."

Jim wondered what Whipple meant by his last remark, but he didn't get to ask.

Concentrating on Irenee, Whipple continued, "You put off your clients for a while. As I recall, the next couple of weeks were going to be a slow time. Do not leave the Center under any circumstances unless John or I arrange a team for you. If you need something from your office, we'll send someone to get it. We think you've gone up a level. You serve your team better if you concentrate on learning, practicing, and testing your skills and spells to match your new potential. There's also the other matter we spoke of. Take care of it tonight."

"But—" Irenee started to protest, and Whipple cut

her off.

"The man needs to understand what's happening. It's the only way he—and you—will be able to deal with the distractions. We need you both at full power as quickly as possible." He turned back to Jim. "Are you getting any hunches about Ubell or his possible actions?"

Jim concentrated for a few seconds, tried to feel movement of his antennae or the back of his brain tickling. He finally had to say, "Nope, not a twitch. Come to think of it, I had no hunch about those guys in the SUVs, either. The previous one, where Ubell found out about Irenee from his Stone, ended there. What about the Stone? Can you demand he give it to you? If we could get it, that would cripple his spell-casting, wouldn't it?"

"Yes, it would," Baldwin answered, "Unfortunately, we don't have definitive proof he actually has the Stone. The way our laws work, Jim, we can't make a claim against an evil item unless we have the proof—which is certification by a trained sensitive like Glynnis Fraser that she has picked up the vibrations of a spell being cast and pinpointed its location and its user. We can't merely accuse someone of having an item and expect him to hand it over. He'd deny it, and if it was well hidden, as this one seems to be, we might never find it. He'd haul us before the High Council in a heartbeat, and we'd have to pay an enormous fine for false accusation."

He pointed at Irenee. "We sent her after Finster's

Stone because we knew exactly who had it and where it was. We also knew Finster would fight us if we marched in and demanded it. Experience has taught us to confiscate the big items as quietly as possible. Their possessors will object, and they don't care what happens to innocent bystanders. Of course, the less attention we draw to ourselves, the better."

"We have these rules," Whipple said, "because otherwise, all you'd have to do is accuse a person and ruin his reputation forever. We Defenders are the only ones who can bring the charge at the present time because in the past, accusations flew, and innocents were punished unjustly. Also, we're not a version of the Inquisition and can't force acquiescence with the practitioner oath. If an item's location is pinpointed, like Finster's was in the safe, we are perfectly within our rules, laws, and practices to confiscate it, and so we did."

"Okay," Jim said, "you have your own due process. My law enforcement experience tells me Ubell is not going to wait long to move against us. He can't be happy his criminal activities are slow and no money's coming in while he deals with his legitimate business. Arms sales have been up and down in the past, but the drug business has been pretty steady. If I was him, I'd be trying to get the Defenders off my back so I could go about my criminal business with no opposition. Once he starts up again, the task force will be after him. He may not know that, or he thinks he's clear because of the cooked books."

"I'll pull in a couple of other sensitives and house them close to the Finster mansion," Baldwin stated. "If he casts, or there's a repeat of last night's communication, maybe they can pick it up."

"I wish there were a way to draw him out, make him cast in the open. We're certainly not going to risk anyone to do so, however. Not against this monster," Whipple said and looked around the table. "What else do we have to say or suggest? Nothing? Let's get to work. Jim, you go with Irenee to her condo. You two have an important matter to discuss. I'll call ahead, so stop at the concierge desk to pick up your room key on the way."

As everyone stood, Jim looked at Irenee. She had the oddest combination of expressions—like she was anticipating something, and fearing it at the same time.

She sighed, said, "Come on," and headed for the door.

He followed, wondering again what he had gotten himself into, but determined to make some things perfectly clear to her. Now if he could only decide exactly what those things were.

CHAPTER SEVENTEEN

Irenee led him out to his car. "We might as well drive to the Center."

"Fine," he said and held the door for her.

Jim seemed still angry, and she had no clue why. Did he not want to stay here overnight? Was he still upset about her lightning bolt? It might be a good idea to get the reasons for his anger out in the open before she hit him with the news of the soul-mate phenomenon. She sighed to herself. Explaining was not going to be easy. Shaking off her thoughts, she directed him to the residents' entrance to the underground parking.

When he pulled up at the gate, he looked at the flat panel with no slot for a card or key. He practically growled, "Another glowing gate. How do I open it?"

Refusing to be pulled into his mood, she answered in a matter-of-fact tone, "Normally, you would place your hand on the pad like I did in the elevator, but we haven't had the chance to put you in the system yet. Punch the green button and look at the camera on the post over there."

He did so, and a woman's voice said, "Security."

She waved at the camera, leaned closer to Jim, and spoke across him. "It's Irenee Sabel. Will you let us in, please?"

"Right away," the security woman said, and the gate lifted into the ceiling.

She showed him the visitor spaces, and he parked the car. "We'll sign you in tomorrow."

"Fine," he said, as she opened her door and climbed out.

She was beginning to wonder if the man knew another word besides *fine*.

He opened the trunk and took out a duffel bag. When she raised her eyebrows at him, he said, "I'm often out overnight or need a change of clothes."

She caught a glimpse of the trunk interior. It held a number of metal boxes, neatly arranged. Come to think of it, the inside of his car was clean and organized also—no loose papers or maps, no bags or cups from fast-food places, none of the usual trash she'd expect a man to have, especially one who probably did overnight stakeouts. She stopped herself from thinking those fateful words, *a man after her own heart*. That was yet to be proven.

They took the elevator up to the lobby level and stopped at the desk for his key card. The concierge asked if Jim would like to have his luggage taken to the room, but he declined.

She waved at the condo side of the building. "My place is on the fourth floor."

They went up in the elevator. Jim still said nothing, only watched the floor numbers change. He followed her to her condo halfway along the hall.

After a swipe of her hand at the key panel, she opened the door and held it for him. "Just put your bag anywhere."

She glanced around as she followed him past the coat closet on her left and the entrance to the kitchen on her right into the dining/living area. Of course her condo was clean and tidy.

He put his bag down by her glass dining table. She watched him while he roamed around the room, looking at the impressionist prints on the wall, the family photos lined up on an end table, the plants in the windows. With the idea the winter landscape outside would be all white and brown and gray and black, she'd chosen deep greens and vibrant blues for the walls and upholstery, accented with bright reds in throw pillows, an afghan, and a colorful oriental rug. All in all, she thought she had a cheerful room with comfortable furniture.

It wasn't quite as happy a space when he turned in the middle between her furniture grouping and her entertainment center to glower at her, however. Well, she wasn't afraid of him, so she asked straight out, "Okay, what's wrong? You're angry, and I don't understand why.

Before we go further—and we have a critical situation to discuss—we need to clear the air."

He gave her one of his accusatory cop looks and folded his arms over his chest. "I'm mad because you keep going off like a rocket, throwing spells before assessing the situation—or, God forbid, asking my opinion. We might have found out more if you hadn't blown that guy away so quick back in the parking lot."

"And not attacking would have given the other two time to get to us," she retorted, conveniently ignoring the fact she hadn't seen them until Jim had pointed them out. "Then we would have had to fight them also."

He shook his head in dismissal of her assertion. "Your lightning bolt was premature, too. I had plenty of time to slip through the left-turn lane and get across the intersection before they caught up. When they followed, they'd have been right in the clutches of the Swords. Again, we could have questioned captives and not had to waste time guessing what Ubell might do next."

She drew herself up straight. "I'm a Sword. I'm trained to act in a crisis, not sit around like a damsel waiting to be rescued."

He put his hands on his hips and looked her up and down like he was a drill sergeant. "If I understand right, this is your first real Sword assignment. That makes you a *rookie*, and rookies make mistakes. I've been a cop for a long time. I know how to handle myself. I know when to wait, how to assess the situation. The last thing I want is to get into another one of these fights with spells going off all over the place, but if we do, for all our sakes, follow my lead, will you? Don't go off half-cocked."

She had no immediate answer to his statements, so she scowled at him. She'd worked hard on becoming a Sword. She'd defeated the thugs. Who was he to be telling her what to do?

She was marshalling her response when he asked, "What would you have done once we had captured those guys? Or if your spells had failed, or worse, backfired? Had you thought about, *do you know*, what to do next? Would you have cast those spells if you were with Whipple instead of me? What about teamwork?"

Oh, damn. He spoke the absolute truth. The Defender principles had been drummed into her with Sword instruction and practice. Be ruthlessly honest about your own abilities. Know your limitations. Don't get caught in a trap of pride. Another, the most important, the bedrock of the entire Defender/Sword combination: function *always* as a team.

Think, Irenee. He's correct, and you still have to tell him about soul mates. Time to back down and restore peace.

She took a deep breath and released it, walked forward and sat on the couch. "No, you're right. I would have waited for Fergus to agree before I threw a spell. I was going to cast stun at the guy you slugged in the parking lot. I didn't have a future plan for after I threw the lightning bolt. I never thought about capturing any of them, only getting away."

She drew herself up to face him squarely. "My biggest mistake was not thinking of you and me as a team. Defenders have always worked in teams. If it hadn't been for the team when we were battling Alton's Stone, I probably wouldn't be here now."

He looked both satisfied and surprised by her answer, and he sat down on the easy chair, from which she usually watched TV. He asked quietly, "How bad was it?"

"We had to call in every Sword and Defender in the complex. That black flame you saw in your dream? The Stone kept shooting energy pulses from it at me and only me. John was on one side of me and Johanna on the other, blocking the attacks as much as they could. Dad was giving me power directly, and the Defenders kept pouring energy on all of us. Fergus and other Swords bombarded the item from all sides. The Stone finally died, but it took a long time. I expect when we take on Ubell's bigger piece, it will be much harder to destroy." She shuddered at the thought.

"If my dream showed even half of it," he said, "I probably have only a small idea of what you went through. I really want to learn exactly how you go about destroying one of these items before we meet it in a fight." His grim expression underlined the determination in his voice and his words.

"I'm sure you'll see it. You may even be involved in it as a team member."

"What? Me? I'm not a Defender."

"That's part of what we have to talk about." She rose. "I'm going to get some water. Do you want some?"

"Yeah, I could use a drink."

"Water or something else? I have wine, beer, soft drinks."

"Water's fine."

She brought out glasses with ice and two water bottles and put his on the side table next to the chair. Taking her seat on the sofa, she busied herself with pouring her water while trying to decide how to begin. With everything going on, she hadn't really had the chance to practice a presentation.

He didn't give her much time to think, however, because he asked, "Okay, what's so critical? What's left I don't know about practitioners? Me, a Defender? Lay it on me. After the past several days, I'm ready for whatever you throw at me."

She decided to get an idea of his general attitude about the result of the phenomenon before hitting him with the big news. "Have you ever been married, Jim?"

He blinked at the question, but answered, "No, not even close."

"Ever thought about it—in general, I mean. Having a family of your own, for example?"

"Nope, too busy." He looked at his hands, reached for the water bottle, uncapped it, took a swig. "Why? What's this have to do with practitioners? I thought bloodlines were all about your ancestors, not descendants."

What a non-answer. So, he'd thought about it, and family was a sore subject. She could see how it might be difficult to discuss when his parents and sister had all died, and he was probably very lonely. She might feel the same way, wanting to wall herself off, not let herself care about someone who might not be there in the future. She, however, could offer him solace and companionship and a family—and more. Good. He should therefore like the concepts she was about to explain—she hoped.

Irenee took a drink of water to soothe her suddenly dry throat. She cleared her throat and plunged into her explanation.

"There's one important part of practitioner life we haven't mentioned, Jim, and it has to do with family, specifically the bonding between a man and a woman and the making of a deep relationship."

Her statement got his attention, all right, because he was staring at her. If his expression was more of "suspicious cop" than "deer in the headlights," that was good, wasn't it? No matter what, she couldn't stop now.

"In the practitioner world we have a concept called the 'soul-mate phenomenon.' According to the circumstance or wonder or situation—people call it by different terms—every practitioner has a soul mate and will find the person, and the two of them will spend the rest of their lives together. *Always.* An ancient force, the soul-mate imperative, helps you identify him or her and makes sure you're together. Soul mates usually have similar interests, likes, dislikes, opinions, and they get along extremely well. Their occupations often complement each other."

She paused—what did she and Jim have in common? She didn't have a clue yet. As for getting along? Was he going to fuss at her for every little thing? Also yet to be seen. Occupations, she wouldn't worry about; she knew lots of couples who had no work connection.

"They're also extremely attracted to each other—sexually." She tried to say the last word nonchalantly, but with so much at stake, she wasn't sure of her total success. It probably didn't matter, however, because the laser beam coming from his eyes told her she had his complete and total attention. She wrenched her gaze away before she got lost in his and forgot her own name. *Concentrate.*

Where was she—oh, yes, attraction. "I'm told this magnetism is far greater than what non-practitioners feel for each other. If that's not enough, the soul-mate imperative, which Fergus calls the 'enforcer,' makes sure the mates can't resist each other. Furthermore, or worse, if you try to reject your mate, the imperative makes your life miserable and causes you all kinds of pain and heartache, particularly in your magic center."

Although he hadn't asked any questions, maybe it was okay. She'd rather tell him at her rate, not submit to an interrogation. Here came the most important part. She spoke quickly to get it all out. "When these soul mates act on their sexual attraction and make love, they share magical energy and create a bond between them. I understand the experience is stupendous. The first time they make love is called the 'first mating.' It's not a single event, though. It's a process. Making love activates and seals the bond. After the mating, the two are bound together, and the bond grows stronger over time. From then on, they're with each other forever in a lifetime commitment."

"What does this have to do with me?" Jim asked in a raspy voice, his only indication of a reaction. She was clueless about what it meant, however. Body language didn't help—he sat absolutely still, and his face could have been carved out of granite.

She took a deep breath and blurted out the answer. "Fergus, Bridget, and my father all think we, you and I, are soul mates."

"Based on what evidence?" More rasp, as though he

was forcing the words out of his throat.

Oh, he was not going to make her explanation easy, but she could almost swear on her sword the tiniest bit of fear had flashed in his golden-green eyes. What did he have to be afraid of? Her?

"Based on how we look at each other," she answered. "On what happened when your magic center woke up, on how you can see through my spells. Soul mates can't cast spells on each other, except for healing and defense. I can cure a headache or make you stronger. I can't cast even one that might make you act against your will. You can see through my spells, like invisibility, for example, but only my spells, not Fergus's. Trying to cast a spell on someone is one of the tests to see if you're soul mates. It's also a safeguard so a person can't decide he wants someone as a mate and casts a spell to make her think they're mates. It's unethical to cast a love spell."

"One of the tests? What are the others?"

He didn't sound like he really wanted to know. Too bad.

"Another is the ability to see each other's spell aura—I can definitely see yours. The definitive one is to make love. If we're not soul mates, we won't be able to . . . do it, to consummate the union." She was certain her face matched her hair after that statement.

He looked at her for a long moment, ran his gaze up and down her body as if memorizing a description—or, a worse thought, testing her worthiness and his attraction. She kept absolutely still, although her insides were jumping like crazy, and her center was humming.

Finally he asked, "What do *you* think? Are we these 'soul mates'?"

"I don't know for sure. The others think so, and we do seem to be attracted to each other. Our lightballs merging is bound to be significant. Therefore, I'm keeping an open mind."

"How do we find out? Have sex? Go through this 'first mating'? What does that entail, screwing each other till we're blue in the face?"

She stifled a sigh. From those words and his sharp, cutting tone, it looked like persuading him to accept the actuality of the phenomenon was going to be more difficult than she originally thought. He'd accepted the reality of being a practitioner, hadn't he? Why couldn't he at least say the phenomenon was possible? Or did he object to her, personally? How could he even frame the idea with the soul-mate phenomenon in full active force?

"Do *you* want us to be soul mates?" he asked. "To have me for a ready-made, automatic, arranged mate with no say of your own?"

That was the question on her side, of course, and she could understand his opposition based on those factors. She could only tell him the truth. "To your first question, I honestly don't know. We've only just met. Neither of us knows the other well. I have no real objection to the idea. I like you—although you can be exasperating at times."

He snorted, and she ignored the derisive noise. "I think you've handled finding out about your talents really well. I admire what you do for the DEA. I think you're a man of integrity, intensity, and purpose. I think you're good-looking—but appearance doesn't really matter to a soul mate. I don't know what you like or dislike yet, except for my throwing spells at what you think are inopportune times."

She said the last with a smile. He didn't smile back, only maintained his relentless scrutiny.

"Granted," she continued, "I'm coming at the possibility from a very different place than you are. I'm used to the idea. I grew up with the certainty that 'someday my soul mate will come,' and I expect to make a life with him. I'm open to the idea of you as my mate."

She expected to fall in love with him, and he with her. Her expectation, however, seemed both too important and too "fairy tale-ish" to mention at this stage, so she tried to lighten the conversation. "When I was young, I did all the foolish daydreaming a girl does about the man in her future. I must tell you, you're nothing like what I expected."

He smiled grimly at her statement. "I'll bet. What did you expect?"

"Some sort of corporate honcho or lawyer, like all

the men I saw at my parents' parties, or maybe one of those very serious, nerdy academic types. Most probably a man who needed my organizational skills. I watched a number of practitioner friends find their mates, and each couple seemed made for each other. Fergus, however, knows a couple who, on the surface, are almost total opposites, even to the way they work magic, and they're together as solidly as those totally compatible mates."

"Great, so there's hope for us yet."

She couldn't let him sit there and make snide comments. They'd never get through this and to his agreement. Time to get him talking.

"All right, those are the basic facts about soul mates and the imperative. What do you think so far?"

He leaned back in the easy chair, put his elbows on the armrests, and steepled his fingers under his chin. His lids half-covered his eyes, and she had no clue as to what he might be thinking.

She made herself sit still and wait.

Finally, he rose, shook his head, and said, "I think it's the biggest load of crap I've ever heard. The idea some magic force would bring two people together for a happily-ever-after is ridiculous. God, talk about a fantasy. You people actually believe this stuff?" He made a scoffing gesture with one hand.

CHAPTER EIGHTEEN

Irenee sighed to herself. Jim was reacting as she was afraid he might, claiming the entire soul-mate phenomenon was their imagination. Thank goodness she hadn't mentioned love. He *really* wasn't ready to face that idea yet. She'd let him fuss and fume and see if he talked himself into accepting the situation. Most of the evidence was indisputable to her, but twistable by someone who didn't believe in or couldn't accept the magic.

Walking around the chair, he began to pace in front of the windows for a few seconds. He finally stopped to lean on the back of the chair and look at her. "You, Whipple, and the rest have thrown a lot of info at me in the past couple of days. Fantastic, surprising stuff I never even thought of and wouldn't have believed possible."

He ticked them off on his fingers. "Practitioners exist and can do magic. I'm one of them. I actually cast a spell—or did something to light a damned candle and put a ball of light in the air."

He straightened up and ran a hand through his hair.

"I've seen you do things that should be impossible—your little 'puff of wind,' for example. I've heard about evil magic items and how Finster and Ubell have been using them. Except for the last, I've seen proof with my own eyes of all those things, and the problems the accountants are having with Finster's books is convincing evidence, too. Yes, magic exists, and yes, you—and I—can cast spells."

Irenee made no movement, said nothing. He was going to deny the phenomenon. He had a surprise coming.

"But you've gone too far with this soul-mate business. It's entirely too much to swallow. Yeah, I'll admit I'm attracted to you. What man wouldn't be? You're a beautiful woman, sexy, smart. I'm certainly up for a fling if you are."

He gave her what she could only think of as a predatory smile before scowling. "I'm definitely not interested in a long-term anything. Never have been, never will be. Soul mates? Bullshit to get you practitioners together and keep the bloodlines going."

She simply looked at him for a few seconds. Sure enough, as she expected, there was a reaction to his rejection of the entire phenomenon, and it didn't come from her.

"Ouch!" He started rubbing his center and almost doubled over. "Damn!"

She stopped herself from grinning. Served him right for not believing. "That's the soul-mate imperative telling you it isn't pleased."

Slowly and still bending over, he made his way around the chair and collapsed into its cushions. He continued to massage his middle. She said nothing; what he decided was between him and the imperative.

"This isn't a spell you threw on me to convince me, is it?"

"Of course not. Weren't you listening? Soul mates can't cast spells on each other except for healing and defense. I can't cause you harm. In our specific case, I can't cast a defense against the imperative either. It's totally out of everybody's power, including Fergus's. You're only looking for an excuse, a way out."

Pressing his hands against his breastbone, he winced and shifted his position several times. The imperative was obviously hitting him hard.

She said nothing. It hurt her to watch him suffering—little jabs were hitting her own center as if goading her to persuade him. She knew from the discussion with Fergus, Bridget, and her father, however, whatever Jim concluded had to be his decision alone.

After a while, he asked through gritted teeth, "How do I get it to stop? Is it one of those 'almost conscious' forces like the items?"

"It seems to be aware and to respond—when it wants to. We've found, if you continue to reject the idea, the pain will only get worse. To stop the torment, I imagine at the least, you have to accept the phenomenon's existence and be open to the possibility of a mate—and you have to mean it. I've been told the imperative won't let you fake it."

"Look, Irenee, the whole concept is crazy, right out of a fairy tale. I'm *not* Prince Charming, Cinderella. How can you believe in it so strongly?"

"I've never known anything else, it's part of my world, and I've seen it in action. My best friend from college found her mate our senior year. My parents are soul mates, like every other practitioner couple I've ever met. It's not supposition or make-believe to me. It's reality, and since you're a practitioner, it's reality for you, too."

"In another universe, maybe."

Obstinate man. Okay, what evidence could she use to persuade him? What argument to convince him of practitioner reality and her as his mate? She almost despaired when no ideas came to mind. Then she took a good look at him. A light blue tinge of an aura surrounded him.

Of course, the absolutely only voice she knew he'd listen to. She looked him straight in the eye. "For you to accept it honestly and not because of coercion, let's ask the question another way. What does your *hunch* tell you about it and me? Are we soul mates?"

The words were no sooner out of her mouth than the blue went from light and faint to dark and bright and surrounded his entire body. He froze and stared at her with big golden-green eyes. This time he did look exactly like the proverbial deer in the headlights.

"Holy shit!" Jim couldn't decide whether to clutch his head or his stomach. His hunch antennae started whipping back and forth like they were in a hurricane. His center burned like the entire country's Fourth-of-July displays were going off right under his breastbone. Through it all, the mother of all hunches was working toward a conclusion he knew would be the absolutely right, totally correct, take-to-the-bank, impossible answer.

He tried to stand, maybe with some goofy idea to get away, but his knees buckled. He slid to the floor and curled up on his side in a ball around the pain.

The hunch mechanism in his head churned on. *Yes*, he was attracted to her. Extremely. *Yes*, he wanted her. *Yes*, he wanted a family. *Yes*, having a soul mate—her, all his—would put an end to his loneliness, his rootlessness, his bone-deep need for someone in his life who gave a damn whether he was alive or dead. *Yes*, he wanted somebody to help him in his cause.

Yes, yes, yes!

But first, he had to recognize what he'd been keeping behind the wall in his head, what he'd been longing for, what was now almost in his grasp.

Out of the torment came a crystal-clear vision of his parents, standing in the kitchen, looking into each other's eyes and saying, "I love you, my soul mate."

Oh, my God.

Yes, deep down, that's what he wanted—her, a family of his own, her, companionship, her, togetherness, love, her, her, her. Was all of it really his, simply for the asking? How could he be truly happy after what he'd let happen to his sister?

"Jim? Jim! Can you hear me? What's going on?" Dimly Irenee's voice made its way through the waves of pain and revelation.

He opened his eyes. She was kneeling by his side, one soothing hand on his forehead, the other gripping his top arm.

"Y-y-yes," he forced the word out, grabbed her hand on his forehead, and pulled it closer to his center. The pain in his middle eased.

"Jim. How do you feel? Can you straighten out? Where does it hurt?"

"Irenee." Her name came out more as a prayer than a call for help—or maybe they were both the same. Saying it brought her gaze to his, and the warmth and caring in her eyes almost made him want to cry. Nobody had looked at him like that in a very long time. It gave him the strength to press her hand against his center.

The pain stopped.

It was gone, just like that.

He blinked up at her, even managed a smile of sorts.

She smiled and sat up.

Her movement took her hand away from contact with his chest.

Wham! And, just like that, the pain returned—doubled.

He pulled her hand to its previous position, reached his bottom arm around her back, and jerked the rest of her down beside him so they were on their sides, facing each other.

The pain vanished.

"What happened?" she asked, her eyes big, brown, and puzzled.

It took him a second to get his breath back before he could croak, "When your hand touched my chest, the pain went away. When you sat up and your hand wasn't touching, it came back worse. Nothing hurts now."

She raised her head and glanced at their parallel bodies, then back at him. A little smirk played around her mouth, and her eyes twinkled when she said, "We can't stay like this forever, though, can we? *I'm fine*, to use your words. *I don't hurt.* The imperative knows I believe in it, and I'm willing to give our relationship a try. What about you? What does your hunch say?"

"Thank you, Ms. Voice of Reason, for your analysis." He closed his eyes. Crunch time. After this episode with such awful agony, he couldn't pretend he was okay or nothing special was going on. His hunch was beating on the back of his forehead with its answers. He took a deep breath—inhale, exhale—and opened his eyes. "Okay. It got me. The damn imperative and whole soul-mate thing are real."

"You're sure."

"Absolutely, positively," he said and realized he meant it, unequivocally.

She smiled, and it turned into a great big grin.

His center cooled to a comforting, contented warmth and vibrated.

A happy notion entered his head—or somewhere—and he acted on it. He gave her a quick kiss and asked, "If we're soul mates, do we get to fool around right away? Don't we have to bond or something? What about our first mating?"

She stared at him with those big chocolate eyes, but said nothing.

So, he kissed her again. This one was not quick.

The idea of their actually mating blew most other thoughts totally out of Irenee's head. His kiss obliterated any left over. Somewhere in the middle of it, she realized there was no possibility in the world she could have anticipated the impact he had on her with a simple touch of his lips.

Simple? No way!

His scent enveloped her, his tongue and lips were fire and satin on her mouth, and he tasted like tiramisu, only better. Her center heated, a warmth that simultaneously comforted and excited. Magic energy skittered along her nerve endings exactly like she was about to cast a big spell, and her blood began to race through her veins.

He deepened the kiss, and she did some deepening of her own, tangling her tongue with his, running hers along his bottom lip. He seemed to like it because he groaned and pulled her closer.

Not close enough. She wanted, needed more, and she managed to get her lower arm around his neck and her top arm around his back so they were chest to chest.

Better.

Worse.

When he pressed his top leg between hers and lifted hers over his hip, the ache started, first in her breasts and then lower. Her cotton shirt and jeans seemed too tight, too constricting, too rough. She could feel how much he wanted her, and she pressed herself to the bulge in his pants.

He grunted, rubbed his hand up and down her back, cupped her backside, and kneaded. Even through the thick denim, he seemed to be touching her bare skin, and she wished she could purr.

Maybe she didn't have to. She could feel his center vibrating, and hers began to oscillate in unison, in harmony. Blissful, absolutely blissful.

He moved his hand from her back to her side, up her

rib cage, and to her front, where he halted, just under the curve of her breast. She could feel her breasts swell, her nipples tighten.

Why did he stop? She needed his touch higher, right where she was aching.

He lifted his head, broke the kiss. "Irenee."

She opened her eyes to look into those golden-green eyes, so hot with desire they almost melted her heart.

"Say the word, and we'll take this to its logical conclusion," he said in a low, gruff, slightly breathless tone.

The question wrenched her mind out of the glorious lethargy into which it had sunk.

She wanted to say yes. Oh, how she wanted to say yes.

Except . . . a feeling, a notion, a voice, a premonition, maybe even a hunch in her was saying it was sooooo soon. Tooooo soon.

She took a deep breath to tell him no.

At the top of her breath before she could say the word, he loosened his arms, separated them a few inches. "Yeah, I can't believe I'm saying it, but I'm somehow not ready either."

She exhaled, let go of him, and flopped back on the carpet. He did the same. Her body was tingling and not happy to stop. She managed, however, to exert some control over her mind. He was right. It was a gigantic step, and she wasn't ready. Not really, not truly.

He still had his bottom arm under her head, and he pulled her to him until she was curled in his arm with her head on his shoulder.

"This is all going so fast," he said. "I'm used to drug deals going wrong in a flash. I know where I stand then—and I can shoot back. There's so much to come to grips with here. My body's saying, 'Go,' but my mind, and maybe my hunch, is saying, 'Slow down.'"

"Yes. It's too fast—even for me, and I have an idea what's coming. We're out of control. And it's like we haven't done something *yet* that needs doing *first*."

"Exactly. I hate that feeling. Hunch or no hunch, I won't be bullied by a phenomenon or an imperative, no matter what other practitioners have put up with. We'll decide when we do whatever we do."

"I agree." She sighed. Why did everything have to be so hard and complicated? "You haven't heard all of it either. There are a couple more things I need to tell you—if I can just remember what they are after your kiss."

He chuckled, a low rumble she felt rather than heard. "I'm almost afraid to ask."

She sat up, smoothed her hair back, and rubbed her face with both hands. He reached up to massage her back, and it felt so good, she could have let him do it for hours. *Be strong, Irenee.*

Propping herself up on one hand, she turned to him. She was about to put her other hand on his chest, before she caught herself. Who knew what reaction touching him anywhere near his center would cause?

He didn't seem to care, because he captured the hand and held it to his chest right over the spot.

"Are you still hurting?" she asked.

He gave her a crooked smile. "Yes, but not where you mean. My center? No, your kiss seems to have made it all better." He wiggled their joined hands. "So does this."

He sat up also, pushed himself back so he could lean against the easy chair. He kept her hand in his. "Okay, what else? Does it have anything to do with what Whipple was saying—something about my understanding and full power?"

He was certainly a quick study and remembered details despite the confusion going on around him, and she supposed it's what cops needed to do. Or . . . "Another hunch?"

"Not really. I noticed how Whipple emphasized the words and you didn't seem to like them."

She scooted around more to face him. "It's part of the pressure to settle the soul-mate issue quickly, and it doesn't come from the imperative. Fergus wasn't talking only about your training in the basics or my trying spells at my new, higher level. Besides bonding mates for life, the first mating carries the probability of enhancing magic abilities, increasing energy, potential, and level. With some matings, only one mate may have an enhancement, or nothing may happen with either. There's no recorded instance of a mate losing power in the process, thank goodness."

"So, with more power, we'd be better equipped to fight the Stone?" He looked both intrigued and skeptical at the same time.

"Yes, theoretically." She shrugged and rubbed her forehead. "The problem under these time constraints is—and I know from my own experience—it still takes a while to get used to your higher level, to learn what it can do, to practice the spells you know. Nothing is easy here, especially the more complicated spells and the precise modulation of energy. When you train with Johanna tomorrow, you'll see that even more than you did today."

"Whipple wants us to mate so we'll have greater power for fighting. He doesn't give a flip about you and me and what our mating might mean to us, does he? He wants us to jump into bed tonight, doesn't he?"

"No, that's not quite right," she answered. "He does care. He also knows what being soul mates means, how it feels, and how wonderful it is. He's trying to speed up the process, that's all. So we're ready for whatever gets thrown at us."

"I'm not trying to reject you, but personally, I'd like a little more time to get used to the idea—to *all* of the ideas. Where do you think our not taking the big step immediately would leave us?"

"Somewhere in the middle. Not totally prepared, but not helpless, either. We're thinking alike—like soul mates—in wanting more time." She had to smile at that thought. What a similarity to have.

He seemed to process the information for a moment before saying, "Okay, then let's proceed at our pace, not someone else's. What's next?"

She felt her face grow warm simply at the thought of the last requirement for mating, and she bent her head in the hopes he hadn't noticed.

Fat chance. Mr. Never-Miss-a-Trick used a forefinger to tilt her head back up and grinned at her. "Oh, man, I bet this is a good one."

She made a face at him and launched into the explanation. Best to get it out of the way. "According to the rules for a first mating, to be sure the bond takes, we can't use artificial barriers. No condoms. No pills."

"Nothing? What about birth control?"

"We witches have our own, in the form of spells. We learn them and start casting in our teens. My personal spell is current."

"I've never had sex without a condom," he said. "You don't have to worry, I'm healthy."

"I'm healthy, too." She wouldn't mention why.

He grinned again. "Honey, if you're going to try to avoid subjects with me, you really need to learn a spell that stops you from blushing. Come on, what else?"

She sighed, looked down, and mumbled, "I'm a virgin."

When he didn't say a word, she glanced up. He was staring at her, an utterly blank look on his face like he'd been hit with a stun spell.

Finally he said, "A virgin? You're what, twenty-five? How can you still be a virgin in this day and age?"

"Well, it's not my fault!" She snatched her hand from his and crossed her arms, tucking her hands under them. "Remember what I said about the test for a soul mate being to try to make love, and if you couldn't do it, you weren't soul mates? The phenomenon or the imperative or a combination won't let female practitioners make love until it's with their soul mates. We feel no attraction or arousal whatsoever. Men can do it all and have sex, too. It's very unfair."

"In that case, why the birth control spells?"

"Because in this day and age, there's a chance of being raped. Besides, the spells help keep a woman regular, if it's any of your business."

As she watched, his expression went from incredulous to blank to possessive. He put his hands on her shoulders and, leaning close, kissed her. She tried to resist him and not move, but he was so persuasive. Her semicooled blood reheated, and she melted again. By the time the kiss ended, she was in his lap and they were both breathless.

"Good," he whispered in her ear, "then you're all mine."

"Remember, the bond works both ways."

"Damn right." He made it a flat declaration, and she knew in her bones he was as much hers as she was his.

They sat there for a few minutes, simply holding each other.

Finally he stirred and looked at his watch. "It's getting late, and we have a big day ahead. You're so damn tempting, if I don't leave now, I never will. What do we do about breakfast tomorrow?"

"Why don't we eat here? One thing I've learned ever since my levels started rising—eat for fuel early. Training usually starts at eight. Come at seven?"

"Fine."

They got up from the carpet. He gave her another searing kiss that left her knees weak, grabbed his bag, and left for his room on the other side of the center.

When she shut the door behind him, a small wave of loneliness swept over her. "Stop it!" she said to the imperative. "We're doing the best we can."

Her center warmed, gave what seemed to her a happy flutter, and subsided.

"Thank you." She wobbled off to bed.

CHAPTER NINETEEN

"You let them get away? You stupid bastard! I give you a simple assignment—bring me Irenee Sabel, and you botch it!" Bruce Ubell struggled to get control of himself before he tried out one of the gifts from his Stone and melted the idiot on the spot.

No, that was not a good idea. The imbecile would be impossible to get out of the carpet. It was bad enough he was still soggy from his trip into the swamp.

"I'm telling you, Mr. Ubell," his highly recommended enforcer whined, "they had some sort of secret weapon. The woman stuck her hand out of the car, and she must have had something in it—a ray gun maybe—and the car just blew up! We couldn't do nothing except get outta there. Good thing we did, because some white Hummers—the big, original kind—came after us."

"You didn't lead them back here, did you?" The last thing he needed—the Swords on his doorstep in the next minute.

"Nah," the man answered. "We lost them, and we'll

ditch the SUV we came back in. We stole both of them, so nobody will be able to trace them to us."

"She had a man with her, you said? Who?"

"Never saw him before. He was a big guy, handled himself well." The thug rubbed his jaw as if in memory. "Probably six-feet-plus, brown hair. I did get his license plate when we followed them to the restaurant."

"Give it to me."

The man dug a limp, still wet piece of paper from a pocket. He unfolded it and handed it over.

Bruce carefully spread the paper out on the yellow pad he'd been writing on. The number was still visible—fortunately for the man standing on the other side of the desk. At least he'd done one thing right.

"What do you want us to do now, Mr. Ubell? Try again?"

"No, they won't come out of the Center without looking for you first, and there's no place to hide where you won't be seen. Go on and get out of here. Tell your boss I won't need you again for a while." As if they'd be allowed a second chance. He wouldn't have used these incompetents in the first place, even if they were "associates" of his primary drug distributor, but they were all he could get his hands on in a hurry.

"Okay, Mr. Ubell." The man left, and Bruce heard Sedgwick meet him in the hall to usher the bungler off the premises.

Bruce leaned back in his chair and swung it around to face Otto Finster's portrait. In the dim light of the study, his grandfather's eyes seem to glint with derision—a trick of the artist's hand or the spirit of the old man somehow stuck in the painting? He nodded at the figure. "I'll bet you're cackling in hell."

Once more, Bruce lamented the lack of good, trustworthy practitioner help. Using his Stone to try to entice someone over to his side was so tempting—with Swords prowling around, however, too dangerous to attempt. He and Alton hadn't gotten where they were by carelessness. Until Alton's bout of utter stupidity ruined so much, they'd had total success. If only his cousin had consulted him before he took his Stone out of its secure hiding place.

Bruce should have known he couldn't trust an addict like Alton had become. Should have seen it sooner. Alton had never been in charge of his Stone the way he himself had. Pity. This line of thought wasn't solving his problem, however.

He reached for his keyboard, typed in a note, and printed it. He read it over, checking the plate number carefully. *Find the owner of this license plate and get back to me ASAP. The messenger will wait.*

He put the note in a blank envelope, sealed it, and printed a name and address in block letters on the front. He rang for Sedgwick. "See that someone delivers this immediately, please. He is to wait for a reply."

After the butler went on his errand, Bruce turned back to his spreadsheets. They made him even unhappier. Under current conditions, the projections for the drug business profit were extremely low for the next three months, and nonexistent for weapons sales, thanks to Alton, his bungling with his Stone, and the subsequent events.

Thank goodness Bruce had his own copy of the books; he'd not been able to find Alton's. Of course they weren't where they were supposed to be, in the old man's secret room. They weren't in Alton's usual hiding places in his bedroom either. Bruce hadn't taken the time to search extensively. The house was simply too big, had too many nooks and crannies, and he was too busy.

As he raised his eyes from his keyboard, his gaze fell on the corner where the floor safe lay.

The floor safe. Why hadn't he thought of it before? If Alton put his Stone there, he'd probably hidden his flash drives in the same place. When Alton collapsed, Bruce barely had time to shut the door and put the carpet over it before the household staff rushed in. He hadn't looked in it at the time or since.

It only took a moment to open the safe. Ah, here were the flash drives in their box. The Sabel bitch hadn't taken them, but why should she? He closed the safe, restored the carpet, and carried the box back to his desk. Now he could work on his spreadsheets in relative peace.

About an hour later, Sedgwick knocked and brought in a brown envelope. Bruce thanked him and told him to go to bed.

As he watched the old man close the door behind him, Bruce entertained the notion of his Stone influencing Sedgwick to become his prime gofer. No, he dismissed it quickly. Sedgwick was only about third level and made the perfect doorkeeper. His honesty practically shone out of his face. No, Bruce needed somebody younger, smarter, and ambitious, not afraid to get physical or throw a harmful spell. Maybe his Stone could help him choose. He wrote "Make list of possibles" on his to-do list for the next day.

For the moment, he had an answer to his most pressing question: who was the man with Irenee Sabel? He slit open the brown envelope, took out his original one, and opened the message. His contact—a very well-paid contact in the police department—had written the name James Booth Tylan, an address, and the words, "No other information at this time. Will look again in the morning when I can get into other systems."

The address wasn't far from the mansion, but in a very different neighborhood. Although Bruce had never heard of the man, lack of such information didn't matter these days. Time to use the Internet. He displayed a search engine on his computer and typed Tylan's name in various configurations. Within seconds, he was reading about the man's parents being killed ten years ago in San Diego.

Tylan was a long way from San Diego. Bruce found another article about a Charity Tylan, who had been killed by a drug overdose in Bakersfield. Only one survivor, James, a brother, a police officer in San Diego. He had to be the same man.

Bruce went to the practitioner registry Web site. No Tylan. Not a one. He breathed a short sigh of relief. The last thing he needed was another Sword or Defender. Or, for that matter, another practitioner of any talent. Who was the man?

Idly he began to play with the box holding the flash drives while he considered scenarios. He flipped the lid open and shut several times before he looked into the box and what he saw registered in his head.

For all his faults, Alton was probably more than a little obsessive-compulsive about certain objects—like how he put them away.

Each drive fit precisely into its own slot. Alton always put them in with the little key rings attached at the ends of the casings facing up, so he could easily hook a finger in to pull one out. The key rings were not in sight. Somebody had put the flash drives into the box upside down.

Alton would never do such a thing.

Somebody copying the drives might.

Bruce slid one of the drives into a USB slot on the back of his laptop. He clicked on the icon for drive contents to be displayed. When the list of files came up, he double-clicked on one. Then he opened the Properties box. The last time the file was accessed was the date of the gala. The time of access was right before the auction began—exactly when Alton was in the ballroom.

So, most likely, somebody had copies. Good luck to them. The spells he'd been able to put on those drives with the help of his Stone should give accountants absolute fits. Even if the police or another agency was investigating the Finster activities, there was no way they could straighten out the financials without the reversing spells. All his other dealings were well hidden. He had nothing to worry about from the law.

Were the Defenders teaming up with a law enforcement agency? Their doing so would be a new tactic. Was the agency aware of the Defenders' abilities? He'd have to be on his guard. Of course he could handle everything either would throw at him, but he didn't need any more surprises.

In fact, he and the Stone would take great pleasure in destroying them all, especially the little Sabel bitch and her boyfriend. They would be the first to go.

The familiar oozing of confidence and hatred from his crystal filled his body, and he allowed himself the luxury of fantasizing about what he would do to them. Should he start with the woman or the man first? Decisions, decisions. His center warmed up, and he laughed in delight. Yes, the Stone agreed with him. Together they could defeat everybody.

CHAPTER TWENTY

"Jim!"

Her scream ringing in her ears, Irenee sat straight up in bed.

Jim was in trouble. He needed her now.

She ran out of the bedroom, out of her condo, down the hall. The elevator took forever to come, and she danced in anxiety until it did. She entered and hit the button for the ground floor, wishing she'd taken the stairs even if it would have taken longer. She needed to be moving.

Once the door opened, she dashed out, conjuring her sword while she ran for the other side of the lobby. She heard someone shout, but didn't stop.

From the hall with the elevators to the hotel, Jim suddenly appeared, gun in hand. "Irenee!"

"Jim!" She canceled the spell for her glowing weapon, and it dissipated when her hands came apart.

They met in the middle of the lobby and flung their arms around each other, holding on tight for a long moment. Then she loosened her grip and separated enough to see his face.

"Are you all right?" she asked as she ran her hands over his naked chest and shoulders to make sure.

"Are you all right?" he asked as he held her to him with one arm and captured her hands with his free hand.

"Fine," they said in unison and hugged again, holding on until . . .

"Excuse me," a voice said from behind her. "I've called Mr. Whipple and Mr. Baldwin. Can we be of assistance?"

Irenee turned in Jim's arms to face the desk clerk and a security guard. Before she could say anything, someone coming from the condo side caught her attention.

With his bathrobe flapping around his bare ankles, Fergus hurried over from the elevators. He relaxed once he looked them up and down. Turning to the desk clerk, he said, "Thank you, Mr. Bennett, I think we have the situation under control."

Irenee was still breathing hard, and her heart was beating like crazy, but she managed to say, "Thanks for calling Fergus so quickly. I'm sorry we disturbed you."

"Perfectly all right. Let us know if we can be help," Bennett replied, and bowed himself and the guard away.

Also in his bathrobe, John Baldwin stalked up from the hotel side. "I take it we're not being invaded."

"Doesn't look like it," Fergus said. "Nobody say a word until we get upstairs to my place."

Her arm still around Jim's waist and his around her shoulders, Irenee walked to the elevator with the men. Only when she saw herself in the long mirror on the wall opposite the doors did she realize how she looked. Her hair was flying about her head, and all she had on were her long sleep T-shirt—one saying "You show me your spell and I'll show you mine"—and a pair of panties. She hadn't even grabbed a robe or slipped on shoes in her rush out the door.

Of course, Jim looked fine—more than fine, actually—barefoot and bare-chested in his jeans with his curly hair disheveled. She jerked her gaze back to the elevator doors. This wasn't the time or place to ogle him.

Bridget was waiting in the Whipple condo. When she saw Irenee's state, she loaned her a robe and gave her a wool throw to put around her feet.

Irenee and Jim took seats on the couch, John and Fergus on the chairs. Jim put his gun on the end table next to him after unloading it.

"What happened?" Fergus asked.

Irenee looked at Jim, who said, "You first."

"I was asleep, and I guess I was dreaming. I was in a big black room. Suddenly a light showed Jim, tied to a chair. Bruce Ubell was standing over him, laughing like a maniac. He had a grotesque, misshapen Stone in his hand, and he threw a fireball at Jim, then a lightning bolt. Jim shouted my name, and I woke up screaming his. I just knew something awful had happened, and he needed me. So I ran to find him."

"I had pretty much the same dream," Jim said, "although it was Irenee in the chair, not me, and it was physical torture, not magic. He hit her. I woke up, threw on some pants, grabbed my gun, and went to find her. We met in the middle of the lobby."

"Interesting." Fergus stroked his beard. "You actually had the dreams at the same time."

"Yeah, and that's not all," Jim stated. "Mine felt exactly like the last one did—the one where you thought Ubell was communicating with his Stone. I was a hell of a lot closer to his house, though, the first time."

"Fergus told me about your episode," John said. "You evidently have some of the qualities of a sensitive Defender, or you could be attuned somehow to this particular Stone."

"Come to think of dreams . . ." Jim rubbed his jaw. "I had an earlier one, the night of the gala—or rather very early the next morning. All I remember is an awful feeling, something like a black hole, and then a flash of white light."

"That was when we destroyed Finster's Stone," Fergus said with a gleeful smile, and he rubbed his hands briskly together. "Oh, this gets more and more interesting."

"There's another possibility," Irenee said, "and it's not all about me, me, me, I assure you. Maybe you're picking up Ubell's and his Stone's animosity aimed at me. Each of your dreams has involved me and the Stone, one way or another. It could be some sort of soul-mate connection triggers your sensitivity."

"Ah, you told him," Fergus said.

"You didn't give me much choice," she answered.

"And?"

"None of your business, Fergus." She wasn't going to get drawn into *that* topic. She'd do what Jim did: stick to the subject at hand. "What about my theory?"

"If this soul-mate thing is so powerful," Jim said, "maybe my dream anxieties are getting sent to you or shared somehow. I may be physically farther from Ubell, but I'm closer to you now in distance."

"We still don't know if Ubell's actually using his item when you have the dreams, do we?" John asked.

"No," Fergus answered, "but I'll bet he's doing something. These dreams don't make sense otherwise, and the timing's right."

"Intriguing theory," Bridget said, "but it would appear none of you have answers, and it's very late. From what Fergus told me, you two, Irenee and Jim, have a big day tomorrow. Speaking as a physician, I recommend you get some rest. Sleep late. I'll tell Johanna to expect you when she sees you."

Everybody thought it was a good idea, so Irenee, Jim, and John said good night and left. John took one elevator down to return to the hotel side. Saying he'd see her to her door, Jim followed Irenee up to her condo on the fourth floor.

All the way to her door, Irenee wondered how to ask him to stay the remainder of the night with her. She simply wasn't sure she'd get even a little bit of sleep unless he was close.

Neither said a word until they were inside and she turned on the lights. Then Jim pulled her into his arms, and they held onto each other for a few minutes.

When they let go enough to pull back, she got no farther than "Jim, I—"

"Irenee, we both may need time," he interrupted, his golden-green eyes very serious, "but I'm staying here with you for the rest of the night. There's no way I'm going to be over in the other wing. I won't be able to sleep unless I'm sure you're safe. Your couch looks long enough, so I'll bunk here."

She was right. They were attuned to each other. "The sofa in my home office is a bed. It will only take a minute to open it."

"No, this is fine."

"Okay, let me get you a pillow." Rather than dig one out of the closet in the office, she walked into her bedroom and pulled one off the bed. For a blanket, he could use the afghan. Coming back out into the living room, she plopped it on one end of the couch and watched as he took his weapon out of the back of his jeans and put it on the coffee table.

"Don't tell me you're afraid of guns, a big bad Sword like you?" he said when he noticed her watching him. As he spoke, he unloaded it again.

"Let's just say, I respect them." She hadn't even noticed him putting the bullets—or clip, or whatever the thing was—back in the weapon before they left the Whipples' place. More proof she was really exhausted.

"That reminds me, what was the glowing stick you had in your hand in the lobby? It disappeared."

"My sword. I'll show you tomorrow."

"Fine. For now . . ." He drew her into his arms and kissed her until they were wrapped around each other like jungle vines.

When they finally broke the kiss, she managed to whisper, "Sleep tight," and wobble off to her room, so tired she wasn't certain if she'd make it to the bed without falling on her face.

After thirty long minutes of tossing and turning—with a nagging flutter in her center—she dragged herself to the bedroom door and down the short hall to the living room. When she came around the corner, he sat up on the couch.

"What's the matter?" he asked.

"I can't sleep."

"Neither can I."

"My center's bugging me."

"Mine is, too."

She hesitated, then blurted out the only remedy she could think of. They really did need to rest. "What if we *only* lie down together? Sleep, not *do* anything else. We'll know where each other is. Maybe the physical proximity will help."

"Works for me." He got up, grabbed his pillow, his weapon, and its pieces, and came toward her. He'd taken off his jeans and had only his boxers on. He stopped when she looked at them. "I can put my jeans back on."

She shook her head. "Too much trouble."

She led him into the bedroom, where he put his gun on the chest next to his side. Between the weapon and her sword, they were ready for all physical threats, and she hoped there'd be no repeat of bad dreams for the rest of the night.

They climbed into bed, he leaned over to give her a little kiss, and she snuggled into his arms.

Exactly where she was supposed to be. She took a deep breath to fill her lungs with his scent, and it was the last thing she remembered.

CHAPTER TWENTY-ONE

Jim woke up the next morning with Irenee's hair tickling his nose. Her head was on his shoulder and her arm flung out across his chest. He couldn't see her bedside clock and he didn't have his wristwatch on, but the sun was shining through a crack in the curtains. Light outside, however, didn't mean it was time to get up. The summer dawn came so damned much earlier in Chicago than his southern California self was used to.

Bridget had told them to sleep late, so he wasn't going to wake Irenee just yet. Instead, he'd lie here and enjoy having her in his arms. She'd had the right idea last night for them to go to bed together. He hadn't slept so well in months. No dreams.

Of course, after that nightmare, who needed another one?

He hadn't really had time to think through all the info and events of the last few days. My God, it was only Wednesday. It felt like he'd been here for days. This mess had only started on Saturday night—when everything seemed so simple in comparison. All he'd had to worry about was catching Finster.

Now he knew about the practitioner world and discovered he was *one of them* and could actually cast spells. He had a soul mate—*a soul mate*—and everything had become so damn complicated. It was a wonder he could think at all.

Strangest of all, however, he was comfortable with the whole situation. Like he finally had the answers to most of his personal problems.

How to reconcile his new situation with his job, he had no clue. If he couldn't, would he even be able to stay with the DEA once his main objective, catching the Finster/Ubell combo, was completed? He'd have to talk to Whipple about fitting magic talents into the everyday world. What would Irenee think of his profession, either way? Please, God, don't let her get the idea as a Sword she could *help* him with it.

No answers came to mind. His antennae didn't even wiggle.

Damn his hunch mechanism. He had to find a way to bring it under control. He couldn't be the first practitioner with the damn premonitions. Somebody had mentioned "probability theory," but he'd always thought that went with games of chance and odds. No, he considered his hunches more akin to data analysis, gathering all the info he could, sifting it through his mind—

consciously or unconsciously—and coming out with a solution for a problem or a correct reading of a situation or a plan of action. He sure would like to be able to turn it on and off at will.

Whatever happened there, it was for future consideration.

More immediate, no, *most* immediate was Irenee. What was he going to do with a soul mate?

One part of his anatomy had no trouble answering the question. Especially in the morning.

His brain, however, was slow to get itself in gear. He'd gone to bed last night and been asleep before his head hit the pillow, despite all the stuff running around in his mind. Then the nightmare, then the sofa, then her bed, and finally true sleep.

Before those events, she'd told him about soul mates and asked what his hunch said about them. As he lay there with her in his arms, all his conclusions came back to him full force. Having her as his soul mate would put an end to so much—loneliness, rootlessness—and he'd have someone to care about and protect and who would do the same for him.

Did he deserve her and all that came with her?

Probably not, but he'd be stupid to turn it down—and he was no fool.

Were they really and truly soul mates? She seemed to think so. The skeptic cop in him wasn't so sure. A small prick in his center warned him to watch his thinking. All right, he'd keep an open mind. He couldn't, however, deny the facts of her world, now his, or magic. He'd have to let the events play out before he truly accepted, fully embraced the soul-mate concept.

He had the sneaking suspicion she hadn't told him everything, either.

None of it mattered. By God, he'd do everything in his power, magic or otherwise, to keep her safe.

His center vibrated a little in agreement, and he suppressed a growl. Every time he turned around, his center was bugging him. The damn thing was worse than swallowing a cell phone.

Right this instant . . . he had a warm woman next to him. Even if she wanted to put off having sex—or, *her* word, *mating*—he could see no reason why they couldn't fool around a little. He inhaled and let her slightly spicy, slightly floral scent float in his lungs. His impatient body responded—as did his magic center, which vibrated harder.

Carefully, he eased her onto her back. She frowned, mumbled something, but didn't wake up. He propped himself up on his elbow and looked his fill. Her dark red hair was spread out on the pillow, and he gently removed a few strands from her face. She was so gorgeous—the porcelain skin of a redhead, slightly arched reddish brows, straight nose, luscious lips. He was looking forward to seeing those dark brown eyes open and make him think of diving into chocolate pools.

Chocolate pools? Where did such a sappy term come from? He shook his head. Would he be spouting poetry next? God, he had it bad for the woman.

His center vibrated again—like it was laughing. Idiot center. The way it got excited at the sight or thought of her? It was worse than his cock.

Enough of this. He was a man of action, not mushy words.

He looked down at the rest of her. Her long T-shirt was hiked up, revealing almost all of her legs, and the sight made him think how they would feel wrapped around him. Yeah, he'd show her his "spell"—his own "sword."

He leaned over and brushed a kiss across her lips. When they opened slightly, he ran his tongue around the soft inner lining. She stirred, and the tip of her pink tongue traced his line. She sighed, and the edges of her lips quirked up in a faint smile.

He traced the V-edge of her shirt with a finger, continued from the bottom of the V over the top of her breast, circled around and up to her nipple. Her shirt was so thin he could see the deep rose of it, and as he played, the nipple became darker and harder, like a raspberry getting ripe. He shook his head again at his flowery thoughts and noted they didn't stop his body from reacting. In fact, they might be encouraging his arousal.

He settled his hand over her breast and gave her another small kiss. Another lingering one.

She sighed again, made a sound like purring, and responded by flicking her tongue into the gap between his lips.

He pulled back, and when she opened her eyes, he murmured, "Good morning, sleepyhead."

She stared at him solemnly for a few seconds, with no sign of recognition.

He grinned at her. "Remember me? Tall guy, wild talent, hunches?"

She grinned back, reached a hand up to his hair, ran her fingers through it. "So, kiss me, Mr. Hunch Man, and tell me what your intuition says about us."

He complied with her command.

And fell headlong into a maelstrom of wanting, of longing, of need. Desire rushed through him, tightening his muscles, speeding up his heartbeat, spreading the heat from his center to every cell in him.

In that instant, without a doubt, he knew *here* was where he belonged, in her bed, in her arms, in her body, in her heart.

When he ended the kiss and came to his senses, he had one leg thrust between hers, her top leg was hooked over and around his hip, and his stiff cock was trying its best to get out of his boxers. His top hand was rubbing her back up under her shirt.

She had one hand on the elastic of his underwear, like she was going to pull it away and dip her hand inside. When she moved the hand to his back and ran it up and down, part of him mourned. His mind told him it was better she hadn't touched him where he so much wanted her to. Stupid mind.

She didn't seem inclined to let go or to talk, and she was breathing as hard as he was. He was content simply to hold her close and rock gently until their breathing slowed. Finally, he loosened his arms and leaned back enough to look her in the face.

"Wow," she mouthed soundlessly.

He had to clear his throat before he could say, "Yeah. My hunches are quiet, but the rest of me sure wants you."

She cupped his jaw and ran her thumb over his cheek. "I had no idea of the strength of this . . . I don't know what to call it. *Attraction* doesn't cover it, and every other word I think of seems too weak."

"Yeah." How could she be thinking about *words*? He was long past coherence. He gave her breast a little squeeze and rubbed his thumb across her nipple. When she gasped and jumped slightly, he knew he wasn't thinking, period. Not with his brain, at least.

Her face was a nice pink when—after clearing *her* throat—she said, "I guess we should get up."

He grinned, refrained from telling her he was "up,"

and slowly let her go. She was right. Today was going to be busy. "What time is it?"

She turned over and sat up to look at her bedside clock. "Oh, it's only seven thirty. Why don't we have breakfast in the restaurant? There's usually a buffet, and it will be quicker than my cooking."

"Works for me." He rose, walked around the bed, and when she stood up, took her in his arms. "Something for you to think about. Let me move my stuff over here. We'll both sleep better."

From her frown and her pause, he thought she was going to say no, but she nodded. "Yes, our being together would probably be for the best. I slept really well."

"So did I, and no dreams. I'll see you downstairs." He gave her a quick kiss and took his protesting body out of her bedroom before it overruled him.

Take it easy. You'll have another chance tonight.

CHAPTER TWENTY-TWO

Irenee watched him leave the room. Within seconds, he called good-bye, and she heard her front door close.

With a sigh of relief tinged by disappointment, she flopped back on the bed. Yes, it was a good thing he had gone. Another minute of that kind of closeness and they might have been making love for sure.

Her center fluttered happily at the thought.

"Oh, stop it." She rubbed the spot at the end of her breastbone.

Should she have said no when he suggested moving in? She almost had. His not being here would definitely remove the temptation to mate.

On the other hand, they would sleep better knowing each other was close by.

How close was the question.

They'd proved last night his being in the same condo wasn't close enough. It hadn't been double insomnia keeping them both awake. It was separation. Once they had physical contact, zap, she was asleep, and she had to assume he was, too.

With no dreams to speak of.

Could they share a bed again and not succumb? Not seal the bond? Despite intense provocation, they'd pulled back twice now. Would they be able to do so again?

Where was the idea they needed to wait coming from? Him or her?

Was it her, not him, delaying acceptance of each other as soul mates? Was he putting it off because of what he was feeling in and from her? Even though she knew in her bones she was his, and everything would work out because the phenomenon guaranteed it?

She wasn't sure Jim had fully accepted her. He did accept the concept, thank goodness. So, what was bothering her? Wasn't that enough?

No, because she wanted and needed a declaration of togetherness from him. A flat-out statement of his belief in her, in their being together always. How insecure was that?

Or was there another factor, an action, a conclusion, a conversation, an event that had not yet happened, but which would turn the tide?

She hadn't a clue.

All either of them could do was wait and see.

"Damn it," she mumbled as she got out of bed and headed for the bathroom. "Why did becoming soul mates have to be so difficult? Nobody ever said a word about having so much trouble."

By noon, while Jim sat in the restaurant with Irenee, Whipple, and his trainer, Johanna Mahler, he wondered if he'd have the energy tonight for "another chance."

Johanna. Teacher, trainer? Hah. More like drill sergeant.

First she'd asked him if he and Irenee had mated. He didn't think it was her business, and he simply answered, "No," with no explanation.

She then proceeded to run him through more versions of *lux* than he dreamed existed. According to theory, once he had mastered the subtle variations and energy controls of the ball of light, everything else was easy.

Some theory.

He'd had much more trouble today than he had when he first cast the spell. Nothing seemed to work. He couldn't change the light's colors easily, he moved it around like he or it was drunk, and he almost burned his fingers when he forgot to make the outer shell cool. He used too much power or too little. The light flickered like an electric bulb in a thunderstorm.

Johanna had explained the "formula" some hotshot theoretical mathematician had thought up, but he couldn't keep track of what all the letters meant and simultaneously cast a spell. When she recited the formula's rap song someone with sense had composed, all the casting steps became a lot clearer.

What really helped him manage his power was her explanation of his "energy bucket." That was his term, not hers. She called it a "well," a "repository," and a "reservoir." Control boiled down to thinking about the energy in his bucket in relative terms, not in absolute ones. In percentages. When he applied ten percent of the energy in a full bucket, he got one result. Twenty gave him another, and so forth.

Once he got used to the concept, he started to get a "feel" for energy application, and spell-casting became much easier.

When they tried putting a defense spell on his own body, however, casting got complicated again. The strength spell would really be helpful—if he could turn the energy inward instead of out. Johanna cast it on him so he could experience it, and the sudden increase in muscle power was exhilarating. Now he knew what a superhero felt like. By himself, he'd only managed a tiny strength boost, however. Damned frustrating.

They'd also gone over a list of low level spells that he might learn—assuming his talents allowed it—and those had him drooling. Oh, to be able to cast lock/unlock, different grades of "invisibility," and his personal favorites, unfasten and unravel. The first would unfasten all of a person's clothing—unbuttoning, unzipping, unbuckling. The second would reduce the spelled object to its basic constituents; a shirt would unravel to threads and buttons, and a device to its casings, screws, gears, and springs. Man, would he like to throw unravel on a bad guy with a weapon. It gave whole new meaning to the idea of a "naked gun."

For now, he had to be patient—and eat like a teenager to replace the calories he'd expended.

Irenee was keeping up with him, bite for bite. Whatever she'd done this morning, it must have been worse than his session. She'd started with two desserts, next attacked a steak and a bunch of shrimp. At the moment, she was working on a mound of vegetables.

He and his soul mate were going to have a hell of a food bill.

Wait. What?

He stared at his juicy steak. In his head he heard the sound of his open mind closing like a vault door—with a big solid thunk and a sign proclaiming "Soul Mates Forever."

Well, hell. Just like that. A decision.

She was in his life, and she was going to stay there. He didn't even need a hunch. A feeling of complete contentment washed through him, his center vibrated, and his entire body relaxed. He silently vowed to do his very best to live up to her, protect her, and keep her safe.

Maybe it would be some atonement for his sister.

"Jim? Jim." Johanna shook his arm. "Are you all right?"

Mentally shaking himself, Jim turned to her. "Sure. The food really rebuilds your energy, doesn't it? I'm surprised it comes back so quickly."

"You looked a little funny there for a minute, but I guess it's to be expected. I did work you rather hard."

"It wasn't so bad. I think I learned a lot."

"Yes, you did," Johanna replied and began telling Whipple what they had gone over.

Jim tuned them out and concentrated on feeding his face. After lunch he was going to move his stuff to her place, practice some more, and go to Irenee's test. When he wondered out loud about it, Whipple said he'd explain how the test was run when they got there.

Fine. She'd probably throw some spells, and it would be over. Until then, he had enough to think about—like applying energy to himself. He finished his steak and asked the waiter for a banana split and, Irenee's favorite, chocolate cake with raspberry sauce.

Jim and Johanna practiced for a couple of hours after lunch. The food helped his energy levels, and he actually increased his strength a small amount over his previous attempt at the spell.

They got nowhere, however, on the Defender ability to transfer energy between them.

Finally, after trying several methods, Johanna said, "It looks like your ability to transfer works only with Irenee. That's normal because of the soul-mate bond."

"About the bond," Jim said. "What goes on? Irenee hasn't given me many details. We make love and that's it? We're bonded?"

Johanna chuckled. "Not exactly. The bonding factor is a spontaneous exchange of energy during the love-making. Usually, it's the only time soul mates can share power. Fergus and John know a non-Defender couple with sharing abilities outside the bonding experience, also only between those two soul mates. Since you and Irenee haven't mated yet, the lack of connection may be holding you back from organizing and manipulating the flow."

"Could Irenee be mistaken when she says she could feel it? I have never noticed movement between us like you've described." He thought Irenee's touch had made the imperative's pain stop, but that circumstance didn't seem to apply here. "I don't see her spell aura either, although she sees mine, and it's weird because I see all these spells glowing."

"Don't confuse seeing spell glow with seeing auras. They're very different," Johanna replied. "I'm sure Irenee is correct about the energy transfer between you. Of necessity, her training has concentrated on the sharing ability. Don't worry, Jim, once you're mated, you'll understand the transfer much better. It may be your sharing does work only with her, and you might also need the mating to see her aura."

"Then, where do she and Whipple get the idea I can share with others?"

"Irenee felt the transfer before she knew you were soul mates and before you were mated. Defenders usually manifest the ability about the time of puberty. Your being a wild talent has thrown the timetable off, I guess, and it seems to affect other abilities, as well."

Not a helpful answer—on the other hand, all he cared to think about at the moment. He knew the ability to share it was important, from the way people were talking about it, but he still wasn't sure why. He didn't question her further; he was tired of showing his ignorance to everyone.

Johanna suggested he work on maintaining several lightballs at once, so Jim put the sharing problem out of his mind. By the end of the practice, he thought he was making real progress, and to be sure, he asked, "Give me some idea of where I am, can you? I'm really in the dark here."

"I teach mostly teens we've identified as having Defender and Sword potential—to see if they truly do have those talents and get them started. They are already well versed in the basics, so I'm not used to pure novices," Johanna replied. "Right now, given your displayed potential and how far we've come in a few short hours, I'd put you at about third grade. Give us another week, and you'll be up to seventh in the very basic spells. Maybe higher, since you concentrate so well."

"Got any notion about what my specific talents might be?"

"No, I can't help you there, Jim. I've never worked with someone who discovered their abilities so late. Most kids have a good idea about theirs by high school, and if they're Defenders, sometimes even earlier. Furthermore, your talents, if they involve hunches or police work, are way beyond my experience. We'll get you to some of the masters who specialize in identification."

"Okay," he said and tried not to be discouraged. Hell, *he* didn't know what he could do. Why should anybody else?

CHAPTER TWENTY-THREE

After their session, Johanna led him to yet another building on the Center's grounds and deep into the basements, where the walls glowed so brightly he thought he was getting a permanent squint. They met up with Whipple there.

The big wizard had a funny look on his face—sort of a combination of glee and warning. "Brace yourself, Tylan," he said. "You're about to meet the family."

"What? Whose?"

"Irenee's mother and brother flew back from New York this morning when they heard about her test. Or that's what they said. The real reason was probably to meet you." He winked at Jim, then looked over his shoulder. "Here they come now."

A striking older woman with dark red hair streaked with silver and a man about his age who looked a lot like Hugh Sabel came along the corridor.

"Oh, there you are, Fergus," the woman said. She gave Whipple a kiss on the cheek before turning to him.

"You must be Jim Tylan. How do you do, Jim, I'm Irenee's mother. Please, call me Catherine."

Jim kept a straight face, said the requisite greetings, and shook hands with the two Sabels.

"We were so happy to hear the news about you and Irenee. We're looking forward to getting to know you better," Catherine Sabel said with a smile. "I've never met a wild talent before."

Jim could tell she meant every word, but he also knew those green eyes of hers didn't miss a trick. He was suddenly scared to death. What if she wouldn't accept him as her daughter's mate? Where was Irenee when *he* needed protection?

He told himself he could handle the situation. He'd act like he was undercover, where a word or expression would give away his position. What went on between him and Irenee was nobody else's business.

Irenee's brother, Dietrich, grinned. "You need help against the onslaught of being thrust into the Sabel family, come see me. We men need to stick together. Mom and Irenee together can be overwhelming."

"Oh, Dietrich," Catherine said, "don't give the man a false impression. We're perfectly nice people. Pay no attention to him, Jim."

"No, ma'am." Thinking furiously, he managed to add, "If Irenee takes after you, I'm sure you're nice people."

Catherine beamed at him, and Dietrich grinned

some more. "Good answer," he stage-whispered.

Jim decided to keep an eye on both of them. The brother was no slouch either.

Thank God, Whipple rescued him. "Come on, we need to get to our seats. Jim, you come with me so I can explain what's going to happen."

They all went through some wooden double doors, carved with glowing runes and glyphs like the ones in the building where he was training. Instead of entering a small stone room, however, they emerged on a balcony with auditorium-style seating overlooking a huge elliptical arena floor at least twenty feet below. The ceiling could easily be sixty or seventy feet high. Jim knew the elevator had descended quite a distance—how far underground would be a pure guess.

The oval arena—at least one hundred by one hundred fifty feet—had stone walls, ceiling, and floor. The lighting consisted both of candles and torches on multibranched wall sconces and of electric spotlights in recessed tubes. If it wasn't for the comfortable modern balcony, all the place needed to look like a medieval castle hall were heraldic flags and shields.

It was no playground, however. The very air reeked of extreme gravity and enormous but dormant power.

The entire arena glowed in rainbows of color with silver and gold mixed in. Jim blinked and, using what Johanna had taught him about dimming spell effects, managed to stop squinting. He found that if he concentrated on people or specific objects, most of the shine receded into the background and was more like bright sunlight.

A shallow two-tiered balcony—they were on the lower level—stretched around the entire structure, and a smattering of other practitioners occupied some of the seats. Shining glass separated the balconies from the arena itself.

"This is our testing and competition arena as well as our largest auditorium for presenting awards, performances, and lectures," Whipple told Jim after they sat down in the front row next to the center aisle. Irenee's mother and brother took seats across the passageway and were soon joined by Hugh. They were in the middle of one of the long sides of the oval.

"As you can undoubtedly see, the entire complex is heavily spelled," Whipple said to him. "We use it to test high level practitioners and for competition between Defender teams and between individual Swords. For protection from spells, the electric lights have covers, and racks with more complex lighting are hidden in the ceiling. We record all tests from behind specially spelled windows."

Movement below captured Jim's attention before he could ask any questions.

Through several doors on the arena floor level, a

number of practitioners entered in a swirl of colorful robes: purple, reds, greens, copper and silver, dark blue, yellow, and black. Five of them were Swords—John Baldwin, and three Jim didn't know, but the way their black robes were shimmering, they had to be high level. The fifth was, of course, Irenee. Despite the raised hoods, he had no difficulty at all picking her out.

"The two in yellow are healers," Whipple told him.

"Can somebody get hurt in this test?" A little breeze of apprehension ruffled his hunch antennae.

"It is possible," Whipple said, "but highly unlikely. They're part of our usual standard precautions. They'll be monitoring everyone, especially Irenee. The amount of energy she expends will help us determine her actual level."

About ten feet out from the walls, an oval line engraved into the floor suddenly glowed silver and gold. A translucent curtain of colors spread from it to the ceiling. Two points lit up in the floor along the line from one end to the other, each about twenty-five feet in from its closest end.

"The test will take place within the ellipse and behind its shield, which John just activated," Whipple said. "Irenee will be inside a pentagonal shield or fortress of her own creation at one of those light points, and a Defender team will be in a similar shield at the other. Normally, a team consists of five Defenders and two Swords, and the

Defenders stand in the points of the pentagon with the Swords on either side of the middle. We're using another Defender team, not our own, and we're adding a third Sword, who will stand in the center and direct the team's spells. It's Kendra Degen in the middle, incidentally—amazing power, by the way. John is in charge of the entire test, and he'll be over to the side at the midpoint."

"Wait a minute," Jim said, feeling a stronger, colder breeze. "It's her against all of them?"

Whipple held up his hands. "Take it easy, Jim. It's simply a test. Basically, they're going to throw spells at each other, measuring Irenee's limits, power, strength, and endurance. Irenee hasn't had time to learn and practice new spells, so she's been working on the ones she knows, to increase their strength. If she's gone up from ten to twelve, and I think she has, her power has increased at least twofold and possibly more."

The wizard put a hand on Jim's shoulder and looked him straight in the eye. "Your part is to sit and watch *calmly.* The balcony is spelled so we'll be able to hear what happens on the floor, and they can't hear us. The spell doesn't, however, stop your emotions from getting through. It's obvious you two are already attuned to each other. Take my word for it, you could disturb her concentration if you react negatively to whatever happens down there."

Catherine spoke from across the aisle. "We've been

through these before as she progressed through the levels, and there's really nothing to worry about, Jim. These Defenders are experienced testers. No one will let anything happen to her, or to the other participants. I'm not telling you it will be easy for you to watch, especially since you're new to all this, but she's safe."

Jim heard the truth in their words, and he struggled to ignore his unease. What had he been thinking at lunch about protecting her? Here she was going to put herself into a situation, the mere thought of which worried him? More than worried—it outright scared him, even though he really wasn't sure what "throwing spells" meant.

The only Sword spell he'd actually seen her use was the puff-of-wind thing. The lightning bolt or whatever she'd cast at Ubell's pursuing thugs had only been a flash in his rearview mirror. The results had been spectacular, however. Were the Swords going to throw stuff like that at her?

He began to wish he'd asked a lot more questions about everything—swords, spells, what they could do and what they couldn't. That way he might feel better prepared for this test. Assuming he could have figured out the questions to ask. His overloaded brain had all it could do to keep up with what had happened so far.

Whatever came, he knew one thing. He had no choice. He had to sit here and watch her test *calmly* like Whipple said. She needed, they all needed, to know what her powers were. Besides, Irenee would be absolutely furious if he disrupted the proceedings, and he would look like a fool to her family. Jim slumped back in his chair. "Okay, I hear you."

The electric lights in the arena were turned off and their covers were closed; the ones in the balconies were dimmed. The candles and torches in the wall sconces came alive with flames, making the scene below even more like a fantasy movie—or was it a horror show?

Baldwin did something with his hands, and the oval in the floor and its translucent curtain glowed brighter. Jim heard a distinct hum and felt the particular tension he was coming to recognize as the presence of magic. This arena, however, held no little drop of energy like he produced from his bucket, but an ocean of power.

Irenee, at one end of the ellipse, and the team at the other both pointed to the floor, and pentagons with similar walls sprang into being. The team's were violet with silver streaks. Irenee's was a mix of blue and indigo with only a few violet swirls.

Inside the pentagons, the combatants settled into place. Finally everyone was still.

Baldwin walked to a point midway between the two fortresses and stood close to the edge of the oval with his back to the balcony where Jim sat. A silver pentagon shot up around him.

"We'll start with a level-six fireball and trade shots, each time increasing in strength by half a level. Irenee, alert us if you think you've reached your limit." Baldwin looked to Irenee and to Kendra. Both nodded. He raised his hand and dropped it. "Begin."

The magic-energy level soared, and in response, Jim's center danced an excited jig in his chest. A crackling sound, then a whoosh filled his ears when a red ball of flame blasted from Kendra's hands straight toward Irenee. Her walls dissipated the energy with apparently no problem, and he relaxed a little bit.

Maybe this wasn't going to be too bad; his lady could obviously take care of herself.

Irenee shot back, and the duel was on. After ten blasts from each side, Baldwin raised his hands, and Irenee and Kendra lowered theirs. "I think we're up to about level eleven, right?" Everybody nodded. "Any problem, Irenee?"

"No," she answered, her voice ringing with total confidence. "I haven't had to strengthen my shield at all, and I have plenty of reserve energy."

"Okay, let's try the same thing again with lightning. Color your bolts to indicate level, starting from eight. Stop on eleven and a half. Ready? Begin."

Again an exchange. Where the fireballs had been relatively silent, lightning brought its own sound effects when green, blue, and indigo bolts flew across the oval and exploded against the pentagons.

Jim cringed as booming cracks of thunder rebounded

off the stone walls and the protective glass in front of him vibrated. When the spells ceased, the resulting silence rang in his ears.

"She's doing very well," Whipple told him. "As you can see, the spells can pass through the walls of their caster's fortress, not those of their opponents. People and objects can pass through the walls in either direction. If Irenee was not as strong as she is, Kendra's bolts could destroy her walls. We won't let that happen, of course."

"Right," Jim muttered. His center stopped dancing and gathered itself into a tight fist.

On the floor, Baldwin spoke again. "Irenee, how are you?"

"Fine. My energy levels are still high. I think my last bolt registered eleven and some." She sounded like she was having great fun.

Jim, on the other hand, was being tortured. It was harder than he'd ever imagined to have to sit there and watch Irenee be attacked. The fireballs had seemed "soft," but when the lightning hit her pentagon, he felt like a true sword had struck him, with a hard, sharp jolt. His heart rate increased, he breathed faster, and his muscles tensed like he himself was in the fight. The "little" breeze of apprehension making his antennae shiver turned into a stronger wind. He gripped the armrests to anchor himself.

"Irenee, push a bolt as much as you can. Kendra,

don't reply," Baldwin ordered. "Go."

Irenee stood still for a moment, then with a flourish pointed her finger at the other citadel and cried, *"Fulmen!"*

An indigo bolt with many violet swirls streaked across the ellipse and shattered on the walls of the Defenders' shield.

"Looked like a twelve to me," Kendra said. "Felt like one, too."

Everybody on the Defender team nodded their agreement.

From behind Irenee and outside the ellipse, the healer spoke up. "She's hardly experienced any diminution of energy levels, John. Her walls are as strong as when she started, and she's regaining energy quickly now at rest."

"All right," the Sword acknowledged and rubbed his hands together. "Let's go to free form and for endurance. Everything goes. Irenee, Swords, we'll build in increments of whole levels this time, no half measures, beginning at six. Irenee, when you reach your high point, keep throwing them to see how long your energy holds out. Healers, tell us instantly if someone has a problem."

He looked at each caster, raised his hand, and brought it down. "Begin."

The concussions and shock waves from the immediate barrage flung Jim back in his seat. Indigo and violet lightning cracked, red and yellow fireballs exploded, and green and blue and lavender laserlike spears of light caromed about the room, off the pentagons and the elliptical shield's interior walls. Winds howled around the oval. The pentagons glowed ever more brightly until two multicolored, five-sided columns reached the ceiling.

Whipple provided a play-by-play analysis of each attack. Knowing exactly what was being thrown at his mate didn't provide Jim with a single reason to relax, however, although the energy and potential in each spell awed him. These guys could kick butt!

His soul mate had power he'd never dreamed of.

All her ability didn't mean, however, she should go off on her own like she'd been doing, he told himself. Teamwork still mattered, and as Whipple had told him, she couldn't stop a bullet.

Both sides began to throw curveballs, spells that wound around to attack the back or sides of their opponent's walls, and from time to time Jim lost sight of Irenee when fireballs and lightning collided.

"How much voltage or amps or whatever do they produce with those bolts?" Jim asked during a slight lull in the action.

"We've never had a true measurement based on modern physics or engineering," Whipple answered. "The use of magic melted the instruments. A couple of electrical-engineer practitioners are working on a new method for calibrating exactly how much energy a team produces. I don't know how successful they'll be. We haven't yet settled on a good measurement term, like a kilowatt, so we're left with level designations by color."

Jim decided he might be better off not knowing how much power they were slinging around down there. He glanced back at the big pentagon. A golden band of light floated in the space between the Defenders at the points and the Swords in the middle. He pointed to it. "What's with the ring?"

"The Defenders create a circle of magical power for the Swords to tap into. It's how they share energy," Whipple replied, sounding extremely satisfied. "Destruction of an evil item takes much more power than one person can produce. We're hoping you can help Irenee by supplying her with an extra source of energy. If you can't help create the ring, you may be able to transfer power directly."

Holy shit! The wind of apprehension he'd felt earlier turned ice cold and gained strength. They actually expected him to produce something like that? Or at least add to it? When all he could cast in reality was a puny lightball? When he could barely control what little he had? When he didn't have one ounce of proof he could actually share the damn stuff? His center seemed to contract into a lump of pain.

My God. What if I can't do what they want? I'm going to fail her.

He rubbed his aching center and watched the group in the pentagon. He could almost feel the enormous amount of energy pouring into the ring and from it to the Swords.

Another wild exchange on the arena floor brought his attention back to Irenee, and he watched the battle with much more trepidation than a few minutes ago.

Kendra changed missiles to throw rainbow-hued energy beams with both hands. When the multicolored lances hit Irenee's walls, her indigo and violet barriers flared. When the torrent increased in number and intensity, her magical fortification bent under the pressure, flexing like the tight skin of a drum. Irenee's defenses held firm under the onslaught, and she appeared unaffected as her walls deepened in color and she returned fire.

Each of the blows, however, hit Jim like a sledgehammer. He couldn't sit still, but dodged and flinched with each strike. With every cell in his body demanding he go help her, his magic center urging him on to *do something*, he tried to rise from his seat. Whipple grabbed his arm and held him down.

"She's all right, Jim," he stated firmly. "You know it, you can feel it. Relax."

Jim stared at the big mage, then abruptly sat back in his chair. Whipple was right. He could feel Irenee's power and confidence, her strength and excitement. His center seemed to take a deep breath and calm down, and hoping it knew more than he did, he followed its lead.

He glanced over at her parents, who were watching the battle closely. Hugh was almost glowing with pride, but the tension in both showed in the way they clasped hands tightly. While the brother appeared relaxed on the surface, he, too, was closely following every move in the arena.

The team had reached twelfth level in their bolts, according to Whipple's commentary.

"What about their swords?" Jim asked. "I only had a glimpse of Irenee's, and I thought they'd be using them."

"A blade is pure magic energy, formed into a column in the shape of a sword. Think of it like a handheld laser," Whipple answered. "They're extremely powerful, but energy eaters. We don't use the Swords' blades in tests—too exhausting, and entirely too dangerous. With enough power from the wielder or against a very weak opponent, the sword beam can cut right through a lesser pentagon's walls. A successful attack on a fortress by a strong enough beam can injure, even kill, the Sword and Defenders inside."

So, from what Whipple was saying, the Swords needed more energy than they could produce individually to destroy an item. Irenee would need her team's—and his, if he could work the transfer. She couldn't do it alone. Okay, those facts perversely gave him cause for optimism. He simply had to make sure she didn't go after Ubell or his Stone by herself, and she'd be safe.

Yeah, *simply.* He'd stop her reckless actions, even if it took a fight. He could probably depend on Whipple's help in that endeavor, too. Jim relaxed a tiny bit and felt his center do the same.

Suddenly, the battle intensified, and the change brought him upright. The three Swords within the pentagon *each* began to hurl separate spells at Irenee instead of only one through Kendra.

"Hey!" Jim yelled.

"Take it easy," Whipple admonished, putting his hand on Jim's shoulder again. "Look, she's fine."

And she was. Previously, Irenee had been standing still while she cast. Now she was moving within her pentagon, almost dancing, hands held up and weaving patterns in the air as if to halt the spell missiles physically and to dodge particularly potent blasts. The glyphs on her robe rippled with colors as the spells swirled around her.

The bombardment seemed to go on for hours, and when Jim looked at his watch, he saw they were indeed into the second hour of the test. He also realized he had been moving in his chair, as though he was evading the bolts. At last he thought he could see her tiring, her energy depleting, her walls weakening ever so slightly. If only he could send her some of his power.

A movement where there had been none drew his

gaze. Baldwin. The presiding Sword had been standing immobile inside his own pentagon throughout the battle, his hands tucked into the sleeves of his gown. Without warning he threw up his hands and brought them together in front of his chest. Out of his fingers flew a huge silver energy bolt, straight at Irenee. Her walls shivered, bent inward almost to the point of touching her slight body, and appeared to be on the verge of collapse.

The son of a bitch!

Jim surged out of the chair. He threw something—energy, fire, he didn't know what or how—at Baldwin just as he saw Irenee rally her defenses, deflect the bolt, and send it careening at the other pentagon where Kendra had to move quickly to parry the blow.

On the balcony, all hell broke loose. Jim's blast bounced off the glass, almost hit him in the head, and ricocheted around the room. He turned in time to see Catherine and Hugh Sabel duck it and Dietrich hit the floor. Whipple grabbed the missile somehow in a spell and dissipated it before it did real damage.

On the arena floor, Baldwin cried, "Enough!"

Irenee dropped her protective walls and swayed, but remained upright. She looked up at Jim, frowned, and, her voice completely audible in the silence, said, "I'm fine. Really." Then she turned to accept the accolades of the testers.

Jim stood rigid for a moment until he satisfied himself Irenee was, in truth, all right—exhausted, but all right. He relaxed with a huge sigh. Relaxation turned to chagrin, however, when he watched the others restore themselves to order after his spell-casting attempt. "Uh, I'm sorry. I guess I lost my head."

"Perfectly understandable, my boy," Whipple chuckled. "You aren't the first and you won't be the last to react when your soul mate's being threatened."

"The most interesting part is, Jim," Hugh interjected, "that you could throw anything at all. What did he cast, Fergus? Could you tell?"

"Sheer energy, spontaneous combustion?" Whipple shrugged. "Jim, we don't know what you are yet, but you pack a hell of a wallop."

Jim didn't care about that. He looked back at Irenee. "Is she really okay?"

"She's fine, and she was spectacular." Whipple smiled like a white-haired bear who had discovered a big pot of honey. "We have a lot of work to do with the both of you in the future."

Fine for Whipple to say. Jim had another take on the performances—both his and hers. They showed Jim exactly how helpless he was here. In his new world, if he didn't do everything exactly right, he wouldn't protect himself and, worse, her.

God, was he doomed to another loss of the person most important to him?

CHAPTER TWENTY-FOUR

Irenee emerged from the arena into the hallway to find her family and Jim waiting.

Her mother reached her first and gave her a big hug. "Irenee, we are so proud of you!"

Her father and even Dietrich followed suit, with her brother, the tease, whispering in her ear, "I'm still a higher level than you." She punched him in the arm, and they grinned at each other.

She was seriously considering fussing at Jim for causing the disruption that almost distracted her at the wrong moment, but he took her in his arms like she was the most precious thing on earth. All the fight went out of her when she felt the anxiety in his hold and he muttered in her ear, "Damn, woman, you scared me half to death."

"I'm fine," she whispered and leaned back to see his face. "Really."

"Let's have a celebratory drink," her father said. "You should be hungry."

"Famished." She kept hold of Jim's hand all the way to the restaurant.

During dinner in the restaurant, her mother quizzed poor Jim up one side and down the other—in a very polite way, of course. He did a good job of telling her enough to satisfy, without divulging what was only between the two of them.

Irenee didn't find out anything new about him from the conversation, but she didn't expect to. He knew how to handle interrogations. She did, however, learn she was even more conscious of his presence next to her than she had been at lunch. If it hadn't been for the need to replenish her energy from the test, she'd have thought seriously about skipping the meal, taking him upstairs, and getting to know him better.

By talking, of course. About their goals, their families, their approaches to life, their likes and dislikes.

With maybe a few of his glorious, exciting, totally arousing kisses thrown in for good measure.

What was to stop her from doing the very thing before they finished eating? Simply get up and go? They were soul mates, after all. Who was going to object?

Jim nudged her with his elbow. When she turned to him, he gave her a look that could have set an iceberg on fire and murmured, "Let's get out of here as soon as we can, okay?"

"I've been thinking along those very same lines," she

whispered back.

He raised his eyebrows at her.

She could feel her face heat and quickly turned her attention back to her plate.

Sitting on her other side, Fergus leaned forward and nodded at both of them. "I need a private word with you two when we're done here, okay?"

Irenee nodded, and Jim said, "Fine."

What now? Or rather, what else? She didn't have a clue what Fergus's "private word" might be, so she applied herself to her fresh strawberry and hot fudge sundae.

"You two must mate tonight," Fergus stated bluntly, when he had them seated next to each other in a small conference room on the first floor of the residence building.

Irenee opened her mouth to refute his statement and closed it again abruptly. Yes, she wanted to make love with Jim, but not be pressured into it. Soul mate or not, she couldn't shake the feeling they were being forced into it and entirely too fast.

Fergus, however, was using his implacable "I am in charge" voice—he would accept no arguments.

Jim obviously didn't realize it—or maybe he didn't care—because he said, "Wait a damn minute, Whipple. Who are you to decide that for us?"

"I'm the leader of Irenee's team, for one. For another, I'm the one who caught the bolt of energy you let loose in the arena." Fergus held up both hands. "Hear me out."

Irenee grimaced. Here came the need for teamwork again, and this time it was infringing on what was supposed to be between her and Jim. She resented Fergus's intrusion—although he did bear the final responsibility for the success of their mission. She put her hand on Jim's arm and sighed. "I think we need to listen to him, Jim."

Jim clasped her hand and sat back with a squinty stare at Fergus. "Okay, but I'm not agreeing to anything in advance."

"You first, Irenee," Fergus said. "The way you've been going up in levels—*spontaneously*—is spectacular and unprecedented."

He pointed to Jim. "We still don't know what you can do. Johanna said it looks like you can't transfer energy the way Defenders do, with other Defenders. On the other hand, Irenee says you can share with her. You have some firepower, as shown by your demonstration in the arena. What kind or how you can control it is a mystery. Do you agree so far?"

Irenee looked at Jim. "I can't disagree with Fergus's assessment. Can you?"

Jim paused, looked like he wanted to object, but said only, "So what?"

"It's inevitable," Fergus continued. "We're going to fight Ubell's bigger, stronger Stone. It's going to throw everything at us, whether Ubell is directing the action or not. Furthermore, we have to assume you'll be its target again, Irenee."

"I think so, too," Irenee said. "What does it have to do with our mating?"

"When you two make love, the soul-mate phenomenon will, most probably, increase the energy and potential in both of you," Fergus stated. "We're going to need every ounce of power in the coming fight. We need both of you at full strength, with Jim pouring power into you. I think he'll be able to share at will after you bond. Jim once said Ubell would think of the most evil way he could to get back at you. I agree. We're meeting with the man tomorrow. We have to be ready for any and all reactions from him."

"Yeah, but what good will it do us to have more energy?" Jim asked. "I don't know how to use mine, and Irenee hasn't practiced the higher spells for her new level. Johanna and I tried to share power, and nothing worked."

"Think of the larger picture. Irenee proved today she can pour more into the spells she has. You're already linked to each other. Soul mates always are. If you can feed her power, that's more for her to use. Once you experience the bonding, where you *will* share energy, you'll have a better idea what I mean."

Jim slumped back in his chair, looking disgruntled and obstinate.

"Irenee, you'll be able to fight longer and stronger," Fergus continued. "Your energy well will increase in size and amount. With more firepower, we'll be able to destroy the thing faster and stop its attacks on Jim or you."

Irenee turned to Jim and shrugged. "He makes a lot of sense. Where going up a level is concerned, I've been explaining it to you mostly in terms of new spells I need to learn, not my overall power increase. Using my increased capacity is what today was all about."

He stared into her eyes with an expression she could only interpret as extremely worried—almost agonized. "Yeah, but . . ."

"Look at it another way," Fergus interrupted with a big smile. "You two are soul mates. You both know it, don't you? Why not capitalize on the connection? Trust me, you won't regret it."

Jim didn't say anything to that.

Irenee studied the man sitting next to her. Something else was bothering Jim, and she . . . , well, she hadn't had time to process her own feelings, much less understand his. They were back to the "I'm not ready" state.

Then she noticed he had a faint blue aura. Whatever was going on in his head, she suddenly, simply *knew* they needed to be alone to work this situation out. The revelation was an interesting sensation, sort of an itching along the scalp. Was Jim's hunch ability transferring to her?

She rose and put a hand on Jim's shoulder. "Thanks for the advice, Fergus. We'll see you tomorrow. Let's go upstairs, Jim. We need to talk—again."

Fergus looked from her to him and back. He offered no argument, only nodded and said, "Have a good evening."

On the way up in the elevator, when Jim didn't say a word, Irenee reviewed her options. Mate or not? The way Fergus laid out the situation, they had no alternative.

She almost snorted in derision at her circumstances. Since when had she had a true choice about anything?

Zip, and her levels increased and she was a Sword.

Zing, and she had met her soul mate—a wild talent, no less.

Zap, and she had an evil item out for her blood, and probably her mate's, too.

Her soul mate. Yes, she'd imagined what would happen when she met him. Days of happiness, nights of rapture. None of it had come true. Where was the time to enjoy the experience, to take pleasure in each other's company, and, yes, to wallow in the sheer *romance* of it all?

What did she get instead?

Zoom! Get in there and mate!

She certainly couldn't deny that every single indication and every individual cell in her body screamed that

Jim was her mate. The few kisses and embraces they'd shared had lived up to all of the phenomenon's legends. A little shiver of expectation and excitement had been running up and down her backbone since Fergus had told them to get on with it.

She almost laughed. If theirs was a "shotgun mating," an "arranged marriage," at least she didn't have to do like women of old—lie there and think of the empire while the man did his thing. No, their actual mating was bound to be stupendous for both of them.

She had to trust in her heritage and her liking and admiration for this man. Love would surely follow—if it wasn't here already.

Was she in love with him? She didn't know, and once again, didn't have the time to think about it. Anyway, not to worry—the phenomenon guaranteed love and a happily-ever-after.

CHAPTER TWENTY-FIVE

When they finally made it to Irenee's, Jim stalked across the living room and stood staring out the window, his arms crossed over his chest. His focus, however, was not on the landscape outside, but inward, on his reaction to Whipple's commands.

What was the matter with him? Why was he suddenly so irritated by the idea of making love with her? Why was he fighting the Sword leader's directive? He'd already decided he would be with her forever.

Wishing he could scratch his hunch antennae wiggling in the recesses of his brain or yank the irritation out by the roots, he rubbed the back of his neck instead. Why couldn't the damn things make up their minds? What the hell was going on?

One hunch was saying he ought to take her straight to bed. A very important body part agreed. Yet, here he was, unsure and angry. He didn't like the idea of "performing" on command—although he certainly didn't doubt his ability. Around her, he had an almost constant hard-on.

So why wasn't he listening to—and acting upon—what his hunch was telling him?

Because Irenee's test had scared the shit out of him. Because Whipple's predictions for the coming fight were awful to even consider. Because now he understood the *absolute need* for him to transfer power from himself to her—if he didn't, the Stone could destroy her. Because he couldn't. He didn't have the ability to share.

Because another hunch had coalesced with Whipple's orders and was beating on the inside of his skull. This one was telling him her Defender team wouldn't be enough. He and only he was *absolutely crucial* to her survival.

How could he be when he couldn't send her energy? He didn't know how, or if it was even possible, no matter what anybody said. He was one big failure.

Where did his failure leave them? Especially her?

Yeah, he knew more now about the awesome power of a Sword, and everything he'd heard about the fight with Finster's Stone meant the one with Ubell's would be worse. Worst of all, the damn item would target her, and he wouldn't be able to help.

"Jim?" Irenee said as she came up behind him and put a hand on his back. "What's going on in your head? Your aura's blue, like it is when you're having a hunch."

He turned, took her in his arms, and held her close, rubbing his cheek on her hair. When her unique scent wound around and into him, he almost grew dizzy with desire. His center practically fainted with happiness. After a minute of wallowing in sheer pleasure, he separated enough to see her face. "I guess I just can't hide a thing from you, can I?"

She grinned. "I turn red, and you turn blue. What a colorful pair we are." She gave him a little shake. "So, tell me."

He let go of her and stepped back to regain his control. "One hunch is telling me Whipple is right. We need to mate. I guess I'm scared. Not so much about the commitment we'll be making, because I certainly want you forever, but . . ."

"You do?"

She had a confused look on her face. Hadn't he told her? He mentally winced. No, there hadn't been time after lunch. When had they had the chance for privacy?

Before he could elaborate on his declaration, she nodded, her expression changed to delight, and she said, "I came to the same conclusion."

Confusion returned when she said, "Well . . . what's the matter, then?"

She came to the same conclusion? She was his? The thoughts hit him like a tidal wave of happiness.

Followed by a hurricane of doubt.

Would she still want him after he told her what he

was really thinking? After he told her he couldn't help her? He stiffened his backbone. Neither hunch helped here. He had to find out. It was time to tell the truth flat-out, whatever the consequences.

He took another step back and a deep breath and began, "Until the little demo you and the Defenders put on, I didn't fully realize what you go through as a Sword—the power you have, the dangers you face. When Baldwin threw that mega-bolt in a cheap shot, I came unglued. If I'd been on the arena floor, I'd have blasted him, or at least decked the guy. I felt so damned helpless up there in the balcony. Whipple's demands and the reasons behind them and his plans for killing the damned Stone underscored another, even bigger problem."

She stepped forward, but he held up his hands. "Let me explain. It'll be easier if we don't touch. I have a hell of a time concentrating when we do."

"I have the same problem." Smiling faintly, Irenee walked over to the couch and, sitting down, looked expectantly at him.

"I've always been about protecting people." Too restless to stand still, too nervous about how she'd accept what he was about to tell her, Jim paced by the windows. "When I was young, I watched out for littler kids. I beat the crap out of a bully who was terrorizing some guys in the seventh grade. I later had the satisfaction of arresting the bastard for abusing his wife."

God, the memory of that was still sweet. He couldn't, however, dwell on the past.

"I'm still all about protection." He ran his fingers through his hair and turned to face her. "But, Irenee, it sure doesn't look like I can help you at all in the fight against Ubell and his damned Stone. Certainly I won't be able to protect you like I want to."

"You *can* help," she said. "You heard Fergus. I need your energy support, not your protection here. I don't expect you to stand in front of me or wield my sword. I need you behind me, holding me up. Together, we'll do the job."

"How? *I* haven't felt *any* transference between us—or *anything* even remotely like what people have described. In your test I watched the team of Defenders share energy. I could see the power pouring off the golden ring in their pentagon right into the Swords. Johanna and I tried the exchange bit, and nothing happened with either of us. My energy only sat there in my bucket and didn't move. I *can't* do what everybody says I *have* to do."

He held up a hand to stop her from interrupting. He was on a roll and absolutely had to get the rest of this out. "Wait, there's more. I have another hunch. It says I'm absolutely *crucial* to your survival in this mess. How on earth can I be if I can't share power?"

He shook his head when she opened her mouth, and he spoke before she could. "Yeah, I know, you felt something when my magic center woke up, and you stopped the pain from the imperative when we were on the floor right here. I felt nothing, so the energy had to be coming from you, not me."

She was clearly worried by his words, but his last statement surprisingly brought a smile. "In that specific instance, I personally did nothing," she said. "The imperative took away the pain when I, your soul mate, touched you, and you accepted it and me. The imperative wants us together. We were. We are. Has it bugged you since then?"

"Only little twitches in my center when I see you again after we've been apart—like when we were training."

"Is it very painful?"

"No," he said and sighed wearily when his center wiggled like it was laughing. "It's more . . . *smug.* Like it's got me exactly where it wants me."

"Mine's happy, too." She gave him a warm smile, and his center grew even more self-satisfied.

"That's all well and good—and useless to me. I want to, *I need to,* help. Actively. I couldn't live with myself if this damn evil Stone destroyed you and"—he took a deep breath as her eyebrows rose, and he blurted it out—"and all *I* could do is stand there like a frigging idiot. I honest-to-God don't know what I'd do if I lost you. What good will going to bed do, outside of making me extremely happy for a while, when afterwards, we're right back where we started? At my total inability to carry my weight here?"

Her brown eyes shining, she stared at him for a long moment. "I don't know what I'd do if I lost you, either," she finally said softly.

Clearing her throat, she sat up straight. "Let's back up a little. I'm the one with the experience here. First, I don't agree you can't help. I *do know* we transferred energy when your magic center woke up. I felt it. We simply have to figure out how to activate the conscious ability in you—like we had to wake up your center in the first place."

He put his hands on his hips to stop from punching the wall in frustration. He wasn't getting through to her about the seriousness of what they faced. She thought she knew it all again. Thought it would be simplistic and easy. A typical rookie mistake.

She kept talking. "Second. Are you getting *a single, even a tiny* hunch about the Stone? Its or our destruction? Or another bad outcome?"

"No. My only active hunches say we should mate and I'm critical," he admitted after concentrating on his mechanism—for all the help it gave him. He jumped when a jab hit him in the stomach. "The damned imperative just took a bite."

"Probably telling you to get on with it. Okay." She

made a shooing motion as if to wave the problem away. "Third. You agree, we're soul mates?"

"Yeah." He had to smile. *That* was the only thing he was sure of. "Commitment and all."

"So do I. Let me think for a minute. How do I share energy?" She grimaced, little stress lines appearing around her mouth, like she was being rushed. He knew how she felt. Frowning, she sat back on the couch and crossed her arms. Stared at the coffee table. Frowned some more.

He was about to interrupt her concentration when a crafty expression crossed her face, and she stood up. Positioning herself in the middle of the room, she pointed to a spot on the rug about three feet from her. "Stand there."

He moved to the spot and faced her. "What now?"

"Fourth. There's something we haven't investigated, and it might bring us closer to sharing. Create a lightball about the size of a baseball, and push all the power you can into it."

"You mean to see if they merge like when I learned to cast *lux*? They coalesced independent of direction from us. What's that got to do with our transfer?"

She put her hands on her hips and gave her one of those shut-up-and-do-it looks his bosses so often used. "If our energies can blend passively, and they melt together like Defenders' power does in the ring, then we ought to be able to move the stuff between us actively. Come on, what do we have to lose by trying?"

"You have a point." In fact, he'd forgotten all about their merged lightball. He revised his estimate of her know-it-all tendencies—rookies often came up with new approaches. Thank God, he had a smart soul mate. If her idea had a remote chance to work, or at least to get them closer to the goal, he'd try it.

"Lux!" His bright blue ball popped into existence, and he grinned at it. "I have to admit, some of this magic stuff is plain old fun."

"And it just gets better all the time," she said with a wink. "*Lux!*"

Her indigo-violet ball floated next to his.

Slowly, they began to merge and grow.

When the combined sphere reached basketball size and the colors were stirring around, forming miniature whirlpools, it looked like a blue version of Jupiter—with a big indigo spot. He and Irenee lifted their hands and cupped them in a cage around the glowing ball.

"Ouch!" Jim jerked, but managed to stay in contact with the surface. "Did you feel the shock?"

"When my fingers touched yours, I got a little jolt."

"Little? My hair stood on end. It didn't do that before."

"We hadn't acknowledged the soul-mate situation at that time, either," she said. "The jolt must be connected to our connection now. This reminds me of holding my sword—like live energy between my hands."

He didn't want to think about how dangerous that must be, so he asked, "What do we do now? Make the cage smaller like before?"

"Let's take it slow. What are you feeling? My hands are tingling, and I can feel a pulse, a throb, in time with my heartbeat."

Gripping the ball a little tighter, he concentrated on the sensations for a few seconds. "Yeah, me, too. I don't think the pulse is coming *from* the ball alone, even though the colors are moving faster. It's beating with my heart, too. All three of us must be in sync."

"Or the two of us are, and the ball's a conduit. Okay, let's do what we did last time."

He pushed as he had before, to compress the ball and intertwine his fingers with hers. This time, however, the light did not dim. Instead, it grew brighter. The tingling began to run up his arms. "Irenee? I can feel prickles up to my shoulders. Is that normal?"

"I don't have the slightest idea," she replied. "I've never done anything like this before, never touched another's lightball, never even heard of two melting together. The way the balls merge looks so much like the energy ring forming in a pentagon, it's got to be related to energy transfer. Isn't it exciting? Keep going."

What? Never done it before? Some expert. Here they

went again, operating on the spur of the moment and without thinking it through. However, the process was certainly causing a different result from the last time. She was right: they couldn't stop now.

The blue-indigo-violet light streamed out of the openings in their cage. When their fingers were laced together and the ball, about the size of a softball, was between their palms, the luminescence suddenly folded back upon itself and surrounded their hands in a shimmering blanket.

"Holy shit! It feels like an electric current all through my body."

"Me, too," Irenee said. "Can you feel the flow, like something's running along your nerves?"

"Yeah. It's beginning to settle, right in my center."

"Hot damn! That's magic energy for sure! Keep pushing."

When their fingers were totally entwined and overlapped the backs of the other's hands, they moved their wrists so his right palm met her left and vice versa with no space between them and with their thumbs touching. The ball vanished, but the glow remained.

"Oh, wow," she whispered. "Okay, don't let go, whatever you do."

"Not a chance," he replied—not with every cell in his body crying out for some of the power flowing around his hands.

"I'm going to send you some of my energy, like we do among Defenders when we share by touch. It's going to come from my center, out my arms, to your hands, exactly like you were my sword. See if you can pull the power into your center. Ready? One, two, three."

The prickles in his hands increased in tempo, like a thousand pins were dancing on his palms, and he felt a force pushing through her palms into his. "Something's coming, the pulse picked up, and I can feel . . . it's like holding a hot cup and feeling the heat warm your hand."

"Imagine pulling the warmth into your center. The energy has to be in your well before you can use it."

"Okay." He felt sweat break out on his forehead as he coaxed, pulled, and tugged at the stuff. He succeeded in moving it only about an inch to his wrist.

"Don't work so hard," Irenee murmured. "Open yourself and let it flow."

Without letting go of her, Jim rolled his shoulders and forced himself to relax. *Flow*, she said.

He closed his eyes and thought of his bucket. How would he get energy from her to it? If her hand was a faucet, he could open it with a twist. He rubbed his palms back and forth across hers, aligned them carefully, and with his fingers on the back of her hands, pushed her palms into his.

Visualizing the waiting energy as water, he twisted their hands ever so slightly. The pressure against his palm, then his wrist, increased. Another little turn, and the warmth moved along his arm to his elbow. One more . . .

Yeeeessssss. Energy poured through his arms, into his chest, and into his bucket until it would hold no more.

"Oh, wow," Irenee whispered. "The dam burst."

"What a rush!" Jim opened his eyes. Though their hands had ceased to glow, they were still warm. He took a second to savor the triumph, before he sobered up. "But how do I send it back to you? That's the key, isn't it?"

She shrugged. "To get energy to my sword when I first started, I'd visualize a line, or a stream, or a pipe coming from my well, up my nerves to my arms and out my hands. I'd concentrate on my supply and pull the power up."

"Okay, here goes." He didn't close his eyes or move his hands. Instead, he imagined "pushing" the energy from his bucket up the path it had created coming down. It worked, but sluggishly and more like a trickle than a good flow. He pushed harder, felt the energy coalesce into a stream and begin to climb his nerves. *Come on, get up there . . .*

Pressure built, first in his bucket, then his chest, when the energy moved. It grew and grew until . . . heat rushed up his chest and down his arms. When it reached his hands, warm magical power gushed directly into hers.

"Yeah!" he shouted. The power poured from him. The feeling—and relief—was almost as good as sex.

"Oh, wow! It's like a flood! Wooo hooo!" she cried.

"Man, are you strong! Back it off if you can. I can only take so much."

He felt her closing the energy stream from her side, and he managed to get better control and turn off his faucet before his bucket emptied.

"Let's try it again, this time slower," she suggested, and they traded a couple of turns of sending, receiving, and moderating the flow.

Once they had established equilibrium, but were still clasping hands, he did what he'd been afraid to do up to now. The last thing he wanted to see on her face was knowledge of his failure. Having succeeded, he could look directly into her eyes. Shining back at him were triumph and satisfaction and . . .

Like a thunderclap, desire shook him from the top of his head to the bottom of his feet. He stretched their still-clasped hands out to the sides, and the movement pulled her flush against him. She came up on her toes and lifted her chin, and he kissed her. As their lips met, their centers aligned, and the energy within them hummed. His entire body hardened.

He let go of her hands to wrap his arms around her and hold on tight. He was hers, and she was his, and he wasn't going to let her go. Oh, God, she felt so good, she smelled like heaven, and she tasted like chocolate-covered strawberries. He let himself indulge.

Eventually, he raised his head and gazed into her eyes

again. They grinned breathlessly at each other like two giddy idiots who'd just won the lottery. He leaned his forehead against hers. He wasn't sure what he referred to—the magic transfer or the kiss—when he managed to gasp, "Oh, honey, that was incredible."

"Yes," she panted. "I've never . . . never experienced . . . anything like this before."

Although he wasn't sure of her reference either, he didn't care. Not with his arms holding her, his center humming, and his body aching.

Still breathing hard, she gave him a victorious smile. "Now do you believe we can exchange power? You can truly help me? We can fight the Stone together?"

Where did she get the lung power to talk? Besides, who gave a crap about power exchange when all he wanted to do was . . . what he was supposed to do. Their energy exchange and that kiss had blown away all his doubts. He took a deep breath and forced the words out, "Yes. I believe. Before we do anything else, though, we follow the rest of Whipple's orders."

She blinked at him. "What orders?"

He swung her up into his arms. "What our leader commanded. We mate."

Laughing, he carried her into the bedroom feeling like he'd won an enormous battle, and he was about to get his reward.

CHAPTER TWENTY-SIX

At Jim's words and especially his actions, Irenee's heart began to race again—not that it had truly returned to normal after his kiss. He was right. She had his declaration they were mates, and he had hers. While neither had been the most romantic thing in the world, both had been sufficient. She had no more doubts. The time for talk and waiting was past.

Still, she might have some mating surprises for him, thanks to her discussion with the Whipples and her father.

She and Jim had already experienced power between them, but the exchange was probably minuscule compared to actual mating. She couldn't even imagine what would happen when they actually came together. Her center fluttered in anticipation.

She didn't have time to think about it, however, because once in the darkened bedroom, he lowered her feet to the floor and kissed her again. She wrapped her arms around his neck and kissed him back.

And fell into a maelstrom of longing and wanting

and craving.

She couldn't get enough of him. Couldn't tangle tongues enough, couldn't run her hands over him enough, couldn't rub herself against him enough. She groaned, both in eager expectation and in response to his touch holding her head, then sliding down her back, around to the front over her breasts, and finally to her waist, to pull her even tighter against him.

When their centers aligned and vibrated in harmony, their heartbeats synchronized, and they drew back and looked straight into each other's eyes.

"You're mine," he murmured.

"You're mine," she answered.

He took her mouth again, hungrier, more demanding, and she reveled in their frenzy of kisses and touching.

Soon, even kisses were not enough. She needed more.

He began to unbutton her blouse. Yes, that was it. They needed less. They had too many clothes on.

She shrugged off her blouse, and he pulled his shirt over his head. She reached behind to undo her bra while he slid the straps down. When the bra hit the floor, she practically threw herself at him.

Oooohhhh! The sensation of being skin to skin was glorious. He was hot as a fireball and as hard as a stone wall. When he fondled her breasts and rubbed her suddenly so-sensitive nipples, internal sparks traveled from them to her center and below. She began to ache.

When he pulled back, she protested and tried to recapture his hands. He grabbed hers instead.

"Wait, honey, and let me look at you for a minute." He released her hands to turn on the bedside lamp.

Oh, good idea. If she had enjoyed observing his bare chest before, the sight of him now stopped her breath. The soft light beautifully illuminated him, all broad shoulders and strong muscles and a light dusting of brown hair on his chest. Her fingers itched to explore.

At the same time, he looked at her, and she could feel the path his gaze took over her own body. When she took a deep breath, trying to get much needed air into her lungs, he groaned.

He swooped her up and deposited her on the bed. Mumbling something about where the unfasten spell was when he needed it, he opened her belt buckle, pants button, and zipper. He slid her pants down and off, taking her underwear, shoes, and socks with them.

"Oh, Irenee, you are so beautiful," he murmured while he leaned over her and raised her hand to his lips. He kissed her palm, and the simple caress made her toes curl.

He placed her hand by her side and straightened to make quick work of taking off the rest of his clothes, while he continued to study her.

She was surprised to realize she had no sense of modesty or shyness at all. In fact, she enjoyed being looked at—by him. He obviously liked it—the heat coming from his gaze would have melted every flake in a twelve-inch Chicago snowfall.

She did some studying of her own. From his muscle definition, he must work out, although he was by no means a bodybuilder. More like extremely fit. The ripple of the muscles under his skin as he bent and rose fascinated her. She noted some scars, one a long gash on his left side, evidence of his dangerous occupation. His sex rose proudly from its nest of dark curls, and even though she knew better, she couldn't help wondering a little if it would fit.

When he lay down beside her and took her in his arms, their bodies met from top to bottom. She ceased worrying about anything.

If she thought it pleasant to be skin to skin with their chests, full body contact far surpassed that mild delight. To touch and be touched was enchanting. To curl a leg around his and slide a foot along his calf was thrilling. To feel his thigh pressing against the aching junction between her legs was marvelous. To kiss and be kissed was glorious.

It was too much to take in all at once, so she gave up trying. The most she could concentrate on was one piece at a time.

First, his mouth. His lips were soft, but firm, his tongue agile as she returned his kiss. When he ended the kiss, he nibbled his way to her ear and neck. She discovered she was ticklish in one particular spot, and he chuckled when she squirmed. He paused to lick the pulse point in her neck—which only made her heart beat faster—before continuing to her shoulder and collarbone.

Then, his hand—large, rough, and callused. He leaned on one elbow above her and with the other hand caressed her from her foot up her leg and her hip to stop right under her breast.

Oh, how she wanted him to touch her there. She could feel her nipples tightening, her breasts swelling, and she pushed the side of her body up as much as she could to give him a hint. When he didn't take it, she ran her fingers into his hair and tugged.

He raised his head and kissed her on the lips before she could tell him what she wanted. His kiss did nothing to lessen her need, so she put her hand on top of his and dragged it up to where she wanted it.

He raised his head again, gave her a devilish smile, and swirled his fingers around her breast, finally tweaking the nipple. She gasped as the contact increased the ache between her legs. She didn't have time, however, to process how it was affecting her because, without a pause, he took her into his mouth and suckled.

Oh, yes! She closed her eyes, arched her back to give him better access, and moaned when new nerve endings sparked again, in her breasts, in her center, in her womb.

He kissed his way to her other breast, and the effects doubled.

They tripled when he cupped her curls and stroked a finger into her folds. They quadrupled when he slid the finger into her. They went off the scale when he also rubbed his thumb over her little nub of nerve endings. She moaned again when every muscle in her clenched.

"Irenee." His voice was hoarse and low.

She opened her eyes. He was staring at her, his face stark, a flush on his cheekbones, his eyes so dark that only a rim of golden green showed.

"I'm yours. Are you mine?"

"Yes," she answered, her voice as throaty as his. "I'm yours, and you're mine."

He gave her a soft kiss, moved between her legs, and braced himself on his arms above her. "Guide me into you."

She took him in her hands, marveling for a second at the heated steel beneath the silky covering before raising her hips and positioning him at her entrance. She lifted her eyes to his, and he slowly pushed inside.

"Jim?" A little panic struck her when the pressure increased and she felt herself stretching. It only hurt a little, and she told herself to relax. It wasn't easy to do, however, as he filled her.

"Shhh. It's all right," Jim assured her in a grating tone. "You're so tight and so wet, and it feels so good."

He leaned down and took her mouth, his tongue pushing deep, retreating, plunging deep again.

His hot kiss took her mind off everything except returning it, and when he raised his head again, she realized he was completely inside her. If there had been pain, she hadn't felt it. She did feel stretched, but not uncomfortable. In fact, when she looked at them joined together, a sense of completeness filled her. Her center fluttered happily. This was the way they were supposed to be.

"Put your legs around me," he grated out.

When she did, he began to move.

Slowly at first. Faster as she picked up his rhythm. He started adding a little twist to his hips when they met hers, a movement that touched her nub and sent shooting stars through her system. She had to be incandescent by now.

He came down on his elbows and kissed her again—deeper, a little more roughly. A claiming, possessive, I'm-yours-you're-mine kiss. She returned it.

Magic energy began to hum around them.

Irenee's world narrowed to Jim's kiss and their bodies moving together. His tongue was matching his body in rhythm. She gripped first his arms, then his sides, as his hips rose and fell. Energy sparked throughout her body, increasingly so where they touched. As she met his thrusts, pressure began to build inside her, a pressure that arched her back, pushed her upward, tightened all her muscles.

She was climbing, striving to reach a point she couldn't see, but knew was just there only a few inches beyond her reach. He must be trying to get there, too, because they were both groaning with each thrust.

The fireworks within her burst faster, bigger, became Roman candles and sparkling flowers on the back of her eyelids and within her.

Just as she reached the peak, the shooting stars, the lightning bolts, the fireballs, all exploded into a conflagration of colors and heat and light . . . and ecstasy.

The shock waves buffeted them both for what seemed like hours and left them tangled together, breathless and exhausted.

The world slowly came back into perspective. He slid off to her side, an action that disconnected them and left her momentarily disoriented. His pulling her against him and her arms about him settled her equilibrium.

How splendid, she thought when her brain began functioning again. How marvelous making love was. How absolutely incredible her soul mate. She kissed his shoulder, the only part of him her lips could reach, and hugged him tight.

After his breathing slowed to a normal rate, he opened his eyes, looked deep into hers, and whispered, "Oh, wow!"

"Holy shit," she answered with a smile.

He laughed and loosened his arms. Leaning back, he brushed a lock of hair from her forehead and gave her a soft kiss.

"I think I was hit by a magic bombshell," she said.

"Good. I'm glad I'm not the only one who feels that way." He ran a finger down her shoulder and around her breast.

She put her hand on top of his to stop his exploration so she could think about what had happened. "Did you hear the energy hum?"

"All I could hear was the blood pounding in my ears. What does a hum mean? Are we bonded now?"

"I don't know about the hum, but I don't think so about the bonding. There's something we need to do in the middle of it. Bridget was explicit."

He didn't let her hand stop him from fondling, when he asked, "Bridget? What's she got to do with us and this?"

"She gave me some tips for mating." She grabbed hold of his busy hand and laced her fingers with his. She looked into his eyes and felt her body respond. She didn't seem to be as tired as all the exertion should have made her. "I'll show you the next time. How soon can we do it again?"

He groaned, seemed to think for a minute, then grinned. "It looks like I'm beginning to recover already. Maybe there's something to the soul-mate stuff after all. Fergus did say something about increased stamina, didn't he? Let me get something to clean us up."

He left the bed for the bathroom and returned in a minute with a damp washcloth.

When he sat on the bed with the clear intention of helping her "clean up," she took the cloth out of his hand. The idea was suddenly too much, too new, too personal. She rose, saying, "I'll be right back."

He was sitting on top of the bedspread, so she couldn't even try to wrap it around her. Naked, she scooted into the bathroom and closed the door behind her. Men, or at least this one, had no sense of propriety, of modesty. She looked at herself in the mirror and rolled her eyes. Of course, considering the intimacy of what they'd been doing . . . She shook her head and watched her hair fly. It was still too much.

Everything else was, however, just right. She gave herself a big grin and turned on the water.

After she'd taken care of the necessities and run a brush through her hair, she opened the door and peeked around it. He had laid the spread back and was sprawled across the bed. Sleeping? She stood for a moment with her hands on her hips. Wasn't that exactly like the stereotype of a man? Falling asleep right away?

She ought to give him some time to recuperate. "Men aren't machines," Fergus had said.

Shc already knew they weren't, of course. Come to

think of it, after the day she'd put in, she could use a nap, too. She climbed into the bed next to him, nudged him until he moved over so she had enough room, and lay down.

She didn't think he woke up, but his arms went around her, and he spooned against her backside.

Oh, wow, was it wonderful, snuggled up against her soul mate. She closed her eyes and let herself drift off, her last thought how stupendous bonding would be.

CHAPTER TWENTY-SEVEN

Feeling absolutely wonderful, Jim floated on his back on the bed while warm, smooth hands glided over his body, massaging his tired muscles, soothing his aches. If he was a big cat, he'd be purring. He tried a purr, sort of a grunting hum. Life was good.

The hands worked on his shoulders, slowly moved to his chest. Not too hard, not too soft, the pressure was just right. They continued down his rib cage and went around the end of his breastbone. His center was quiet, for which he was grateful. Damned disturbing—and painful—the way it intruded itself into his business.

He would have frowned, except he felt too damn . . . content. That was the word, *content.* He didn't even have the energy to open his eyes. He did a purr again. Life was *really* good.

The hands moved to his sides and met in the middle over his navel. His cock twitched. It wanted those hands lower. It grew and hardened, in anticipation—or was it invitation?

Whatever.

Slowly, so slowly, the hands drifted farther. By the time they reached its base, his cock was fully erect and wanted to be touched so badly, it was almost crying.

He squirmed, trying to bring it in contact with those hands.

The hands moved again, encircled him, slid up . . . and down . . . and up—oh, yes!—and down . . . and stopped.

The hands were attached to a woman—his soul mate. He knew and was glad, but he wanted more. She was straddling his legs and hadn't let go of him. Could he hope . . . ?

He felt her warm breath on him. He froze, hoping, praying . . .

She gave him a little lick. Then another. And took him in her mouth.

Thank you, God!

The pleasure speared through him so acutely that he opened his eyes—and stared right into two pools of twinkling dark chocolate. She gave him another lick and sat up.

"I wondered when you'd wake up," she said as she played with him, running those clever fingers up and down his length, giving him a little swirl over the tip. She was smiling and looked like temptation personified.

The combination of her touch and his vision tightened every muscle in his body and made him harder than steel.

He held out his arms. "Come here." The words came out in a rasp. His throat was so tight, his blood nowhere near his brain, he was surprised he could think, much less speak, at all.

She released her hold and moved up on her hands and knees to hover over him.

Perfect. All he had to do was reach up and fondle to his heart's content. Which he did.

She settled her lower half right where he wanted it, with his cock between her legs. Smirking at him, she slid her slick folds up and down along him. His eyes almost crossed with pleasure.

She grinned. Bent over and gave him a little kiss. Grinned some more.

"You're pleased with yourself, aren't you?" he managed to force out.

"Yep," she answered, "and I have something to show you."

"Yeah?" What was left? He'd seen it all.

"Yeah." She raised up, positioned him, and took him inside her all the way.

As her tight muscles enveloped him, he took a deep breath and closed his eyes at the sheer satisfaction of being back inside her. God in heaven, the practitioners had it right with this no-barriers stuff. His hips made a little thrust up without his thinking about it.

"You need to take your hands off my chest for a minute," she said.

He opened his eyes at the suggestion. She was serious. His center gave a lurch, seemed to rev up its vibrations. He moved his hands to her hips.

"To bond, we need to be making love and to touch each other's center at the same time."

"That's it?"

"Bridget's instructions. The man needs to be inside the woman."

Despite the "location" right where he wanted to be, the process seemed weird, too simple, and somewhat anticlimactic to him. Being inside her was fine. Only touching her center? He shrugged mentally. It certainly wouldn't hurt to go along with her, however—especially with the "inside" part.

"So, I touch you . . ." He placed the tips of the fingers of his right hand on her breastbone. "Do you feel anything?"

"Not really. Put your whole hand on me."

He did so.

"Hmmm. Still nothing. Maybe if I . . ." She did the same to him with her right hand. "Ahhh."

"Yeah, my center started vibrating." Not to be left out of their activities, his cock started throbbing to remind him exactly where it was and what it wanted.

"Mine, too. I can feel warmth spreading, but it's not

different from before." She frowned. "I wonder what we're doing wrong."

"Maybe it will come to us. Right now . . ." He ran his free hand up her side. "Right now, let's not waste the opportunity. I'm inside you, and if one of us doesn't start moving, I'm going to suffer great bodily harm."

Her eyebrows went up, and she said in a mock-serious tone, "Oh, by all means, we don't want that to happen."

With his free hand, he pulled her down and kissed her. Their hands still caught between them, she began to move also. He set a slow rhythm she easily matched, and he took his time with the kisses, teasing her tongue, giving her little pecks, then delving deep.

Slow, leisurely lovemaking, exactly as he liked it.

His deliberate pace didn't last long, however.

Within a minute, pressure began to build inside him. Serious pressure. Climatic pressure. Unlike he'd ever felt before, not centered only in his groin, but in his middle, too.

His center warmed, heated, flamed, sent sparks along his nerves to every part of his body.

He moved faster, kissed harder, held her tighter.

It wasn't enough.

She must be feeling the same thing because she moved faster, kissed harder, held him tighter.

It still wasn't enough.

Surrender! Stop thinking! Give in to all of it! Become

soul mates! Whether he was having a hunch or hearing from the imperative, he didn't know and didn't care. He had to do what it was telling him.

He threw himself and her into the most tumultuous lovemaking he'd ever experienced.

Jim knew the exact moment he lost control. His conscious mind went blank, his kiss turned voracious, his free hand roamed all over her, his thrusts lifted his hips clear off the bed. She responded like a possessed woman, riding him wildly, plundering his mouth, sucking on his tongue.

To every part of his body, the sparks shot out of his center like from a machine gun. He knew if he opened his eyes, he'd see fireworks all around them.

Then he felt it—magic energy flowing from him to her, from her to him, around in a course through their hands, their centers, their mouths, their joined bodies.

More than fireworks were going off. Power, sheer *power* raged through them as they both convulsed, their simultaneous climaxes fusing them together for a long moment.

She collapsed on top of him, and he couldn't gather the strength to even take his hand out from between them.

Holy . . . He didn't finish the expletive either before he slept.

Irenee opened her eyes, but she didn't move. Her

muscles ached in the most interesting places. She was still on top of Jim, and their hands were still caught between them. Her head, turned toward his face, lay on her free arm, which was stretched up on the pillow next to his head. She took a deep breath, and a combination of his unique scent and pure sex filled her lungs. Her center fluttered—*smugly*.

Just when she decided he wasn't awake, his hand moved slowly over her back, and his chest rose on his own inhalation.

She knew she ought to change position, at least get their hands out from between them. It was so hard, however, to raise even her head, much less her body.

"Irenee? Are you all right?" His voice sounded strained.

She nodded. "I think so. How about you?"

"Fine, I think. What a ride."

"Did you have sparks?"

"I had the entire Chicago Fourth-of-July and New-Years fireworks shows combined."

"I could have lit up the lakefront clear to Milwaukee." She straightened out her legs and managed to slide to her right off his body and into the curve of his left arm.

He flapped his right hand around. "Thanks. It was going to sleep."

She propped herself up on her right elbow—it wasn't easy when her muscles protested—and turned to him.

"We *must* be bonded now."

"God, I hope so. I'm all for good sex, but if that's what happens to us every time, I won't live to see forty." He laid his hand on his stomach and rubbed his center. "Okay, how do we tell?"

"Cast *lux*, I guess. If we've gone up in level potential, we're bonded."

"Lux!" they said at the same time. His lightball glowed indigo with blue swirls. Hers shone violet with indigo streaks.

The two balls quickly merged.

"Wow!" she said. "I think the mating worked."

"I still can't read the color gradations. How much did we gain?"

"Before you were a nine to ten, a solid blue. Mostly indigo with blue means a level eleven, for sure. I was a twelve, indigo with violet. I'm probably a thirteen now with more violet than indigo. How does your center feel?"

"Happy. A little bigger than it was. Or deeper. Or something. More."

"Mine, too." She sat up straighter and scooted over to the edge of the bed so they weren't touching. "We need to see if we can exchange energy like Defenders do. Cut your power to the lightball."

The large ball vanished.

Jim sat up slowly, gave her a skeptical look. "God, woman, I don't understand how you can even move, much less think, after all the energy we just used. I'm surprised I even got *lux* out."

"I'm exhilarated, and maybe I'm more accustomed to spell-casting and energy use than you are. We can always wait if you'd like."

"No, I'm game, I guess." He rubbed his center. "It's fine. What do I do?"

"Gather your energy, push it out your hands, and see if you can make it coalesce in front of you. That's what Defenders do. When I'm receiving energy, I usually think of it as a stream."

"Okay, here goes." He held out his hands, palms up. After a few seconds, he said, "I'm holding some. I can see it. Do you?"

"I can see an amorphous, glowing, very pale blue blob. Send it this way."

The blob floated over to her. She tried to grasp it, first with her hand, then with her mind, finally by reaching out from her center with her own energy, except . . . "I can't get hold of it. I tried three different ways. It bumps up against me, but won't come inside."

"Great." He flopped back down on the bed.

"However." She sat up straighter when a notion came to her. "Let's try something."

He gave her a what-kind-of-idea-do-you-have-now look. "What?"

"I touch your center, and you touch mine."

"What will that do? I don't think I could survive another experience like the last one so soon."

"Dad can transfer his energy both across space and by touch. Maybe, since you're not technically a Defender, you can only use physical contact. Every time we exchanged energy, when your center woke up, and when we worked with the merged lightballs, and when we bonded, it's been through touch."

"Okay, I guess it won't hurt." Although he still looked dubious, he turned to face her and placed his right hand on her center.

She put her left hand on his center. "I can feel your center vibrating. It feels like it's purring."

"I feel yours, too, and it's warm."

"Try sending me some energy, like you did when we were holding hands."

He stared off into space for a few seconds. "Okay, here comes some, I hope."

Power poured from his hand directly into her energy well. "Oh, oh, oh. Great. Can you slow it down a little?"

He squinted his eyes and concentrated. The rate of energy flow decreased and stopped altogether. "I think I slowed it first and stopped it. I'll have to work more on modulation."

"Yes, the flow did cease. Don't worry about putting me on overload. I can only take so much at a time when

I'm not sending it out my sword, but when I am, I'll need a lot more. We don't want you to expend energy needlessly, either." She took her hand off his chest.

"Okay." He looked at his hand and smiled like he'd made a discovery. "Speaking of expending energy . . ." He moved it over to cup her breast.

Damn, the man's touch sent little lightning bolts flying through her, no matter what. She leaned over and kissed him, and one thing led to another—without the total combustion of the previous time.

CHAPTER TWENTY-EIGHT

The next morning while they were eating breakfast, Whipple came to call. He accepted a cup of coffee, scrutinized them both up and down, and got straight to the point. "Excellent! You're soul mates and bonded. I'm glad that's settled. Can you transfer energy?"

Jim looked from him to Irenee, who shrugged.

"Why are you so sure?" Jim asked.

"The happiness in the room is so thick," Whipple answered with a grin, "I feel like I'm swimming through chocolate pudding. What about the energy? Did you try to make an exchange, uh, 'independently' of anything else?"

As a vivid memory of the "anything else" ran through his brain, Jim hoped he wasn't blushing for the first time in his life. He concentrated on the question. "Yes, we did. We tried it both touching and not touching. It appears touching is the only way I can transfer energy to her."

"We've both gone up a level, me to thirteen, and Jim to eleven, from what I can tell by the colors of our lightballs," Irenee said.

"Splendid! You two practice today. Several of us are going to visit Bruce Ubell this afternoon, whether he wants to see us or not. We'll meet later to report the outcome." With those orders, the big wizard left.

After cleaning up the dishes, Jim and Irenee called Johanna, told her of their progress, and met her in the Defenders' building in one of the underground rooms.

Jim blinked when they went into the large five-sided space. "Whoa. Much stronger spells. What goes on here?"

"It's a Sword room, where we practice by destroying tiny, relatively weak evil items," Irenee answered while she put on her black robe. "If we were actually destroying an item, we'd put it in the crystal bowl on the pedestal in the middle."

"We're not going to destroy anything today," Johanna said, also donning her Sword garment. "We need to get an idea of your strength and the flow-through from you to Irenee and out her sword."

Jim put on his gray novice robe and joined them next to the pedestal. "What do I do?"

"I'm going to activate a protective pentagon," Johanna answered. "It won't let uncontrolled energy in or out. You stand behind Irenee with your hands on her waist. She'll draw her sword and send a beam out the end and into the bowl to expend energy. You start transferring your energy to her, and we'll see how it goes from there."

"Okay," Jim said. He wasn't totally certain of his ability—after all, they had clothes on now, where their previous transfers had been skin to skin. He shrugged mentally; he wouldn't know if he could until he tried. Funny, he seemed to be coming to that conclusion a lot lately.

They got into position, and Johanna cast *castellum*. Glowing multicolored walls extended to the ceiling. Jim squinted and concentrated on Irenee. As he did, the glow faded to a manageable level.

"I'm going to draw my sword," Irenee said. "Whatever you do, don't touch it. I'll have it at a very low level, but it can hurt you just the same."

Standing behind her, Jim put his hands on her waist. "I'm ready whenever you are."

She brought her hands together in front of her in what looked like an interlocking golf-club grip, little finger on her right hand hooked between her left index and middle fingers. Through the robe, he could feel her energy moving. It was swirling around inside her without a real direction.

Whoa. He blinked when suddenly she held a glowing sword in her hands. The blade was about two-and-a-half feet long, and it was red.

The sword hummed and shimmered with live magic power. Jim knew he was looking at a fine, hand—or rather *mind*—crafted weapon, beautiful and deadly at the same time. For her, it had to be like holding a live electrical line, and she held it in her unprotected hands. One slip and who knew what could happen? A cold chill settled in his bones. The obvious and inherent danger to her was not pleasant to contemplate.

"Not so tight, Jim," Irenee said.

With an effort, he took a deep breath and loosened his fingers, which he had gripped harder without realizing it. He told himself to relax. She was calm and in control of her sword. She knew what she was doing. There was no threat here.

Why then, were his antennae wiggling?

He had no time to consider a nebulous hunch. She pointed her sword at the pedestal, and a red beam of energy shot out the end into the bowl.

"What can you feel, Jim?" Johanna asked.

Ah, now her internal power had direction. "A little stream of energy is leaving her center, going out her arms to her sword. Uh . . ."

He dropped his hands from her waist when he realized what he was seeing.

"What?" both women asked.

"I can see an aura around you, Irenee. It's still there, even though I'm not touching you."

"What color is it?" Irenee looked back at him over her shoulder.

"Violet."

"Well, it sure took long enough for your ability to kick in," Irenee said.

"Let's keep going," Johanna instructed.

Jim returned his hands to her waist. "I'm ready. I can feel your energy moving."

"Good," Johanna said. "Irenee, increase the power."

The sword's colors changed to orange, to yellow, to green, and the beam matched the shades.

"I can feel her using more energy," Jim said. "The stream's bigger and faster, and there's a sort of vibration inside her. It's like what you feel if you put your hand on a microwave when it's cooking."

Irenee laughed. "I never thought of it that way. Start transmitting."

He took a deep breath and concentrated. The power moved up from his center as he directed, down his arms and out his hands, directly into her body.

"Reduce the flow a little," she said. "Move your hands more to my back, right behind my center."

He followed her instructions, and they played with placement for several minutes. She was finally satisfied with the transfer when his hands were inverted so his fingers pointed downward. Because of their height difference, the position was more comfortable for him also.

They practiced, varying the flow from none all the way up to Irenee's new level, until lunch. Then they ate like they were both in the defensive line of the Chicago Bears and went back to her condo for a nap. Johanna had suggested they get some rest, and Jim was happy to go along. He was exhausted.

Irenee had a couple of calls to make—yeah, she was used to the magic stuff and had energy to burn while he was still a wimp—so he stripped to his underwear and flopped on the bed. Sleep, however, didn't come immediately like it usually did. His hunch antennae gave a wiggle every once in a while. Try though he might, he couldn't figure out what their problem was.

When she came to bed, he pulled her into his arms. Everything quickly got a lot better.

CHAPTER TWENTY-NINE

"There are some people here to see you, Mr. Bruce," Sedgwick said from the doorway of the study, his voice shaking. "They're Defenders, I think."

Bruce looked up from the financial newspaper he was reading. It was about time they showed up. "Who are they?"

"Only one gave his name, a Mr. Fergus Whipple. When I explained you weren't receiving visitors, he told me they were here on official practitioner business and you'd want to see them. He emphasized the word *want*. What shall I tell them?"

Bruce put the paper aside. At first he'd thought about receiving the expected delegation in the living room, but soon discarded the idea. The study was a much better place. Not only because his grandfather was "watching over" the proceedings. Alton—the idiot—had actually cast with his Stone here. The residue from his foolhardy actions would mask emanations from Bruce's own Stone below in its secret room—if there was the slightest leakage.

The old man had really done a magnificent job shielding the Stone's hiding place and its use. Bruce, however, wasn't about to take chances with Defenders in the house. He'd choose the time and place for a battle—and he knew there would be one.

What kind of heavyweights would the Defenders send? He'd heard of Whipple. Who else? "Show them in here, Sedgwick. We won't be having refreshments."

The butler nodded and left. Within a minute, he ushered four people into the study.

Bruce rose, came around the desk, and shook hands with them as they introduced themselves: Fergus Whipple, Sword; John Baldwin, Sword, member of the Defender Council; Miriam Chandler, president of the Defender Council; and Rachel Goldfarb, member of the High Council.

Bruce smiled to himself; heavyweights, indeed, but no one he and his Stone couldn't handle.

He offered them chairs around the rectangular conference table he'd had placed in the corner, right over the floor safe where Alton had hidden his Stone. If one picked up even a whiff of either his or his cousin's item, none gave any indication. Good. He'd play the complete innocent and give them no grounds for a preemptive search. When all were seated, he asked, "What can I do for you?"

Whipple began the interrogation with no preliminaries. "What's the prognosis on your cousin?"

"Not good. Nobody can decide what caused his collapse. All the doctors have diagnosed is some sort of brain seizure. They won't predict when he might return to consciousness." He kept his expression completely sad. What a great mourner he made.

Whipple responded with scorn. "Oh, come, Mr. Ubell. We're all aware of what happened to Alton Finster. He had in his possession an item of evil magic. We confiscated it as is our right and duty, and when we destroyed it, its death also damaged him. In its place, we left a notice of confiscation. Do you expect us to believe you don't know any of this?"

"What? An evil item? Alton had it? Oh, my God! No, I didn't know a thing about it. Where was the item? When did you find it? How?" Bruce sat back in pretended shock and then forward in fake concern. He really ought to take up acting. He was giving a performance worthy of an award.

"That's bull, Ubell," Baldwin stated. "You were with Finster when he collapsed. The item was in the safe right under this table."

"What? What safe?" Bruce leaned to glance under the table, shrugged, and, shaking his head, resumed his upright position. He met Baldwin's unfriendly gaze.

"The only safe I have seen in this room is the one behind my grandfather's portrait. The night after the gala, or more accurately in the early morning, Alton called me at home and said to come here quickly. He sounded ill. I came and found him collapsed on the floor right there." He pointed to a spot in front of the desk.

"Alton was in no shape to speak at all, certainly not about a safe or a magic item. May I remind you, this isn't my house. I don't know all its nooks and crannies or what Alton may have hidden here." Bruce made sure to speak clearly and forcefully, without so much as a tiny quiver in his voice. It wasn't difficult. After all, he wasn't afraid of these people. They couldn't hurt him.

Miriam Chandler, a six-foot-tall woman who looked like she could bench press three hundred pounds without the aid of a strength spell and lead an army to victory at the same time, spoke with a soft voice. "In that case, you have no reason to deny us permission to search the property."

Bruce had met CEOs before who used low voices to command; he knew how to handle them. He looked from one visitor to the next and replied in the same tone, calmly, deliberately. "It's not my place to give you such permission. I'm holding onto the property and our family company for Alton and our stockholders. I can assure you I will conduct a thorough search of the premises for a confiscation notice and magical anomalies. I don't dispute your statements that you confiscated an evil item from Alton, although I can't conceive of my cousin with such an object. I don't quarrel with your seizure of it.

Your confiscation would be totally within practitioner law as I understand it."

He spread his arms in a conciliatory gesture. "Whatever Alton had, you now possess. I had nothing to do with whatever he might have done. Unless you have an order from the High Council with indisputable evidence there is some other problem item in this house, however, I must deny your request and exert my rights to protect the family, the company, and our good name."

There. Let them answer that. Did they think he didn't know the laws? What fun to use practitioner rules against them.

High Council member Rachel Goldfarb turned her gray eyes on Bruce, and the impact of her gaze confirmed the immense power rumored to be residing in her tiny body. This visitor meant business.

Bruce steeled himself to keep still and betray no emotion. He was stronger than they were, and he didn't want to call on his Stone for help—not yet.

"Mr. Ubell," Goldfarb said, "we have cause to believe an item of ancient evil magic is on these premises. Not the one Alton Finster possessed. Another. Consider my statement here today your official notification. If you have knowledge of the item, you are in violation of practitioner oath and law, and all the power of both councils will be brought to bear against you when it comes to light. If you truly do not know of the item, but find it, you are bound by oath and law to turn it over to the Defenders immediately."

Her voice and her gaze turned as hard as granite. "If you attempt to use the item, we will know it. We will come after it. Rest assured, we will find it, and we will destroy it. Your cousin played a very dangerous game. He paid a horrendous price. Take care that you do not do the same."

"I'll start searching Alton's things immediately." Bruce kept his expression serene. *What a bitch! Too bad he couldn't show her his Stone right now. Wouldn't he and it have some fun?*

With raised eyebrows, Chandler looked at her three cohorts, who each nodded slightly. She faced Bruce. "I believe we've said everything necessary. Good day to you, sir."

The foursome rose as one and left the room without another word.

Supercilious, overbearing idiots. Bruce sat in his chair and watched them go. Who did they think they were, ordering him around? They had no proof, or they would have brought the orders with them.

To expect him to give up his Stone like a good little boy. How ridiculous. Arrogant bastards and bitches, every single one of them. He hit the table with his fist at the last thought. It felt so good, he hit it three more times, once for each of his visitors.

What could he do to teach them a lesson, to show them his power, to force them to acknowledge the truth? He was inviolable, untouchable, above the world of mundane practitioners.

The familiar and wonderful and seductive oozing of his Stone's power began to swirl in his mind and his center, bringing with it truly diabolical ideas. It seemed to be trying to tell him something else, but he couldn't quite understand what. Something to do with power? No matter. He understood—and agreed with—all of its other schemes. He smiled, then chuckled, then broke out in laughter. *Oh, thank you, Stone!*

He went to his desk and pulled out of a drawer a cheap, limited-minute cell phone. He punched in a number. When the call was answered, he said, "Burt, get all the inventory out of the warehouse and start moving it. It's time to make some money."

They discussed tactics for a couple of minutes. Before he hung up, he had one more order. "Send that man of yours over here for instructions. I have another job for him. This time he'd better do it right."

He put the phone away, walked over to the decanters on a side table, and poured himself a celebratory bourbon. He held up the drink to his grandfather's portrait. "Here's to you, old man. Thanks for the Stone. Here's to death for the thieving Sabel bitch and her DEA boyfriend. They'll pay for what they did to us."

He knocked back the drink and poured himself another. Laughing again, he headed downstairs. He loved spending time communing with his Stone and contemplating revenge.

CHAPTER THIRTY

"Irenee!" Jim came awake holding his gun, standing by the side of the bed, and looking around for the threat. When he saw none, he straightened slowly from his fighting crouch. Irenee was standing on the other side, her sword glowing violet and indigo in her hands.

He looked at his own weapon. Fat lot of good it would have done him. It was exactly as he had originally placed it on the bedside chest—unloaded. He put it down again before turning to her.

"Oh, my God," she whispered, blinking at him, then at her shining blade. She separated her hands, and the sword disappeared.

They met at the foot of the bed and held each other until they stopped shaking.

"If we don't put an end to Ubell and his tricks soon, I'm going to have to kill him to get some sleep," Jim said, only half-joking. He put his hands on her shoulders and pushed back to see her face. "What was your dream like this time?"

"I was running, trying to get somewhere. Something awful was going to happen if I didn't. Suddenly I was there, wherever 'there' was, and somebody was hurling fireballs and lightning bolts at me, like in my test, and I was fighting and fighting and fighting. And then I woke up." She stopped to take a deep breath. "What was yours?"

"An horrible, big, black *thing* was coming after you. It was huge, it had glowing eyes, and it absorbed all the light around it. It was attacking you with laser beams. I was the only one who could save you. But I couldn't move. Ropes or chains were wrapped around me. I struggled, and fought, and couldn't lift so much as a finger. It was going to kill you, and I couldn't do a damn thing to stop it."

He let go of her, sat on the end of the bed, put his elbows on his knees and his head in his hands. There it was again, that awful feeling of complete helplessness.

She sat down beside him and rubbed his back. "It was just a dream, Jim. We're both all right."

"Ubell must be playing with his Stone again. It's the only explanation making any sense. What time is it? Four in the afternoon? Whipple said they were meeting with him today. Could they have had problems? Been attacked?"

"No, alarms would be going off all over the place if Ubell tried to fight them. Besides, I'm sure they took backup."

He scrubbed his face and stood up. Paced around the bed. Why was he still feeling helpless, incompetent, and inadequate? He thought he'd gotten rid of this particular demon when he'd exchanged energy with her. Evidently not—or had he made it worse? Why wasn't his hunch ability working? Was the present going to be like the past had been?

Irenee leaned back on her arms and frowned at him. "Jim, you have a blue aura. Even though it's very faint, I can still see it. What's going on?"

He shook his head, put his hands on his hips. "My hunch antennae are wiggling and driving me crazy. Outside of a very strong feeling something bad is going to happen, I can't seem to focus on real possibilities or conclusions. I only know *absolutely* that, whatever is coming, it's aimed at you, and I won't be able to help."

"But we proved you *are* able to help me. You and I can exchange energy. Your energy will be an enormous help when we destroy the Stone."

"It won't be enough." He shook his head again.

She stood, reached up to grab his shoulders, and gave him a shake. "Stop! Don't degenerate into defeatist talk. You've about solving problems, not creating them, especially out of thin air. Where is your attitude coming from?"

Jim looked at her, so brave, so sure of herself and

her talent. So certain she would prevail. He didn't want to burst her bubble. She simply needed to understand where he was in his head and how he felt. She needed to be prepared for what was to come—his failure. "It's happened before, with disastrous results. Sit down, and I'll tell you."

When she did, he rubbed his hand over his chest while he considered how to begin. His center gave an encouraging hum—a direct counter to the negative confusion in his head. "Okay, this isn't going to be easy for me, but here goes. I told you my parents and sister are dead."

"Yes, you said your parents were killed by a drug addict." She pulled her feet under her.

God, she was so adorable, sitting there in her lacy underwear. He had to be strong and not join her like he wanted to. He had to get through his explanation, then see if she still wanted him.

"I had the same kind of nonspecific hunch that day—something awful was going to happen, and I needed to be there—but I had to take my last final before graduation. I knew my dad would be extremely upset if I didn't take the exam simply because of some idiotic hunch, so I took it and rushed right over to the store afterward. The cops were already there, and my mom and dad were dead. I hadn't been there to help them."

She held her hands out to him. "Oh, Jim, their deaths were not your fault. For all you know, if you'd been there, the addict would have killed you, too."

He took her hands, kissed them, and let them go. "Yeah, I know. I *might* have stopped it, though. Look, regardless of my feelings, I've come to terms with this event, believe me. It's not the real problem."

"Go on," she said with an encouraging gesture.

"My sister, Charity, was fourteen when they died. She'd been a typical teenager, full of drama about every little thing and not happy with the limits my parents put on her, but she was basically a good kid. Afterward, she wanted to live with me until she could go to college. I was starting police training, and I knew there was no way I could provide the kind of home she needed. Hell, my own life wasn't stable. How could I give her any supervision, or even my presence at home every night?

"We talked it over, and she accepted it would be better if she had someone who could be there. My Aunt Mary, my mom's sister, lived in San Diego also, and she agreed with us. Charity moved in with my aunt. I was leery of the arrangement from the get-go—for no good reason other than one of my hunches again. I simply could see no other alternative."

"That sounds like a good plan," Irenee said. "It's what I would have done if I'd lost my parents."

"Yeah, well, it didn't turn out to be. My aunt had her real estate business to run, and you know how realtors are always out at night. We knew this going in, and we thought it could still work because Charity could go to the realty office after school. Things went okay for a couple of years."

He ran a hand through his hair. Here came the bad part. "When she was a junior in high school, old enough to date and everything, Charity began to run with a bad crowd. I tried to talk with her, get her to change her ways. Charity wouldn't listen to me or our aunt, and she wouldn't talk to a counselor. As a big, bad cop, I tried scaring her buddies, and they blew me off. My hunches about my sister—something was really, truly wrong—kept getting stronger. I hadn't learned to trust them yet, and nothing I did or said got through to her at all."

He paced for a minute while the memories of her and her problems returned in a tidal wave of regret, sorrow, and anger. He shoved them aside somehow and managed to say, "Long story short, Charity ran away, disappeared after her high school graduation with some of her scumbag friends. I looked for her, *man*, did I look for her. Found her once, even talked her into rehab since she was an addict herself by then. She took off the day she got out. I'd get reports from various cities around southern California, and she'd be gone by the time I could get there. She and her buddies pulled some convenience-store heists, so there were warrants out."

He stopped, took a deep breath, struggled for control, and forced the final words out of a throat tight with grief. "One day, not long after Aunt Mary died from cancer, I got a phone call. Charity had been found in Bakersfield, dead from an overdose. She was twenty years old. I couldn't do a thing for her except bury her."

He lost it on the last word. He'd never told anyone the entire story. The wall he'd built to hold in his feelings broke, and the rushing memories—the anguish of his search, the devastation of her death, the loneliness of his life—overwhelmed him, and he broke down.

Irenee was up off the bed in an instant, holding him tight as he cried.

Finally cried for his sister, and his parents, and all he'd lost.

After a while, he regained control of himself and let her coax him to sit on the bed. She handed him a box of tissues, and he blew his nose. When she took one of the tissues, he realized she'd been crying, too. He hauled her into his lap, gave her a kiss, and whispered, "Thanks."

"I'm so sorry you lost your family. Those are terrible things to live through. I can only imagine how it felt. But, Jim, listen to me. None of what happened is your fault."

He sighed. That's what he expected her to say. "Yes, it was. I couldn't help any of them when they needed it the most. I should have been there. I should have listened to my hunches. I should have protected Charity. I should—"

She put a finger on his lips. "You couldn't. Your

parents' deaths are a terrible tragedy. Your sister's is, too. She made a lot of bad choices and didn't take your help, and it killed her. You and your aunt couldn't have locked her up. This may sound harsh, but *you* are *not* to blame. You did everything you could. What happened afterward—to you? What did you do?"

"Afterward, I went out for revenge and started looking for the people who provided the drugs to my parents' killer and to Charity's suppliers. Ended up in the DEA as a result. Found out the ultimate supplier was Finster, and now Ubell."

He smiled, a small one generated by one of his best memories. "Found you, burglarizing a safe."

"And I found you, a wild talent. So, here we are, full circle," she said after she gave him a kiss. "I don't understand, though, how any of the past affects our situation today."

"Because I've learned how to trust my hunches. Even when they're vague at times, they're right. The ones I'm having now are all bad. You're in terrible danger, and I won't be able to help you. Like with my sister, I don't know *what* to do. Unlike with her, I know I have to do *something.* I'll try my best, but I could end up doing the worst possible thing, and my actions could get you killed."

Her expression turned to one of sheer exasperation, and she poked him in the chest. "No, you won't. These hunches are too vague to be meaningful. Besides, we're in this together. We're soul mates, and if whatever happens is too much for the two of us, we have a lot of people to help. I've just found you, and I'm not letting you go. So if you have some idiotic idea about taking on Ubell and the Stone by yourself, forget it. We're a team."

"Yes, ma'am." What else could he say? Her declaration of their togetherness gladdened his heart. On the other hand, her words also meant she didn't completely understand. His hunches were never wrong.

What could he do? Hell, what would he do when he had to go back to work? Could he depend on Whipple and the rest to take care of her, restrain her recklessness? Was there another way to protect her—by keeping her away from the fight altogether? "Is there a single chance in the world you won't be part of Ubell's Stone's destruction?"

She shook her head. "I don't see how. I don't have a choice. The evil in the item has targeted me. When the Defenders destroy it, it will come after me no matter where I am. I'm much safer with the team and fighting back. I'm sure Fergus will bring in all the Swords and Defenders around. Besides . . ."

Her expression changed from the previous sympathy for him to anticipation—excited anticipation. He almost groaned. He didn't need a hunch to tell him what she'd say next. Sure enough . . .

"Besides, I'm a Sword, and destroying evil items is

my duty. I must do this, Jim. It's my calling."

Jim opened his mouth and shut it again. What could he say to change her mind when her reckless side was in control? Not a damn thing. The worst part of it was he understood deep in his bones what she meant. He had his own calling.

"Be careful, that's all I ask," he told her. He sighed and held her close. Now he only had to figure out how to protect her despite her nature and his hunches.

If determination counted for anything, he'd be successful. She was his soul mate, damn it! Of course he would protect her—or die trying.

His center began to heat when he kissed her. Time to change the subject.

CHAPTER THIRTY-ONE

That evening for dinner, Irenee and Jim joined Fergus, John, the high-ranking visitors, and the others working on the problem of Ubell's Stone. Irenee was so excited, she thought she'd burst. Wow, both the head of the Defender Council and a member of the High Council itself. She told herself to be on her best behavior, especially with her soul mate at her side.

Surely, these experienced practitioners would be able to handle Bruce Ubell and his piece of the Cataclysm Stone. Jim's fears would prove groundless. She just knew it.

The poor man had been through so much. How her heart went out to him for the loss of his entire family. She couldn't imagine how she'd feel in his circumstances—probably hardly able to function. He'd held all his grief in, of course. She saw the proof in the difficulty he had telling her the story. Today was probably the first time he'd cried in a long time—if he had let himself cry at all when it happened.

If it hadn't been for Charity's death and his search for the drug suppliers, she might not have met him at all. No. She squashed that horrible thought. The soul-mate imperative was at work here. It would somehow have brought him to her, no matter what the previous events.

Besides, he was alone no longer. He had her now. In fact, he had her whole family, if he stopped to think about it. They'd already welcomed him with open arms—although he might not think so from her mother's interrogation. When the current mess was over, they'd have the chance to get to know each other. Dad already liked Jim, she could tell. Did Jim realize it? She made a mental note to emphasize their togetherness—she was learning her "obvious" and his were often two different animals.

Her soul mate did have a strong overprotective streak, though. She understood where it came from, but he had to stop blaming himself or taking on the responsibility for those tragedies.

What was all his nonsense about not being able to help her? They'd proved he could. Men could be such wrong-headed thinkers at times.

He hadn't mentioned his hunches again, even though she knew he was still having them. His aura remained a faint blue. Yes, she found them disturbing also, if too vague to take action. He was simply feeling the effects of Ubell's using his Stone and those horrible dreams, and his hunches were coming from that.

Well, until he became sure of their meaning, she could do nothing. Besides, she had a bunch of other problems to think about—like learning how to use her upgraded powers for the battle to come.

When they destroyed the Stone, of course she'd be there, with him right behind her supplying energy. The shoe would be on the other foot then—*she'd* be protecting *him*. After the difficult episode with Finster's Stone, all the Swords and half the Defenders in the country would be there, too. Nobody was going to get hurt.

Irenee snuck a look at her soul mate sitting next to her. *Her soul mate!* The thought was still mind-boggling. The reality even more awesome. All the love scenes in all the romance novels she and her friends read in high school? Put together they didn't come close to the true experience. How could they? She had the soul-mate phenomenon and a truly magical connection on her side. Simply the thought of making love again tonight was enough to get her blood flowing.

Jim glanced at her out of the corner of his eye, turned to wink, and whispered, "Later."

She coughed and hid behind her napkin. She was sure she'd turned the color of the tomatoes in the salad. Was he reading her mind now?

She composed herself when Fergus clinked his spoon against his glass to get everyone's attention. Thank goodness, Fergus was to her other side so she didn't have to look past Jim to see the head of the table. The man, in even an unfocused glimpse, was a distraction to her thought processes.

After reporting on the meeting at the Finster mansion, Fergus said, "In light of Ubell's intransigence, we must use other means to obtain his part of the Cataclysm Stone. We'll begin with the legal. After we finish here, Rachel, Miriam, and I will fly to Washington tonight to meet with both councils tomorrow. We have already ordered the legal masters to find every precedent that would compel a search of the property."

"From past experience with these items," Miriam stated, "we know Ubell will not abandon his, nor will he ever be physically far from it. The object is in the Finster mansion. He won't leave without it. Conversely, we don't want him to leave and take the Stone out of its shielding, even though it would give us actionable proof of its existence. The Stone might precipitate a fight in the open—a situation to be avoided if possible."

"It's too bad," Rachel added thoughtfully, "we went after the first Stone clandestinely. A direct confrontation with Alton Finster under council warrants would have put us in the house and automatically given us search rights."

"We followed proper procedure, but I do understand the attraction of putting the question to him in person," John said. "You, however, didn't take part in the struggle with the smaller remnant. In the light of that battle, I would have hated to face Finster's piece, *in the hands of its possessor*, opposing its confiscation. We could have burned the house down, at the very least, and a worst-case scenario would have involved *both* Finster and Ubell *and* their Stones fighting us."

"What do you mean?" Jim interjected.

"Destroying an item by itself is difficult enough," Fergus answered. "Battling a practitioner wielding the item from within a pentagon fortress, using it to focus offensive and defensive spells, is a long, dangerous, nasty fight. You saw Irenee's test. Multiply it by ten or twenty, throw in our blades and their energy beams, and you'll have an idea of the possible damage."

"I'm going to make some calls tonight," John said, "to put other teams and unaffiliated Swords and Defenders around the country on standby. Ubell's larger Stone will be stronger than its smaller third. Once we have our hands on it, we'll need every ounce of firepower we can get, and in very short order."

After John's statement, the discussion changed to revolve around tactics—which depended on the type of precedents they found and the strength of the orders from either council. Irenee listened carefully to the experts. She'd need every bit of knowledge when they faced the Stone.

"Oh, damn, my phone," Jim whispered, as he reached

into his pocket and pulled out his cell phone. After he looked at the caller ID, he excused himself to take the call out in the hall. When he returned, he had a grim look on his face, and Irenee's center vibrated in a way she hadn't felt before. Was it anger? Or trepidation?

"Folks," Jim said into a break in the conversation, "I have some news of another kind. Ubell's revved up his drug business again. A lieutenant of one of the biggest dealers paid a visit to the Finster mansion late this afternoon after your visit. Drugs have already appeared for sale on the street—by the truckload. Ubell's wasting no time making up his losses. I have to report to my headquarters tomorrow morning."

An icicle of apprehension ran down Irenee's back, and her center quivered again. He wasn't going to stay with her in the safety of the HeatherRidge.

"Any ideas what brought on his activity at this particular moment?" John asked.

"Several possibilities from my task force, but nothing definitive," Jim answered. "Could be Ubell got tired of not making money. The pent-up demand created by withholding his merchandise raised prices, so he stands to make a bigger profit. Could be pressure from upstream, if more inventory is headed here and can't be stopped, and the warehouses are full. Could be he has some big bills due or his distributors are unhappy. Or . . . my idea, because it's happening so soon after your meeting, he could be sending a message he can do what he wants and you can't touch him."

"Isn't your last reason a little far-fetched?" Miriam asked. "We're not involved with the drug business or law enforcement."

Jim shrugged. "Anything's possible here."

"I agree," John stated. "The Stone's influence could certainly have warped Ubell's reasoning."

"Jim, keep us apprised of events on your end. Ubell's drug business is out of our jurisdiction. His preoccupation with it may work for us, however," Fergus said. "If he uses the Stone to enhance his dealings, he may trigger our sensitives to pinpoint its location. In the meantime, I suggest everyone use the lull to clear calendars and finish outstanding tasks at your regular jobs. Get some rest. We'll need to move fast and in full strength when we get the go-ahead from the councils." He rose and walked around the table. "The rest of you keep on with the contingency plans. Jim, Irenee, let's talk in the hall for a minute."

Once in the hall, Fergus came straight to the point, "Do you want a Sword for a shadow, Jim?"

"No," Jim answered. "I have no way to explain one, and if I'm with another agent, or worse, an informant, and he notices somebody tailing me, it will cause even more problems. By the way, our surveillance people noted your visit and are making nothing of it at the moment. You looked like normal business traffic."

"What if—" Irenee started to say.

Using his cop voice, he cut her off. "No, honey, you can't come, either."

"That wasn't what I was going to say." She folded her arms over her chest. Well, maybe she was going to suggest it, but she had another idea, too. "What if you call in on a regular timetable? Then we'll know where you are."

"I'm sure I'm going to be stuck in a planning meeting or trying to contact informants most of the morning. If I leave the building, I'll phone. Oh, and don't call me either, not unless it's vital."

As though she'd bug him at work. She knew better. He had his stubborn cop look again, so she said only, "Okay."

"John will be here if you need help while we're gone." Fergus pulled a card out of his pocket and wrote on it. "Here are both my and John's cell numbers. Will you be back tomorrow night, even if it's only to sleep?"

"I don't really know. It depends on what Ubell's up to. My boss did say the accountants and computer techs got nowhere with the info from Finster's safe. Some even higher-powered techies are looking at it now, trying to hack Ubell's programming. Let me ask you something I've wondered about. Suppose you do take Ubell out. Destroy the Stone. What happens to the financial info and everything he's set up by magic?"

Good question, Irenee thought and turned to Fergus for an answer.

"Hmmm." Fergus stroked his beard and looked off into the distance for a few seconds. "As you know, for a spell to be ongoing, it has to have energy from somewhere. For example, if you don't supply it to your lightball, it goes out."

"Yeah, I'm learning 'maintenance,' as Johanna puts it."

"In this particular case, I would think the maintenance must be coming from the Stone, and it, not Ubell or Finster before him, has been supplying the spelled computer programs. It definitely has the range. If so, when we destroy the Stone, we stop the supply, and the programs lose their enchantment. Your accountants should have no trouble with them."

"Okay," Jim said with a smile. "I hope you get both him and his Stone soon."

"You two get some rest," Fergus said. He nodded toward the conference room. "There's no need for you to stay. The bunch in there will argue every possible scenario, but we can't come to a real plan until we hear what the legal masters and both councils say."

"Sounds good to me," Jim said. "I hate those kind of meetings. Let's go, honey."

Irenee was about to protest—she wanted to hear

what the scenarios were. She might need them in the future. Then Jim looked at her, took her hand, and said, "It's 'later.'"

If she said good-bye to Fergus, she didn't remember it. Jim's golden-green gaze sent excitement skittering up her backbone, and his touch warmed her to the core. Other parts of her body came alert, too. She practically raced him to the elevator.

Fortunately, no one else entered with them because, even before the door closed, he wrapped his arms around her and kissed her. Exactly what she had in mind, so she kissed him back. By the time the car stopped on the fourth floor, she was practically climbing his body. They stumbled out into the hall, almost straight into another couple waiting to enter.

"Oh, sorry!" she managed to mumble.

Jim just grinned, and the guy—probably as old as Fergus!—grinned to match Jim's and said, "Oh, we understand completely."

Mortified, she dragged her soul mate down the hall.

CHAPTER THIRTY-TWO

Once inside her condo, Jim pulled Irenee into his arms and took up where they left off. Her embarrassment went out the window in the heat of his embrace and the fire in his kisses. They left a trail of shirts, her bra, and her shoes in the short hall and fell onto the bed. After rolling back and forth in a tangle of limbs, she managed to land on top and straddle his thighs.

"Wait, wait," Jim gasped and captured her hands when she attacked his belt buckle.

"Why, why?" she asked, laughing and stretching their arms to each side, which had the effect of bringing them chest to chest.

"Because," he said, letting go of her hands, flipping her over, and making himself comfortable between her legs, "I want to take this slow. We might not see each other for days, and I want something to remember you by."

She was still pushing at his shoulders and trying to figure out how he'd managed to put her on the bottom so effortlessly when the meaning of his statement hit. She stopped struggling. "Oh."

"Oh," he repeated and kissed her softly, leisurely, like they had all the time in the world. From her mouth, he worked his way slowly down her neck to her breasts, where he fondled one while he licked and suckled the other.

She luxuriated in his touch while her body warmed and tingled—her usual response to him, she realized.

They'd made love, she couldn't remember how many times since yesterday. Yesterday? Yes, it was only last night they'd truly become soul mates. Their first mating had been glorious, but . . .. this time felt different, somehow. Less hurried, less stressful, more sure.

As in all the others, her blood was singing through her veins, and his hands and his lips were causing sparks to excite her entire system.

But . . . this time, all her senses were heightened. All sensations more intense, more alluring, more . . .

The smell of him, his lemon-lime shaving cream, his shampoo, himself. She took a deeper breath.

The feel of him when she slid her hands over his skin. Rough in places, smooth in others. His hard muscles bunching, relaxing. The puckered slash he'd told her had come from "an idiot with a machete who thought he was a pirate." The silky curls in his hair that gave him a boyish look at times and that she loved to twine around her fingers. His morning whiskers scratchy on her lips; his smooth cheek now after his shave. All she could reach right now were his hair, back, and shoulders. It would do—for the moment.

She didn't have to open her eyes to see him. She had him memorized, from the top of his brown hair to the golden green in his eyes to his firm lips, to his strong jaw. Down to his broad shoulders, down to the smattering of dark hair on his chest arrowing to his sex, down to his long legs to his feet . . . and back up.

All she could hear were her occasional moans and the slight creak of the bed. That was okay. She knew the sound of his deep voice, could pick it out from a crowd, and loved to hear him say her name.

His taste. Salty, sweet, like no other. His kisses possessed her.

Then there was his touch on her—of his lips, of his tongue, of his hands. If his kisses were passionate, his touch possessed, claimed, enticed, excited.

She couldn't get enough of him. Now or ever.

She opened her eyes when he kissed his way to her navel. She still had her long suit pants on, but so did he. She slid her hand to her buckle, and he stopped her from unfastening it. He glanced up, gave her navel a little kiss, and murmured, "I'll get there, honey."

She squirmed, groaned, "Faster." He only kissed his way back up to her breasts and played there a while, until her nerves were sparking, and she was arching into him.

Finally, *finally*, he undid her buckle, lowered her

zipper, and slid her pants and panties down her legs and off. Standing quickly, he stripped off his own clothes.

He held still for a couple of seconds at the foot of the bed, simply looking at her. Before she could demand, or ask, or *beg* him to come into her arms, he leaned over and started kissing his way back up her legs, climbing on the bed as he did so.

If his previous touches and kisses had aroused, these caresses inflamed and enthralled. When he finally kissed her most intimately, she quivered all over. When he licked and sucked her most sensitive spot, she began to writhe, then moan. Sparks began racing through her, and every muscle tightened, to the point of pain. Tension built and built, and she thought she would burst. She grabbed the bedspread for an anchor in the storm and pressed herself into his mouth. Ecstatic release came with her cry, "Jim!"

She was still shaking when he moved swiftly up, drawing her legs around him.

"Open your eyes, Irenee," he said in a low voice that sent more sparks through her center.

She did, to look right into his. The golden green was darkened, his expression serious, his skin pulled taut on his face. Her laughing lover had become passion personified.

He was poised at her entrance, braced over her on his arms. "Touch my center."

When she did, he balanced himself on one arm and placed his palm right over her breastbone. Slowly, oh, so slowly, he pushed into her. She raised her hips to accept him, glorying in the connection, the possession, the becoming one.

When he was totally inside her, he lowered his face close to hers and stared into her eyes. His voice was raspy when he declared, "No matter what happens, I'm yours, and you're mine, and we will belong to each other forever. I'll do everything in my power to keep you safe."

His words thrilled her to the core and inexplicably made her want to cry at the same time. All she could whisper was, "Oh, Jim, yes," before he was kissing her, obliterating all thought.

Magic energy, more powerful than ever before, began to swirl through their linked bodies. Stronger and stronger, as their heartbeats increased. Faster and faster, as they began to move.

He possessed her, as she did him. Each thrust, each acceptance proclaimed their oneness, their merging, their mating.

The tension in their bodies grew, multiplied, as she grasped him tightly when he was deepest inside her. At first he paused momentarily each time, but soon they were meeting each other, stroke for stroke, both straining, reaching . . . reaching . . .

"Jim!" She cried out his name as she climaxed,

waves of ecstasy rolling through her. Through the roar of blood in her ears, she heard him shout, "Irenee!"

He poured himself into her, and she rejoiced. He collapsed into her arms, and she held on tight. She would never let him go.

How long it was before either moved, she didn't know. Eventually he rolled to the side and pulled her to face him.

After a while, she managed to open her eyes about halfway. His eyes were closed, and his lips were smiling. He looked . . . relaxed, satisfied, happy—no, stronger than happy. Blissful.

She felt the same.

She ran her fingers through his hair, played with the curls until he captured her hand and kissed the palm.

He blinked at her and smiled again, his eyes twinkling. She could hear the laughter in his voice when he said, "Now I understand why the men around here have goofy expressions on their faces practically all the time."

"What? Really? They do? I never noticed it." She ransacked her memories, but had no clue what he was talking about.

He chuckled, kissed her softly on the lips. "It's a guy thing, honey. You wouldn't notice."

The light dawned. "Oh."

"Have you got any ice cream?"

"I think there's several pints in the freezer. Why?"

"After our expenditure of energy, I need replenishment. After that, we really need to get some sleep. I have to leave early and stop by my apartment in the morning before I go to the office."

She had the nagging notion they needed to discuss something, but whatever it was would have to wait. She was too tired to think, and besides, ice cream sounded good to her, too—especially with chocolate raspberry syrup.

CHAPTER THIRTY-THREE

Jim woke when she started kissing his chest. He lay there for a few seconds enjoying the feeling of her lips moving up from his navel. Then he realized his cock was already awake and even more thoroughly enjoyed being held in her hand.

He glanced at the clock. Five in the morning, just getting light, and the alarm was about to go off. He should be exhausted. They'd been awake again at two, going at it like rabbits. Or was it minks? Whatever. Instead, here she was, and there he certainly was, ready to go again. Where was all his "stamina" coming from? Must be the soul-mate phenomenon. After all the pain, this must be the payoff.

Damn, what a time to have to get up, and he didn't mean this kind of "up."

He shut off the alarm before it could sound. A couple more horizontal minutes couldn't hurt.

When she reached his magic center, it began to vibrate. The pulsations heated his blood and warmed his muscles—and gave him another idea. Maybe it would be better to spend the couple of minutes in a more active—although still horizontal—manner.

He reached a hand under her chin and tilted it up. He couldn't see her smile, but he could hear it when she said, low and sultry, "Good morning."

"Good morning," he answered with a scratchy voice. With her hand doing what it was doing, it was a miracle he could speak at all. "Come up here."

She slid up his body and, lying on him full length, captured his cock between her legs. An elbow on each side of his head to brace above him, she bent and gave him a little kiss on the lips. "Do we have time for this?"

He shifted, lifted her hips, and slid inside. His filling her almost took his breath away, it was so perfect, so right, so complete. "Let me introduce you to the concept of the 'quickie.'"

Breakfast turned out to be a slightly more hurried meal than he had originally planned.

Over the rim of his coffee cup, he watched her peruse the newspaper advertisements. Her dark red hair was still disheveled, her porcelain skin was a little flushed, and her big emerald-green T-shirt displayed a longsword and the words, *A Forged Blade, Finely Tempered.* She looked good enough to eat.

"Going to practice some today?" he asked.

"Maybe, if Johanna's around. I need to go shopping,

though, and it looks like there are some good sales over at Woodfield Mall." She turned the page of one of the flyers.

What? She was thinking about leaving the secure Center? "No. Don't go shopping."

She looked up, her eyebrows lifting. "Excuse me? Don't go shopping?"

"Look, honey, it's still not safe out there for you. Ubell hasn't forgotten about you, and just because he's occupied with the drug business, it doesn't mean he doesn't have some bad guys out looking for you."

"Jim, I need some things nobody else can get for me." She squinted at him. "Or, are you saying I can't take care of myself?"

"What I'm saying is we can't take Ubell or his possible actions for granted."

She made a face, rolled her eyes. "Okay, just to keep the peace, I'll say it: I'll take someone with me. Maybe Johanna would like to go. Give me a little credit here. How would you feel if I made the same comment to you? You're going out *by yourself*."

Oh, brother! She had the stubborn look again. He should have known better than to phrase his "request" as a command. All the sex had rattled his brain. Best to calm her down. To avoid sounding like he was wimping out, he spoke in a matter-of-fact manner. "I didn't mean it that way, Irenee. I'm worried about you with this maniac running around loose. Knowing you're not in the Center will really hurt my concentration on the job. We've only found each other a few days ago. I don't want anything to happen to you."

"Oh," she said, her tight mouth showing she was only slightly mollified. "I'll be careful. You be, too."

"I will, I promise."

Then she smiled, and it was like the sun shone. "I feel the same way. Oh, speaking of the bad guys, have you had another hunch? Your aura is barely blue."

Jim relaxed. Looks like he dodged that bullet. To answer her question, he shook his head. "Nothing strong. I still get wiggles every once in a while if I'm not actively thinking of something else—like you, for instance. Still, nothing comes together. It's never been like this in the middle of an operation before—so quiet, almost confused."

He looked at his watch and stood up. "I'm sure it will work itself out. Right now, I've got to move if I want to pick up those papers at my apartment before I go to the meeting. Why don't I call you around noon? I should have an idea of my schedule."

She thought it was a good idea, and after a big hug and an even bigger kiss, he left. It was not easy to do so. That damned nagging worry still plagued him. Why wasn't his mechanism working better?

Ten minutes later, he was driving Interstate 90 headed for the city. Traffic was fairly light—for Chicago—at six twenty on a Friday, so he let his mind wander a bit.

Irenee. Of course, his first thought. He knew he had an idiotic grin on his face again. Him and all the other male soul mates. Lord have mercy, what great sex! No, he had to think like a practitioner—what great *mating*!

He couldn't get enough of her. He wanted to spend the entire day in bed with her. The thought stirred a particular part of his anatomy. Holy shit, he was becoming downright . . . what was the word? Oh, yeah, *insatiable*. He hadn't been this horny when he was eighteen. If he could bottle the phenomenon's ability to increase stamina, he'd make a fortune.

He didn't like being away from her, especially if she was in a reckless mood. Shopping, for God's sake. Johanna had common sense. Maybe she could keep Irenee home. She would listen to another Sword.

He'd meant what he said last night. He was hers, and she was his. Forever. He'd do all he could, give his life if necessary, to keep her safe.

He had to make that declaration. He wanted it said at least once, to hear it come out of his mouth, to set the words in his heart, forever.

He wasn't sure she completely understood him yet. Neither of them had used the word *love*. Certainly he hadn't expected to fall so far, so fast. Here he was, however, and he knew she was with him. He'd tell her in no uncertain terms when he returned to the HeatherRidge.

He'd show her, too.

As for today and her shopping trip, he was probably worrying about nothing. If someone or something was going to attack Irenee, wouldn't he be having stronger hunches? Shouldn't all his bells and whistles be going off to alert him? He checked the inside of his head.

Nothing, not even a wiggle where she was concerned. Yeah, the faint foreboding was still there, only no greater help than it was before.

Wait a minute. Given the difficulties he was having, could something be repressing his hunches or hiding Ubell's plans? The Stone? The Defenders talked about this Stone's ability to hide its location. Whipple said it could supply magic energy across distances—to those flash drives, for example. Maybe it could affect his ability to put info together and come up with hunches. Or, more possibly, he simply didn't have enough info to begin with. He'd talk to John or Johanna about it tonight—assuming he actually made it back. At any rate, the idea was not one he could explore in depth at the moment.

Right now, despite his desire for Irenee, it did feel good to be going back to work and doing something active on the case. He wasn't meant for the sidelines.

He turned up the radio to catch the sports news.

Forty-five minutes later, he walked toward his apartment building from the parking space he'd found down the block. A yellow van with a plumber's logo pulled into an alleyway about fifty feet in front of him. He hoped it wasn't his building with a plumbing problem.

When he crossed the alley, four big guys jumped him. Despite his elbowing one in the stomach and kicking another in the knee, they grabbed his arms, overpowered him, and tossed him into the van.

He hit his head on the seat, and pain lanced through his skull. He felt one more blow, a falling sensation, and nothing more.

CHAPTER THIRTY-FOUR

"Uhhhh." Jim came to with a groan. His face and various body parts ached, and his head felt like a sledgehammer had hit it. He was sitting on something hard and upright, but couldn't seem to move.

"Open your eyes, Mr. Tylan," a smooth, almost oily voice murmured.

Jim cracked his eyelids apart enough to gaze straight into the smirking face of Bruce Ubell. The man had changed since the last time Jim saw him—just six days ago. At the ball, Ubell had appeared thin and fit, with a healthy color to his face. Now he looked like shit. Gaunt, almost skeletal, with dark bags under his eyes, and a sour smell about his body. Evidently, having and using the Stone came with a cost.

Ubell's pale, yellowish-brown eyes glowed with hatred.

Jim launched himself at the son of a bitch. Or tried to. He couldn't even raise his arms or get his butt out of the chair. He was bound—tied to a great throne of a chair with a high back and carved arms. The chair itself did not even budge from his attempt.

A large, muscular, bald man, probably one of his attackers, stood next to Ubell, and when Jim looked at him, the guy gave him a backhand that whipped his head to the side.

"Enough, Leroy." Ubell laughed, a sharp, staccato bark, and sneered, "You're mine, Mr. Tylan."

Whatever else he was—crooked, evil, overconfident, devious—Ubell was also crazy. Jim knew it in his bones. Something terrible and inhuman burned in the back of the man's weird eyes—probably his Stone shining through.

Ubell turned to a table next to the chair. "Let's see what you brought with you."

Tasting his own blood from the thug's hit, Jim swiveled his head to see his wallet, ID case, phone, two ammo clips, handcuffs, and pocket stuff on the dark surface. Where was his gun?

Leroy swept back the side of his jacket, and Jim saw it, stuck in the guy's belt. Maybe the thug would shoot off his own balls—an optimistic thought, unfortunately not very plausible.

He didn't see his watch on the table. No, it was still on his wrist, and he could see the time. Almost noon. His task force would be wondering about him. Were they still on watch outside? He doubted it. Erlanger would have pulled everybody to help with the drug raids.

He could expect no help from that quarter.

Irenee would be worrying about him, too. *Please, don't come looking for me*, he prayed.

"Ah, you're DEA," Ubell said, flipping the case open. "My source thought you worked for either it or Alcohol, Tobacco, and Firearms. No matter. Neither agency will be able to catch me."

He spoke in a matter-of-fact, totally calm, oh-so-rational tone that sent shivers up and down Jim's back. He revised his conclusion. *Crazy* didn't begin to describe Ubell. The man was *totally insane, unhinged, possessed, wacko.*

Jim jerked his eyes away from Ubell to study his location for a means to escape. They were in the gold-and-white, two-story-high ballroom of the Finster mansion. Weird. He would have expected to be at a remote place—where torture wouldn't be heard. Then he remembered what Miriam had said: the Stone was here, and Ubell wouldn't be far away from it.

Facing the room, the throne sat on the small elevated stage between the thick round columns defining the space. Behind him was solid wall, set back about fifteen feet from his chair. French doors on either side opened to a balcony, and light poured in from the clerestory windows above. Another side door to his right—the one Irenee had used to evade him only a few days ago—was open to a hall.

Their facets flashing in occasional rainbows, crystal

chandeliers hung from the ceiling. The pale-brown wooden floor gleamed with wax and age. The rest of the large, formal, open space held no furniture except for a few chairs lined up against the left wall, and the big double doors of the main entrance were closed.

He might be able to make a break for the balcony or even the side door, but he had to get out of the ropes first. Why hadn't he tried to learn the unfasten spell? Or unravel?

Leroy slapped him again, and he grunted at the pain.

"What do you want from me, Ubell?" Jim growled at his captor. "Do you expect me to talk?"

"Oh, no, Mr. Tylan. I don't want you to talk. You have nothing to tell me. I know everything." He picked up Jim's telephone, flipped it open, and punched some of the buttons. "I want you to scream."

CHAPTER THIRTY-FIVE

Irenee finished her lunch and looked out the window of her condo. It was almost noon. When would Jim call?

She'd practiced increasing power to her offensive spells all morning alone, Johanna having gone to visit friends. Most Defenders and Swords were taking advantage of the day off Fergus had suggested. Although a shopping trip had lost its attraction, she still might go later, once she knew what was happening with Jim. What had he found out about Ubell?

She'd also been nagged by a persistent . . . she couldn't think of the correct word. *Fear* was too strong. *Anticipation*, too weak. *Premonition*? Possibly. *Dread*? What did you call the thing hanging over you? Waiting for the other shoe to drop? A sword of Damocles?

Whatever it was, the sensation both aggravated and exhausted her. She was so antsy she'd declined lunch with a couple of Defenders who were going to a nearby Mexican food restaurant she liked. She didn't feel like being good company. Besides, she wanted to be alone when talking with Jim.

Jim. Her soul mate. She smiled to herself. What had he said about goofy smiles? She'd looked around at the women today. Many of them had little secret smiles lurking. It wasn't only a guy thing.

What he'd said last night—about being hers and she being his. Forever. She'd meant to repeat the words to him, but she'd not had the chance. Passion had actually swept her away. She'd always thought the phrase trite. No, it was real.

Just as he was.

Just as her love was. She'd tell him so the minute they were alone.

The question was, where was the man right this instant? Why didn't he call?

All of a sudden, her center began to flutter, and not in a good way. In a scared way. Something was going on in the back of her brain, too. A feeling worse than dread. Alarm. Danger. Heading toward terror. She almost drew her sword by sheer reflex.

Her cell phone rang.

Oh, thank heaven. Jim's number showed on the display. She flipped open the phone.

"Jim! I've been thinking about you!"

"Hello there, Irenee, I hope you are well." The voice coming from the speaker sounded calm and reasonable—

and with such an undertone of vicious malevolence that she almost dropped the phone.

"Who is this!"

"Bruce Ubell, my dear little Stone thief."

"Where's Jim Tylan? How did you get his phone?"

"I have his phone because I have him. Soon, I will have you."

"What are you talking about? Put Jim on."

"The phone's on speaker, so he can already hear you. Just listen, and you'll hear him."

A sound like a slap came over the phone. Then another. Louder, like Ubell had moved the phone closer. And another.

The third time, she heard a groan.

"That was Tylan, Irenee."

More sounds of hitting. More and louder thuds. More and louder groans and grunts.

"I won't scream, you son of a bitch." It was Jim's voice, low and grating.

"Stop it, Ubell! Stop it right now!" She grabbed her purse and headed for the door. She didn't know where they were, but she'd find them.

"All right, Irenee, I'll stop it—for a price."

Ubell's oily tone halted her with her free hand outstretched for the knob. "What?"

"You come here, and I'll give him to you."

"No! Stay where you're safe!" Jim shouted.

She heard more hitting sounds and a couple of grunts. "Where's 'here'?"

"The Finster mansion, of course. There's also a requirement on your part, of course." He was gloating, so full of oiliness she thought the phone would slip out of her fingers.

She ground her teeth together in frustration and spoke through them. "What's the catch?"

"You have to get here by one o'clock, or only pieces of your boyfriend will be left to find. My Stone is hungry."

"No!" She heard Jim yell again.

Although it hurt to do so, she ignored him. "An hour? I can't get there that fast."

"Too bad for both of you. Oh, don't bring anyone with you, either."

"I'm coming, you piece of slime, but if you hurt him, I'm going to slice you into ribbons and fry the pieces like bacon. You'll learn firsthand what a Sword can do. The same goes for your puny, putrid Stone, too."

She punched the hang-up button before he could make more demands, and then ran for the elevator.

CHAPTER THIRTY-SIX

"Bitch!" Ubell screamed and threw Jim's cell phone against the back wall of the stage. Leroy went to pick it up.

Jim sagged back into the chair. He felt like screaming in frustration himself. Irenee was coming here, right into Ubell's arms.

And he couldn't do a damn thing to stop her.

Tied to the throne, he couldn't do a damn thing to help her once she got here, either.

Maybe, just maybe, *please* maybe, she'd think before rushing over and bring along help—another Sword, a couple of Defenders, somebody. Ubell wasn't going to kill him before she showed up. The bastard wanted to torture both of them while they watched each other's suffering.

Leroy brought Ubell the phone, and he punched some buttons. Then he punched some more. He shook the instrument. From the glimpse Jim got, the screen was black.

A snarling, infuriated Ubell raised his hand like he

was going to throw the phone again, but he suddenly froze for a few seconds. With an exaggerated slow motion, he lowered his hand, closed the instrument, and gripped it tightly. He placed it softly on the table, clasped his hands in front of his belt buckle, closed his eyes, and took several deep breaths.

With his hunch antennae dancing in a frenzy of foreboding, Jim watched an unnatural composure slide down Ubell's face, feature by feature, and down his body. To calm himself so suddenly and thoroughly, the man had to be communicating with his hellish Stone. When he opened his eyes, the maniacal gleam in them was stronger than before.

Jim had to do something, *anything* to disrupt Ubell's plans and give him some grief. So he tried the one thing he knew he could do—he cast *flamma* on Ubell's jacket.

A little flame appeared right above the first buttonhole. Jim tried to put more energy into it, but the flicker only fluttered.

"Oh, really, Tylan, you'll have to do much better than that." Ubell waved his hand, and the flame sputtered out. He laughed, that short bark, and looked puzzled. "You're not a practitioner. How did you acquire practitioner talents?"

Jim said nothing.

"I'll bet I know," Ubell crowed. "You and the Sabel bitch are soul mates! The talents came with your mating!

Oh, this is too good."

He was quiet for a few seconds, his eyes seeming to go unfocused. Then he perked up again. "That's what my Stone has been trying to explain—it's been opposing another source of magic. You! And now you're here, and she's coming. I can't tell you how happy my Stone is! What *fun* we're going to have—the four of us!"

After telling Leroy he had to prepare for the witch's arrival, Ubell sauntered out, still laughing like a demented dog.

After the double doors closed behind Ubell, a great weight descended on Jim's thinking processes, as though it was trying to crush them. It had to be the damn Stone. His hunch antennae wiggled feebly. What was he going to do? With the Stone suppressing his abilities, his hunches couldn't even give him ideas, much less solutions. He closed his eyes and concentrated on pushing back against the nauseating force. All he could do was wait for Irenee—and pray she brought reinforcements.

CHAPTER THIRTY-SEVEN

On the way down in the elevator, Irenee hit the Defender hotline speed dial and the speaker-phone buttons. "This is Irenee Sabel. Get me John Baldwin and put everyone on alert. Bruce Ubell has kidnapped Jim Tylan and is holding him at the Finster mansion. Ubell is going to kill Jim. I'm heading there right now."

She ran out of the elevator and took the stairs to the parking garage. By the time she was in her car and heading for the HeatherRidge entrance, the hotline had patched her through to John. She told him what Ubell had said and where she was.

"Irenee, wait at the entrance, and I'll send some people with you," John ordered.

"I can't wait, John. It will take me every minute to get to Jim, even if I don't run into traffic. I'm turning out of the HeatherRidge entrance right now."

She heard him sigh before he spoke briskly. "Okay. I'm in Naperville, and I'll get to Ubell's as soon as I can. I'm scrambling everybody we can find. With luck, somebody will be at the mansion waiting for you. Stay on the line. The hotline will let you know ETAs for everybody."

"Roger. I won't hang up. I have to be there with him by one, or he'll hurt Jim. If there's no help out front, I have to go in. I'll find some way to stall him until backup arrives."

"Be careful," was all John said.

Ubell may have told her to come alone. He hadn't mentioned others coming separately. The man was an idiot. She only hoped he didn't try to call her and took it out on Jim when he couldn't get through. She put the phone in her lap and concentrated on driving.

Fifty-three minutes later, having driven like a complete maniac through heavy traffic, she pulled up to the Finster mansion. Seven minutes to one—seven minutes to spare. Unfortunately, dispatch reported no other Defender or Sword could arrive for another twenty to thirty minutes at the earliest. She had to go in alone, or Ubell would follow through with his promise. It was up to her to get Jim out of there.

The Finster butler—what was his name?—was standing in an empty parking spot right in front. When he saw her, he motioned for her to take it, and she pulled in.

Picking up her phone, she told the dispatcher she had reached the mansion and was going in. She climbed out of the car and left the phone on the seat. The magic spells thrown inside—and she expected a bunch—would fry its chips.

Wringing his hands and visibly trembling, the old man came over to her when she left the car. "Oh, Miss Sabel, I'm so sorry, I don't know what's wrong with Mr. Bruce. He hasn't been himself since that meeting he had with those Defenders. He told me to be sure you had a parking place."

"Take it easy, Mr. . . ."

"Sedgwick, miss, just Sedgwick."

"Calm down, Sedgwick. Where's Ubell?"

"Mr. Bruce is in the ballroom. He said to tell you. He sent all the servants except me away this morning and told them not to come back until Monday. After you arrived, I'm supposed to do the same."

"Is anybody else with him?"

"A very large, rough-looking man. He and three other men carried in another man through the kitchen—he looked unconscious. Then the three left."

"Could they have been seen doing it?" After all, some of Jim's people were supposed to be on surveillance.

"I don't think so. Delivery trucks pull in by the kitchen under a portico for weather protection. I didn't see a soul when I opened the door."

Damn. No help there, and time was running out. "Okay, thanks, Sedgwick. You've done your duty. You can go now."

"Oh, thank you, miss." Looking tremendously relieved to be dismissed, the old man bowed deeply before adding, "The front door is unlocked, miss." He hurried away.

Irenee studied the house for a moment. No signs of life inside. No stirring of a curtain or shadow of a watcher. She took a deep breath, told herself to be calm and alert. It was time to find Jim, get him out of there, and wait for the Defenders.

CHAPTER THIRTY-EIGHT

Irenee ran up the front steps of the mansion, opened the outer door slowly, and slid into the vestibule through the smallest crack possible. She closed it carefully, so the lock made only the slightest click. Her back to the door, she looked around and listened hard.

Nothing and no one appeared. She crept past the vestibule's coat closets, up the two steps, and through the open inner double doors. The halls to either side were dark. The only light came from the upper floor.

She stopped, tried to relax to slow her rapidly beating heart, and listened again.

Total silence. Utter stillness.

Not even a whirr of an appliance, or a whisper of a voice, or a breath of an air current.

Thankful for her sneakers, she silently crossed the marble entry and made her way to the stairs and up. No one lurked in the upstairs hall. Its wide double doors closed, the ballroom entrance loomed in front of her.

No, she wasn't going to waltz in the main entrance

and be a sitting duck. Not when she knew of the side door.

She kept to the carpet to muffle her steps and snuck to the left and around the corner. The doorway was in the middle of the side hall. She heard low voices, mutterings really.

Wishing she'd grabbed her robe for protection, she crept up to the door. This one was open. She peeked around its frame. No one was in her line of sight.

She did, however, hear Jim say hoarsely, "He's crazy, you know, totally insane, and he'll kill you, too."

A man said, "That pansy? He doesn't even have the balls to hit you himself. Shut up." She heard a sound like a fist hitting flesh. The voices were coming from the left.

If she remembered the room correctly, they were probably on the stage or close to it. The room appeared to be bare of furniture, so she'd have a clear shot with her spells.

She took a deep breath and sidled around the door. Jim was in a chair on the stage, and a big thug had his hand raised to strike again.

"Hey!" she yelled.

The guy turned.

"Typhonicus flabra!" She hit him with puff of wind at tornado force.

He flew spinning through the air and, with a satisfying THUMP, hit the wall behind the column to the right of the stage. He slid down to the floor and didn't move.

She rushed to Jim. He had cuts and bruises and the beginnings of a black eye, and his nose and lip were bleeding. At least he was sitting upright. "Can you walk?"

"Yeah," he answered, "but . . ." He looked at his hands on the chair arms.

"Oh." She cast unfasten, and the ropes fell off.

"Oh, honey, I'm so glad to see you." He stood up and gave her a hug. He winced when she hugged him back, and she quickly loosened her hold.

"Me, too." Difficult though it was to do, she pushed out of his arms. "Come on, we have to get out of here."

"Where's everybody else? Don't tell me you came alone . . ."

"They're on their way." She took his hand, stepped back, and tugged. "Let's go."

"Uh-oh." He wasn't looking at her, but at the main doorway.

From behind her, she heard the sound of the double doors closing.

CHAPTER THIRTY-NINE

"Irenee, what a pleasure to see you again." The smarmy voice seemed to slither down her backbone, trailing behind it a little snake of fear.

She pivoted and froze.

His red-and-black accountant's robe hanging limply, Ubell stood before the closed double doors with a long staff at his side. The pole's black wood split at the top into a grotesque hand, in which a misshapen black crystal sat, its fractured side facing outward.

Like its smaller remnant, this segment of the Cataclysm Stone drank in the light and surrounded Ubell, the staff, and itself in a pool of shadow.

When Irenee looked at the hideous monstrosity, a black flare lit up its insides and reached for her. The snake running along her back turned into a python trying to squeeze her spine. A icy knot formed in her stomach, and sudden nausea made her feel like throwing up.

Her Sword defenses met the challenge automatically, however, and her center immediately warmed and aimed its heat at the cold spot. She threw her shoulders back to stand tall and angry. No way was this perversion of magic going to destroy her or her soul mate.

"Castellum!" She set her pentagon. Indigo walls with violet streaks sprang up around her and Jim.

"Fulmen!" She shot an indigo lightning bolt at the Stone.

Jim grabbed her shoulders as if to pull her behind him.

"No! Feed me power!" She sent a blue energy bolt after the lightning.

The Stone absorbed the two bolts, but Ubell didn't return fire. Surprisingly, he didn't seem to know what to do for a moment. Then he laughed, like a dog's bark, and braced himself, the staff in his left hand and held toward her.

Jim put his hands on her back, and she felt her well fill with his energy.

With his right hand, Ubell threw a fireball. At least she thought it's what he intended. The pitiful spark, no better than *flamma* to light a candle, wobbled across the space between them, finally fizzling on her barricade.

Ubell evidently didn't have the skill to lay down a fortress or shoot an offensive missile. Good! That made him vulnerable.

Irenee fired directly at the warlock, and he ducked, using the staff as a shield.

"Dodge this." She shot a lightning blast, and the boom rebounded off the walls and windows. The Stone drew the indigo arc into itself and dissipated the effect.

"We only have to hold out a little while until the others get here," she told Jim over her shoulder. "We can do it!"

She threw another lightning bolt. The Stone deflected it to the side, and plaster flew when it hit the wall by the door.

Ubell was talking to the crystal, although she couldn't make out the words. He put both hands on the staff and sent her a concentrated look of hatred. Out of the Stone flew several rainbow-colored bolts that rattled her fortress walls only slightly.

She had expected more power from the monster on top of the staff. It appeared, however, Ubell was manipulating the Stone, not the other way around, and her human opponent didn't know how to use his crystal. This might be his first actual fight with the abomination, and his inexperience and ineptitude would give her an advantage.

The battle with Finster's remnant had not given the team a problem until the item was in its death throes and its other section came to help. She knew she couldn't destroy Ubell's Stone by herself, even if it didn't have outside aid. In her favor, the monster didn't have an expert wielding it, either. Therefore, all she had to do was hold off the attacks and stall for time and the Defenders' arrival. With Ubell obviously being more hindrance than help, her chances for success were good.

Time to get serious. She drew her sword, and the blade glowed almost pure violet when she shot an indigo beam directly out of its tip. She hit the Stone in the middle of its fractured face.

Ubell howled when the Stone deflected the beam, and the energy stream splintered around it, one piece almost hitting him. The Stone returned a crackling ray of its own, and her fortress repulsed it, but her walls definitely rippled from the hit.

Oops! Slight miscalculation. The last shot held more power, greater ferocity, better focus. That blow definitely came from the Stone, not Ubell. It was probably giving up on its "master" to run its attacks.

She and the Stone traded hits back and forth for several minutes, each shot more powerful—and energy consuming—than the last.

The good news? From the color of her blade, she was rising in level again. The bad? She was using power faster than she wanted to. She had to ration and couldn't shoot a continuous beam at Ubell, or she'd run out even quicker. Jim was helping her maintain her necessary amount, but how long would his last?

The Stone's bolts were not diminishing in strength and, an ominous note, were becoming tinged with black. Was it realizing its potential? More bad news for her and Jim.

Where was John? Where were the Defenders and Swords?

Another blast from the Stone shook the floor, which was scored now with black ruts from the deflected lightning bolts and energy beams. Although scorched in places from the fireballs, the wood wasn't burning—yet.

Irenee looked closely at the smirking man behind the staff. What was she thinking? She'd never get anywhere going directly at the Stone. Ubell was an attractive target of a weaker sort.

She gathered herself and aimed a violet, searing beam at the base of his robe. Maybe she could give him a hot foot!

A hit! Ubell jumped, took one of his hands off the staff, and bent over to shake his smoking robe. His movement turned the Stone's face away from her.

"Yes!" She pointed her sword directly at Ubell and fired several bursts in succession.

The monster had to be complaining to its so-called wielder because Ubell quickly put both hands on the shaft and aimed the smooth, sloping face at her again. She could see his mouth moving, but couldn't hear his words in the din of thunderclaps and beam whooshes as the Stone answered her shots. He looked like he was apologizing.

She blasted him again, and after three more shots, he was definitely cringing, held upright only by his grip on the staff. Her attention to the man seemed to take the Stone's concentration away from attacking her, and the evil item was working more to deflect her bolts than to strike at her fortress.

The problem was, her well was definitely running out of power. Jim's stream into her had slowed and greatly lessened in strength. Surely the others would get here soon. She put more power into the walls of her pentagon. If she had to, she'd divert all her energy to her fortress.

"I need more if you have it," she told Jim.

"I'm about to run out," Jim gasped in her ear.

CHAPTER FORTY

Jim was so weary. He'd wasted some of his power earlier on that miserable excuse of a *flamma* to set Ubell's coat on fire. With Ubell out of the room, he'd almost managed the strength spell he and Johanna had been working on, when Leroy hit him again and broke his concentration. The beating hadn't helped his reserves, either.

Somehow he had to keep going, keep supplying Irenee with energy. Where in hell would he get it? He could feel her power diminishing, and his bucket was almost dry. Nobody had ever explained what happened when a practitioner ran out of energy. He probably would need a transfusion of some kind—or he might simply fall over.

If they both ran out, Ubell and his Stone would kill them.

What could he do? There had to be something!

He looked around wildly. No ammunition. Nothing to throw. Where was a good rock when he needed one? Or even better, a cannon.

His eyes fell on Leroy collapsed behind the column.

Oh, wait. Could he get to the guy?

He threw the last of his power into Irenee. At this point, what did he have to lose?

"I don't have any more energy," he told her, "but I have an idea. Cover me."

She didn't reply, only nodded, and sent another beam from her sword at Ubell.

Jim let her go, took two running steps, and dove for Leroy. He slid on his stomach across the stage, ending up behind the stout column and almost on top of the thug. A chunk exploded from the column plaster just after he reached its protection.

He grabbed his gun out of the man's belt and stood up, keeping his back against the column. He made sure a round was in the weapon's chamber and braced himself, ready to turn and fire. When he looked at Irenee, she was looking back at him. He leaned enough to peer around the column at Ubell. "Ready!"

"Ready!" she answered.

"I love you!" he shouted.

"I love you!" she yelled back to him. "One, two, *three*!"

On three she threw a brilliantly violet beam at Ubell's head. He yelped and ducked, and his sharp movement jerked the staff and the Stone's face to the side.

Jim came out from behind the column. His first shot missed because Ubell was moving to the side, dodging Irenee's beam. He aimed at Ubell's head and fired, just as the man swung the staff his way.

CRACK!

His bullet hit the Stone dead center, and crystal shards flew from it in a black cloud.

"AAAARRRRRRGGGGHHHH!" Ubell clutched his head and collapsed. The smoking black staff fell over by his side.

When the walls stopped shaking and silence returned, Jim took three steps to Irenee and caught her as she threw herself into his arms and held on tight. They only raised their heads when someone yelled, "Irenee! Jim!"

Swords blazing in their hands, Baldwin and Johanna, with a bunch of Defenders behind them, threw open the ballroom doors, only to stop abruptly at the threshold.

"Nobody move," Baldwin ordered, staring at them and the collapsed Ubell. "Are you two all right?"

Jim had only the strength to nod, and Irenee did the same.

"That was gunfire we heard? You shot the Stone?"

Jim nodded again.

"Were either of you hit by the splinters?"

"No," Jim and Irenee said together.

"Well, it's one way to kill the thing." Baldwin

cancelled his sword and put his hands on his hips while he surveyed the room.

Jim also looked around, now that he had the chance. Ricocheting energy beams had gouged hunks of plaster out of the walls, and yellow and white bits lay scattered in clumps about the room. The ruts in the floor had stopped smoking, and the surface had buckled in places. Obsidian shards were stuck in the floor, walls, and doors in about a ten-foot radius around Ubell's body. Miraculously, the crystal chandeliers had hardly lost a single prismatic drop and those not covered in soot still reflected rainbows.

"Okay, here's what we're going to do," Baldwin said. "Jim and Irenee, you stay there until we get the Stone fragments out of the way. Healers, see if you can reach them by the side door. Everybody, be careful where you step."

He pointed at the obsidian shards. "Defenders, get the removal kits and start collecting every piece of the Stone. Every little bit. Watch out for those big chunks by the staff. Use extreme caution with them. Remember, the pieces are still evil and hold power, so use tongs or pliers to pick them up. We don't want any evil rubbing off on anybody. Looks like we'll be able to give every Defender team in the country a chance to destroy several of them."

He turned to Johanna. "You and I will get Ubell and his henchman out of here. Ubell doesn't appear to have any shards in his face, but I see some in his robe. Somebody bag the robe after we get him out of it and put it and what's left of the staff in the Hummer. Let's take the men downstairs to the study where Finster collapsed. You know, some medical problem must run in this family. This cousin seems to have suffered a similar affliction."

CHAPTER FORTY-ONE

After he and Johanna took Ubell and Leroy downstairs, and while the others worked to pick up the Stone fragments, Baldwin came to the stage.

Jim was sitting in the throne, holding Irenee on his lap. He couldn't let go of her, and she wouldn't let go of him. Just the way he wanted it.

"The healers say you're going to be fine," Baldwin reported. "They applied some quick fixes and will look you over again back at the center. How are you feeling?"

"Tired, very tired," Jim answered. Now he knew what happened when you ran out of energy. He was staying upright by sheer willpower.

Irenee, her head on Jim's shoulder, only nodded.

"I have to call my boss," Jim said and picked up his phone from the table. Except for his weapon and ammo clips, he'd already put the rest of his stuff in his pockets.

"Does it still work?" Irenee mumbled.

"Ubell threw it across the room after you hung up

on him. It didn't seem to work after that." He flipped the lid and punched the *on* button. Nothing happened. "No, it's dead."

"All the magic killed it, not the throw," Baldwin said. "It would be better—and traceable—to call from the phone in Ubell's study. Before you do, however, I'd like to ask, are you going to tell him and the agency about us?"

"What good would it do? Even if I did, I doubt he'd believe me." He rubbed his free hand through his hair and winced when he brushed the bump on his head he'd received in the van.

"Let's get the two of you to the study. While we were clearing a path through the crystal pieces, I alerted Fergus, Miriam, and Rachel about the situation. They said to tell you both congratulations and thanks. You have done some excellent work here. We also came up with some suggestions for handling the situation concerning your task force."

In the Finster study, Jim listened to their ideas while he and Irenee ate candy bars for energy restoration, and somebody cast a spell that dissipated the smoky smell left from the fireworks. Feeling more energetic, though still tired, Jim agreed with the suggestions. He trusted Ken Erlanger, but if he himself hadn't been part of the battle, he'd never believe the tale from someone else.

Baldwin knocked over a chair and did a little more

"set decoration," since the interrogation was supposed to have taken place in the study and the fight with Leroy in the hall. Somebody dragged the still-unconscious muscle out. Ubell was stretched out on the floor in front of the desk—where, John remarked, he had said Finster originally collapsed.

Jim sat in the big chair behind Ubell's desk and pulled Irenee into his lap. He called his boss from the desk phone and put it on speaker.

"It's Tylan."

"Jim! Where have you been? Where are you? We're about ready to move on Ubell."

"Hold on, boss. Ubell's moved ahead of us. He kidnapped me, brought me to the Finster mansion, and had a thug beat me up, trying to get info on what we're up to. He tricked my fiancée"—he winked at Irenee, who looked quite startled at the word—"to come over here with the idea of using threats against her to make me talk. When she came in, she distracted the muscle so I could jump him and knock him out. Ubell started screaming at me and then had a fit, literally, and he keeled over. He's lying on the floor right in front of me. He's still breathing, and his heart is beating, and that's about it. We need the paramedics."

"You stay there. We'll be right over."

Jim disconnected the call. "Here they come. Irenee, when they get here, let me do all the talking, okay?"

"I won't say a word," she answered.

"We're headed out the back," Baldwin said. "Leroy is in the hall, still unconscious, shackled with your handcuffs around one of the newel posts on the stairs. Here's your gun and one clip. We cleaned and reloaded it, so it doesn't appear to have been fired. You have your other stuff."

He waved toward the upper floor. "Upstairs is clean—still damaged, of course, but with no trace of you or Irenee, including the bullets you fired and their shell casings. After your people are finished here, we'll be back to check for any pieces of the Stone we missed. I'd like to find its hiding place, too. We'll see you later at the HeatherRidge."

"Thanks," Jim and Irenee said in unison.

"You two did real good," Baldwin said with a grin and left.

Almost immediately, Jim heard sirens.

He held Irenee close, swiveled the chair, and glanced up at Otto Finster's portrait. "You know," he said, "I think the old man is mad as hell."

Irenee stirred and tilted her head to stare at the painting. "I think he looks crazy, as crazy as his grandsons."

Jim leaned to see it from her angle. Finster's eyes seemed to glint with deranged malice. "You're right. A psycho if there ever was one."

CHAPTER FORTY-TWO

The sirens died outside the house, and for the next several minutes, people were everywhere. One set of paramedics hauled Ubell away. Another set separated and checked over Jim and Irenee. When they wanted to take Jim to the hospital, he refused, saying he'd see a doctor later.

At the beginning of the invasion, Ken Erlanger made sure Jim was all right and left to investigate the rest of the house. When things were organized, he returned. Erlanger was a big, burly man with dark brown skin and a deep voice, which reminded Jim of James Earl Jones. He could sound like a jovial, kindly man one instant and the wrath of God the next.

He walked straight up to their chair—Jim had her on his lap again after the paramedic exam—and held out his hand to Irenee. "Ken Erlanger, Ms. . . ."

Irenee sat up straight, smiled, and shook hands. "Irenee Sabel."

Erlanger's eyebrows shot up. "Of the Sabel Industries

Sabels?"

"Yes."

"I understand congratulations are in order." He looked from Jim to Irenee and back with a smile. Jim could see Ken was still surprised by the news. Hell, so was he.

"Thank you. We're very happy," Irenee said with a big grin before Jim could say anything. She pulled Jim's arm tighter around her.

He winced. "Careful, honey."

"Okay, what exactly happened here?" Erlanger asked, all business again, as he pulled up a chair and sat down.

"I spent the night with Irenee and went back to my apartment early to get ready for the meeting. Four of Ubell's guys jumped me there and knocked me out," Jim explained. "When I woke up, I was here. Ubell tried to question me about our plans. When I wouldn't talk, the one piece of muscle still here—Leroy—beat on me for an incentive. When I still wouldn't talk, Ubell called Irenee on my phone and told her he'd kill me if she didn't come here."

"So, I came," Irenee put in.

"Yeah, even though I told you not to." Jim frowned, gave her a "keep quiet" squeeze, and continued, "I figured he was going to threaten to beat her—or worse—to get me to talk. While she was on her way, Ubell left the gorilla with me and went somewhere. I don't know where. When Irenee came in, her entrance distracted Leroy, and I was able to take him down. Ubell came back and started yelling and screaming—something about killing both of us. I told him he was under arrest for assault, and he turned white as a sheet and fell over, shaking like he was having a seizure. After a few seconds, he went limp. I made sure he was breathing and called you."

"You didn't hit him or struggle with him?"

"I didn't lay a finger on him." *And that was the God's honest truth.*

"What happened in the big room upstairs?"

"The ballroom?" Jim shook his head, did his best to look puzzled. Better to offer no explanation. "Why?"

"It looks like somebody fought World War Three up there."

The best defense being a good offense, Jim said only, "I thought we had people watching this house. They didn't see a ruckus?"

"We pulled the surveillance to put more people on the increased drug sales last night. It paid off because we caught a couple of the major distributors in the warehouses. One of them is so mad at Ubell for moving too fast that he's willing to give him up as the guy behind the scheme. If I had any notion we were going to capture them, I'd have had you come in when I called you. I know how much you want those guys."

Erlanger shook his head. "Anyway, no, we didn't see a fight. The damage upstairs is weird—burn marks and plaster all over the place. On the other hand, it doesn't appear to have relevance to our investigation. Maybe Ubell had a temper tantrum and beat on the walls or maybe he liked to play games with blowtorches. It's too bad we weren't here, though. We might have seen you brought in and been able to spare you a beating."

"Yeah, and moving in might have brought about a hostage situation and a bigger mess. Ubell wasn't acting rational. I doubt he'd have given up without a fight." Jim waved the hand not holding Irenee's at the room. "Look on the bright side. We're here now. We're in the house. Assaulting me is a felony. *It's a crime scene.*"

Erlanger smiled, a showing of his predator teeth. "I've called in a request for a search warrant for the entire property. We're not going to let Ubell get out of paying for his crimes on a technicality."

"That has to be Ubell's laptop," Jim said, pointing to the one on the desk. "Maybe we can get straight accounting records here."

Erlanger's phone rang. After a couple of minutes of conversation, he hung up, a very satisfied look on his face. "Looks like everything is coming together. The computer guys reported they've cracked Ubell and Finster's code on the drive copies you made. We're going to nail those bastards and their entire operation to the wall.

I can't wait for them to wake up."

"Assuming they ever do," Jim said. Whipple had been right—cut the power and the spells disappeared. "Listen, Ubell said something about knowing I was either DEA or ATF from a source. He didn't name the guy, but I'll bet it's somebody in law enforcement."

"I'll look into it. We need to get busy rounding up all their associates and closing their operations. Oh, Leroy in the hall woke up and started yelling for a lawyer. Wait until he finds his boss in the next cell." Looking extremely satisfied, Erlanger rubbed his hands together and stood. "Jim, you look awful. Get to a doctor. You tend to your wounds and Ms. Sabel this weekend. The paperwork can wait until Monday."

Since Jim's phone was fried, they gave Erlanger Irenee's number and walked out of the mansion hand in hand. While they were waiting in her car for the police to move some of their vehicles, her phone rang. She answered, said "yes" a couple of times, and hung up.

"That was Johanna. We're getting an escort home." When the exit was available, she pulled out, turned left at the corner, went down the street two blocks, and turned right. A big white Hummer was waiting.

Johanna came over. "Get in the other car, you two. We have some food. We don't want you driving in your condition."

Jim was perfectly happy to do so. He knew he was

in no shape to drive. He'd been worried about Irenee's strength also. If she was even half as exhausted as he was, she'd have a hard time staying awake on the road.

On the way to the Center, they ate some chocolate and a couple of apples and drank two bottles of water each, and fell asleep in the backseat of the Hummer.

CHAPTER FORTY-THREE

Johanna roused Jim and Irenee at the HeatherRidge and shepherded them into a private dining room full of Defenders. Everybody gave them a standing ovation. Catherine and Hugh Sabel and Bridget Whipple hugged them both.

All Jim wanted to do was go to bed. He was still hurting in places—the healers' quick fixes had only done so much. How long would he have to be here? What time was it? He looked at his watch. Fried, exactly like his phone.

"Eat," Bridget commanded. "You have to replenish your magical and physical energy. That requires food, then sleep."

So, they ate.

Irenee was certainly recouping her energy faster than he was, Jim noted while he shoveled in whatever they brought him. Sitting next to him and between bites, she gave an avid audience a blow-by-blow account of the battle.

She closed with, "I had no idea what Jim was planning when he dumped all his energy into me and ran over to Leroy, but I had no options left. I was about to run out of power, and I didn't know if my fortress could withstand too many more bolts from the Stone. Jim's been in shoot-outs before, and I trusted him to get us out of this one. When I saw the gun in his hand, I knew we had a chance."

"Here's to our wild talent," Hugh Sabel said and raised his glass. Everyone followed suit.

Jim felt his face grow hot. He knew he was blushing as much as Irenee usually did. "Only doing my job," he mumbled and kept on eating.

"I may have gone up part of another level," Irenee announced. "I was throwing pure violet at the end."

"Let's see," her father said.

"Lux!" A violet lightball with indigo streaks floated in the air over her plate. She stared at it for a few seconds and frowned. "That's funny. I'm pushing it to the limit, and I have plenty of power."

"Here, honey," Jim said and put his hand on her back, "have some of mine."

When he shared some of his energy, the lightball glowed pure violet.

Several people made exclamations.

"Take your hand away, Jim," Baldwin said. "Irenee, keep pumping power into your ball."

Jim did as instructed and used his hand to pick up another piece of bread to dip in the olive oil/parmesan cheese mixture. The stuff was addictive.

Irenee's lightball retained its pure violet for a while, then reverted to her former color combination.

"Oh, wait until Fergus and the Defender masters see this!" Baldwin chortled. "You two are really something. We have to run some tests soon."

"I'm nobody's lab rat," Jim growled.

"Of course not," Baldwin said, with a smile belying his statement.

Well, Jim would fight that battle later. Right now he had other things on his mind. "What's for dessert?"

After dinner, a couple of healers examined him and Irenee again. They cast some spells to take away most of his remaining pain from the beating and told them to get some sleep. Fine with him. Even with his aches gone, he was still bone tired and getting more so by the second.

Before they could head for the elevators, however, the Sabels drew him and Irenee aside. "Speaking for both of us," her father said, "we want to thank you, Jim, for keeping our daughter safe and putting an end to all those monsters."

"My stupidity was the reason she was there in the first place," Jim protested. "If I'd been more alert, I could have stopped those guys from taking me, and we could have followed the original plan."

"Jim, you can't take responsibility for things out of your control," Irenee scolded. "Ubell would have found another way to get one or the other of us in his clutches."

"She's correct," Sabel said, "or we would have gone in with a large force, possibly suffered a lot of injuries. Worse, we would probably have left the mansion as a burned-out shell and been on the evening news. No, if you hadn't shot the damn Stone, there's no telling what destruction Ubell and it would have caused. No Defender would have thought of using a gun. We certainly don't carry them. We've always used magic weapons."

"I was aiming at Ubell," Jim said, certain beyond doubt his face resembled Irenee's red hair. He wasn't used to such compliments. He and Irenee had been damn lucky, too. "He turned the Stone into my line of fire."

"It doesn't matter how you shot it. You did, and both of you are safe," Catherine said. "Since all the excitement is over, I have a more pressing concern." She gave Irenee a penetrating look.

Irenee must understand "mother-speech" better than he did because she blushed now. "Mom, give us a break. We're exhausted. Everything will work out fine. You know that. Right, Jim?"

Jim didn't have the slightest idea what she was talking about, so he simply nodded.

Sabel grinned at him, then gave his wife a kiss. "Let the kids get some rest, Catherine. Irenee's pale and Jim's about to pass out."

"All right," Catherine sighed. "I understand I'm

pushing. Yes, Irenee, I know you and Jim need to talk. We love you both."

She gave both of them a hug and a kiss.

All Jim could do was smile and hope Irenee could get them up to her place because Sabel was right, he was about to fall over. Whatever Catherine and Irenee were talking about could wait.

When they got upstairs, Irenee made him take a shower. He did feel more human, but all he could do afterward was fall into bed. The last thing he remembered was her kiss.

CHAPTER FORTY-FOUR

Jim opened his eyes to darkness. Closed them again. Nothing to see.

Plenty to feel. Irenee was curled up in his arms, her head on his shoulder, her arm across his chest, her leg draped over his. He ran his hand up and down her back, enjoying the silken smoothness, the curve of her hip, the lushness of her butt.

No, he wasn't simply enjoying. He was . . . relishing, that was the word, *relishing.*

Plenty to smell, too. He took a deep breath, let the scents run around in his lungs. Flowers from her shampoo and soap and the indefinable something that was pure Irenee.

No, he wasn't only relishing. He was . . . savoring. A better word, *savoring.*

He gave her hip a little squeeze.

"Hmmmmm," she purred and snuggled closer, just like a cat would, rubbing herself against him. Her fingers lying on his rib cage flexed to give him a little scratch back for the squeeze.

Taste. He'd taste her in a little while, when he conjured—now, there was a great word—*conjured* up the energy to move. He'd taste her all over. He licked his lips in anticipation.

Right this moment, he'd indulge himself by simply lying here with his soul mate. He'd certainly earned it.

He tested some of his muscles, the ones that had been aching from Leroy's punches. Nothing hurt. He wiggled his jaw and felt not even a twinge. Those healers really knew their stuff.

He checked his magic center. It was full to overflowing and vibrated like it was quite happy.

The damn thing should be ecstatic.

Just like he was. He smiled in the dark. Petted Irenee's back again. Gave her bottom a little pat and a little squeeze.

"Hmmmmm," she purred again, and her hand began to roam, across his chest, over his magic center—where it paused until he felt her heat warming his entire torso—and down toward his cock, which was already reaching for her.

No, he wanted to be able to think a little longer, and he captured the hand before it reached its destination.

She raised her head, gave his shoulder a little kiss. "How do you feel?"

"Fine. What about you?"

"Blissful."

A perfect word. "Yeah, me, too."

She put her head down and snuggled closer. He felt her relax into sleep.

He smiled and followed.

When he woke the next time, a glimmer of light was cutting around a corner of the curtains. He turned his head to the clock. Six thirty. The room was still dim, but enough light came in so he could see.

Good. He really liked to look at her.

Slowly he shifted to roll Irenee onto her back and to raise himself up, propped on an elbow. She was so damn gorgeous, with her red hair spread on the pillow and her fair skin so creamy and smooth. And her breasts, with their rosy tips, just begging . . .

He leaned over to give the nearest one a kiss, a lick, another kiss, and, when the temptation grew too great, he suckled. His hand roamed automatically to play with her other side.

Irenee stirred, hummed, arched, and moaned when he sucked harder and used his tongue. Her fingers tangled in his hair and held his head to her.

He kissed his way across her breastbone—he could feel her center vibrating—and concentrated on her other nipple for a while before reaching to cup her dark red curls at the apex of her thighs.

When his finger slid between her wet folds, she

groaned and pulled on his hair until he raised his head. "Come inside me, soul mate," she murmured.

"Yes, ma'am." He moved between her legs to stop on his hands and knees, poised at her entrance. He put a hand on her center, and his began to vibrate in sync with hers.

When she placed her hand on his chest, heat spread all over him.

Sliding into her in one smooth thrust put him exactly where he wanted to be—home.

He held himself still and looked into her eyes. He needed to make sure she understood him. "Irenee, I meant what I said at the end of the fight. I love you."

"I love you, and I meant it, too."

"I'm yours, and you're mine, and we will belong to each other forever."

"Forever. We'll keep each other safe. You're not alone anymore."

The words reverberated in his skull, and a wonderful, miraculous warmth of satisfaction, contentment, and delight spread throughout his body.

"Jim," she whispered and tugged his head down.

"Irenee." Her name came out of his mouth like a prayer and a pledge. He kissed her and began to move.

Magic energy flowed through them and around them, sending the usual sparks throughout his body, but it felt different this time. No frenzy to mate drove him, no desperation to climax took over his mind or his body, no uncertainty about their feelings for each other frightened him. In this moment, only she and he existed, demonstrating their love and commitment to each other.

Release, when it came, overwhelmed him with its heat and depth and power, fused them together in a long moment of sheer ecstasy, and filled his heart with joy.

He was hers, and she was his. What he had done to deserve her, he didn't know. He was sure, however, he'd spend his lifetime keeping her safe and making her happy.

He rolled to the side and gathered her in his arms. They snuggled while their breathing slowed, he cupping her breast, she running a hand up and down his back.

After a while, his mind started working again, and he leaned enough to see her face. "What happens next?"

"Hmmm? Next? . . . Breakfast, I guess."

"No, honey, next with all this practitioner stuff? Where do we go from here? While I'd be perfectly happy to stay here in bed with you forever, I assume Whipple and the rest have plans."

"Oh, that." She thought for a few seconds. "Yes, you need training, and we need to have you evaluated by the masters who study talents. I think your specialty will be hunches, but you may have other secondary ones."

"I hope they can help me get control of the damned things. Oh, I almost forgot—you remember how so many of my hunches seemed vague? Ubell's Stone was suppressing them. Before you came, he told me the thing was trying to tell him about another magic source—me."

"We need to see about your robe, too," she said. "How can we represent hunches? Maybe a moiré pattern."

"A what?"

"It's the pattern you see on silk with wavy lines that also look like ripples in water. It seems to change or move if you look at it from a different angle. I think your hunches come from you looking at the evidence from different angles than everybody else. You'll recognize it when you see it. As for the color, maybe a green with some gold to match your eyes."

Oh, brother. All he said was, "Whatever."

"Speaking of hunches, do you have any right now?" she asked with a wide-eyed expression of false innocence.

He focused on the back of his brain—not a wiggle of the antennae. "No, why?"

"Nothing about us?"

"No . . ." What was she talking about? Then he remembered . . . "Your mother said something about our needing to talk. You and she exchanged funny looks. Is that what you mean? Am I supposed to have a hunch about us? Let me tell you, it's not a hunch. I have a certainty we're supposed to be together."

She turned as red as her hair, and he was fascinated to see her blush reached down to her breasts. Her words brought his eyes back to hers. "What about marriage?"

"What about it?"

"What about it? Are we going to get married?"

He stared at her. So that's what this was all about. He opened his mouth, but shut it again when he remembered her dislike of commands. He gave her breast a small caress and her mouth a tiny kiss. "Irenee Sabel, will you marry me?"

She must have been prepared for an order, not a question, because her eyes went wide, and her lips went from an *O* to a broad smile. "Yes, I will."

"As soon as possible." He made it a firm statement.

"Yes . . . only . . ."

"What?"

"Mom will want to help, and she'll have a guest list as long as your arm."

"Do we have to go through a big hoopla? You're an event planner. Plan a small one."

"No wedding is small," she replied. "There's the place, and the dress, and the flowers, and the cake, and the reception, and the food, and the mmmph . . ."

He shut her up the only way he could. By the time he raised his lips from hers, she was wrapped around him like the paper on a gift.

"We'll worry about all that later," he murmured. He reminded himself he needed to talk to Whipple about being a practitioner on the job, and his thought brought up another possible problem. "Irenee, how do you feel about my job?"

"As a DEA agent? Well, I'm not happy about the idea of your being in danger, but I can't imagine you being anything else."

He gave a silent sigh of relief. He couldn't imagine being anything else, either.

Then she asked, "What about me and my being a Sword?"

He had to answer this one honestly. "I'll admit, it scares the hell out of me. I can live with it, though—as long as you always work with your team."

She gave him a wonderful smile. "Good."

He turned onto his back, and she did the same so they were lying side by side. "I sure hope I can cast some of those spells Johanna was telling me about. If I'd known 'unfasten,' I would have been able to get out of Ubell's ropes."

"We're back to your need for training again. Having gone through it, I can tell you it won't be easy. But if you have the talent, the spell will come."

"Yeah, I look at all the stuff you and the Swords can do, and I start drooling. Right now, the only one I'm sure of is *lux*." As he said the word, he held out his hand, and his blue-indigo lightball formed and floated above them.

Irenee pointed, and hers appeared, glowing violet and indigo.

The balls began to merge.

Irenee shifted to prop her head on one hand and run her other across his chest, his center, and down. She gave him that oh-so-innocent look again and kissed his shoulder. "It's not only the men who have secret smiles on their faces, you know."

Her hand reached the part of him that had awakened when the lightballs touched each other.

"Come here, soul mate." His voice was rough when he pulled her on top of him.

As their lightballs merged, so did they.

ANN MACELA

DO YOU BELIEVE IN MAGIC?

According to lore, an ancient force called the soulmate imperative brings together magic practitioners and their mates. They always nearly fall into each other's arms at first sight. Always . . . or so the story goes.

But what happens if they don't? What happens when one mate rejects the other—in fact won't have anything to do with him? Who doesn't even believe in magic to begin with?

Computer wizard Clay Morgan is in just such a position. Francie Stevens has been badly hurt by a charming and good looking man and has decided to avoid any further involvements. Although the hacker plaguing her company's system forces her into an investigation led by the handsome practitioner, she vows to keep her distance from Clay.

The imperative has other ideas, however, and so does Clay. He must convince Francie that magic exists and he can wield it. It's a prickly problem. Especially when Francie uses the imperative itself against him in ways neither it, nor Clay, ever anticipated.

ISBN#9781933836164
US $7.95 / CDN $9.99
Paranormal Romance

ANN MACELA

YOUR MAGIC OR MINE?

A battle over the "correct" way to cast spells is brewing in the magic practitioner community. Theoretical mathematician Marcus Forscher has created an equation, a formula to bring the science of casting into the twenty-first century. Botanist Gloriana Morgan, however, maintains spell casting is an art, as individual as each caster, and warns against throwing out old casting methods and forcing use of the new. A series of heated debates across the country ensues.

Enter the soulmate phenomenon, an ancient compulsion that brings practitioners together and has persuasive techniques and powers—the soulmate imperative—to convince the selected couple they belong together. Marcus and Gloriana, prospective soulmates, want nothing to do with each other, however. To make matters worse, their factions have turned to violence. One adherent in particular, blaming Marcus and Gloriana for the mess, wants to destroy the soulmates.

Something's got to give, or there will be dire consequences. The magic will work for them…or against them. But with two powerful practitioners bent on having their own way, which will it be—Your Magic Or Mine?—and if they don't unite, will either survive?

ISBN#9781933836324

US $7.95 / CDN $8.95

Paranormal Romance

Available Now

www.annmacela.com

ANN MACELA

UNEXPECTED MAGIC

Johanna Mahler is a gifted Sword practitioner—a modern witch with superior ability. At eighteen she loses her adolescent sweetheart, Billy Johnson, in an accident at the HeatherRidge Center near Chicago. In an arrogant act of bravery to prove his worth to Johanna, he tries to demolish an evil artifact without assistance.

Her grief inspires her to teach young Swords and Defenders how to use their magic skills without killing themselves. Only mating within the bond of love allows practitioners to enhance their natural talents, giving them power to decimate dangerous sorcery objects. This is a sacred, ancient force accepted by their clandestine social order.

Seventeen years later she meets Saxton Falkner, a member of the Defender Council and chairman of the Committee on Swords. A born leader, Saxton knows how to apply medieval concepts to the present day without disrupting traditionalists or thwarting innovators. Johanna knows this sophisticated, sexy man is her mate . . . her destiny.

Thieves have stolen pieces of the infamous Cataclysm Stone from their high-security vault, intending to reconstitute the cursed relic for destructive use. This rock is powerful, capable of disabling curiosity seekers and annihilating upright protectors who attempt its obliteration. Now Johanna and Saxton must embark on a perilous assignment for only the best of mates.

ISBN#9781605421223

US $7.95 / CDN $8.95

Paranormal Romance

SEPTEMBER 2010

www.annmacela.com